OLD
ABE

OLD ABE

FIRST EDITION

Copyright 2020 John Cribb

ISBN: 9781645720164 (Hardcover)

ISBN: 9781645720171 (ebook)

For inquiries about volume orders, please contact:

Republic Book Publishers

501 Slaters Lane #206

Alexandria VA 22314

editor@republicbookpublishers.com

Published in the United States by Republic Book Publishers

Distributed by Independent Publishers Group

www.ipgbook.com

Cover designed by Laura Klynstra

Interior designed by Mark Karis

Printed in the United States of America

Cover Images:

American Civil War Era By Patricia Turner From Arcangel Images Inc

Grand Review of the Armies at the end of the Civil War on Pennsylvania Avenue in Washington DC May 1865. Color lithograph

Contributor: North Wind Picture Archives / Alamy Stock Photo

OLD ABE

—⁓— A NOVEL —⁓—

JOHN CRIBB

REPUBLIC

BOOK PUBLISHERS

To Kirsten, Molly, and Sarah

CONTENTS

FOREWORD

Thousands of books have been published about Lincoln—more than 15,000, according to one count several years ago. More, of course, have been added since. The vast majority are nonfiction. More books, it is said, have been written about Lincoln than any other person in history except Jesus Christ. But you must read this book.

This is the best book about Abraham Lincoln I've ever read. Why? In most books about him, you learn something about his life and times, his policies, the Civil War, and so on. But in the end, there is still something unapproachable about him. He's still that rigid, copper image staring toward the edge of the penny.

This novel turns that copper face into a walking, talking, breathing fellow. And we walk right beside him, through the most catastrophic years in American history. John Cribb has brought Lincoln to life for us. We are with him for every blow and triumph of his journey and come to know his heart and soul as he fights to save the Union.

In this novel, we pace the White House hallways with Lincoln, groping for answers. We stand with him over the hospital beds of wounded Union and Confederate soldiers, and we walk the streets of a smoldering, fallen Richmond with him, studying the faces of defeated countrymen.

Old Abe bulges with epic scenes from American history, but it's also full of those moments, sometime crushing, that make up life. The afternoons Lincoln sits alone in the bedroom where his son Willie died. The night he tries, without success, to dash inside the blazing White House stables to save his boys' ponies. The day he realizes that all the destruction and loss is too much for Mary, his wife, and that they are slipping away from each other.

I asked John Cribb why he wrote this book, and he said, "Because I love Lincoln, and I want others to know and love him, too." That you will. This book makes you love Lincoln. We all know what happens to him in the end, but as the end draws near, you will not want it to happen, and you'll weep for him when it does.

Since his death, Lincoln has fascinated people, both in his own country and abroad. Leo Tolstoy once told a journalist from the *New York World* about a time he was traveling in a wild region of the Caucasus and stayed with a tribe of mountain horsemen. After sharing a meal, he told the chief and "a score of wild-looking riders" about famous statesmen and generals such as Napoleon.

"When I declared that I had finished my talk," Tolstoy related, "my host, a gray-bearded, tall rider, rose, lifted his hand and said very gravely:

> *But you have not told us a syllable about the greatest general and greatest ruler of the world. We want to know something about him. He was a hero. He spoke with a voice of thunder; he laughed like the sunrise and his deeds were strong as the rock and as sweet as the fragrance of roses.... His name was Lincoln, and the country in which he lived is called America, which is so far away that if a youth should journey to reach it, he would be an old man when he arrived. Tell us of that man.*

"'Tell us, please, and we will present you with the best horse of our stock,' shouted the others."

Tolstoy told them of Lincoln's wisdom, home life, and youth. "They asked me ten questions to one which I was able to answer. They wanted to know all about his habits, his influence upon the people and his physical strength.... After all my knowledge of Lincoln was exhausted they seemed to be satisfied. I can hardly forget the great enthusiasm which they expressed in their wild thanks.... This little incident proves how largely the name of Lincoln is worshipped throughout the world and how legendary his personality has become."

If a score of wild-looking riders in the remote Caucasus were so eager to learn about Lincoln, then surely we Americans should want to know him, too, even now in the twenty-first century when he often seems as far away as he did to those horsemen.

Why is his life still so worth knowing?

One answer is his deeds, deeds as "strong as the rock and as sweet as the fragrance of roses," as the chieftain put it. He led the effort to save the Union and free the slaves. For those actions alone, he deserves to be studied and remembered.

Another answer lies in the principles he defended, especially those enshrined in the Declaration of Independence, his favorite founding document. Growing up on the American frontier, he soaked up the ideals that all are created equal and endowed by their Creator with the right to life, liberty, and the pursuit of happiness. He fought for those ideals until his last breath.

Lincoln once called America "the last best hope of earth," a phrase I borrowed for the title of my history of the United States, *America: The Last Best Hope,* because it perfectly captures how millions have viewed this nation. Lincoln knew that throughout history, the vast majority of people had lived with little or no freedom under the rule of kings, emperors, and tyrants. He realized that the world had been waiting centuries for the kind of liberty America stood for. He believed that if the Union fractured and the American experiment failed, it would be a severe blow to worldwide hopes for freedom for a very long time. His wisdom regarding America and its principles is still worth learning.

A third answer comes in the magnificent words he left behind. The late Lincoln scholar Don E. Fehrenbacher wrote that Lincoln's words have become part of "the permanent literary treasure of the nation." Generations of schoolchildren have memorized the Gettysburg Address. (One hopes that some still do.) Millions have stood enraptured at the Lincoln Memorial, in the shadow of the giant statue of the seated Lincoln, reading the words of the Gettysburg Address and Second

Inaugural Address carved on the memorial's walls. His words will live as long as the idea of America lives.

The fourth answer to the question "Why know this man's life?" is his life itself. Tolstoy said that Lincoln's greatness "expresses itself altogether in his peculiar moral power and in the greatness of his character." There is much to learn from the example of the virtues he embodied.

His perseverance is awe inspiring. It was a trait he no doubt learned growing up on the frontier, where you either persevered or died. During the Civil War, he suffered through four years of loss and destruction. Many in the North were willing to give up. Not Lincoln. He used to compare himself to a man trying to keep a storm from blowing down his tent. He kept driving tent pegs into the ground as fast as the wind could pull them up. "I mean to keep pegging away, pegging away," he told people.

His boundless compassion was, I think, one reason he often struck people as looking sad. He reveled at any chance to pardon a soldier who had been court-martialed for falling asleep on duty or going home without leave to see his family. Slavery offended not only his great sense of justice, but his sense of compassion. It is no coincidence that the president who issued the Emancipation Proclamation was a man of tremendous empathy.

He possessed a humble eagerness to learn. The boy who had less than a year of formal schooling really would walk miles on the Indiana frontier to lay his hands on a book. As president, he borrowed books from the Library of Congress to study up on military tactics. He was a great listener and chose his cabinet, which included political rivals, in part because he knew they were men from whom he could learn.

We can't say that the man called Honest Abe never told a lie, but he was a man of the highest integrity. As a young fellow, he famously walked several miles to return six and a quarter cents overpaid by a customer at the store where he clerked. A bit later, when a little general store he co-owned went belly-up, he repaid every penny of his debt, even though it took several years. When the Civil War went badly, political enemies called him confused, incompetent, out of his league. But his allies knew that he was a good, decent man, and that helped them be sure they were fighting for a cause that was good and decent.

He was a man of great faith, even though he never formally joined a church. He knew the Bible perhaps better than any president before or since and turned to it frequently in the White House. As the war deepened, he came to view himself as a "humble instrument in the hands of the Almighty." His faith not only gave him strength; at war's end it gave him the wisdom to tell Northerners that the time had come not for revenge, but for charity.

This is the man we find in the pages of this wonderful novel, a giant of a man, but also a real man, the man those wild riders in the Caucasus wanted to know.

In the past few decades, there has been a strong inclination in American letters to knock great figures off their pedestals, often, it seems, for no other reason than to see them shatter. *Old Abe* is something different. It portrays Lincoln as a flesh-and-blood man but also a great man—the great American hero who embodies this country's finest ideals. And that, I believe, is exactly who he was.

As Tolstoy said, "He was great through his simplicity and was noble through his charity. Lincoln is a strong type of those who make for truth and justice, for brotherhood and freedom. Love is the foundation of his life. That is what makes him immortal and that is the quality of a giant."

In these pages, as we grow close to Lincoln, we come to know his deeds, his words, and those principles he so fiercely defended. Most of all, we come to know his life and his virtues. He was not a perfect man, but he was a darned good one. And darned good men are worth knowing and loving.

As Lincoln's journey unfolds, *Old Abe* chronicles the times in which he lived. It probes the character and spirit of America. This is a story that involves much suffering and loss, but in the end it is a hopeful story, both for Lincoln and the nation.

We live in a time in which many Americans feel uncertain about the future and worry about the direction the country is headed. Distrust of major institutions is at historic highs. People yearn for true leaders. They will find such a leader in this novel—one of the greatest American leaders, the one who set the country on track to becoming a great nation.

—WILLIAM J. BENNETT

AUTHOR'S NOTE

This is a work of fiction. There are many fine biographies of Abraham Lincoln, but because of nonfiction's constraints, they can go only so far in portraying his thoughts and feelings. I've chosen to tell Lincoln's story through fiction so you and I can step into his world, walk with him, and intimately know this extraordinary man.

Though this is a novel, I've tried to give an accurate depiction of Lincoln in the last five years of his life. I've turned to hundreds of primary and secondary sources, drawing on the words of Lincoln and his contemporaries when possible. For example, in the first chapter, when I write that the Illinois Republicans picked him up and passed him hand-to-hand over their heads to the front of their makeshift convention hall in Decatur, and that Lincoln says the split rails his cousin John Hanks brought to the convention "don't look like they're a credit to their maker," it's because an eyewitness tells us that is what happened. In many cases, I've taken artistic license to provide details of action and dialogue, and I've occasionally bent the timeline for minor events, but I've tried to stay faithful to the historical record.

I hope this book brings Lincoln to life and that it helps you better understand the tragic circumstances he faced and the heroic service he rendered to a nation that seemed hopelessly divided.

PART ONE

THE ASCENT

May 1860 to February 1861

CHAPTER 1

MAY 9, 1860

H e squatted on his heels at the back of the huge Wigwam, head down, whittling on a pine stick while three thousand farmers and shopkeepers whooped for joy around him. Men jostled past each other in the aisles of the convention hall, which the citizens of Decatur had thrown together with a few sticks of lumber and a rented circus tent. A blacksmith with too much corn whiskey in his belly climbed one of the poles holding up the Wigwam's canvas roof and shouted that he could see the Promised Land. Nearby, a miller and a grocer started a good-natured brawl over the rights of man that ended with the blacksmith dropping an empty flask from atop the pole onto the grocer's head.

Outside, one or two thousand more people milled about Decatur's streets, taking turns sticking their heads through the tent flaps to see what the Illinois Republicans were doing at their state convention.

A booming, determined voice from the front of the hall broke over the crowd: "I am informed that a distinguished citizen of Illinois, one whom Illinois will ever delight to honor, is present, and I wish to move that this body invite him to a seat on the platform—Abraham Lincoln!"

He barely had time to drop the pine stick before a dozen hands grabbed him and hoisted him into the air. A roar of assent shook the Wigwam's timbers and set its canvas roof flapping. The next thing he knew, he was being passed forward, rolling and sprawling, hand-to-hand over laughing, upturned faces. He went dangling and turning to the platform, clutching his stovepipe hat and wondering if the tumultuous ride would make his undergarments show.

More hands grabbed him and set him down on the stage. A tempest of cheering burst over three thousand heads. Hats went soaring to the roof as if men would never again need hats.

"Speech! Speech!"

He tried to say something, but the booming, determined voice that had called out his name beat him to it.

"An old Democrat outside has something he wants to present to this meeting!" it announced.

"Receive it! Receive it!" the delegates shouted.

The crowd parted, and Abraham saw his cousin John Hanks enter the hall. For an instant, thirty years melted away, and it seemed like it was only yesterday that the two of them had been rough-hewn youths toiling beside the lazy Sangamon River and Decatur was little more than an unfinished log courthouse in a stump-filled clearing. Together they had split fence rails by the hundred and busted sod to plant corn on acres of hard-baked Illinois prairie. They had loaded a raft with pork, corn, and wheat and floated it down the Sangamon into the Illinois River and then down the great Mississippi itself all the way to New Orleans, just about the grandest adventure any frontier boy could hope to have.

Now here came good old John Hanks marching down the aisle, sporting a bushy gray beard. Another grizzled farmer came with him. Each carried upright a gray fence rail decorated with red, white, and blue streamers. Stretched between the two rails was a banner reading, "Abraham Lincoln—The Rail Candidate for President in 1860."

Hats, canes, coats, and newspapers went flying into the air again. Men stamped their feet and pounded their seats so hard, part of the canvas roof came down on their heads.

Abraham shook John's hand while some of the delegates fixed the tent. His cousin's face was weathered from seasons of burning suns and driving snows, but it was still the good, solid face Abraham had always known, with an honest gaze carved into it.

"It took a while, but I found some of the fences we built still standing," John grinned. "They asked me what kind of work you used to be good at. I told them not much of any kind but dreaming, though we did split a lot of rails when we were clearing land."

A chant rose from the crowd: "Identify your work! Identify your work!"

Abraham blushed. "I don't know that I can. That was a long time ago."

"Identify your work!"

He examined the rails, peering through the colored streamers to see the wood.

"What kind of timber are they?" he asked.

"Honey locust and black walnut."

"They don't look like they're a credit to their maker."

"Identify your work!"

"Well, boys, it may be that I mauled these rails. I can only say that I've split a great many better-looking ones."

There was enough screaming and shaking to put the whole roof in danger of falling, and heaven with it. Delegates shouted that Old Abe was the original Rail Splitter. They yelled to each other that his politics, like his rails, were straight and made of sound timber. Everyone whooped until they were hoarse, and then they set about passing a resolution that Abraham Lincoln was the choice of the Republican Party of Illinois to be president of all the United States.

☙ ❧ ☙

That evening he sprawled on the grass in a patch of woods near the Wigwam to talk over his next move with friends. Clouds of pink hung on the far side of tender yellow-green leaves. Pollen on the ground left yellow-green smudges on the seats of the men's black trousers and the elbows of their sleeves.

The Republicans' national convention, to be held in Chicago, was only a week away. Judge David Davis, who had ruled on scores of cases Abraham had tried, would go as the head of the Lincoln delegation. A huge man who tipped the scales at nearly three hundred pounds, Davis handled the prairie lawyers appearing before his bench like a firm, genial father presiding over two or three dozen rowdy sons at the dinner table. Norman Judd, a friend who served on the Republican National Committee, would also be a Lincoln delegate in Chicago.

"I want Gustave Koerner to go," Abraham said. "He'll carry weight with the German vote. And Orville Browning. We'll need his ties to the old-line Whigs."

"We'll need Logan and Swett and Jesse Fell there with us, too," Judge Davis said. He wallowed in the pollen like a big goose plum rolled in sugar. "And Yates and Dubois."

"Yes. And take Hill Lamon. He knows how to twist a few arms. And Billy Herndon, of course."

Excitement pulsed through the circle of men laying plans in the grove. Arguments over protecting slavery had begun to splinter the Democratic Party. Whoever won the Republican nomination in Chicago stood an excellent chance of becoming the next president.

"All the Illinois delegates will give you their votes on the first ballot," Judd said in a candid tone. "After that, they'll start to drift away to

Seward or Bates."

"That's right," Abraham said. "I might get around a hundred votes. I have a notion that'll be the high mark for me."

The others nodded. None expected him to be the national party's nominee. It was best to say it aloud. But deep inside each of them, including Abraham, a little voice whispered: there's always the slim chance things could go our way.

After all, stranger things have happened in politics, he thought. It's a long shot, but it's a shot all the same. Anyway, it's a triumph to have my name in the running, no matter how it turns out. It's hard to believe I've made it this far.

They assessed the other candidates' weaknesses. William Henry Seward of New York, the favorite to win the nomination, was immensely popular, but to many voters unacceptably radical. He would not be able to carry Pennsylvania, Indiana, Illinois, or New Jersey—crucial states in the general election. Salmon Chase of Ohio was even more radical than Seward and had made plenty of enemies. More than a few Ohio Republicans said they would vote for anyone but Chase. Simon Cameron of Pennsylvania was plagued by rumors of greed and corruption. There were some who believed strongly that he was better suited for the penitentiary than the White House. Edward Bates of Missouri was a good man, but his association with the anti-immigrant Know Nothing Party in years past had angered German voters.

"You have the advantage of being none of those other fellows," Davis said. "Give them space, and they might knock each other out of the running."

"If I have any chance, it's that most of the delegates will have no strong objection to me," Abraham said. "I'm not the first choice of many, but most wouldn't mind voting for me if they can't have the man they prefer. Our policy should be to give no offense to others. Leave them in a mood to come to us if they have to give up their first love."

Judge Davis grunted his approval. Everyone looked satisfied.

"Should I go to Chicago or stay behind?" Abraham asked.

"Stay home," Davis said. "None of the other candidates will be there. If you go, it'll look like you're grasping. We'll keep you informed."

"All right."

"A pledge or two may be necessary to round up votes when the pinch comes."

"Make no contracts that will bind me," Abraham cautioned. "I can't be bound by promises I don't make myself."

The meeting broke up. He shook each man's hand and thanked him as they walked out of the grove.

"Keep the faith and stick to your guns," he told them. "Stand together, ready, with match in hand."

His outlook turned doubtful again as he walked to the hotel with Judge Davis. All this talk about being president is just foolishness, he thought. My father would tell me to stop dreaming my life away.

"I reckon I haven't a chance in a hundred," he said. "But it's honor enough to be talked about for the job. Anyway, who knows what will happen."

He brushed the pollen off his pants.

Events, not a man's exertions on his own behalf, make presidents, he told himself.

CHAPTER 2

MAY 18, 1860

This was no day for sleeping late. He was up before the rest of Springfield, stirring coals, fetching wood, feeding the horse. His morning chores finished, he went to the sitting room, stretched out on the floor with his shoulders against an overturned chair, and pored over a black notebook containing information he had compiled about delegates to the Republicans' national convention in Chicago and the candidates they were likely to support. He ran his finger down columns showing clues—who could be trusted to stand fast, who might be swayed, who was a lost cause.

When he ran out of columns and figures to ponder, he rose and went to the kitchen. Mary was stewing some rhubarb to make jam. Like Abraham, she had tossed and turned all night.

"Well, Mr. Lincoln, I've always said you would be president someday," she reminded him cheerfully.

"Yes, you have."

It was true. Since the days of their courtship, when he was a young lawyer and representative in the Illinois legislature, struggling to make a name for himself, she had told friends he was destined for the White House. Her tone had often left people wondering if the prediction was a joke or not. She was dead serious about it. Mary had always carried more passion and resolve than her five-foot-two-inch frame would seem to hold.

"After today they'll begin to understand how right I was," she said.

"I wish I had your confidence."

"I have enough in you for both of us." She said it matter-of-factly, but he could tell by the little crease in her brow that she was just as nervous as he was.

Willie and Tad came scampering through the kitchen in pursuit of Fido, their yellow mutt, who was in pursuit of a black-and-white cat Abraham had never seen before.

"G'ab him, Papa-day, g'ab him!" Tad yelled as they raced by.

Cat, dog, and boys tumbled out the door into the backyard.

"I don't trust that man Seward," Mary said darkly. "He's a snake in the grass. If we lose, it will be because the New Yorkers have spread their dirty bribe money all the way from Manhattan to Chicago."

She gave him an egg with a piece of toast for breakfast. He wasn't hungry but ate anyway to please her, then gulped down a cup of coffee as he put on his tie and coat.

"Send word when you know anything certain," she said.

"I'll bring you word myself," he promised, kissing her on top of her head.

He walked two blocks west on Jackson Street, past white picket fences and tidy clapboard homes, then three blocks north on Sixth. The sharp, pleasant smell of chimney smoke mixed with the fragrance of lilacs in bloom. The sun was just touching the golden-brown limestone walls of the statehouse when he stepped onto Springfield's town square. At Candless & Co. Groceries on Fifth Street, a clerk set bags of flour on the sidewalk for display. Horses stood at hitching posts, heads down, daydreaming on their hooves. A farmer with spring planting on his mind sauntered by, scouting windows of hardware stores before going inside to make his purchases.

Abraham climbed the stairs to his second-floor law office on the west side of the public square, flopped onto the firm's old sofa, and tried to read a newspaper. Two hundred miles away in Chicago, ten thousand men with political fire in their bellies and last night's whiskey on their breaths were converging on a ramshackle wooden Wigwam, this one cavernous enough to swallow whole the meeting hall in Decatur.

Judge Davis and his team of operatives had been up there for days, prodding and sweet-talking delegates from other states, telling them why they must pass over William Henry Seward, and that Abraham Lincoln was as true and honest a man as ever lived, the right man to split rails and maul Democrats. Today the delegates would choose their nominee, and Abraham was more fidgety than he had expected.

My God, what will I do if I actually win? he thought.

Cryptic telegrams had been arriving from Davis and his team the past few days. "We are quiet but moving heaven and earth. Nothing will beat us but old fogy politicians." Who knew what sort of horse-trading they were doing up there to win votes? Probably gambling him all around and selling him a hundred times. He had fired off a telegram, reminding them of his instructions: "I authorize no bargains and will be bound by none." More cryptic messages had come back. "Am very hopeful. Don't be excited. Nearly dead with fatigue." And yesterday, this one: "Things are working; keep up a good nerve—be not surprised at any result."

Reading the newspaper was no good. He went back outside and crossed the square to the ball alley. A few friends were there for a morning game of fives, which involved knocking a handball against a brick wall in a vacant lot. They asked him to join them and were good enough to not talk much about the convention. Whacking the hand-ball helped calm him down. One of the fellows mentioned that Jim Conkling, another attorney, had returned from Chicago on the night train. Abraham walked back over to Fifth Street, climbed the stairs to Conkling's law office above Chatterton's jewelry store, and stretched out on an old settee to interrogate his friend.

"The Sewardites have repulsed more votes than they've bought," Conkling chortled. "They're a horde of political pirates, strutting around trying to buy off anyone in sight with their filthy New York lucre."

"Did you talk to Davis?"

"You should see him, sitting behind his table at the Tremont House, dispatching operatives here and there. The man is a genius. Indiana is ready to go for you. So are a good number from Pennsylvania and New Jersey. If Seward isn't nominated on the first ballot, you'll win."

"I think Chase or Bates will win, if not Seward."

"You'll be nominated by sundown."

Abraham studied his shoes dangling over the end of the settee. That's wishful thinking, he told himself. That's all it is. Don't start to believe it.

"Judd and Lamon have a little surprise," Conkling laughed again. "They've printed up extra tickets to the convention and handed them out to Lincoln men with voices loud enough to shout across Lake Michigan. I imagine there are more than a few Sewardite spectators who can't find a seat in the Wigwam right about now."

Abraham winced. He would rather not know about such tricks. Still, it was a good one.

"Well, Conkling, I believe I'll go to my office and practice law," he said.

By the time he got back to his office, a couple of young law students had taken up their stations and were busy flourishing pens against paper, copying something. "Hello, boys, what do you know?" he asked. They had heard nothing. He sat at his desk and shuffled through a stack of documents.

The Wigwam must be a bedlam, he thought. Names have been placed into nomination by now. They might even have gone through the first ballot. If Lamon and Judd had really managed to pack the hall, like Conkling said, there would be more noise than all the hogs in Illinois squealing all at once. Seward would have a few thousand backers of his own on hand to scream and yell just as loud. You would be able to drop a thousand steam whistles and a tribe of shrieking Comanches into that Wigwam and never hear a difference. He wished he could be there.

E. L. Baker, editor of the *Illinois State Journal,* burst through the door, waving a telegram. "First ballot results!" He threw it down on the desk and collapsed in a chair.

Seward 173 ½, Lincoln 102, Bates 48, Cameron 50 ½, Chase 49.

Abraham scrutinized the numbers, struggling to keep a blank face. His vote total was about what Davis was aiming for on the first round. That much was encouraging. But two hundred and thirty-three votes were needed to win. He was less than halfway there. Seward was already drawing close to the mark.

"It's good news, don't you think?" E. L. declared. "Better than we had a right to expect."

"I'm not sure I like the looks of it," Abraham frowned. "About forty of my votes come from men pledged to me on the first ballot only. They're mostly friends of Bates. If I lose them on the next ballot, I'm finished."

He scoured the numbers for another minute, trying to solve a half-written equation that held the sum of his future.

"Why don't we go over to your office," he suggested. "We'll get news faster there."

On the way to the *Journal,* they passed the telegraph office on the north side of the square.

"Let's stop here for a minute," Abraham said. "It's about time for the second ballot to come."

Upstairs, a cluster of men giddy with anticipation surrounded the telegraph. The key was clattering away. The operator wrote out a message and handed it to Abraham in the cool, professional way the telegraph men dispensed all news, from the birth of a baby to the end of the world.

Seward 184 ½ votes, Lincoln 181.

He stared hard at the numbers, shocked at the collapse in the margin between them. He was only three and a half votes behind now. The other candidates were fading.

Davis and his team were doing it—by God, somehow they were actually doing it. He tried to think where seventy-nine new votes could have come from. The Pennsylvanians must have come through. Seward had gained only eleven votes. All the color would be draining out of the New Yorkers' faces right about now.

No one spoke a word in the telegraph office. All eyes were on him.

"I have no fault to find with this," he said weakly. "I believe they might well nominate me on the next ballot."

No one offered congratulations. They didn't want to jinx it. The little crowd followed him out of the telegraph office to the *Journal*'s office on Sixth Street. Abraham dropped into a chair and made small talk with friends gathering in the room. It was hard to focus on what they were saying. The scene before him appeared strangely remote and subdued. He had the same feeling he had experienced on his wedding day more than seventeen years earlier, the sensation that it was all happening to some other fellow named Abraham Lincoln. The sharp, heady smell of ink and paper filled the office, the smell of liberty and struggle and corruption and redemption all mixed together.

E. L. pushed into the room, waving two new dispatches. He pumped Abraham's right hand and thrust the telegrams into his left.

One was from John Wilson, superintendent of the Illinois and Mississippi Telegraph Company. It read simply, *To Lincoln: You are nominated.*

The other telegram came from Nathan Knapp, one of Judge Davis's army in Chicago: *We did it. Glory to God!*

He had won on the third ballot with three hundred and sixty-four votes.

Good God, he thought. Is this true?

The newsroom broke out in hurrahs. Every man wanted to shake every other man's hand. Everyone wanted to read the dispatches for himself, to make sure it was really true. Someone called for three cheers for the next president. Someone else yelled out a window, "Lincoln is nominated! Lincoln is nominated!" Through the noise, they could almost hear the pandemonium erupting far away at Chicago's Wigwam, where thousands shouted through tears of joy, black hats went flying into the air like swarms of hornets, steam whistles in boatyards and train yards screamed, and telegraph machines furiously clicked away to spread the news across the land.

Abraham accepted the congratulations as calmly as he could. He felt excited but not euphoric—more like numbness tinged with disbelief. Perhaps euphoria would come later.

"Gentlemen, there is a little woman over on Eighth Street who is probably more interested in this news than I am," he said after a minute. "If you'll excuse me, I'll go home and give it to her."

Most of the men followed him out of the newspaper office. Word had already traveled around the square. Shoppers and storekeepers hurried out of doorways to share the news. Church bells began to ring. The ballplayers in the alley stopped their game to salute him.

"Well, boys, you'd better shake my hand now while you can," he laughed, beginning to feel a little giddy. "Honors elevate some men, you know."

Friends and strangers reached toward him. Guns fired into the air. A man stuck his head out an upstairs window to sound a bugle as he passed. People trailed him, laughing and shouting like children skipping after the tall, thin Pied Piper.

There would be no need to tell Mary. The news had gone faster than he could. As he strode down Eighth Street, anxious to embrace her, he saw her standing at their front gate, beaming, waiting with reassurance and joy.

CHAPTER 3

MAY 19, 1860

The next morning he took a long walk, heading away from town on roads that cut through prairies and fresh green fields of corn. He couldn't decide whether he felt like a man lost at sea or one with opportunities as wide as the blue sky.

He had always been a walker, starting back in his Kentucky childhood when he had followed his sister Sarah into the woods to fill pails with wild grapes and blueberries. In southern Indiana, where he had done most of his growing up, he would walk miles to lay his hands on a book. His cousin Dennis Hanks had teased him about it, saying, "There's something peculiarsome about you, Abe, wanting to read so many books." Abraham would smile and tell him: "The things I want to know are in books, Denny. My best friend is a man who can get me a book."

During his teenage years, he often hiked to the Ohio River to sit on the bank and dream of being a captain on one of the proud, white steamboats that churned the water. The river was a good place to get away from his father, who was always pestering him to split rails or pull fodder. "Don't fool around with more learning than you need," Tom Lincoln would say. "Books don't put food in your mouth. You can't eat a book."

Sometimes he had wandered the Indiana woods at night, pausing to sit beside his mother's grave on a knoll close to the Lincoln cabin. He would try hard to remember Nancy Hanks Lincoln's voice as she sang hymns at her spinning wheel before she grew ill, when he was only nine. She had called Abraham and Sarah to her bedside, told them to always be good, smiled her sweet smile for them to remember her by, and died. Tom sawed planks for her coffin while Abraham whittled the pegs to nail them together, and they lowered her into the ground.

Sister Sarah's grave was nearby, next to the Little Pigeon Baptist Church. She died in childbirth along with her baby about ten years after their mother had passed away. Her grave was a good place to sit and ponder the knowledge that life was as swift as an arrow.

A stepmother had come into his life, Sally Johnston Lincoln, a tall, handsome woman with blue-gray eyes and black hair she always wore curled. She had been a godsend. When his father groused about the foolishness of wanting too much education, she found ways to help Abraham get his hands on books. She laughed at his jokes, like the time he dipped a young cousin's feet in mud and lifted her up to make footprints that walked across the cabin ceiling. Sally Lincoln had always understood him better than Tom Lincoln could.

After Abraham helped his family move to Illinois, where the woods gave way to prairies covered with grass that stood taller than a man, he had struck out on his own. As postmaster of the village of New Salem, he had trekked into the countryside with letters for farmers' wives, and his job as a surveyor had him lugging a compass and chain across Sangamon County. Running a general store, on the other hand, had not required much walking. Customers came to him, what few he had. But he had tramped from farm to farm while campaigning for the state legislature, and often he had walked with his eyes on Blackstone's *Commentaries* while studying law.

In 1837, he had moved to Springfield, Illinois's new state capital, to begin his law career while serving in the legislature. Almost three years later he began courting Mary Todd. From the beginning, friends had commented on how different they were. He was six-feet-four and rail thin. His face was leathery and craggy, with a nose too large, a jaw too long, and ears that stuck out too far. His course, dark hair rambled whichever direction it wanted. Folks used to laugh that he was the awkwardest fellow that ever stepped over a ten-rail snake fence.

Mary was more than a foot shorter and pleasingly plump. Her pretty face and charm had drawn the bachelors of Springfield toward her. The daughter of a prosperous Lexington, Kentucky, businessman, she grew up in luxury and attended the finest private academies, even learning to speak French. Abraham had grown up in one-room log cabins and done his schooling by littles—a little here and a little there whenever his father could spare him in the fields. But their quick wits, ambitions, and love of politics drew them together. During their courtship, Abraham had worn out the cow paths around Springfield, asking himself if it was lunacy for a fellow like him to propose to a girl like Mary Todd.

Their marriage wasn't perfect, but whose is? Each had faults the other had to live with. Mary was spirited but had a temper. She had thrown hot coffee at him and even hit him across the nose with a piece of firewood in fits of rage. He was often moody, given to telling jokes and spinning yarns one minute, withdrawing and brooding the next.

But they loved each other deeply and leaned on one another. Their marriage had produced four wonderful sons. One of them, Eddie, had died of consumption when he was not yet four. The loss devastated them, but the shared pain brought them closer.

Bob, nearly seventeen, had always been a bright young fellow, though sometimes a little aloof. He resembled his mother more than his father, thank goodness. He had Mary's firm smile and blue-gray eyes. He was getting ready to enter Harvard and talked of becoming a lawyer like his father, a prospect that filled Abraham with pride.

Willie, nine, was a gentle boy who loved books and writing poems. Mathematics and things mechanical fascinated him. He had a remarkable talent for memorizing railroad timetables and could recite them as easily as nursery rhymes.

"Illinois Central southbound, Galena to Cairo and all points between, departing Galena 6:45 p.m., arriving Amboy 12:50 a.m., Wapella 6:45, Centralia three o'clock, Cairo 9:45—*All aboard!*"

Willie liked to climb onto chairs and make his parents giggle at fire-and-brimstone campaign speeches full of hurrahs for the memory of Henry Clay and shouts of "Down with Stephen Douglas!" People said that Willie Lincoln was the true picture of his father, even in the way he carried his head tilted slightly toward his left shoulder when lost in thought. Abraham had not realized he carried his own head that way, but he asked Mary, and she laughed and said it was so.

Little Tad, seven, was sweet and lovable, too, though he sometimes showed flashes of the Todd temper. When he flew into one of his rages, Abraham would pick him up, hold him at arm's length, and laugh while the boy flailed at the air and tried to kick his father in the face. But most of the time Tad was a happy little fellow, a bundle of energy, always bolting into a room in search of one toy or another he'd misplaced, hurling himself at his father like a miniature thunderbolt to give him a hug, then dashing away again. Abraham loved to carry Tad on his shoulders to market with a basket on one arm and Willie skipping along at the end of the other.

Tad was born with a cleft palate, which caused a speech defect. Mary fretted over the woes she feared it would eventually cause him. His teeth had come in crooked, which didn't help. He had trouble saying his *r*'s. His attempts to say "Papa dear" came out as "Papa-day."

"Papa-day! I don't want to go to chu'ch!"

"But you must go to church, son."

"I hate the suh-mons."

"You mustn't say that to Mr. Smith, Tad. You'll hurt his feelings. He tries to give nice sermons."

"He gives ho'ible suh-mons."

"Now, Tad, don't say that."

"Plaguey old suh-mons, Papa-day! Plaguey old suh-mons!"

Politics had fascinated Abraham since his youth at the Little Pigeon Creek settlement on the Indiana frontier, where neighbors had gathered around fireplaces to read aloud from newspapers about the exploits of Andy Jackson and speeches of Henry Clay. In Illinois, the villagers of New Salem had taken a liking to him and convinced him to run for the statehouse. He had served four terms in the legislature, building a reputation as an able Whig politician. A two-year term in the United States House of Representatives gave him a glimpse of politics in Washington, DC. In 1855, he had run for the United States Senate but had lost.

He tried for the Senate again in 1858, this time running against his longtime rival Stephen Douglas, a bantam rooster Democrat who stood just over five feet tall yet who, with ambition and fiery eloquence, had come to be known throughout the country as the Little Giant. In seven debates in eight weeks, in towns across Illinois, the two had traded arguments over the direction the country should take, especially involving slavery.

Abraham had brought to bear all his skills as a speechifier and courtroom lawyer, laying out his best arguments as to why slavery violated the sacred rights in the Declaration of Independence. Newspapers across the country took note of the debates. Many editors thought that Abraham got the better of Douglas in his arguments. In the end, Douglas had won election to the Senate, and it seemed that Abraham's political career was over.

Now here he was, less than two years later, the nominee of the new Republican Party that had been founded to combat the evil of slavery. Yet as his star rose, the country was rushing toward an abyss.

Violence was in the air. Less than a year before, the white-bearded abolitionist fanatic John Brown had tried to incite a slave revolt by attacking the federal armory in the Virginia town of Harper's Ferry. The raid, quickly put down by troops led by Colonel Robert E. Lee, had horrified North and South. Brown had gone to the gallows with a prophecy: "*I, John Brown, am now quite certain that the crimes of this guilty land will never be purged away but with blood.*"

Abraham had always hated slavery. But he had never been an abolitionist. Like many, he distrusted abolitionists' thundering demands for immediate emancipation. Sudden freedom for millions of Negroes would be too much of a shock to the nation. It would be cruel to penniless, uneducated slaves to simply tell them, "All right, you are free. Now go and fend for yourselves."

The best solution, it seemed to him, was to keep slavery from spreading beyond the South. Leave it alone where it already existed, but keep it out of the western territories, which would eventually enter the Union as new states. If slavery could be held in check, it could be gradually done away with. Allowing it to spread risked perpetuating it forever.

The nation was quickly coming to a place of stark moral choice between freedom and slavery, between right and wrong. A house divided cannot stand, he had warned during his second run for the Senate. The country could not endure forever half slave and half free. Eventually it had to be one or the other.

The choice was clear. The Declaration of Independence was right. *All* men, regardless of color, were created equal. All were meant to be free.

He walked as the sun climbed the prairie sky, listening to the wind pass over the corn and contemplating all these things: ambitions fulfilled and unfulfilled, struggles between right and wrong, and life as swift as an arrow.

CHAPTER 4

SUMMER 1860

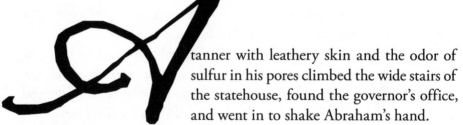A tanner with leathery skin and the odor of sulfur in his pores climbed the wide stairs of the statehouse, found the governor's office, and went in to shake Abraham's hand.

"Best of luck to you, Mr. President," he said.

"Not yet," Abraham smiled. "We shouldn't count our chickens before they hatch."

"Maybe yourn ain't quite hatched," the tanner said, "but they're peeping sure."

An old lady came with a pair of woolen socks she had knit to keep his feet warm in the White House.

"Thank you, madam," he said, holding them up. "It looks like you got my latitude and longitude just right." He handed the socks to his new secretary, John Nicolay, who gave a quiet "Humph!" before adding them to the day's pile of gifts: two hats, an ax, a wedge, three flags, some books, a whistle made from a pig's tail, a little statue of Abraham carved from a fence rail, and the rib of a huge buffalo fish someone had caught.

A long fellow from Missouri came to say he thought he was as tall as the Republican nominee. He looked confident until the nominee straightened himself up to stand back-to-back for measuring, then straightened himself up even more.

"There's a good deal of come-out in me," Abraham said. He came out a whole inch taller.

So it went, day in and day out, morning until evening. He received visitors in the governor's office on the second floor of the statehouse, which Governor John Wood had kindly put at his disposal for the campaign. The door to the hall stayed open. Friends and strangers stopped by. They came to wish him luck or see what he looked like. Some wanted to stay and talk about slavery, some about tariffs, others about the Pony Express, or the failure of the Atlantic cable, or the Frenchman who had crossed the gorge at Niagara Falls on a tightrope. Some just stood and stared with open mouths. Abraham shook their hands, told them a joke or story, and sent them on their way.

Nicolay sat at a corner desk, working away with an occasional "Humph!" at a pile of incoming mail that, despite his best efforts, always seemed to grow. Twenty-eight years old, Bavarian born, efficient as a mechanical reaper, reliable as an ox, he was exactly what the besieged candidate required. His stern freckled face gave visitors pause. Nicolay organized the mail, took dictation, and answered queries, discretely when necessary. Some letters begged for an autograph and needed only a one-line response: "Dear Sir: You request an autograph, and here it is. Yours truly, A. Lincoln." Responses to old friends like Nat Grigsby, a schoolmate during his youth on the Indiana frontier, needed more care: "You can vote for me if your neighbors will let you. I would advise you not to get into any trouble about it. Give my kindest regards to your brother Charles."

A journalist from Baltimore came asking when Mr. Lincoln expected the divided house to fall.

"My friend, if I say anything new, someone will just twist it out of shape," Abraham told him. "You'll find everything you need to know about my positions in the speeches and statements I've made to date."

"Can you assure the citizens of the South that their property will be safe?"

"I've given my views on that many times. It's in print and open to all who will read. Those who won't read or heed what I've already said publicly won't read or heed a repetition of it."

The journalist left disappointed. Nicolay scowled and let out a "Humph!" as he went out the door.

Republicans had decided to follow the custom of keeping their candidate at home in a dignified state of inactivity while allies campaigned for him. Hannibal Hamlin of Maine, the vice presidential candidate, was laying low as well. Abraham knew it was the right thing to do. There was no point in asking for trouble. But it made him feel like exactly what he was: a man used to roaming the prairies suddenly caged inside four walls.

He was left to read about the hurly-burly of the campaign—the Wide-Awake clubs marching through city streets at night in black capes while holding aloft bright, smoking torches; the rowdy barbecues; the orators braving rotten eggs; the giant banners proclaiming "Prairies on Fire for Lincoln!" and the faithful relieving their lungs with "Old Abe Lincoln came out of the wilderness, Out of the wilderness, Out of the wilderness. . . ." to the tune of "The Old Gray Mare."

A vast Republican campaign machine stayed busy manufacturing an image of Honest Old Abe the Rail Splitter. Republican newspapers boasted how he had split enough rails in his youth to reach from the North Pole to the South Pole. Old Abe was a scrupulous teller of truth, had never wronged anyone of a cent or spent a dollar not honestly earned. He possessed wisdom born of the log cabin, the rifle, the ax, and the plow. It was a strange and unsettling thing for Abraham to see them making him into something more than he was.

As many expected, the Democratic Party split over the slavery issue. Northern Democrats were running Stephen Douglas for president. The Little Giant broke with tradition and took to the stump, campaigning his heart out from New England to the West, stamping his feet and waving his fists, denouncing Republicans in his deep, booming voice. Southern Democrats nominated John Breckinridge of Kentucky. And a new party, the Constitutional Union Party, put forward John Bell of Tennessee.

The Democratic press had fun taking cracks at the Republican nominee. "Old Ape" was so ugly he could split rails by looking at them. He was a second-rate bumpkin, third-rate lawyer, and fourth-rate politician, a leader only in that he could lead cows to water.

The jibes did not bother Abraham. With the opposition divided, he was starting to believe he might actually win.

A banker from Chicago came to see him. The man waved a Southern newspaper, incensed over things it said. "They call you a mulatto, 'an African gorilla,' and 'a nigger in principle,'" he fumed.

"They've said worse. I'm still standing."

"They say that Republicans will destroy the white man, so the black man might be free!"

"I've said time and again I would not interfere with the institution of slavery in the states. But we can't allow it to spread into the territories. I can't make it any clearer."

"They threaten to secede if you are elected."

"The people of the South have too much good sense and good temper to attempt the ruin of the government."

An artist came to paint his portrait. The man looked distraught when Abraham threw his angular form into a chair before the easel and ran his fingers through his hair until it stood out like an oven broom. The artist looked even more distraught when he realized his subject would keep hopping up to greet visitors.

Elmer Ellsworth dropped by with Willie and Tad hanging onto

his coattails. The young man had recently moved from Chicago to Springfield to study law in Abraham's office, though he spent most of his time campaigning for Republicans and enjoying his fame as colonel of the US Zouave Cadets, the most famous drill team in the land. He stood only five foot six, but his dark hazel eyes and enthusiasm for everything he tried always brought men under his spell. Abraham's sons adored him.

"Elmer says he'll teach us to march!" Willie announced.

"He's going to make us Zouaves, Papa-day!" Tad said happily.

"I told them that if they want to march in my company, they must undergo the strictest discipline," Ellsworth winked.

Abraham got down on the floor to spin a top that Willie had brought along. Tad wandered the room, investigating everything he could lay his hands on. He discovered the unfinished portrait of his father. "Look, Elme'! It's anothe' Old Abe!" he shouted in delight. Before anyone could stop him, he got hold of the paint, squeezed bright yellow and blue onto his palms, and smeared it on a wall. Ellsworth marched the boys home to have their hands and faces washed.

An old Democrat who said he was thinking of leaving his party stomped in to size up the Republican candidate. "They say you're a self-made man," he growled.

"Yes, sir. What there is of me is self-made."

The man surveyed him with a careful eye. "Well, all I've got to say is that it was a damned bad job!" he said, and stomped out.

Another old Democrat came to see him in the evening, this one perhaps with more sympathy for rough-hewn edges.

"I'll vote for you, Mr. Lincoln," he said, "not because you once split rails for a living, but because you rose from a common laborer to the position you occupy today, without stooping to a mean thing or tampering with your integrity."

"That's a good one to end on," Abraham told Nicolay. "I'm going home. We'll do it again tomorrow."

He found Willie and Tad standing on the terrace in front of the house, shouting "Vote for Old Abe!" at anyone coming down the street. Mary was in high spirits over some flattering words about her in the *New York Evening Post.*

"'Whatever of awkwardness may be ascribed to her husband, there is none of it in her,'" she read aloud. "'She converses with freedom and grace, and is thoroughly *au fait* in all the little amenities of society.'"

"What does 'oh fay' mean?" Abraham asked.

"It means, Mr. Lincoln, that I know the proper way to hold a fork, and you do not."

He kicked off his shoes to let his feet breathe. "I received a letter from a little girl in Chautauqua County, New York," he said. "She thinks I should grow a beard. She says all the ladies like whiskers, and that if I had a beard, they would tease their husbands to vote for me."

"You might try it," she said. That surprised him.

"You don't think people would call it a piece of silly affection?"

"I think you would look like a statesman." That surprised him, too.

"I'll take that under advisement, Mrs. Lincoln," he said. "There are some who would say that covering any portion of my face would do no injustice to the world."

CHAPTER 5

SUMMER 1860

H is law office just off the public square was a refuge from the stream of visitors at the statehouse. He sprawled out on the firm's old sofa and rifled through a pile of newspapers.

"How's your bones philosophy this morning?" he asked Billy Herndon, his junior partner.

"Fine-tuned as ever, Mr. Lincoln."

"What news on the Rialto?"

"Widow Chase fell on a sidewalk and broke her leg. She wants to talk to you about suing the city."

"Widow Chase is a good-looking woman. Half the fellows on the jury will vote to give her a thousand dollars in hopes of marrying her afterwards. What else?"

"Ben Horne owes us five dollars and says he can't pay in cash. He wants to pay in chickens and firewood instead."

"That's all right. A big pile of firewood is as good as money in the bank. Anything else?"

"The Illinois Central sent a note for two hundred dollars. They'll send two hundred more when proceedings in DeWitt County are concluded."

"Well, Billy, all I can say is, thank the Lord for the Illinois Central."

Billy grunted. He was by nature suspicious of big corporations like railroads, but he liked the retainers they paid.

Abraham rummaged more through the newspapers. "Looks like President Buchanan will veto the Homestead Bill. Says he fears the government doesn't have the power to give away land to settlers."

"That's not what he fears," Bill snorted. "He's scared of western lands filling up with free-soilers who'll vote to keep slavery out. He's kowtowing to the South."

"I suspect you're right."

"The man is an embarrassment to the republic. He's enough to make a patriot's cheek burn with shame!"

His cheeks were, in fact, aglow. Billy was like that, always quick to light up like a torch for noble causes. A lover of books and collector of knowledge—his office bookshelves were crammed with writers from John Locke to Emmanuel Kant—he declared he could feel truth in his bones when he found it. His backwoods bones philosophy guided his politics and a dreamy idealism.

"Well, Buchanan does have the whole country to think about, including the South," Abraham mused. "A considerable portion of the country's wealth is invested in slaves."

"Ill-gotten wealth does no man any good."

"That's true."

"It's as true of nations as individuals," Billy avowed. "All the ill-gotten gain wrenched by us from the Negro will eventually be taken from us, and we'll be set back where we began."

"That's a rather direful prophecy."

"Mark my words, Mr. Lincoln. I can see to the gizzard of the question."

Abraham smiled. "I wonder if either of us will live to see the righting of so great a wrong."

"We should put it to rights today, no matter the cost."

"Billy, you're too rampant and spontaneous."

The younger man's face fell.

"But only when it comes to your bones philosophy," Abraham quickly added. "In matters of law, no one could ask for a better partner."

He said it in all sincerity. Billy Herndon had long ago proven himself to be a loyal friend, hard worker, and able attorney. He was a skilled researcher and more than capable at drafting legal documents, leaving Abraham time for courtroom arguments and politics.

Abraham put down the newspaper and surveyed his office. It looked to be in its usual untidy state. Dusty stacks of pleadings and affidavits piled on the floor. Old secretary with pigeonholes stuffed full of papers. Bookcase crammed with musty legal tomes. Everything pretty much as it had been since the day fifteen years before when they first hung up a shingle reading *Lincoln and Herndon* outside their door.

He was fond of his office, but his favorite thing about work was traveling Illinois's Eighth Judicial Circuit, which sprawled across much of the state. A small army of lawyers rode from town to town, along with Judge David Davis or another judge, trying cases as they went. When they reached a county seat, they shopped for clients, prepared their cases, went to trial, and collected their fees, sometimes all in one day. After court adjourned in one place, they followed the judge to the next courthouse. Along the way, they slept in dingy, flea-ridden taverns, two or three to a bed, eight or more to a room. A lawyer brave enough to travel the whole circuit faced a trip that covered hundreds of miles and took several weeks.

He liked the freedom of moving across the open prairies in the springtime, when the smell of moist loam was in the air and wildflowers covered the hills, and again in the autumn, when a soft golden haze filled the space between brown grass and sky. He rode behind Old Bob, his horse, in a buggy made for him by a Springfield blacksmith, his books and clean shirts stuffed into a striped carpet bag, important papers tucked away in his tall hat. On the seat next to him rode a faded green umbrella, its knob gone, the name "A. Lincoln" sewn in white muslin letters inside, a piece of string tied around its middle to keep it from flapping open.

It always had the feel of a traveling circus, this biannual migration from courthouse to courthouse, with the lawyers joking and singing as they rode along, old friends stretching out arms to shake hands when they reached the next town, and crowds pressing into courtrooms to see the attorneys put on a show. Into Judge Davis's courtroom came litigants dragging behind them a tangled skein of human motives and passions. Neighbors suing neighbors for stealing hogs or allowing cows to trample each other's corn. A village accusing the owners of a lard factory of operating an "unwholesome business" that was polluting the town. A man refusing to pay alimony to the mother of his children because, he said, she was a vicious, hard-hearted woman.

On the Eighth Circuit, he sharpened his skills as a lawyer and reader of men. He learned to use homespun expressions to drive home a point in court, as when he made a jury understand that someone was crooked by telling them about a fence so crooked that a hog trying to go through an opening kept coming out on the side where it started. Pretty soon he had gained the reputation as one of the cleverest attorneys in Illinois.

The other lawyers had started calling him Old Abe in a good-natured way. He sometimes wondered about it. He did not look particularly old. They had given him the name when he was still in the full vigor of life, with only a few lines on his leathery face. No, it wasn't his looks that invited the nickname. Perhaps it was because he was a good old fellow. Or maybe his life had been kept so crowded with the work of living, he seemed older than his years. He could not quite put his finger on it.

They called him Honest Abe, too, and said he held himself to the highest standards of integrity in practicing law. He was not afraid to tell a client, "My friend, you are in the wrong—I would advise you to drop the matter." He liked settling a case better than going to trial and had even been known to tell a client, "If you settle, I will charge nothing for what I have done, and thank you to boot."

He was the best storyteller on the circuit. Everyone agreed on that. If you found a knot of men gathered around a fireplace, slapping their thighs with laughter, you'd likely find Old Abe in the middle, spinning one of his yarns. Folks said he could make a cat laugh.

But then there were times he would abruptly turn inward, times he wanted to be off by himself. There were shades of melancholy in his eyes. Perhaps that was part of the reason people called him Old Abe. More than once, a lawyer had awakened early in some dusty tavern room, when the snoring of eight or nine men filled the darkness, and seen him sitting alone by the hearth, legs drawn up, hands clasping his knees, brooding by firelight.

The coming of the railroads changed his legal practice. Instead of traveling the Eighth Circuit by buggy, he took trains from town to town. Springfield had changed as well, growing from a prairie village where hogs roamed the public square into a thriving capital city of nearly ten thousand inhabitants. City blocks pushed back cornfields. Locomotives chugged in and out of town, and telegraph wires brought messages riding electric currents from far away. The Lincoln home at Eighth and Jackson, which had started out as a modest one-and-a-half story cottage, was remodeled into a handsome two-story residence with pilasters adorning its corners and a balustrade of iron grillwork running along a side porch—a house befitting a prosperous lawyer whose name was known in legal and political circles throughout Illinois and beyond.

Billy pulled a copy of the *Illinois State Register* from Abraham's stack of newspapers and perused reports from the Southern presses.

"I'm afraid the South means to cause real trouble if you're elected."

"Think so?"

"They say you're an abolitionist in disguise and that they'll secede the minute you show your real face."

"If they're waiting for me to do something to make them secede, they'll wait all their lives."

"They say you'll put hordes of abolitionists into federal offices," Billy said. "They'll have Negroes at their polls, Negroes in their schools, Negroes in their legislatures."

"That's the firebrands talking, Billy. They talk the loudest, so what they say ends up in the papers."

"That's true."

Abraham leaned back and hung his feet over the sofa's end.

"Elections in this country are like big boils," he mused. "They cause a great deal of pain before they come to a head, but after the trouble is over, the body is in better health than before. The bitterness of this canvass will pass away as easily as the core of a boil. At least I hope so."

"I hope so, too," Billy said.

He didn't sound very hopeful. If the newspapers were to be believed, across the South, discouraged, frightened men were reaching dire conclusions. Hysterical voices warned that the moment Lincoln was in the presidency, the North would invade the South. Already wild rumors of slave revolts were sweeping the countryside—wells poisoned, fires set to plantation houses, white women seized and violated in ways too appalling to say aloud. Shootings and hangings were certain to follow. "Let the boys arm. Every one that can point a shotgun or revolver should have one," the *Montgomery Mail* was telling its readers. "Abolitionism is at your doors, with torch and knife in hand!"

Abraham studied Billy's face. "Look on the bright side," he said. "Maybe I won't be elected."

Billy shook his head. "I'm afraid there's a storm coming, either way."

"You really think so?"

"I know it. A big storm. I can feel it in my bones."

He raised his arm as if to show a divining rod.

"I just hate to see you in the middle of it, Mr. Lincoln."

Abraham's mood turned somber. It struck him head-on for the first time that the life he had known in Springfield was going to disappear, perhaps forever. He looked at the old familiar trappings of his office—rickety sofa, stacks of pleadings, dusty secretary, crowded bookcase—and for a moment the room seemed to dissolve before him.

CHAPTER 6

SUMMER AND AUTUMN 1860

It was a summer of jumbled nerves and approaching storms. One August afternoon, the townspeople watched a distant black wall build to the top of the western sky. The air lay motionless, like water behind a dam just before it gives way. Abraham hurried home from the statehouse to calm Mary. She had been terrified of storms ever since she was a girl, when she would stand crying, "Hide me, O my Savior!" in her father's parlor every time thunder rolled through Lexington.

The maelstrom hit in early evening. Fire dropped from the sky. Wind rushed past the house and pried at the clapboards. Thunder crashed around them like mountains falling. They huddled on the stairway, away from windows, Mary whimpering that the noise was hurting her head, the boys trying to be brave.

When the storm passed, and it grew still again, they crept outside with their neighbors to see the damage: uprooted trees, missing roofs, broken windows. Their own house had suffered no major damage, thank goodness. Downtown, plank sidewalks lay splintered. Crowder's stable on Washington Street had been hit by lightning and burned to the ground. The brick walls of Withey's carriage factory had collapsed and smashed dozens of carriages.

The pounding of hammers and scraping of saws filled the air as thoughts turned back to the campaign. The Republicans repaired their Springfield Wigwam, a round frame building at the corner of Sixth and Monroe Streets built to hold more than three thousand people. Nearby stood their campaign pole, one hundred and twenty feet high, made of ash timbers, with a broom lashed to the top to symbolize Old Abe's determination to sweep corruption out of Washington and, below the broom, a weathervane shaped like an ax. Next to the pole sat the mighty Lincoln Cannon, cast especially for the campaign, ready to boom out the call for Republicans to flock to the Wigwam for speeches and rallies.

"Will they fi'e the cannon if you win, Papa-day?" Tad asked.

"I suppose so."

"Do they have cannon in Washington?"

"I believe they have many cannon in Washington."

Elmer Ellsworth's US Zouave Cadets put on an exhibition drill one afternoon in an open lot down the street from the Wigwam. Thousands gathered for the show. The Lincolns stood in the shade of a cottonwood tree, Abraham letting Tad and Willie take turns sitting on his shoulders to see until the boys determined to push forward and squat in front. Fifty Zouaves marched onto the field in jaunty red caps, blue jackets trimmed with gold, and loose scarlet trousers. Young ladies tracked Colonel Ellsworth with their eyes, taking note of the dark brown curls that spilled from his cap down his neck. With flawless precision, he put his cadets through the maneuvers of war: advancing, retiring, rallying by fours, firing while standing and kneeling. They formed a line that coiled like a serpent until the head met the tail, tied itself into a Gordian knot, and at a signal from Ellsworth, miraculously untangled itself.

After the drill, Ellsworth showed Willie and Tad how to stand at attention with musket on shoulder.

"Backs straight, eyes forward. Good boys."

"Do you think I'll make a good Zouave?" Willie asked, eyes shining.

"You'll make a fine cadet," Ellsworth promised. "I'll have you ready in no time."

"What do I have to do?"

"Before you can become a Zouave, you must climb an eighty-foot rope, hand over hand, with a barrel of flour dangling from your heels. Then balance yourself atop a forty-foot ladder and shoot a dozen wild pigeons on the wing, one at a time, just behind the eye, at a distance of three hundred yards, and never miss a shot."

"In truth?"

"Yes. But more important, you must improve yourself morally and conduct yourself in an honorable way."

"How do I do that?"

"Love your father and mother more than life, stand ready to give your last cent to a brother in need, and stay away from drinking saloons."

"I'll do it," Willie pledged solemnly.

The Republicans staged a grand rally to beat all rallies, the largest demonstration ever held in the West. Fifty thousand people converged by train and wagon on Springfield, from all over Illinois and beyond. The town of ten thousand had no place to put them. They slept in taverns six to a bed, pitched tents in backyards, curled up in stables. On the appointed day, the pilgrims lined up and streamed down Eighth Street past Abraham's door.

First came a huge rolling ball inscribed with the slogan, "The people mourn insulted laws, and curse Steve Douglas as the cause." Then came the Wide-Awake clubs, the glee clubs, and the wagonloads of visiting delegations. Willie and Tad leaned out upstairs windows and shouted with joy whenever a float came along: a flatboat on wheels; a log cabin on wheels with a settler in its yard, splitting rails; a power loom on wheels with men weaving yards of jean cloth to make pants for Mr. Lincoln. It took nearly three hours for the column to pass the house and wind its way to the fairgrounds.

Ward Hill Lamon, a fellow attorney and good friend, came by to watch the parade. A Virginian by birth, the tall, stout Lamon had a way of causing a party if not a ruckus wherever he went. His colleagues, who called him Hill, liked to hear him strum his banjo and sing "The Blue Tail Fly" after a long day before Judge Davis's bench. Davis always said that Hill Lamon could take more out of a pint of whiskey than a pint of whiskey took out of him. He could swing his two fists as hard as he drank, and though friends said he had probably never read a book from first chapter to last, he had a fine appreciation for jokes too rough for ladies' ears.

"Let's go out to the fairgrounds and take a look at the rally," Hill suggested. "The Wide-Awakes have built five platforms for speakers."

"All right," Abraham said, "so long as I'm not called upon to do any speechifying myself."

They climbed into a carriage and trailed the parade to the fairgrounds, west of the city, but when the people saw him arrive, they rushed the carriage from all sides, shrieking with joy. Several climbed on top and danced like savages. Hands stuck through the windows, trying to touch him. One man pried the carriage door open and started to haul himself through until Lamon grabbed him by the shoulders and pushed him out.

"They're drunk on politics and corn liquor, damn them," Lamon swore.

The cheering mass pressed harder. Men started throwing punches. The innermost layer of people, crushed against the vehicle's sides, cried out in pain.

"Why don't we go?" Lamon yelled to the driver.

"We can't go! Some fool unhitched the damned horses!"

A band of Wide-Awakes muscled their way through with a horse.

They brought the animal alongside the rocking carriage, pulled Abraham out, slipped him over the horse's tail while they held the onslaught at bay, then forced their way out of the crowd like a wedge being driven through a log. Abraham, holding hard with both hands to the knob of the saddle, watched his hat disappear into the throng.

Lamon caught up with him as he reached the deserted public square.

"My God," he panted, "if they'd caught you, they'd have crushed the life out of you."

"They meant no harm," Abraham said, trying not to sound shaken.

"That's what worries me. Those fellows are your friends. Think of what a bunch of rascals who don't like you might do if they got hold of you."

The campaign moved into the fall, and the closer the election drew, the more likely it seemed he would win. "I hesitate to say it," he wrote a friend in Oregon, "but it really appears now as if the success of the Republican ticket is inevitable." From New York to Chicago, newspapers were predicting that Abraham Lincoln would be the next president. It seemed unreal.

He felt as if he were on the eve of a long voyage, though he could not be sure the winds wouldn't turn against him before he could sail. Was it possible that Stephen Douglas, who seemed to know how to gain power and fame better than any man alive, would somehow manage to beat him again?

At Southern crossroads and over store counters, citizens swore to one another that they would never submit to a Lincoln presidency. It would be a fine thing if the Union would break into pieces, they said. If the South were to set up its own government, it could appoint diplomats, acquire territories, and negotiate treaties with other countries, including what was left of the United States. Across the South, governors, senators, and congressman, one by one, were going on record in favor of secession.

Election day, November 6, when it finally arrived, came as a blur of anticipations, like dimly lit impressions cast on a wall at a magic lantern show.

The Lincoln Cannon booming at dawn.

A wagon rolling down the street hauling a brass band and some Wide-Awakes singing, "Ain't I glad I've joined the Republicans, joined the Republicans, joined the Republicans!"

Nicolay sitting at his corner desk in the governor's office, directing a low guttural "Humph!" at well-wishers as they filed through the door.

An afternoon trip across the square through a cheering crowd to cast his vote at the courthouse, Hill Lamon marching proudly on his right, Elmer Ellsworth on his left, Billy Herndon and John Nicolay bringing up the rear.

The telegraph briskly tapping out returns from Wisconsin, Iowa, New Jersey, and New York as friends shouted, howled, embraced.

Judge Davis throwing his hat against the ceiling again and again.

Billy rolling back and forth on the floor.

Hill strumming his banjo as loud as he could until the strings popped off.

And finally men running through the streets, yelling from the rooftops, firing guns in celebration as Abraham thought *God help me* and walked home as calmly as he could to deliver the news: "Mary, Mary, we are elected!"

CHAPTER 7

AUTUMN 1860

The South's response to his election was swift. Word came that citizens of Pensacola, Florida, had hung him in effigy. In South Carolina, leaders gathered to consider leaving the Union. "The tea has been thrown overboard," the *Charleston Mercury* proclaimed, "the revolution of 1860 has been initiated." Down in Alabama, men were wearing ribbons that read "Resistance to Lincoln is obedience to God."

In Washington, DC, President James Buchanan fretted and groaned that a Republican president would divide the country beyond repair. He let it be known that although he did not like the idea of secession and thought it was wrong, he did not see that there was much the federal government could do about it.

Men came to Abraham with panic in their voices, urging him to say something to calm their Southern countrymen before it was too late.

"I don't take office for four months," he reminded them. "Until then, I'm a private citizen. It's not my place."

"They will listen to you anyway."

"I can say nothing I've not already said or written. If I say anything to comfort the South, it will agitate the North. If I say anything to please the North, it will inflame the South."

"If you will compromise, even a little, on the question of allowing slavery in the territories, it would save the day."

"I can't shift the ground on which I was elected."

"Not even to keep the country in one piece?"

"The instant I made any concession, the loudest voices would just shout for more. Do you know Aesop's fable of the lion who fell in love with a beautiful maiden and asked for her hand in marriage? Her parents didn't like the idea, but they told the beast they would give their consent if he would have his fangs and claws removed, to be sure he never hurt her by accident. The lion was so desperately in love, he did as they asked. When his claws and teeth were gone, the maiden's father took a club and knocked him on the head."

"If you don't do something, by the time you get to Washington, this land will be whitened by tents."

"Well, we won't jump that ditch 'til we come to it. At any rate, I believe that most Southerners are loyal to the Union. If they'll give me a chance, they'll see I won't interfere with them in any way. This threat of secession is a bluff. It's the trick by which the South breaks down every Northern man."

More people than ever flocked to see him. They came by the train-load to shake hands, give advice, ask questions. He received visitors at the governor's office in the statehouse for two hours every morning and again for two hours every afternoon. Often the line stretched out the door, along the hallway, and down the big staircase.

"You're going to wear yourself out seeing so many people," Billy

Herndon warned.

"Each one of them considers his business with me important," Abraham said. "I must gratify them."

A lawyer he'd known a long time came begging him to reassure the South. "Don't let them make a rumpus," the man sobbed like a child. "I live just across the river from Missouri. If there's war, I know I'll be killed or hurt."

An old woman in a homespun woolen dress whose farm he had helped save from creditors long ago waited in line to see him and squinted into his face. "It *is* him," she mumbled to herself. "It's the same. God preserve you, Mr. Lincoln."

Letters poured in. People wrote to congratulate or castigate him. Some urged him to resign and hand the reins of power to Stephen Douglas. Some called him an Illinois ape, a baboon, a mulatto, an abortion. More than a few poked fun.

"Deformed Sir—The Ugly Club, in full meeting, have elected you an Honorary Member of the Hard-Favored Fraternity," read one. "Prince Harry was lean, Falstaff was fat, Thersites was hunchbacked, and Slawkenbergius was renowned for the eminent miscalculation which Nature had made in the length of his nose; but it remained for you to unite all species of deformity, and stand forth the Prince of Ugly Fellows." It was signed, in the bonds of ugliness, by Hinchaway Beeswax, President of the Ugly Club, and Eagle-eyed Carbuncle, Secretary.

The flood of mail threatened to drown poor Nicolay. He recruited a friend, John Hay, a recent graduate of Brown University studying law in Springfield, to help. Red-cheeked and black-eyed, given to wearing derby hats and dashing off lines of poetry, Hay grinned when Nicolay frowned and laughed when Nicolay growled. His smooth face and slight figure gave him the look of a schoolboy. The young men sat together at the office's corner table, reading, sorting, and scribbling away until, just when they had fought off one deluge of letters, the United States Post Office Department arrived with another. Visitors to the president-elect, especially ones who had never learned to write, stared bemused at the sight of two heads disappearing and reemerging behind rising and falling waves of mail.

Office seekers swarmed without restraint. They waylaid Abraham on the square, appeared in his parlor at night, and practically crawled through the windows and down the chimneys of the statehouse. They came hoping to be turned into judges, marshals, postmasters, patent examiners, customs inspectors, and more.

"The Republican Party has never been fed, and it's vigorously hungry," Billy observed, eyeing the long line of supplicants. "Does every one of them expect a teat at the government crib?"

A man with smooth hands and a threadbare coat came looking for something along the lines of a government clerk. "Poverty is no disgrace, but I find it damned inconvenient," he explained. "I should like to get something that would keep my nose and the grindstone apart for a while." He went away looking hungrier than ever.

Another came hinting strongly that he deserved a plum appointment in reward for invaluable campaign work.

"So you made me president, did you?" Abraham asked.

"Yes, I believe I did."

"Well, then, it's a fine mess you've got me into, isn't it?"

Willie burst into the office, looking for a quarter.

"What do you want it for?" Abraham asked.

"I want to buy candy!"

"I can't let you have twenty-five cents," he said, putting his thumb and finger into his vest pocket, "but I'll give you five cents." He laid the pennies on the desk's edge. Willie put on a scornful face, turned his back, and sulked off down the hallway.

"He'll be back in a few minutes," Abraham told the man hoping for the plum office. "As soon as he realizes he'll get no more, he'll come get it."

A short while later, Willie crept into the room, scooped up the pennies, and left without a word. The office-seeker departed with a thoughtful look on his brow.

The task of choosing men to serve in the cabinet took an enormous amount of time and energy. If he was going to hold his government together, he needed advisors with the administrative experience he lacked. He needed a mix of lieutenants representing the rival factions of the Republican Party, as well as men with ties to the Democrats, men from the East and West and, if possible, even someone from the South.

William H. Seward, still considered by many to be the leading Republican in the nation, would be best for secretary of state. Salmon Chase of Ohio, admired by antislavery radicals, would make a good head of the Treasury Department. Simon Cameron of Pennsylvania could perhaps lead the War Department, though his enemies would protest that he had a reputation for corruption. And Edward Bates of Missouri would make a fine attorney general. All four of those men had lost the election to Abraham. Would they be willing to serve under him now? Montgomery Blair of Maryland, Gideon Welles of Connecticut, and Caleb Smith of Indiana would make good choices for postmaster general, secretary of the navy, and secretary of the interior.

He made a quick trip to Chicago to meet with Hannibal Hamlin, the vice president-elect, and talk over cabinet selections with him. An old dear friend, Josh Speed, came up from Louisville at Abraham's request to meet while he was there.

"Speed, you're a sight for these sore eyes," he almost shouted. They sprawled out in Josh's room at the Tremont House, marveling that they had both turned into middle-aged men, and talked over old times.

Josh had been the first soul to welcome him to Springfield in 1837 on the day he rode into town on a sorry-looking horse, looking for a place to stay while he got his start as a lawyer. When Abraham wandered into Josh's general store on Fifth Street, the young merchant had taken pity on him and suggested they become roommates in a bedroom above the store. From then on, they had shared jokes, plans, worries, and dreams. Josh had long since returned to his family home in Kentucky, just outside of Louisville, to oversee operations of the Speed plantation. He had put on a few pounds since their younger days, and his beard showed traces of gray, but his smile had lost none of its warmth.

"Tell me something, Speed," Abraham ventured. "What are your pecuniary conditions—are you rich or poor these days?"

Josh's smile took on shades of regret. "I think I know what you're after. I'll speak candidly. My pecuniary conditions are good. I don't think there's an office you can offer that I could afford to take."

"I thought so," Abraham sighed, "but it was worth asking. It would have been a fine thing to have you with me in Washington."

He told him the names he was considering for his cabinet.

"You'll have your hands full," Josh said. "Some of those men think they are bigger than you are."

"Do you know any other men who think they're bigger than I am? I'll put them all in my cabinet. I'll need them."

"Seems as if truly big men are scarcer than they used to be."

"I wish I could take all my friends that rode the Eighth Circuit with me and make a cabinet out of them. I could head off any trouble with that bunch of fellows."

"A good many of those lawyers are Democrats."

"That's all right. I'd rather have Democrats I know than Republicans I don't know."

Abraham fidgeted with his hat for a moment.

"Tell me something else, Speed," he said. "How is the mood in Kentucky these days?"

"I know more than a few men who aren't happy about your election."

You'd no doubt be among them if we weren't friends, Abraham thought. That dozens of slaves worked the Speed plantation growing hemp to make rope and bags hung as a painful, unspoken fact between them.

"Can I count on your friends' loyalty to the Union?"

"You can if they'll listen to me, which I believe most of them will."

"Thank you," Abraham said. "I'll need your help. If Kentucky were to give me trouble, it would be a very bad sign."

The year 1860 moved into its final days, and the country drifted.

Editors and politicians clamored for the president-elect to say something making clear his intentions, and the president-elect stuck to his policy of issuing no public statements. "They seek a sign, and no sign shall be given them," he told his friends.

He did, in fact, give one sign. One that might signal to people that they were getting an elder statesman for a president. Or perhaps a learned Western lawyer. Or a prairie philosopher, or the son of a humble farmer. People could take it as they might.

He decided to follow the advice of that little girl in Westfield, New York, and grow a beard.

CHAPTER 8

LATE 1860 AND
EARLY 1861

The Union was dissolved. The news came as a shock despite years of warnings. When it raced over the telegraph wires and the dispatch was put into his hands, Abraham did his best to look calm, but inside he trembled. A South Carolina convention had unanimously passed an ordinance of secession, and already state troops were preparing to occupy federal forts at Charleston Harbor. Now that one state had dared to go, secession fever would likely sweep the Cotton Belt, and states across the lower South would quickly follow.

Oh, Lord, this can't be happening, he thought.

Rumors flew that President Buchanan planned to give up the forts at Charleston if attacked.

"If it's true, they ought to hang him!" Abraham muttered to Nicolay. "If he surrenders those forts, we'll have to retake them after the inauguration."

He lay in bed at night, cold and sleepless, listening to a mantel clock that seemed to be counting down the last hours of the United States. How could that old fool Buchanan have let things get so far out of hand? Surely to God the secession fires would die down when Southerners realized Republicans meant them no harm. The South was still full of men loyal to the Union. Given the chance, they would gain the upper hand over the hotheads. A little time was what they needed.

Down in Georgia, Alexander Stephens, a frail, stooped man whom Abraham knew fondly as Little Aleck when they had served together in Congress, was telling anyone who would listen that the election of Abraham Lincoln was no reason to leave the Union. Bob Toombs, another friend from Georgia who had been in Congress, was urging Southerners to bring their sons home from the federal army, withhold their taxes, and use the money to buy arms.

Desperate for reassurance, Abraham wrote to Aleck, asking if Southerners really believed that a Republican administration would interfere with their slaves—and assuring him it would not. Aleck's reply came back full of resignation and warning: "Do what you can to save our common country."

Nine days into the new year, South Carolina guns opened fire on the *Star of the West,* a merchant vessel carrying supplies and reinforcements for the federal garrison at Fort Sumter in Charleston Harbor. The unarmed steamer reversed course and headed out to sea. That same day, Mississippi left the Union, followed closely by Florida, Alabama, and Georgia. Louisiana and Texas were not far behind.

Across the South, state troops seized federal installations. Southern congressman and senators resigned in droves, packed their bags, and left Washington. In Savannah, the mayor saluted his state's new independence with a toast: "Southern civilization—it must be maintained at any costs and at all hazards!"

Every morning, Abraham put on his shirt and tie, went downtown, and gave out the message to Republican allies that they must hold firm as a chain of steel. Every night he went home, lay in bed, and shivered.

Death threats and pleas to be on guard arrived almost daily. The mail brought drawings of guns, daggers, and Abraham being tossed into hell on a devil's pitchfork. A farm boy came to see him at the statehouse, hat in hand, saying, "Father sent me to tell you that you might be poisoned. He says you must look out and eat nothing but what your old woman cooks. Mother says so, too."

Abraham came home one evening and found Mary looking grim.

"This came today, from South Carolina," she said. She handed him a canvas painting that depicted him with a rope around his neck, feet chained, body tarred and feathered. Its viciousness jolted him.

"My God, Mary, I'm sorry you had to see this."

"I won't let it alarm me!" she vowed. "Anyone cowardly enough to send this would never be man enough to carry it through."

"That's my girl." He pulled her close, staring over her shoulder at the crude image.

Tense rumors filtered out of the nation's capital—whispers of schemes to prevent the counting of electoral votes and plots to kidnap the president-elect. He sat beside a potbellied stove in the statehouse on a snowy evening, whittling on a stick and discussing the reports with a circle of friends.

"We got a letter from someone in Washington who says that he and nine others have sworn to shoot you during the inaugural procession," Nicolay reported.

"I'll go outside and hang myself in my backyard before they'll scare me off."

"And another saying ten thousand men have organized in Maryland and Virginia. They've pledged to seize the capital before you can take the oath of office."

"We should put out a call for a hundred thousand Wide-Awakes to make their way to Washington," Hill Lamon growled. "That'll guarantee the result we want."

"My fifty Zouaves could handle ten thousand traitors!" Elmer Ellsworth's eyes glowed. "I'd lay down my life to see you installed, Mr. Lincoln."

The men warmed their feet and contemplated the situation.

"Our wayward friends might yet come back," Abraham said. "We've got to convince them we'll let them alone as long as they're in the Union."

"Convincing don't have much to do with it," Lamon grunted. "Most seceshes are no better than horse thieves."

"Well, I wish I could have got to Washington to lock the door before the horse was stolen. But when I get to the spot, I can find the tracks."

It was hard to know if the threats of violence at his inauguration were real. He sent queries to General Winfield Scott, general-in-chief of the army. Scott sent back word from Washington that he would plant cannon at both ends of Pennsylvania Avenue, and that if any secessionists showed their faces or raised a finger, he would blow them to hell.

Mary dealt with the mounting stress in her own way. She went shopping. "I'll go to New York," she announced. "I can find what I need there. When we get to Washington, I want to arrive in style."

"Is it necessary?" he asked gingerly.

"If I'm to play the part of first lady, I can't go looking like a frontier wife."

"That's true," he conceded, though it seemed to him that she had never looked like a frontier wife.

"I also want to get some things in the way of curtains and bedclothes for the Executive Mansion."

"But we don't even know what's already in the house."

"Whatever is there, I'm sure I can improve on Mr. Buchanan's touch. It will be our home for at least four years, you know."

"How much will all this cost?" he asked, again carefully.

"Abraham, the presidency pays five times as much as you make now. You can afford it. We've advanced in the world, and we must have a few nice things to advance with us."

He let it go. There were more important things to worry over. Besides, it would do her good to get away for a while.

She was gone for almost two weeks. It was lonely in the house without her, even though he had Willie and Tad on his hands in the evenings. The kitchen and sitting room rapidly fell into disorder. When the boys were in bed, he sprawled on the floor beside a stove and rubbed Fido's raggedy ears as he jotted down thoughts to put into his inaugural address.

The night she was due to return was cold and snowy. He bundled up in his overcoat and walked up Tenth Street under an umbrella to the depot to greet her. Bob, now enrolled at Harvard, had joined her in New York and was coming home as well. They would all be together again.

The train was late. He waited inside the depot for a while, then stood outside under the platform's shelter, peering down the empty tracks. The locomotive finally pulled in, and the passengers disembarked. He stood watching until the last figures had climbed out of the coaches and melted into the dark. No Mary. He turned, put up his umbrella, and tromped back down Tenth Street alone.

The next two nights he went back again through the cold and snow, and waited for more slow trains. Still no Mary. Why hadn't she telegrammed to let him know when she was coming? Being elected president didn't do much in the way of making trains or women run on time, he told himself as he walked home.

She finally arrived on the fourth night, full of high spirits over her New York sojourn. Bob was with her, looking very much like a genteel young Bostonian. Two porters unloaded a mountain of parcels onto a dray.

Mary chattered like a schoolgirl. She couldn't wait to tell him all about the dresses and jewelry and lace curtains she'd bought, about the tour of the Brooklyn Navy Yard that an admiral had given her, the private box she'd enjoyed at the Academy of Music, and the special car the president of the railroad had put at her disposal. It was good to have her back. By the time they reached home, he was wondering how he had stood so much peace and quiet while she was gone.

He stayed up for a while with Bob to hear all about Harvard, but everyone was fatigued, so they blew out the lamps in the sitting room and went upstairs. Abraham threw himself down on a lounge in his chamber and tried to read a couple of letters he had brought home from the office. Drowsiness overtook him, and he closed his eyes. He needed to undress but was too tired to move. Half of him wanted to just lie there, and half wanted to make the effort to climb into bed. If he didn't get up now, he'd end up sleeping all night on the sofa and wake up sore. He forced his eyes open and gave a start.

Near the lounge sat a bureau with a mirror on its front. He found himself looking at his own reflection sprawled out on the sofa. Only there was something odd about it. His face had two separate and distinct images, with the tip of one nose about three inches from the tip of the other.

He sat up and looked in the glass. At once the illusion vanished. He rose and went closer to study his face. It looked weary from the pressures of the last few weeks. A few more lines around his eyes than the last time he had looked. A few specks of gray in his new beard. Perhaps he really was beginning to look like an Old Abe.

He lay back down, eyes on the mirror. There it was a second time, the double-image, even plainer than before. One of the faces looked vivid, full of the glow of life. The twin, dim and gray, stared back at him. A shudder passed through him. He jumped up, and the ghost melted away.

He tried a few more times to resurrect it, but the thing would not reappear. The clock struck eleven. He needed to be up early tomorrow. His clothes dropped to the floor, and he crawled into bed, worrying over what the double-image could mean.

CHAPTER 9

LATE JANUARY 1861

*H*e needed to say goodbye to his stepmother. Sally Lincoln lived in Coles County, eighty miles southeast of Springfield, on a stretch of prairie where she and Abraham's father had settled after their move from Indiana. Abraham knew the land and its people well. Between visiting his family, politicking, and trying cases in Charleston, the county seat, he had spent a good bit of time there over the years.

A series of three trains carried him over winter-stiff prairies, the last one a freight train, and by the time he climbed off a caboose after sunset and hiked along the tracks through slush and ice, toting his carpetbag to the platform at the Charleston depot, his feet were close to freezing.

Old friends and kinfolk gathered to congratulate him, half-bursting with pride from his achievement, half-wanting him to know that to them, he would always be plain old Abe Lincoln. Good, honest John Hanks was there, taking quiet pleasure in his role as the cousin who had split rails with the Rail Candidate. His cousin Dennis Hanks was there, too, boasting that it was he who had taught young Abe to write with buzzard-quill pens and maple-bark ink when they lived in the Indiana wilderness. It wasn't quite true, though it was true that Dennis had taught him a lot growing up, from how to find the North Star to how to skin a rabbit.

"I always said there was something peculiarsome about you, Abe," he laughed, "and now you've gone and proved it."

"I reckon so, Denny."

"When you get to be president, you can just reach up and set the last stones on top of that monument to General Washington they've been trying to build and finish it off for 'em."

Folks came unsure of how familiar to be until he put them at ease with, "Lord A'mighty, Jim, it's good to see you," or, "Tell me, Harriet, do you still make gooseberry cobbler as good as you used to?" A young fellow with fuzz on his cheeks came to say he would shed his last drop of blood to help save the country. An old client appeared, saying he hoped Abraham would make as good a president as he was an attorney.

"I still own the mare you gained for me in that suit long ago," the man said. "I rode Old Trim to the election to vote for you, and I've rode her here today. Do you remember that lawsuit?"

"I remember it well. It was 1837, more than twenty-three years ago."

The next morning, he climbed into a two-horse buggy with Dennis and drove ten miles into the country. The land was as still as only land buried under cold can be. Kickapoo Creek flowed under a skin of ice just thick enough to give the horses trouble, and it took some urging to get them across. Sally was staying with her daughter Tildy, Abraham's stepsister, because the chimney on her own cabin had fallen.

"I believe I spy three sparrow eggs in there," she teased, stroking his beard. "It looks good on you, Abe. Makes you look like a president should look."

She was seventy-two years old now, and her black hair had finally turned completely gray. For the first time he could remember, she looked small as she rocked by the fire in the chair that Tildy had brought from her cabin. As he watched her, his thoughts drifted back more than four decades to Little Pigeon Creek in Indiana.

After his mother had passed away, his father had left him with his sister Sarah and cousin Dennis to fend for themselves while he went back to Kentucky to fetch a new wife. Lonely, wretched weeks had passed, and then one evening they heard the rattle of wheels and ran outside to find Tom Lincoln pulling up to their cabin with a wagonload of furniture. Beside him sat a woman they did not know, and behind her, two girls and a boy. "Children, this is your new ma," Tom had announced. The tall, handsome woman had climbed down, smiled, and taken them into her arms.

That was her first act of motherly love. The second was to look over the Lincoln cabin and tell her new husband, "This place isn't fitting for pigs to live in, let alone children. We'll commence cleaning now." The third was to see Abraham running his fingers over one of the few books she had brought with her and say, "Abe, you can read these all you want." It had taken only a few weeks for Abraham and his sister Sarah to begin calling her "Mama," and she had remained just that to him ever since.

"How are you getting along?" he asked her.

"Tolerably well. Still spry enough to dodge a chimney now and then. Did you bring Mrs. Lincoln and those boys of yours?"

"No, Mama, they couldn't come." The question gave him a pang of guilt, though he knew she had not meant it to. He had never brought Mary or the boys out to Coles County to meet her. "Mary sent you this, with her love," he said quickly. From his carpetbag he pulled a black cape that Mary had bought in New York for the old woman. Sally pressed it to her face for a minute, rocking quietly.

"It's beautiful, Abe. Thank you."

"When we get settled in Washington, you can come for a good, long visit."

"You just want me to come whitewash that mansion you're going to live in," she smiled. "No, I believe I'll stay here."

They sat beside each other, holding hands, while she looked into his eyes and stroked his face.

"It seems like just yesterday that I pulled up to the cabin at Little Pigeon Creek with your father and found you and Sarah and Dennis looking half-human," she said. "I'm so proud of you, son. I wish your father could have lived. He would be proud of you, too."

Yes, he finally would, Abraham thought. But he might be too stubborn to admit his pride.

"I wish Washington weren't so far away," she said. "I can hardly stand to think of you being so far gone."

"It's not forever. If they let me, maybe I can sneak back here every once in a while to put footprints all over your ceiling."

"That would be just fine," she chuckled.

He left her for a short while to ride to Shiloh Cemetery. His father's grave, nearly ten years old now, was marked by only a fieldstone. It looked neglected, covered by shriveled ragweed. Another pang of guilt. He had not been at his father's bedside when he died, and he had not made the trip from Springfield to Coles County for the funeral.

I really must get a proper headstone and have it engraved, he thought. Marble, even though it will cost more. What should it say? *Thomas Lincoln: Farmer, Carpenter, Father of a President.* No, people would say it was vain of him to put that on his own father's stone. What, then? *Six days shalt thou work, but on the seventh day thou shalt rest.* Perhaps. He must think about it when he had time.

He stood beside the grave and prayed for his father's soul, and for all of their souls. Black-limbed hickories and oaks congregated about the cemetery, haggard strangers offering their respects. Crusty gray fields stretched beyond. Yes, Tom Lincoln surely would have been proud. And if he had lived another decade, perhaps they could have told each other they were sorry, Tom for failing to accept that his son had not wanted to spend the rest of his life breaking his back in a cornfield, Abraham for not recognizing that his father had only wanted the best for his son as he saw it. It was too late for that now. But he would like to think that old Tom was looking down at him from someplace, grinning and saying, "Well, boy, maybe you wasn't fooling yourself with too much learning after all."

He rode back through the cold to Tildy's house for dinner, and then it was time to say goodbye. He knelt beside Sally's rocker and gently put his arms around her.

"I'll make sure you're taken care of while I'm gone," he said.

He had not expected to feel so bad about leaving her. They had seen so little of each other during the last several years. Perhaps he should have made more of an effort.

"When you're in Washington, think of me in my old log farmhouse," she said.

"I will. You know I will."

For a few seconds, neither said anything. She studied his bearded face, searching perhaps for that rawboned youth with an ax in one hand and a book in the other. She fought to hold back tears.

"You never gave me a cross word or look," she said softly. "Scarcely one mother in a thousand can say that. You're the best boy I ever saw, or ever expect to see."

She clung to him, unwilling for him to go just yet.

"They say there's going to be a war. Is that true?"

"I don't know. I hope not. If we have a war, I expect it won't last long."

Somehow I thought she would never grow truly old, he thought. She always had more strength than anyone I knew. But the vigor in her blue-gray eyes had faded.

"I didn't want you to run for president, Abe. I didn't want you elected. I'm afraid something will befall you, and I'll see you no more."

The tears she had been holding back came.

"They'll kill you, Abe."

"No, I won't let them do that," he murmured, kissing her forehead.

"They'll assassinate you," she cried, "and I'll never see you again."

He pulled her tight, wondering if it really would be for the last time.

"No, no, Mama. They won't do that. Trust in the Lord, and all will be well. We'll see each other again."

CHAPTER 10

FEBRUARY 1861

There were more tasks to complete before he left Spring-field than kernels on a corn cob. He still had to finish deciding who would serve in his cabinet. It seemed like every time he settled on a name for a post, a hundred political enemies of that man appeared, each armed with a hundred reasons why the appointment should go to someone else. And he must plan the train trip to Washington—who would accompany him, what route they would take, which cities they would stop in, how many receptions he must attend.

Gaunt, efficient John Nicolay and dapper, fresh-faced John Hay would go as his private secretaries. That was for certain. Elmer Ellsworth was urging Abraham to take along his regiment of Zouaves for protection. That was going overboard. Colonel Ellsworth himself should come, though. The fellow was no bigger than half a piece of soap, but no one was better at organizing and inspiring men. He could coordinate security at each stop.

Hard-drinking, hard-fighting Ward Hill Lamon would make a good personal bodyguard if he was willing to give up his law practice for a while.

"Hill, it looks as if we might have war," Abraham told him. "It'll be handy to have you around. Get yourself ready and come along."

"I'll bring my pistol."

"We'll need a weapon to keep up our spirits, too. Bring your banjo."

A whole congress of political friends wanted to go part or all of the way—Judge Davis, Norman Judd, Orville Browning, Jesse Dubois, Ozias Hatch, and more. And there would have to be journalists. The list for the traveling party grew by the day. He didn't see how they would cram everybody onto the train.

Wide-eyed folks kept flocking to see what he looked like. The office-seekers kept coming, too. They nearly tortured him to death. A stranger stopped him on the street and gave him a wink.

"Mr. Lincoln, I just want to say good luck," he said. "I don't want any office or any part of Washington. But if you ever need help, I'll do anything I can."

Abraham grasped his hand for joy. "Hurry home, before you repent," he said.

He needed a quiet place, hidden from all visitors, where he could sit and write his inaugural address. Clark Smith, husband of Mary's sister Ann, led him up some dusty stairs to a third-story room above his grocery store, across Adams Street from the statehouse. It was a dingy, neglected back room with a slant-front, pigeonhole desk—a perfect refuge. Billy Herndon supplied him with copies of a few texts he needed, including the Constitution, Andrew Jackson's proclamation against nullification, and Henry Clay's great Compromise of 1850 speech. Inside his own head he carried works he knew by heart, like the preamble of the Declaration and snatches of Webster's "Liberty and Union" oration. He secluded himself for a few hours a day and scribbled away with a steel-nibbed pen until he had a draft that pleased him.

The question of what to do about their house vexed him. "I don't think we ought to sell ourselves out of a home," he told Mary.

"Why don't we lease it to someone?"

"We could, but I'm afraid it'll be pretty well used up before we get back."

"We can find a renter who'll take good care of it."

"Who?"

"I don't know. Mr. Lincoln, you are president-elect of the United States. Surely you can use your good name to locate a good renter."

"You're right." He ran his fingers along the parlor mantel. "It's just that we've been in this house for seventeen years. It makes me sad to think of leaving, and someone else being here."

They ended up renting the house to Lucian Tilton, president of the Great Western Railroad, for three hundred fifty dollars a year. Then came several frenzied days of sorting through, throwing out, and packing up their earthly possessions. Mary carried stacks of old letters to the alley behind the house and fed them to a bonfire. A newspaper advertisement lured buyers for most of the house's innards: sofas, chairs, tables, wardrobes, carpets, bedsteads, stoves. The barn's innards—Old Bob the horse, their carriage, the cow—were sold off or given away. Willie and Tad broke into wails of grief when Abraham told them they must leave their dog, Fido, behind.

"But he's part of our family!" Willie cried.

"I know, boys, but he wouldn't be happy moving so far away."

The floppy-eared Fido gazed sadly at them from beneath a horsehair sofa.

"We'll take good ca'e of him in Washington, Papa-day!" Tad promised.

"I know you would. But I don't think he could stand the long train ride. A train's no place for a dog. We'll find some friends to take care of him, just until we get back."

"Can we come visit him sometimes?" Willie sniffed.

"Of course you can."

They gave a farewell reception for seven hundred guests. From evening until past midnight, Abraham stood in the parlor shaking hands. Mary stood nearby, showing off a new gown of white moiré silk. People waited in line for twenty minutes to get through the front door into the jammed house. They tromped up and down the stairs, poked into corners, opened drawers.

Our lives are no longer our own, at least for a few years, he thought. I've traded them away. For what?

Two days later, they packed up the last of the things they were taking with them. Neighbors who had bought furniture came and carted it away. Abraham made a last tour of the hollow rooms, feeling like a ghost. He turned the key in the front door lock, stepped through the gate onto Eighth Street, and walked in the direction of the Chenery House, where they would spend their final nights in Springfield. He almost turned to take one last look. No, it will be too hard, he thought, and he went on his way, head down.

There was little time for nostalgia. The telegraph brought reports that delegates from several slave states had met in Montgomery, Alabama, and organized the Confederate States of America. More Southern states were debating whether to join them. The delegates elected Jefferson Davis of Mississippi as provisional president. Most shocking of all was the news that Alexander Stephens, who only a few short weeks ago was urging his fellow Georgians to remain loyal to the Union, had accepted the office of vice president of the Confederacy.

My God, Abraham thought. If even Aleck is gone, who'll be left to speak for the Union down there?

Rumors of assassination plots kept arriving, including reports of schemes to blow up the tracks and ambush the presidential train on the way to Washington.

"I'm beginning to think you and the boys shouldn't travel with me," he told Mary.

"We most certainly will," she said, as if that were the end of it.

"We can't know how safe it will be."

"I'm not going to begin these next four years by playing the coward." The old Kentucky fire showed in her eyes.

"Has anyone informed you that I've been elected commander-in-chief?" he inquired. "I can order you off my train, Mrs. Lincoln."

"That may impress a bunch of gold-braided colonels and captains. It does not impress me."

General Scott weighed in with a dispatch from Washington, advising that the presence of the first family might lessen the chances of trouble. They reached a compromise. Abraham and Bob would go ahead on a separate train; Mary, Willie, and Tad would stay behind for a short while, in case of violence at the trip's outset, then join them the following day in Indianapolis. From there they would proceed together.

The afternoon before he left town, Abraham climbed the steps to his law office for a last conference with Billy Herndon. They went over the books and talked about how to handle a few pending cases. When business was done, he threw himself down on the old sofa and lay there looking up at the ceiling.

"Billy, how long have we been together?" he asked after a while.

"Over sixteen years."

"Sixteen years. . . . We've never had a cross word during all that time, have we?"

"No, indeed, we have not," Billy said emphatically.

"It's been a good partnership. There are those who are better lawyers than friends, but you've been mighty fine at both."

"Thank you. I feel the same way."

"We've won a few cases, helped a few neighbors, and made a little money in our time, haven't we?"

"Yes, we have."

They were both quiet a while longer, thinking back over so many years. The silence was as eloquent as any words of affection.

"You're just about my only friend who hasn't asked for a favor or job. Is there an appointment you'd like?"

"No, I've no desire for federal office."

Good old Billy. The most undemanding fellow he knew, in many ways.

"You may not know this," Abraham said, "but there's been more than one occasion when other lawyers have tried to talk me into dropping you as my partner and taking them on instead."

"No, I never knew that."

"I want you to know that I told every one of them that you're the best law partner a man could have, that I believe in you, and I would never desert you."

"Thank you," Billy said humbly.

Abraham stretched his limbs and got up. "Well, I guess I'd best be going." He gathered a few books and papers he wanted to take with him. "What do your bones tell you, Billy?"

"They tell me you're going to make a damn fine president."

They went down the stairs together. Abraham paused at the bottom and glanced up at the little shingle announcing the names *Lincoln & Herndon,* swinging on rusty hinges.

"Let it hang there undisturbed," he said. "If I live, I'm coming back some time, and then we'll go right on practicing law as if nothing ever happened."

They stepped into the evening's faded light. A cluster of men down the street caught sight of them, called out to Abraham, and hurried forward to ask him something. Abraham grimaced.

"I'm sick of office-holding already," he sighed.

The two friends clasped hands.

"Goodbye, Billy."

65

"Goodbye, Mr. Lincoln."

He left his law partner standing beneath their signboard, looking pensive and lonely.

CHAPTER 11

FEBRUARY 11, 1861

They were all up early the next morning: Abraham double-checking to make certain his inaugural address and other important papers were carefully stored in a small black gripsack he'd set aside for the trip; Mary suddenly agitated because she wasn't sure if a brooch purchased in New York had been packed; Willie and Tad racing up and down the stairs of the Chenery House, rousing other guests with yells of "Old Abe's coming out of the wilderness!" Abraham gulped down a cup of coffee and stepped into the hotel office to rope some trunks that would go on the train with them. He took a few Chenery House note cards, wrote "A. Lincoln, White House, Washington, DC" on the back sides, and tacked them onto the chests.

Hill Lamon and Elmer Ellsworth appeared to escort him to the Great Western Railroad depot.

"The train leaves at eight sharp," he reminded Mary.

"You go on," she said. "Don't worry, we'll be there to see you off." He wondered. Willie and Tad were still only half-dressed.

He and Bob climbed onto an omnibus hired to carry members of the president-elect's traveling party to the station. Nicolay and Hay were already on board, along with Judge Davis, Governor Yates, Orville Browning, Norman Judd, and several other friends. There was little talk during the short ride. A cold drizzle spilled from gray clouds pressed low against the earth. Hooves and wheels struggled through ruts of black mud, the same mud that had filled the streets the day he had ridden into Springfield two dozen years before.

The size of the crowd at the little brick depot surprised him. There must have been a thousand people huddled under a canopy of umbrellas. They let out a cheer when they saw him coming. A locomotive waited on the track, steam hissing into the drizzle, ready to pull a three-car train festooned with flags and bunting. The crowd made a path for him to get into the station. Friends reached to shake hands and slap him on the back as he passed by.

The waiting room was dank and smelled of the hundred men pressed inside to greet him. They gazed up into his craggy face and told him that they looked forward to the day when he would come back home to pass stories around wood stoves, whittle sticks on courthouse steps, and shoot marbles with boys again. Memories tore into him: thoughts of fording prairie streams with a caravan of lawyer friends; of dried corn stalks rattling in September winds; of staying up late arguing politics in the back of Josh Speed's store; of stepping inside Chatterton's jewelry shop to buy Mary's wedding ring. He could manage little more than "Thank you" and "Bless you" in response to all the goodbyes.

The train bell called that it was time to go. Mary and the boys arrived just in time. He held her for a minute and lifted Tad and Willie to kiss their cheeks.

"I'll see you tomorrow," he told them.

Again the crowd parted respectfully as he made his way to the tracks. More arms reached to shake hands one last time. He climbed the steps of the rear passenger car and turned to face the throng. A thousand faces looked up at him from beneath their umbrellas, waiting. Almost all of them he recognized. Mary stood with them, holding hands with Willie and Tad. The rain was turning to snow. A hush broken only by the hiss of the locomotive fell over them all.

He had not planned to say anything, but the upturned faces in the gray mist touched something deep inside him. Here were neighbors who had trusted him to draw up their wills, draft their laws, secure their land, and make peace among their warring factions. They wanted to hear him say goodbye. He stood for a moment, head down, then raised his chin and doffed his hat. The men in the crowd uncovered their heads in the cold wind as he began to speak in choked phrases:

My friends, no one, not in my situation, can appreciate my feeling of sadness at this parting. To this place, and the kindness of these people, I owe everything. Here I have lived a quarter of a century, and have passed from a young to an old man. Here my children have been born, and one is buried. I now leave, not knowing when, or whether ever, I may return, with a task before me greater than that which rested upon Washington. Without the assistance of that Divine Being, who ever attended him, I cannot succeed. With that assistance I cannot fail. Trusting in Him, who can go with me, and remain with you and be everywhere for good, let us confidently hope that all will yet be well. To His care commending you, as I hope in your prayers you will commend me, I bid you an affectionate farewell.

Three loud cheers rose from the tracks, along with cries of "We'll do it! We'll do it!" Bells clanged, the whistle shrieked, wheels jerked forward. The flags decorating the train stirred. Abraham stepped into the car as it pulled slowly away from the depot. Behind him, voices called through the wet snow. "Goodbye, Abe!"

CHAPTER 12

FEBRUARY 1861

The journey to Washington would take twelve days and cover two thousand miles of tracks passing through countless cities, towns, and villages. Indianapolis. Cincinnati. Pittsburgh. Cleveland. Buffalo. Albany. New York. Philadelphia. Sometimes it seemed the entire winding route was lined with people, tens of thousands of them, cheering, waving hats and handkerchiefs, craning their necks, scratching their heads, all of them come to catch a glimpse of the tall stranger going to the nation's capital to try his hand at being president. He spoke from balconies, windows, podiums and makeshift stages, in hotels, statehouses, and meeting halls, giving more than a hundred speeches along the way, his voice growing so hoarse at times his orations came out as whispers.

In smaller towns, he made whistle stops, stepping onto the train's rear platform to greet the crowds and tell them he could stay only a moment while the iron horse watered itself. "I have come to see you and allow you to see me," he told them, "and in this arrangement I have the best of the bargain, especially regarding the ladies."

Sometimes, after Mary joined the entourage, he convinced her to step onto the platform with him so people could see her as well. They stood side by side, the top of her head barely reaching his shoulder. "Now you have the long and the short of it," he told them. A joke or two more, and the whistle would screech as the train jolted forward. Bands strained, and artillery bellowed. He stood on the platform, bowing his uncovered head until each town had shrunk from sight.

In larger cities, where the traveling party spent nights, masses wild with excitement turned out to see the president-elect. Local police could not hold them back. They pushed and clawed to get near, crushing in from all sides until he felt like the arms of a bear had wrapped tight around him. More than once the burly Lamon and boyish Ellsworth had to throw a few elbows and clear a path to safety.

Outside Cincinnati, the crowd was so huge it blocked the train tracks. In Buffalo, frenzied people shoved so hard they dislocated the shoulder of Major Hunter, one of the military escorts. In Albany, men and boys climbed all over the train when it pulled into the depot. Policemen fought with ruffians until soldiers arrived to break it up.

The throngs delighted Tad and Willie, who took to shouting, "Do you want to see Old Abe?" and then pointing out someone else. Mary was a little unnerved, especially after enthusiasts in Alliance, Ohio, fired a cannon salute too close to the hotel where they were dining, shattering a window and sprinkling her with bits of glass. She somehow went on smiling and chatting, determined to be a charming first lady.

"If the other side don't kill us, ours will," Abraham whispered.

"It's nothing," she told their hosts. "Our boys can break more glass than that just sitting down for dinner."

Disaster threatened to strike in the first part of the trip, while overnighting at the Bates House hotel in Indianapolis. Abraham had asked Bob to take charge of the gripsack containing his inaugural address. When he asked to have it back, the boy looked stupefied.

"I don't have it with me," he confessed. The words came out a little slurred. He had been sipping Catawba wine with several local teens.

"Well, where it is?"

"I'm not sure. I think I gave it to the porter as we came in. Or maybe the clerk at the desk."

Abraham's heart went up into his mouth. His only copies of the speech were in that bag. Visions of it on the front pages of tomorrow's newspapers raced through his mind.

"Who has it, the porter or clerk?" he demanded.

"The clerk, I think."

"And what did the clerk do with it?"

"I think he set it on the floor, behind the counter."

Abraham opened the door of his room, pushed his way through the crowded hallway to the hotel office, and in a single motion swung his long legs across the clerk's counter. A mountain of handbags, most of them black like his own, covered the floor. He took a small key from his pocket and began testing locks, one after another. The fourth satchel he tried opened. Thank God, he thought. He looked inside and found a soiled shirt, several paper collars, a pack of cards, and a bottle of whisky, nearly full.

"Looks more like my gripsack," Lamon said, peering over his shoulder.

Abraham closed the bag and kept digging into the pile.

"I feel like the old Methodist who lost his wife at the camp meeting and went up to the preacher to ask where in hell she was," he grumbled. "Except I'm in a worse fix. If it were only my wife missing, she'd be sure to pop up somewhere on her own."

A few tries later, he located his satchel. Relief washed over him, though he still counted pages to make sure they were all there.

"I'll keep it under my own hands and eyes from here on," he

snapped at Bob. The teen withdrew, sulking. It was one of the few times Abraham could recall being genuinely angry with one of his children.

In Westfield, New York, where the inaugural train made a brief stop, he told a crowd at the station he would like to meet the young lady who wrote him suggesting he grow a beard.

"Her name is Grace Bedell," he told them.

"There she is, Mr. Lincoln!" a boy called out.

A beautiful eleven-year-old girl with black eyes stepped forward, blushing and holding a bouquet of roses. Abraham stepped off his car onto the freight platform, lifted her up, and kissed her.

"You see, I let these whiskers grow for you, Grace," he said, running his hands over his beard. He put her down, shook her hand, and stepped back onto the train. It pulled away to cheers as Grace scurried to the arms of her mother and reporters scribbled, "Old Abe Kisses Pretty Girl."

At every stop, people asked him the same question: "What are you going to do about the South?" Mostly he tried to answer without saying much, reminding folks he wasn't president quite yet. He told them that back home in Illinois, the Fox River was one of the trickiest streams to ford, and that it worried a good many travelers, but that he had one rule about the Fox River: he never tried to cross it until he reached it.

In every town, he appealed for devotion to the Union. At Dunkirk, New York, he grasped the staff of an American flag and urged the crowd "to stand by me so long as I stand beside it."

Occasionally his statements bred uncertainty. In Pittsburgh, he said there was no crisis except an artificial one, that nothing was really wrong, and that if the American people would only keep their temper, on both sides of the line, the troubles would come to an end. But in Trenton, he told the state assembly that although he hoped for a peaceful settlement, "it may be necessary to put the foot down firmly," lifting his boot and setting it down again on the floor as he spoke, a gesture that brought wild cheers from legislators.

Hostile editors sniffed that his comments were foolish, out of touch, and "ludicrous to the destruction of buttons." Southern newspapers scoffed that he was a weak, dangerous, dumbfounded man.

As he rode east, the telegraph wires brought news that Jefferson Davis had completed his own triumphant inaugural tour of the South, arriving in Montgomery to strains of "Dixie." Davis had stood on the portico of the Alabama statehouse, amid columns soaring three stories high, and taken the oath as president of the Confederacy, telling an exultant crowd that it was "joyous in the midst of perilous times to look around upon a people united in heart." An actress, Maggie Mitchell, danced on the American flag. Two of Mary Todd Lincoln's sisters, Martha and Elodie, were on hand in Montgomery to jest with President Davis that they could not be held responsible for their sibling's taste when it came to a husband. That same day, General David E. Twiggs surrendered his entire command in Texas, including military posts and soldiers, to the secessionists.

While citizens of the new Confederacy held funeral services to bury the United States flag, the president-elect of the United States, hundreds of miles to the north, pushed on. Scout trains ran ahead of him, scouring the tracks for signs of trouble. State militia guarded trestles and switches until the presidential train had gone safely through. On board, Hill Lamon sang "Camptown Races" to the strums of his banjo. Elmer Ellsworth double-checked arrangements for upcoming stops. Nicolay and Hay took notes in lurching pen strokes, Nicolay giving off an occasional "Humph!" while Hay grinned like a schoolboy on a lark. Mary read stories to Willie and Tad.

Abraham sat at the rear of the car, resting his hoarse voice and reading newspapers that praised, condemned, critiqued, or questioned every word he uttered along the way. The closer he drew to Washington, the more it felt as though he were straddling a cyclone he had no idea how to ride.

CHAPTER 13

FEBRUARY 1861

n Philadelphia, he got word that Norman Judd, traveling with the presidential party, needed to see him right away, in private. Judd was an old Chicago friend, a good railroad lawyer who over the years had sent business Abraham's way and helped navigate political currents. He was a man worth listening to. Abraham disengaged himself from a receiving line in the grand parlor of the Continental Hotel, went upstairs, and rapped on the door of Judd's room.

He found his friend chewing a cigar in the presence of a small, black-bearded man with brows that ran in a straight line over deep-set eyes. It was Allan Pinkerton, a well-regarded Chicago detective.

"You need to hear what he has to say," Judd said firmly.

Abraham sat and crossed his legs.

"We've learned of a plot to assassinate you," Pinkerton began. The burr of the Scottish Lowlands tinged his speech. "It exists beyond a shadow of a doubt. The attempt will be made day after tomorrow, on your way through Baltimore. I'm here to help you outwit the assassins."

Abraham's chest tightened. "I'm listening."

"The leader is a barber, a man named Ferrandini. Born in Corsica. Lived in the South for many years. Full of the fires of hate for the North. My operatives and I spent weeks penetrating his councils."

"Go on."

"This man Ferrandini considers you a tyrant. He says, in his own words"—the detective paused to consult his notes—"'Murder of any kind is justifiable and right to save the rights of the Southern people.' He says that you shall never be president, that his own life is of no consequence, and that he is willing to give it to take yours."

"How many are with him?"

"He's got fifteen, perhaps twenty conspirators brave enough to aid him. No man's life is safe around these bullies. They've all sworn that by the time you leave Baltimore, you'll be a corpse."

"How do they plan to do it?" He tried to keep his voice analytical.

"Your train will arrive in Baltimore at the Calvert Street Station. From there your party must cross town by carriage to the Camden Street Station and board a B&O special for Washington. They aim to attack as you leave the Calvert Street Station."

Pinkerton spoke in a matter-of-fact tone, as if reciting from a shipping manifest.

"There's a narrow vestibule you must pass through to get to the street. The moment you enter that passageway, they'll start a brawl outside the depot. The police will rush out to stop it, leaving you unprotected. Ferrandini and a chosen few will surround you. They've drawn cards for the honor of striking the fatal blow."

For the honor of it, Abraham thought. Like in Shakespeare. *For Brutus is an honorable man; so are they all, all honorable men.*

"They've chartered a steamer to take them to Virginia afterwards," Pinkerton said. "It's lying in wait in the Chesapeake Bay now."

"Can't you warn the police?"

"The Baltimore police are entirely in the hands of the secessionists. Their chief, George Kane, is a rabid rebel. It would be wise to distrust any local escort there."

"The mayor and city council have refused any ceremonies to greet you," Judd pointed out.

"And you really believe these men are capable of accomplishing their aims?"

"A few reckless men can accomplish a great deal, Mr. Lincoln," Pinkerton said.

Abraham sat immobile. He did not want to believe it. But Pinkerton sounded certain.

"What do you propose?"

"Leave for Washington on the train tonight."

"That I can't do. I'm to hoist the flag at Independence Hall tomorrow morning, and then go on to Harrisburg to address the state assembly. I mean to fulfill those engagements."

"Then you could proceed to Washington tomorrow night from Harrisburg, after you've finished there," Pinkerton said. "You'll have to travel with only one or two men if we're to slip you past the assassins."

Good Lord, is this how I'm to begin my presidency? he thought. By sneaking into the capital in the dead of night?

"There'll be some sneering in the newspapers," Judd conceded, reading his mind.

"I can stand that. I'm more concerned about the safety of Mary and the boys."

"We can assure their safety, once you are through," Pinkerton said.

She's going to hate this, Abraham thought. Well, they'll have to be the ones to argue with her about it. I won't have time.

"All right, gentlemen. I'll go on to Harrisburg tomorrow, as planned. If tomorrow evening you still believe this threat is real, I'm disposed to carry out your plan. I'll place myself in your hands."

"Good. I'll make the arrangements," Pinkerton said. "Tell no one except the few who absolutely must know. Keep it quiet, and I'll answer for your safety with my life."

Abraham stood at Independence Hall the next morning just after sunrise, on George Washington's birthday, and told his audience he never had a feeling that did not spring from the sentiments embodied in the Declaration of Independence. It gave not only liberty to Americans but hope to all the world that in due time the weight of oppression should be lifted from all shoulders, and that all should have an equal chance.

"But if this country cannot be saved without giving up that principle," he told them—pausing an instant as his thoughts flashed to Baltimore—"I was about to say I would rather be assassinated on this spot than to surrender it."

He raised a giant Star-Spangled Banner with thirty-four stars, including a new star for the free state of Kansas, and watched it unfold in the glowing sunshine. Then it was on to Harrisburg, where he told crowds that if he could help it, "this country shall never witness the shedding of one drop of blood in fraternal strife."

By night he was backtracking toward Philadelphia, an old overcoat thrown loosely over his shoulders to disguise his lean frame, a soft wool hat in place of his usual stovepipe. Hill Lamon rode beside him on the special train Pinkerton had arranged. Lamon traveled with two derringers, a pair of brass knuckles, a black-jack, and a long bowie knife.

"Want a pistol?" he asked Abraham. "How about a knife?"

"No thanks. It's probably not a good idea for the man about to be president to enter Washington armed."

The moment they steamed out of Harrisburg, Pinkerton's men cut the telegraph wires leading from the city. As far as the outside world knew, the president-elect was sticking to his published schedule.

Pinkerton was waiting for them in Philadelphia.

"I've secured berths in the sleeping car on the train to Baltimore," he told them. "We'll board through the rear. Mr. Lincoln, I want you to stoop a little as we pass through the depot. No sense in calling attention to your height. Once we're on board, stay in bed until I tell you it's safe to come out."

His berth was too short—he had to lie on his side and draw up his legs to squeeze in. He drew the curtains, and the train started forward.

They pushed south through hills once settled by Swedes, Dutch, Scots-Irish, and English; past the Mason-Dixon Line into the slave-holding South; over the long and winding Susquehanna River, bearing waters from high Allegheny Ridges to the broad Chesapeake Bay. It all passed in the dark of night amid sleepless, uneven rocking. Pinkerton was the only one to stir from his berth, rising from time to time to step onto the car's rear platform and scan the tracks for lanterns set by his operatives to signal that all was well along that portion of the route.

This is a mistake, Abraham thought. I shouldn't have let them talk me into it. They've made me the first president smuggled into office. He realized, with sudden shame, that Mary and the boys had been turned into decoys. What if Ferrandini and his conspirators got hold of them? But Pinkerton had guaranteed their safety.

They reached Baltimore's Calvert Street Station at about half past three. A railroad crew uncoupled their car, hitched it to a team of horses, and pulled it a rattling mile to the Camden Street depot, where they waited to be hooked to a Baltimore & Ohio Railroad engine. A night watchman shattered the early morning stillness by banging his club on the side of a shed and yelling "Captain, it's four o'clock!" at a sleepy ticket agent. A drunkard on the station platform launched into "Dixie," caroling at the top of his lungs that he would take his stand to live and die in the Land of Cotton.

"No doubt there will be a great time in Dixie by and by," Abraham muttered.

The B&O engine arrived, and they started on the short final leg to Washington. The eastern sun still lay below the rim of the Atlantic. Somewhere off to the west, past hills rolling to the Blue Ridge, spread the bluegrass of Kentucky and prairies of Illinois. And beyond those, infinite plains, deserts, and heights reaching to the Pacific shore.

The twelve-day trip was coming to an end. It had been a dozen years since he served in Congress. Nearly three decades since his first run for the Illinois state legislature. Now he was going to take on a job as large as the country itself, or what was left of it.

He wondered if it would prove to be too large for him. Some people were already saying so. The *Cincinnati Enquirer* had reported that the Republicans had "elected an ignoramus for a president." The *New York Argus* had declared that his speeches should "cause the hearts of our citizens to sink within them." Perhaps the job was too big for any man. Well, they would all have to see.

The train followed a gentle descent into the valley of the Potomac, slowed, and pulled into the cold, dark capital city.

PART TWO

THE INFERNO

March 1861 to January 1863

MARCH 4, 1861

Nine days later, he sat in an open barouche clattering over cobblestones on Pennsylvania Avenue toward Capitol Hill. A raw wind came off the river, driving whirlwinds of dust through the street. Overhead, dark clouds were raveling to shreds, and the sun was trying to break through.

The Stars and Stripes flapped from windowsills along the street. People jammed the sidewalks, though it was hard to see them through the mounted soldiers that trotted alongside the carriage. He glimpsed hats waving and fingers pointing. Broad smiles were on a good many faces, probably Western men. Polite, anxious nods from Easterners. Sullen looks on faces with Southern leanings. Cheers mixed with the trills of a fife and drum, along with an occasional, "Hurray for Jeff Davis!"

Abraham doffed his tall, black hat and made little sitting bows, right and left. He tried to look self-possessed. The soldiers shielding the barouche closed ranks. Folks can't see me any better than I can see them, he thought. Well, they'll be able to see what's coming behind— the bands, Wide-Awakes, veterans of the Mexican War, wagons loaded with pretty girls.

General Scott had made good on his promise to muster all the power at his disposal to head off the rumored attacks. Sharpshooters gazed down from rooftops. Cavalry patrolled cross streets. Two batteries of light artillery stood ready near the Capitol.

James Buchanan sat beside Abraham, sighing as though he had not a friend in the world. He was a large, portly man. His head slumped a little toward his left shoulder, like it was ready to fall off. Weary lines crossed his face, from thinning white hair to sagging cheeks. Opposite, in the seat facing Abraham, sat Ned Baker, an old friend from Illinois and now a United States senator representing Oregon. Ned gave a wink that said, 'Well, old boy, you've come a long way from giving speeches on tree stumps to rows of corn stalks.' Abraham was grateful to have him close by. He was feeling like he would need all the friends he could get in the coming four years.

He tried making small talk with Buchanan. "All these guards and rifles make me feel more like a prisoner heading to the gallows than a president to his inauguration," he offered.

Buchanan rolled his head and looked as though he'd rather be anywhere else in the world. Abraham waited, but no answer came. He tried again.

"Any last-minute words of advice?"

The outgoing president furrowed his brow.

"I think you will find the water of the right-hand well at the White House better than that at the left," he moaned at last.

Abraham gave up. He glanced at Ned, who gave another sly wink and a shrug. He stared down for a while at the gold tip of a new ebony cane wedged between his knees, then over the heads of the mounted soldiers at what he could see of the capital city.

Washington had grown in the dozen years since he had been a congressman, but in many ways it still looked like a straggling cow town, with its grand public edifices scattered like Greek temples among shanties and pastures. The obelisk of the Washington Monument stood unfinished, surrounded by a field where cattle and sheep roamed. The red sandstone castle of the Smithsonian Institution looked complete, its towers rising above the bare treetops. At the Capitol, directly ahead, workers had torn away the building's old wooden dome and begun the gargantuan task of constructing a cast-iron one. A huge crane loomed above the gaping hole in the roof. Giant columns and blocks of stone lay about the grounds, waiting to be hoisted into place.

They pulled up to the Capitol, entered the building through a high tunnel of boards put up to shield them from attack, and watched the swearing in of Hannibal Hamlin as vice president in the Senate chamber. Then they stepped back outside, into sunshine now, onto a massive wooden platform erected over the steps of the building's east portico. Applause rippled across the lawn below.

He took a seat on the front row of the platform, blinking in the bright light. Off to one side of the crowd, several men were pulling down a little fellow with red whiskers who evidently thought he was president and had climbed a tree to give his own speech. The platform was packed with senators, congressmen, justices, and diplomats. It looked like half of Illinois was there, too. Stephen Douglas sat nearby. There was Bob, looking on proudly with John Nicolay and John Hay. Elmer Ellsworth was all decked out in his Zouave uniform. And there was David Davis, all three hundred pounds of him. *I hope they reckoned on him when they built this stage,* Abraham thought. He spotted Mary, Willie, and Tad sitting further back, in a section for women, along with Mary's sisters, Elizabeth and Margaret, and assorted Todd kin.

If someone is going to take a shot at me, this is where it will happen, out here in the open, he thought. *Some drunken hothead might try it.* He knew the chance of his actually being hit from a distance by an assassin in the crowd was remote. But the ball would likely strike someone on the stage. Then there would be blood in the streets for sure.

When everyone was seated, Ned Baker stepped to a rickety little speaker's table and announced, "Fellow citizens, I introduce you to Abraham Lincoln, the president-elect of the United States of America!" Abraham rose, heart pounding a little quicker. Where was he supposed to put his hat? He wasn't sure. Steve Douglas reached out with a, "Permit me, sir," and took it from him. "If I can't be president," the Little Giant whispered, smiling, "I can at least be his hat-bearer."

He moved toward the speaker's table, half-expecting to hear the crack of gunfire. He took his address from his vest pocket, laid it on the table, and put the cane on top to keep the pages from blowing away while he put his spectacles on his nose. Glasses adjusted, he took a deep breath and forcefully read his speech in the chilly March breeze.

He reminded the anxious crowd that he had no intention of interfering with slavery in states where it already existed. Yet no state, by its own action, could lawfully get out of the Union. There would be no invasion of the South, he stressed, but he would use the power given him to hold, occupy, and possess the property and places belonging to the federal government.

"In your hands, my dissatisfied fellow countrymen, and not in mine, is the momentous issue of civil war," he told Southerners. "The government will not assail you. You can have no conflict, without being yourselves the aggressors. You have no oath registered in Heaven to destroy the government, while I shall have the most solemn one to 'preserve, protect, and defend' it."

He closed the half-hour address with a plea for amity. "We are not enemies, but friends. We must not be enemies. Though passion may have strained, it must not break our bonds of affection. The mystic chords of memory, stretching from every battlefield, and patriot grave, to every living heart and hearthstone, all over this broad land, will yet swell the chorus of the Union, when again touched, as surely they will be, by the better angels of our nature."

Shriveled and stooped Chief Justice Taney tottered forward to administer the oath. Abraham placed his left hand on an old Bible, raised his right hand, and swore to protect the Constitution. Cheers rolled over the lawn. Cannon boomed as the Marine Band struck up "God Save Our President," and every soul on the platform rushed forward to shake his hand. He looked for Mary to give her a smile but could not see her behind all the swarming men.

On the ride back down Pennsylvania Avenue to the White House, with Buchanan sitting beside him again, he felt mainly relief that there had been no violence. The barouche pulled up the sweeping driveway to the door of the Executive Mansion. The forlorn ex-president shook his hand and wished him good luck.

"If you are as happy, my dear sir, on entering this house as I am in leaving it, you are the happiest man in this country," he said. With that, James Buchanan went home to Pennsylvania.

Mary and the boys arrived from Capitol Hill, giddy from pomp and pageantry. They had a few hours to explore their new home before the inaugural ball. Old Edward, the Irish doorkeeper, and Stackpole, a watchman, gave them a tour. They wandered downstairs through the mammoth East Room with its glittering chandeliers, the oval Blue Room with its grand view toward the Potomac, and the State Dining Room, where princes and presidents ate together. It was overwhelming to think they would be living in a mansion with thirty-one rooms. The upstairs, they discovered, was divided roughly in half, with offices on the east wing and family space on the west. The more they looked, the more they realized that most of the building was devoted to working and public space. The private quarters were not as roomy as they had imagined.

Abraham made a quick tour of his office, making note of its furnishings. A big oak table covered with cloth and surrounded by chairs for meetings. An old upright mahogany writing desk with pigeonholes. An armchair and a couple of horsehair sofas. Over the mantel, a faded portrait of Andy Jackson, looking as fierce as ever.

This should work fine, he thought.

Mary was less impressed. "The place looks like a third-rate hotel," she sniffed.

"It seems all right."

"The wallpaper is peeling. And most of the furniture looks like it was brought in by John Adams. I wouldn't have those chairs if I lived in the humblest cabin."

"The house has seen some use," Abraham admitted.

"We'll have to make some changes, Mr. Lincoln. That's all there is to it."

Willie and Tad came running full speed down the corridor, chasing each other with wooden pistols a soldier had given them.

"Call off the attack, boys!" Abraham ordered. Too late. They ran straight into a table. A red and blue vase went splintering across the floor. Mary gasped.

"It's all right, ma'am," Stackpole said. "It was nothing of value."

"I should think not," Mary smiled. "Taddie, are you all right?"

Abraham stooped to pick up the pieces. "I don't know if I'll succeed in governing the nation," he told Old Edward, "but I do believe I'll fail in ruling my own household."

He was exhausted by the time they arrived at the Palace of Aladdin, a wood-and-canvas pavilion built for the inaugural ball. The Marine Band struck up "Hail Columbia" while he led the Grand March arm-in-arm with the mayor, as custom required. Mary, dressed in blue silk with bracelets of gold, promenaded with Stephen Douglas. The pageantry brought back her good spirits.

"Always the belle of the ball," Abraham teased.

"Good. I want all of these Eastern ladies to go home green with envy," she said, "especially the Democrats."

Hoopskirts revolved to waltzes and mazurkas in the glow of gas chandeliers. Abraham accepted all the congratulations he could stand, while Mary accepted invitations to dance. He was pleased to see her dance a quadrille with Douglas. It was a good symbol that both parties must work together to resolve the national crisis.

"This hand-shaking is harder work than rail-splitting," he told her, fidgeting with his white kid gloves.

"You look spent. Perhaps you should retire."

"I think I will."

"Do you mind if I stay a while longer?" she asked. "People will be disappointed if we both leave so soon."

"Stay as long as you like. Have a good time. You deserve it."

He took her hand and squeezed it. "I've barely had a chance to stop and think that I'm actually the president of the United States," he whispered.

"I always knew you would be president!"

"And I always thought you would make a first-rate first lady."

She glowed with exultation. "Good night, Mr. President!"

"Good night, Madame President."

He left her on the ballroom floor, dancing through the night.

CHAPTER 15

MARCH AND APRIL

1861

The next morning he strode into his office, ready to get to work, and found on his desk a batch of communications from Major Robert Anderson, commander of the federal garrison inside Fort Sumter in Charleston Harbor. Anderson reported that his provisions would be exhausted in a matter of weeks. If not resupplied soon, he would have to abandon the fort to the Confederate forces ringing the harbor.

Abraham sank hard into a chair. My God, I'm not ready for this, he thought. The Senate hasn't even approved my cabinet. I barely know my way to the War Department.

He sent for General Winfield Scott. The old warrior came lumbering up the stairs and heaved himself onto a sofa. He was too fat and gouty to mount a horse anymore, and his bulbous head looked like a cauliflower set atop a bag of potatoes. But his fine blue coat with velvet cuffs and rows of fierce eagles perching on shiny brass buttons reminded everyone that he had once been a hero of the Mexican War and that the Duke of Wellington had proclaimed him the greatest living general.

"I told President Buchanan months ago that we ought to reinforce Sumter, before the secessionists had a chance to surround it with batteries," he wheezed. "He would not do it."

"How long can Anderson maintain his position without fresh supplies?" Abraham asked.

"He's got hard bread, flour, and rice for about twenty-six days, and salt meat for about forty-eight. He'll be starved out in six weeks. That's assuming he's not attacked first."

"Can you resupply him?"

"No, not for several months."

Abraham blanched. "Why not?"

"As I say, it would have been easy last fall. Now the Southerners have blocked the harbor channels and brought in heavy guns. I would need a fleet of war vessels, five thousand regular troops, and twenty thousand volunteers to take the batteries in the harbor and outer bay."

"But there are barely sixteen thousand men in the entire army!"

"That's correct. And most of those are scattered across the western frontier. It would take six to eight months to raise and train the force we'd need."

Abraham could barely believe what he was hearing. It had never entered his mind that the United States Army was incapable of relieving a single fortress.

"What do you advise?" he asked.

"Instruct Major Anderson to evacuate the fort."

"I can't do that, General! I promised just yesterday in my inaugural address to hold and occupy all federal property."

"I understand that, sir," the old man said in a professional way, "but as a practical military question, I see no alternative but a surrender. It is merely a question of time."

Perhaps not. A few navy men studied the charts of Charleston Harbor, scratched their heads, and suggested that something might be tried. It might be possible for a fleet of warships to carry supplies to Charleston and transfer them offshore to small boats, which could make a dash to the fort under cover of night. That might at least buy Anderson's men more time.

The cabinet assembled around the big oak table in Abraham's office to grope for a solution. He studied the somber faces of the men he had chosen to help preserve the ruptured Union.

"Gentlemen, the question upon us is urgent," he told them. "Assuming it is possible to provision Fort Sumter, is it wise to attempt it?"

William Henry Seward, his secretary of state, the man he had beat for the Republican nomination, chomped on a fat cigar. Lively eyes gauged Abraham over a beaklike nose. "No," he said firmly. "It would probably initiate civil war. After that, reunion would be hopeless."

Salmon Chase, his secretary of the treasury, who had also run for president, sat straight with squared shoulders. His handsome face with its one slight imperfection of a drooping right eyelid looked humorless. "If the attempt will inflame civil war, I cannot advise it," he said carefully. "But if war seems improbable, as I think it is, then I say resupply."

Simon Cameron, his secretary of war, voted to take Scott's advice: "Even if the attempt to resupply did succeed, the surrender of the fort is an inevitable necessity." White-bearded Edward Bates, his attorney general, yet another defeated political rival, nodded slowly like a wise man: "Don't do anything which may have the semblance of beginning a civil war."

Gideon Welles of Connecticut, his secretary of the navy, looking like Neptune himself with his billowing gray wig and flowing gray beard: "If we do this, they'll claim we made war on their state and its citizens in their own harbor." And Caleb Smith, his interior secretary: "It would not be wise under these circumstances."

Only his postmaster general, the stormy, hatchet-faced Montgomery

Blair, insisted on reinforcement. "These Southerners don't think we'll fight," he growled. "Provisioning that fort will show them we're determined to maintain the authority of the government."

Abraham surveyed his advisors' faces again. A circle of masks around the table, hiding doubt, stared back. They don't think I'm up to this, he realized. I see it in their eyes. But they don't know what to do, either. That's in their eyes as well. They don't know any better than I do.

Vacillating, exhausting days followed, full of hours spent bending over maps of Charleston, listening to officers give conflicting opinions. Reading countless Northern editorials that thundered, "Let the Southern states go in peace!" or, "If Fort Sumter is evacuated, the new administration is done forever!"

He sent Ward Hill Lamon and other men he trusted down to Charleston to test the breezes of public opinion. Lamon was a Virginian by birth. He would be able to find out what the Carolinians were thinking. Lamon and the others came back discouraged, reporting that they found no attachment to the Union in Charleston, and that nothing but giving in to secession would prevent war.

Seward came to his office to urge evacuation. "If we surrender the fort, Virginia and the other Upper South states will likely stay in the Union," he said. "Virginia is all-important."

"Well, a state for a fort is no bad business," Abraham conceded.

"That's right. And with time, the gesture might win back the seceded states."

"Perhaps. But giving up Sumter would also discourage friends of the Union and embolden our enemies. It would divide the North. Let go of that fort, and there will be no end of Southern demands to yield other places until I finally gave in to disunion."

The secretary of state puffed a cigar while he thought it over, as if calculating how to blow some sense into the new president.

"This plan to resupply the fort is not likely to succeed," he pointed out.

"We can't know that unless we try," Abraham countered. "If we try, it will show the world we mean to hold the Union together, and make other states think twice about leaving."

"But if it ends in bloodshed, it will sweep the country into war, and the Southerners will blame you for starting it."

Seward departed, looking dissatisfied. Abraham sat in his office alone and pondered Major Anderson, the commander at Sumter. He searched old memories of his one brush with military service, when he had marched in 1832 in Illinois as a volunteer in the Black Hawk War, a conflict with the Sauk and Fox Indians. He had seen no actual combat, though he sometimes joked that he had a good many bloody struggles with mosquitoes. A young officer named Robert Anderson had mustered him into service. Yes, it was the same man—a graduate of West Point and a good, stiff-backed officer. Later, he had fought gallantly in the Mexican War. But Anderson was a Kentuckian and had once owned slaves. His wife was from Georgia. Was his loyalty to be trusted? The generals said yes, but did they really know?

It was too much to think about, too much for any one man to decide. By each afternoon he felt like his head would crack open, like a rail splitting right down the center by an iron wedge pounded with a maul.

"If being the head of hell is as hard as what I have to undergo here, I could find it in my heart to pity Satan himself," he grumbled.

From the White House, he looked out south-facing windows toward the Potomac, past the hills of Virginia, far beyond his range of sight, down toward the cotton fields of South Carolina, and tried to understand the hearts of the people there. Back in the days of the Revolution, they had been overrun by the British but refused to give in, had taken to the saddle and finally given Cornwallis's men a devil of a whipping. They had taken as their motto, "While I breathe, I hope." His thoughts ranged up to the rocky hills of New England, where farmers had stood before advancing red-coated lines and yelled to each other, "Don't fire until you see the whites of their eyes!" And out West, past the prairies, where men and women with little more than clothes on strong backs rumbled in white canvas-covered wagons toward claims where they might scratch out lives for themselves under a wide, promising sky.

All was at stake now. All the toil, the sacrifice, the high-minded phrases about liberty and equality and unalienable rights. If the nation were to break apart, it would show the world that the American experiment was a failure, that the idea of people governing themselves was wrong. All the ideals his countrymen had inherited would be gone. Democracy would shrivel and die, and with it, a centuries-long hope of freedom.

He summoned the cabinet and gave them his decision. "We'll send in the supply boats with provisions only—no troops, ammunition, or arms. I'll notify the governor of South Carolina that the ships are on their way. If the secessionists open fire, they must bear the blame for aggression."

He dozed off sitting at his desk that evening, listening to rain beat against the windows. He was thinking, as he fell asleep, that perhaps cooler heads would prevail in Charleston. There was always the chance that the Confederates would let the boats through.

He dreamed that he was on the water, standing on the deck of a vessel of some sort, moving toward a dark and indefinite shore. Perhaps he was on the bow of a warship being swept by the tide into Charleston's bay. Or on a flatboat, drifting on the wide Mississippi. He could not tell. There was no wind, no sound of an engine. Mist hung over the water and obscured the low, pale strip of land ahead. The indescribable vessel floated slowly at first, as if caught in the fog, then picked up speed, moving in silence, until it was gliding rapidly across the gray water. But the faster it moved, the further the dim shore receded.

He felt suddenly weighed down and opened his eyes to find Willie sitting in his lap.

"Were you having a bad dream?" the boy asked.

"No, I don't think so," Abraham said, not quite fully awake.

"Your face looked like you were having a bad dream."

"I was just taking a little nap, that's all."

"Mother says to come to dinner."

"All right."

The boy gave his father a hug and kissed his cheek. "Does being president give you bad dreams?" he asked.

What a question. Abraham wasn't sure how to answer truthfully.

"No, but being president is a very hard job."

"Don't worry, Papa dear," Willie said. "Mother says everything will turn out fine."

"That's right," Abraham smiled. "Everything will turn out fine."

But it didn't. The telegraph wires brought the news. The secessionists had bombarded Fort Sumter before the relief ships could arrive. The country was at war with itself.

CHAPTER 16

APRIL 1861

*H*e paced his office, from window to fireplace and back, pausing every few rounds to take hold of a large spyglass mounted on a tripod and scan the Potomac.

"Why don't they come? Why don't they come?"

"They'll come," John Hay said. He was trying to strike a nonchalant pose by leaning against a bookcase, but the boyish face looked dark. "They're mustering all across the North. They'll come."

"I'm beginning to believe there is no North."

He swept the spyglass over the river again. Beyond the Long Bridge, a lonely government sloop of war cruised the approach to the city. Further downstream, past the mouth of the Eastern Branch, the

Confederate Stars and Bars floated over Alexandria's rooftops. Smoke from rebel campfires curled above the far bank—the campfires of fifteen thousand Virginia militiamen, if reports could be trusted, all sharpening their bayonets, ready to take Washington.

On his desk lay a stack of telegrams from Northern governors, fervent responses to the call for seventy-five thousand troops he had issued after Fort Sumter fell. From Massachusetts: "Dispatch received. By what route shall I send?" From Ohio: "Will furnish the largest number you will receive." Indiana promised ten thousand men, Michigan fifty thousand if needed.

Republicans and Northern Democrats alike were thundering allegiance to the Stars and Stripes. Even Stephen Douglas had come to see him, pledging to do everything in his power to help. It was as if their rivalry had been blown away by the cannonade at Charleston. Thank God for the Little Giant. He had looked bloated and spent as they sat talking for two hours in the office Douglas had fought hard to gain for himself. But he still had fight left in him. He was back in Illinois now, campaigning his heart out again, this time to raise troops and support for the Union, telling Democrats out West that they may have voted against Abraham Lincoln, but now they all must stand beside him.

Yet no Union troops had shown up in the capital. Every day came fresh reports that they were on their way, and people gathered at the depot to greet them, only to drift away with long faces when no soldiers arrived. The District of Columbia claimed thirty home-grown militia companies, but they looked scraggly and raw. A good many were probably less than one hundred percent loyal. There was no one to hold back a rebel attack. The *Richmond Examiner* was gloating that it would take only "one wild shout of fierce resolve to capture Washington City."

"They're closing their coils around us," Abraham said, lowering the spyglass. "If I were them, I'd have attacked by now."

A deep boom came rolling over the Potomac flats and up the South Lawn. He jumped.

"What was that?"

"What was what?" Hay asked.

"It sounded like cannon fire." A signal of some kind? The start of an assault?

"I didn't hear it."

They both stood at the window, listening. Nothing. Abraham stuck his head into Nicolay's office.

"Did you hear anything?"

His private secretary looked up from behind a high rampart of correspondence. He shook his head and gave an emphatic "Humph!"

"Well, I know I heard *something,*" Abraham insisted.

He bounded downstairs, followed by Hay, to the East Room, where the Frontier Guards were bivouacking. Senator-elect Jim Lane of Kansas had rounded up the motley gang—about fifty clerks, lawyers, and out-of-work Kansans looking for jobs—to guard the Executive Mansion. Their blankets and open ammunition boxes covered the velvet carpet.

"Did anyone hear artillery fire?"

A dozen blank faces looked his way. A young Jayhawker left off polishing his shiny new musket. "No, sir, not me, sir."

"How about you other men?"

More blank looks from the Frontier Guards. "Should we go to our posts, sir?"

"No, it's probably nothing. I'll go see."

He walked outside with Hay. The day was warming up, and the air felt thick with treason. The streets lay mostly deserted, with shops closed and boarded up. Next door at the Treasury Department, General Scott's men had thrown up barricades of sandbags behind towering columns. Sentries paced the doors. Wild rumors were going around that the secessionists had planted mines under the building. On Pennsylvania Avenue, someone was playing "Dixie" on a piano beside an open window. But no one seemed to have heard any cannon fire.

They crossed the Washington City Canal and walked south along the river, past the stump of the unfinished Washington Monument, to the Arsenal at Greenleaf Point. All was quiet there as well—no alarms, no soldiers in sight. Inside the Arsenal, through open doors, they saw rows of muskets and casks of powder, waiting for battle. Nearby, the Eastern Branch flowed lazily into the Potomac. A pair of mallards flew by, the male's head flashing bright green, and landed with a quiet splash.

"It must have been my imagination," Abraham admitted.

He felt relieved for a moment, until he realized that the Virginians, if they wanted to, could simply row across the river, walk through the unguarded doors of the Arsenal, and clean the whole place out.

Each day brought the resignations of army and navy officers. No one could tell who would go next. Joseph E. Johnston, the quartermaster general, was making noises about going home to Virginia. Commodore Franklin Buchanan, a native of Maryland, was said to be on the verge of defecting, along with a good many of his officers at the Navy Yard. There were rumors that the bombshells being made at the yard were filled with sand and sawdust.

It was hard to know which civil servants to trust. Clerks and messengers could be seen on sidewalks wearing blue secession badges. Some of the White House staff had quietly disappeared. Lawyers acquainted with the Supreme Court were laying bets that Justice John Campbell would soon put aside his black robe and return to Alabama.

General Scott heaved himself up the stairs to Abraham's office to talk about who should lead the new Federal army, if it ever materialized. He recommended Colonel Robert E. Lee, in his opinion the best officer in the whole service. Abraham told him to make the offer, and Scott went away, but later came back with a long face. Lee was against secession, but he had told Scott that he could never raise his sword against his native Virginia. The colonel had ridden away across the Long Bridge to his columned mansion on Arlington Heights, just over the Potomac River.

The crisis was tearing Mary's family apart. Letters from Kentucky brought news that brothers George, Sam, and David were joining the Confederate army. Baby brother Aleck was saying he would join, too. At first Mary tried to make light of it.

"If you'll give me my own regiment, Mr. President, I'll go South and give them each a good spanking," she said. She grew somber. "I hope the day will come when the Todds are united again. But I fear there may be some missing from the family circle."

One of Mary's younger sisters, Emilie, had married Benjamin Hardin Helm, a Kentucky lawyer and graduate of West Point. Abraham called him to the White House, sat him down, and put into his hands a sealed envelope containing the offer of a commission as paymaster in the army, with the rank of major. It was a valuable post, paying three thousand a year.

"Ben, here's something for you," he said. "Think it over, and let me know what you'll do."

Helm came back the next afternoon with tears in his eyes.

"I'm going home to Kentucky, and I'll answer from there," he said. "The position you've offered is beyond my most hopeful dreams." He struggled for words. "I wish I could see my way. I'll try to do what's right. Don't let this offer be made public yet. You'll have my answer in a few days."

They shook hands, and Abraham knew by the despair in his brother-in-law's voice that he would cast his lot with the rebels.

Chilling news came from Baltimore. The Sixth Massachusetts Volunteer Infantry, en route to Washington, had been attacked by a secessionist mob. Four soldiers and a dozen citizens were dead, and more wounded. On the eighty-sixth anniversary of the battles of Lexington and Concord, which had begun the Revolutionary War, Massachusetts men had again spilled blood, this time fighting their own countrymen.

Trains stopped arriving in Washington, then the telegraph went dead. Marylanders had severed the tracks and cut the wires. Mail service halted. Men on boats and horses brought vague reports from the outside world. They said that Maryland was about to go out of the Union, that the District would be completely surrounded, that an assault from all directions was coming any hour.

Panic swept the capital. Hotels emptied. Carriages piled high with luggage, groceries, and women and children headed out of town. Men searched frantically for carts to hire. Southerners clamored for passes to get over the Long Bridge to Virginia.

Abraham stood at his office window again, watching the scramble. Out on the White House lawn, some of the Frontier Guards marched back and forth, trying to keep a straight line. Up at the Capitol, workmen were turning iron plates meant for the new dome into breastworks. Perhaps the dome would never be finished, and the stones of the Capitol would be carried south. He raised his spyglass to examine a steamer coming up the river, wondering if it had soldiers on board.

My God, does the North know our condition? he thought. If the troops don't get here soon, we'll die like rats in a heap.

A call bell in a nearby room jangled. Then a second bell, and a third. Abraham lowered the spyglass. Every bell in the mansion was suddenly going off, like a dozen fire alarms at once. What was happening? This wasn't his imagination, not this time.

John Hay hurried into the room. "Did you need something?" he asked.

"No. What's happening?"

"Did you ring me?"

"No."

"Is it some sort of alarm?"

"I don't know."

Stewards and messengers came running to see what the president wanted. The call bells kept jangling away, as if the whole house were bewitched. Old Edward the doorkeeper went to investigate, and a few minutes later the ringing stopped. He came back with Tad and Willie in tow. Both boys were full of glee.

"I found them in the garret," Old Edward said. "They got their hands on the yoke of the system. They were pulling every bell cord in sight."

"I p'omise I won't do it again, Papa-day!" Tad giggled. "I p'omise!"

They all laughed, even Nicolay. They couldn't help themselves. Anything to break the tension of the last several days. Abraham was just starting to issue an executive order banning the boys from the garret when another sound broke across the city—the shriek of a locomotive whistle.

It was the Seventh New York Regiment, coming down the tracks at last.

They all stood outside watching the soldiers parade through the spring sunshine down Pennsylvania Avenue. Rank after rank of them, flags flying, bands playing, marching in brisk step, weary and dusty from their long journey but still looking smart in gray uniforms with shiny, white crossbelts. Bayonets glistened like a river of steel points flowing down the road. The city, which had seemed nearly deserted only hours ago, poured out to grasp their hands. Men slipped cigars into the soldiers' knapsacks, and women put flowers in their buttonholes. People danced in the street. The officers said that more troops from Massachusetts, Pennsylvania, and Rhode Island were following close behind.

The point of danger was passed. The capital was safe. For the first time since taking office, Abraham felt hopeful. He gave John Hay a wink.

"I believe we'll go down to Charleston and pay her that little debt we're owing her," he said.

CHAPTER 17

MAY 1861

Even civil war could not deter men ravenous for public office. They rushed the White House like a pack of wolves, howling for post offices, clerkships, consulates, generalships, and Indian agencies. They clogged the Green Room, Red Room, Blue Room, vestibules, and closets. A long jostling line crowded the staircase, so that anyone wanting to go up or down had to squeeze his way past. Some camped out for the night, waiting to see the president. In the early mornings, Abraham stepped over their snoring bodies in the corridor on the way to his office.

"I'll have to start checking under the bed for them before I put out the light," he told Mary. "It was bad enough in Springfield, but that was child's play compared with the tussle here."

There were far more applicants than offices to dispense. He did what he could for them, which often was no more than send them away with the honor of having met the president.

"A federal judgeship would suit me," a Republican from Ohio told him.

"But you have no experience with the law," Abraham pointed out.

"Well, then, being a postmaster will do."

"There are no vacancies in your town."

"Then you can make me a lighthouse keeper. Anywhere on the Atlantic coast will be fine."

"I must give this some thought," Abraham said, consigning the man's letters of recommendation to one of the pigeonholes of his desk.

Another man came wanting to be doorkeeper of the House of Representatives.

"Do you have any experience as a doorkeeper?" Abraham asked.

"No, sir, no actual experience."

"Any theoretical experience? Any instruction in the duties of doorkeeping?"

"Well, no."

"Ever attended a lecture on doorkeeping?"

"No, sir."

"Ever read any books on the subject?"

"No."

"Ever conversed with anyone who has read such a book?"

"Not to my knowledge."

"My friend, don't you see that you possess not a single qualification for this post?"

"I know how to open and close a door. Ain't that enough?"

A delegation came seeking the appointment of a friend as commissioner to the Sandwich Islands. "He's in poor health," their spokesman said. "An appointment to a place with a balmy climate would do him no end of good."

"I hope he gets well," Abraham said, seeing them to the door, "but I must tell you there are eight other applicants for that place, and they're all sicker than your man."

Sometimes women joined the line, seeking appointments for loved ones. A bossy lady came wanting a colonel's commission for her son. "Sir, I demand it not as a favor, but as a right," she said. "My grandfather fought at Lexington. My uncle was the only man who did not run away at Bladensburg. My father fought at New Orleans, and my husband was killed at Monterey."

"Madam, your family has done enough for the country," he smiled. "It's time to give someone else a chance."

The country was falling apart, and he found himself spending hours a day greeting the horde of political beggars. "I feel like a man letting out lodgings at one end of his house while the other end burns down," he sighed.

"If I were you, I'd turn the army's bayonets against them and drive them out of the city," Hill Lamon growled. He had agreed to stay in Washington as marshal of the District of Columbia, a post that allowed him to serve as Abraham's unofficial bodyguard.

"They don't want much, and they get very little, so I must see them. I know how I would feel in their place." He thought back to his younger days when he was poor and hungry for work. "Besides, it's important. We've got to have good, loyal people in office if we're to stand a chance of making this government work."

Mary pestered him about jobs for friends and relatives. It rankled him, and he knew it rankled his cabinet as well. Already the newspapers had begun to complain about a hundred Todd kin grunting at the hog trough, all wanting offices.

"I'd like to find a customhouse post for Grantham Shanks," she told him.

"What makes him fit for an appointment like that?"

"He's quite suitable in intelligence, manners, and morals. He's a distant relation, and he's our friend."

"Mother, I made nearly two million friends the day I was elected, and they all want positions."

"A true friend, then. You fail to realize that if you don't take care of your friends, you make enemies of them."

"I still don't see why I should bestow a customhouse post on Shanks."

"Because if you don't, Mr. Lincoln, I shall go out onto Pennsylvania Avenue and roll about on the sidewalk."

"I'll see what I can do."

Mary soon turned her mind to refurbishing their new home. The carpet was worn, the drapes threadbare, the plaster moldy. She discovered that Congress had appropriated twenty thousand dollars to restore the White House, and immediately took a train to go shopping in New York. She returned with chairs, sofas, French wallpaper, velvet carpets, a Haviland dinner service, gold flatware, and more.

"If we're to have a first-rate presidency, we must show the world a first-rate Executive Mansion," she said, running her fingers over a Swiss lace curtain.

"I suppose you're right," Abraham said. If it kept her from meddling in appointments, fine. Far more important matters were pressing him. Arkansas, Tennessee, and North Carolina had followed Virginia out of the Union. He had to figure out a way to keep the border states of Maryland, Delaware, Kentucky, and Missouri from joining them—and persuade Europe from taking the South's side. There had been so much trouble with secessionists destroying tracks and snipping telegraph wires between Philadelphia and Washington, he had authorized the army to arrest and detain suspected traitors without charges. That was threatening to cause an uproar. Meanwhile, the swarms of office seekers kept coming.

I could bail out the Potomac with a teaspoon before I could fix all these problems, he thought.

❧❧❧

Within days of Fort Sumter's fall, Elmer Ellsworth hurried north to recruit volunteer soldiers from the ranks of New York City's firemen.

He came back to Washington with a jaunty red-capped regiment of Fire Zouaves. Eleven hundred men marched up Pennsylvania Avenue in crisp red shirts and gray jackets, with swords and foot-long bowie knives swinging from their belts. They bivouacked in the south wing of the Capitol and had fun playing cards in the Rotunda. Congressmen found them hanging like monkeys from the unfinished dome. They abolished the House of Representatives, elected their own Congress, dissolved the Union, then went to dinner. They knocked down sentinels, scared old ladies, and left restaurants without paying for extravagant meals, telling the owners to send the bill to Jeff Davis or Uncle Abe. When a fire broke out near the Willard Hotel, they rushed to the scene and put it out in a two-hour battle with the flames. Half the town said the Fire Zouaves were a menace to civilization, and the other half swore they were the best men God ever made.

Willie and Tad raised their own regiment of neighborhood boys they dubbed "Mrs. Lincoln's Zouaves." Colonel Ellsworth stopped by the White House nearly every day to review their troops. Abraham climbed with him up through a trapdoor to the roof to see a fort the boys had constructed. They had a small log cannon and a few broken muskets that poured withering fire on suspicious-looking vessels coming up the river.

"I'm a colonel," Willie said.

"I'm a d'um majuh," Tad said. "I have a d'um. If I can get a pistol, Willie says I can be a co'po'al."

"This is our spyglass," Willie said. "We can spot any rebels coming from up here."

"If you spot any, send word to me," Ellsworth told them gravely. "I'll send reinforcements."

"Can you show us your Arkansas toothpick?" Willie asked.

Ellsworth showed them his long gleaming bowie knife and a gold medal inscribed *Non solum nobis sed pro patria.*

"What does it mean?" Willie asked.

"'Not for ourselves alone, but for country.' It's a good motto, don't you think?"

"That'll be the motto of Mrs. Lincoln's Zouaves!"

Abraham stood with his young friend at the roof's stone balustrade, looking over the city. The capital was turning into an armed camp. Infantry patrolled the streets, halting people outside public buildings with the demand, "What's your business here?" Lines of quartermaster wagons tore up roads. Rows of white tents sprouted in fields. Through the boys' spyglass, they could see the rebel flag over the Marshall House, a hotel across the river in Alexandria.

"That flag's an insult," Abraham grumbled.

"It's meant to be," Ellsworth said. "They must know we can see it from here."

Well, whatever happens next, Virginia has brought it on herself, Abraham thought. She's allowed this insurrection to make its nest within her borders. We have no choice but to clean out the nest where we find it.

"We'll have to move over the river soon," he said. "We can't give them time to mount guns on those ridges."

"My men request the honor of being in the vanguard," Ellsworth said quickly.

"This first movement needs to be handled with delicacy. The rebels will view it as a pollution of sacred soil."

"We may meet with a warm reception," Ellsworth nodded.

"I wish no violence, if possible. I want nothing to occur that will incense Southerners still loyal to the Union."

"I'll give strict orders. We'll show them we're men as well as soldiers."

Abraham smiled. Everything that Ellsworth said and did brimmed with passion. His hand rested on the hilt of his sword as he leaned slightly against the balustrade. His face, smooth as a girl's, was flushed. I'll be a fortunate man if my boys turn out as well, Abraham thought.

A few days later, in predawn hours lit by a bright gold moon, Union troops crossed the Potomac by bridges and vessels to take the Virginia shore. The Fire Zouaves landed at Alexandria just as daylight was coming on. A message had been sent ahead to warn that they were coming, and the outnumbered Confederates slipped away with the rising sun. Barely a shot was fired.

Abraham was sitting in the oval library room next to his office, breathing a sigh of relief, when a grim-faced captain appeared in the doorway to inform him that Colonel Ellsworth was dead. He tried to hold himself together, gripping the arms of the chair, while the officer told it: The colonel had gone to the Marshall House in Alexandria to remove the odious rebel flag, had dashed up to the roof to haul it down, was coming back down the stairs when a man had jumped out of a dark passage with a shotgun and shot him point blank. The blast drove the medal inscribed *Non solum nobis sed pro patria* into his chest.

Oh Lord, not this, he thought. What am I going to tell my boys? He motioned for the captain to leave and buried his face in his hands.

For two days, he moved numbly through rituals made necessary by death. Images of sacrifice, the kind he had once imagined from books and newspaper articles, now surrounded him. The body lying in state in the East Room, dressed in the Zouave uniform, white lilies at the breast. The bloodstained Confederate flag that Ellsworth had given his life to capture. The military procession to the depot, to send him home to Mechanicville, New York. The letter to his parents, trying to offer some comfort. At night he lay in bed asking himself, *Is this what it will take?*

Ten days after Ellsworth was killed, word came from Chicago that Stephen Douglas was dead. He had worn out his body telling crowds they must rally to preserve the Union.

CHAPTER 18

JULY 1861

Forward to Richmond! Stamp out the rebellion! The drumbeat rolled across the North. *Crush the rebel army!* Thousands of Yankees left their plows standing in fields and headed for Washington. Northwest farm boys kissed their sweethearts goodbye. New Yorkers formed a new regiment they called "Ellsworth's Avengers."

Abraham called his top generals to his office and urged them to attack a Confederate army under General Pierre G.T. Beauregard that was gathered at Manassas, Virginia, a rail junction thirty miles from Washington. The generals were not so sure.

"There's no reason for a battle just now," General Scott said. He had propped a big gouty foot up on a stool. "Blockade their ports. Send gunboats and men down the Mississippi. Isolate the South and squeeze it like a boa constrictor until they come to their senses. That's the way to do it."

"Isn't it better to whip them here and now?" Abraham asked. "That may drench the secessionist fires."

"Our army just arrived," General Irvin McDowell pointed out. He was a big, broad-shouldered man, stern and forthright, with a reputation for being a more than hearty eater. It was said he could gulp down a whole watermelon for dessert. "It's not even an army yet. It's a rabble. We need time to train them."

"But our boys are itching for a fight," Abraham said. "They don't understand why we let a hostile army sit there, almost in sight of the Capitol."

"They may want to fight, but they're not ready. They're green."

"They're green, it's true," Abraham said, "but the other side is green as well. You're all green alike."

Several days later, he stood on the White House lawn and watched the troops head for Manassas, led by General McDowell. Zouaves in tasseled fezzes and billowy pantaloons. Minnesota lumberjacks in checkered flannel shirts. Bay Staters in sea-blue jackets. Boys who had scribbled "18" on a scrap of paper and stuck it in a shoe so they could stand and swear in all honesty "I'm over eighteen" when signing up. Some grinned and waved carelessly as they marched by.

Yes, we're green, Abraham told himself. But cautious men don't win wars. If we can beat them in one big fight, maybe we can end this mess once and for all.

The Sunday morning of the battle started off warm and muggy. A battalion of congressmen, senators, journalists, and ladies rode out of the city toward Manassas to watch the fighting. They took along picnic baskets, bottles of wine, and opera glasses. Abraham put on a good suit and went with Mary to the New York Avenue Presbyterian Church to hear Dr. Phineas Gurley preach. It was hard to sit still in the pew. The rumble of distant cannon filled the spaces between the words of the sermon.

What am I supposed to pray for? he wondered. That we kill more of them than they kill of us?

After church he went to the telegraph office at the War Department, next door to the White House. He put his feet up on a table, adjusted his spectacles, and read the dispatches coming from Fairfax Court House, near the fighting at Manassas. The two armies had met along the banks of a wooded stream called Bull Run. The reports clicking over the wires seemed encouraging. "Columns advancing. . . . Gaining ground. . . . Converging on enemy's left flank. . . ."

The officers in the telegraph office looked anxious but satisfied. But here was a dispatch that said something about an enemy counterattack. That sounded worrisome, though none of the officers acted alarmed. Perhaps they didn't know what it meant any more than he did. They were all busy. He didn't want to distract them in the thick of battle. He decided to go ask General Scott.

He found the old warrior asleep in his office. The general roused himself, looked over the dispatch, and nodded.

"No need for concern," he said. "Battles surge back and forth, and these reports in the midst of struggle mean little. McDowell is a good soldier. He'll win the day." The Grand Old Man of the Army rubbed his eyes and settled down for another nap.

By afternoon, the dispatches were pointing to victory at Manassas. McDowell seemed to have the situation in hand.

"Let's go for a carriage ride," Mary said. "You need the fresh air. There's nothing you can do here."

They rode to the Navy Yard with Willie and Tad. The Eastern Branch, smooth and unhurried, slipped past the hulls of steamers and tugs. The flag on the yard's tall mast hung idle in the thick heat, but clouds were moving in from the west. They heard more faint booms— artillery or thunder?

I hope they get finished before rain comes, he thought.

"Are we going to win?" the boys asked. The booms made their eyes wide with excitement.

"I expect we'll whip them."

"It sounds like they're fighting hard," Willie said.

"They're fighting hard, but the other side's getting the worst of it."

When they got back to the White House, he found Nicolay and Hay waiting under the portico, ashen-faced.

"Seward was just here," Nicolay whispered. "He says we're beaten. He said to tell you to go to Scott's office."

Abraham stared at his two young assistants. They both looked frightened. That can't be right, he thought. How would Seward know? It's a mistake. He turned and strode across the lawn to the War Department.

Scott's headquarters was full of officers and cabinet members, all gathered around a big map of the Manassas battlefield, looking dumbfounded. Seward was there, a cigar hanging at a discouraging angle from his mouth. He handed Abraham a shocking telegram from an army captain in the field: "The day is lost. Save Washington and the remnants of this army. . . . The routed troops will not re-form."

"I don't believe it," Scott insisted. "McDowell would have sent word if it's true."

But a dispatch from McDowell soon arrived: "The larger part of the men are a confused mob, entirely demoralized." His commanders did not think they could make a stand on the far side of the Potomac.

"How did this happen?" Abraham demanded. "How did it happen?"

Scott and his officers looked at him as if they suddenly could not tell one end of a cannon from the other.

"Send him all the reserves we've got," Abraham snapped. "And put more troops at the bridges. Do it now."

They stayed at the War Department until after midnight, absorbing the blows of dispatches that got worse and worse. A message came saying the secretary of war's brother, James Cameron, was killed fighting in Colonel William T. Sherman's brigade. Then suddenly the dispatches stopped coming. The telegraph station at Fairfax Court House had been abandoned.

Abraham walked back to his office and threw himself down on a sofa. Word of the disaster was beginning to spread. He could hear the murmur of a crowd outside on Pennsylvania Avenue, standing in the drizzle that was beginning to fall. Rumors flew that Beauregard's men were coming straight for the White House. The sightseers who had ridden into the countryside with their picnic baskets that morning straggled back over the bridges, jabbering about bodies choking Bull Run and soldiers bolting like jackrabbits. Senators and congressmen appeared at the White House to tell of roads clogged with smashed wagons, bleeding horses, writhing men.

He sprawled on the sofa, listening glassy-eyed. A Pennsylvania artilleryman had been seen wandering a field, two bloody stumps at the ends of his arms, looking for his hands. A Bible had stopped a bullet that hit a New York lad; as he took the book out of his breast pocket, gazing in wonder, another shot came along and cut him through to the heart. Senator Ben Wade of Ohio had leaped from his wagon, pointed his rifle at fleeing soldiers, called them cowards, and yelled, "We'll stop this damned run-away!" It had done nothing to end the human stampede.

General Scott came to the White House to urge that Mary, Willie, and Tad leave the city until it could be secured.

"Will you go with us?" Mary asked Abraham.

"No, I will not leave at this juncture."

"Then *I* will not leave *you* at this juncture."

By dawn, the rain was falling in torrents. The soldiers came streaming across the Long Bridge, beaten, drenched, and footsore. Abraham watched them through an upstairs window. They staggered like men walking in their sleep, many without shoes or coats. They collapsed on doorsteps and lay down on sidewalks with their heads in the mud. Women stood outside their houses, offering cups of coffee and bowls of hot stew. Some opened their homes to the ambulances that came splashing into town with loads of wounded.

By late morning, he had pieced together what happened. McDowell had hit the Confederates hard on their left flank, where they were not expecting him, and forced them into a retreat. But the Union drive was disorganized, and the Southerners hit back. General Thomas J. Jackson, commanding a Virginia brigade, had earned a name of honor when General Bee of South Carolina, trying to inspire his troops, pointed and shouted, "There is Jackson standing like a stone wall! Rally behind the Virginians!" Already men were calling him Stonewall. When nine thousand Southern reinforcements arrived by rail from the Shenandoah Valley, seemingly out of nowhere, the weary Union men broke and ran. Hundreds lay dead on each side and hundreds more wounded. Now the capital shuddered and braced itself for a Confederate assault.

"If they're going to attack, why don't they get it over with?" Mary asked.

"I don't know," Abraham said vacantly. "Maybe this downpour's too much for them. Maybe their boys are just as spent as ours." Whatever the reason, the expected invasion did not come.

The next day, he rode across the river in an open hack with his secretary of state to visit the troops. Everywhere they looked, they saw companies busy digging, building, dressing each other's wounds, fixing rifles, cleaning camps. Young men with serious, determined faces put their muscles to the task of throwing up defensive works.

"These boys don't look as scared and lost as we'd heard," Seward said, puffing vigorously on his cigar.

"No, they don't. They look like an old gamecock I used to know back in Illinois. He always got nicked up pretty bad in a contest, but every time he went back into the ring, he had more fight in him than before."

The more they talked to the officers and men, the more it seemed like it wasn't as bad as they'd thought. McDowell had come within a hair's breadth of victory at Manassas. Most of the troops, farm boys and city fellows alike, had fought well. And many had, in fact, retreated in good order when the time came. Some of the panic had been the work of teamsters, sightseers, and volunteers whose enlistments were about to expire anyway. The army was bruised but not smashed.

"I reckon they did their duty," Abraham told Seward. "I'm satisfied with their conduct. As for the fellows that ran, I'm not sure I wouldn't have done the same."

He watched a young corporal trying to kick a stubborn log into place on a redoubt. The more the log resisted, the harder he kicked.

"These boys got whipped, but now they've got their dander up. Give them a little time, and they'll be yelling 'Forward to Richmond!' again. And no Stone-walls will stop them."

CHAPTER 19

SUMMER 1861

*H*e summoned George B. McClellan to come to Washington and take charge of the army. The general arrived a few days later and stood in Abraham's office, smiling with youthful confidence, gray eyes reconnoitering above a fine Roman nose and a thick reddish-brown mustache. He was on the short side, but his muscular chest and broad shoulders gave him the look of a man who ought to have authority. Abraham had known him back in Illinois when he was vice president of the Illinois Central Railroad and had liked him, even though McClellan was a Democrat and had let Steve Douglas use his private railroad car during the 1858 debates. No matter. They were all in this together now. The army needed Democrats and Republicans alike if it was going to win this war.

"George, this army is like a railroad with its tracks bent out of shape. I need you to fix the rails and get the trains running on time."

"I'll do better than that. I'll lay new tracks and build a juggernaut engine that will crush this rebellion."

He was only thirty-four years old. The son of a Philadelphia doctor. Had graduated second in his class at West Point and fought valiantly under Winfield Scott in Mexico. He had spent time in Europe studying armies there, had invented a cavalry saddle, and risen to the rank of major general. Everyone agreed he was a born leader of men, though some added he was the only man ever born who could strut while sitting down. He had recently won two battles at Rich Mountain and Corrick's Ford in the western part of Virginia—small-scale battles, to be sure, but they were the biggest wins any Union general could claim so far, and they had cleared that part of the state of rebel forces.

"I'll start early tomorrow on a tour of our lines," McClellan said. "Then I'll be able to make up my mind as to the state of things."

"Our ranks are swelling," Abraham said. "More three-year men arrive every day. But I'm afraid you'll find them all very raw."

"It's no doubt an immense task that I have on my hands, but I believe I can accomplish it."

"I believe so, too."

"I flatter myself that Beauregard has gained his last victory."

By week's end, the capital city was calling him "the man on horseback." He spent twelve hours or more a day in the saddle, dashing from camp to camp. He chose not to sleep in a tent, but set up his headquarters in a large house on H Street, near the White House. Every day he rose early, held a quick staff meeting, jumped onto Dan Webster, his big bay horse, and raced off to see his troops. It was nothing for him to gallop from the Chain Bridge to Bailey's Crossroads to Alexandria and return to headquarters well after dark.

"I must ride much every day. My army covers much space, and unfortunately I have no one on my staff I can trust with the safety of affairs," he explained to Abraham. "It is necessary to see as much as I can. And more than that, to let the men see me and gain confidence in me."

He trained the men hard: polished them up, made them stand straight, marched them until they were too tired to complain, gave them target practice until they could shoot something like straight. He cleared out barrooms and rounded up loafers. Good men were promoted, bad officers dismissed. The troops dug, hammered, sawed, and sweated until a network of forts and batteries encircled the capital. It quickly became one of the most protected cities in the world.

McClellan was everywhere at once, even in the air. Abraham took Willie and Tad to watch him go up in Professor Thaddeus Lowe's hydrogen balloon to peer over the river at the Confederate lines. The general staged massive parades to show how the men were learning to drill in close order. Congressmen and senators fawned whenever he visited Capitol Hill. He went to Mathew Brady's photographic studio and posed with his right hand shoved into the front of his coat. Newspapers dubbed him the Young Napoleon.

Abraham rode out with him to inspect the troops and fortifications. Everywhere they went, the men broke into wild cheers and yelled "Little Mac! Little Mac!" The general snatched off his cap, raised it high, and gave it a sparkling twirl on his finger as he passed by.

"You have no idea how the men brighten up when I go among them," he confided. "I can see every eye glisten. Yesterday they nearly pulled me to pieces in one regiment."

In every camp, McClellan reined Dan Webster to a stop and chatted with the soldiers.

"Ready for a brush with the rebels, my friends?"

Cheers and shouts.

"I've come to place myself at your head and share every danger with you. Boys, I promise that every foot of ground taken by us hereafter will be held!"

Even wilder cheers, whoops, and hollers.

Throughout the summer, the volunteers kept pouring in. A great army—General McClellan named it the Army of the Potomac—was born. The various red, gray, and harlequin uniforms of the Zouaves and state militias gave way to a standard Union blue. The parades of troops grew immense. Huge tent cities sprawled around Washington's edges. The ring of forts bristled with cannon. Not far away, the Confederates were erecting batteries of their own.

Early one morning, Abraham and General Scott walked across Lafayette Square to McClellan's office. The Young Napoleon came bounding downstairs from his sleeping quarters, riding boots on. For an instant he did not look pleased to see them, but he invited them to sit.

"Well, George, when do you reckon the army will be ready to move against the rebels?" Abraham asked.

"Not until the city is adequately defended. Once it's secure, I can embark on a campaign of maneuver."

"It's pretty well defended now, don't you think?"

McClellan shook his head. "No, sir, I do not. In fact, we are in a terrible spot. The army is entirely insufficient for the emergency we face."

"What do you mean?"

"The enemy has at least one hundred thousand troops in front of us."

Abraham looked at Scott, flabbergasted. Scott gave him the same look back.

"Are you certain it's that many? How do you know?"

"From reliable intelligence reports. They vastly outnumber us. And their army is highly trained."

"I find that assessment hard to believe," Scott huffed.

McClellan smiled with polite contempt. "Were I in Beauregard's place, with his force at my disposal, I would attack our lines on the other side of the Potomac, and at the same time cross the river above the city in force. In fact, if Beauregard does not attack this week, he's a fool."

"Let him come," Scott growled. "I have not the slightest apprehension for the safety of the government here."

"What leads you to think he intends to attack?" Abraham pressed.

"I know full well the capacity of the generals opposing me. Not long ago, they were my most intimate friends."

Abraham groaned inwardly. And I barely know enough about military affairs to tell the butt of a musket from the back end of a mule, he thought.

"How many men will you require?"

"More than we have now," McClellan said evasively. "The best course is to build an army of overwhelming strength. Then I will advance and force the rebels into battle on a field of my own selection."

"How long will that take?"

"I am trying to follow a lesson I learned long ago—not to move until I know everything is ready, and then move with the utmost rapidity and energy."

"Yes, of course," Abraham yielded. "You can't move until you are ready."

McClellan rose. "Now if you will excuse me, gentlemen, I must go see my men."

He moved toward the door but turned before going out. He swept his cap through the air, as if about to give it a twirl on his finger.

"You have made me responsible for our country's fate," he said. "Place the necessary resources at my disposal, and I feel sure I can save this great nation."

He put on his cap, mounted Dan Webster, and galloped away.

CHAPTER 20

LATE SUMMER AND EARLY AUTUMN 1861

With almost the first shots of the war, Abraham was besieged by calls for emancipation. They came from generals like John C. Frémont in Missouri, who wanted to play politician and free the slaves of rebels himself. They came from Radical Republicans like Senator Charles Sumner of Massachusetts and Senator Ben Wade of Ohio, who declaimed in self-righteous tones that it was folly to preserve slavery while conducting war against slave holders; that emancipation was the only noble and true thing to do; that by failing to strike a fatal blow against bondage the president was murdering the country by inches—but then what else could you expect from a man born in a slave state?

The abolitionist agitators came at him thundering their ideals, the editorial writers sharpening their pens, the red-faced ministers waving their Bibles like clubs. They complained that the president was timid, foolish, and narrow-minded. They ranted that the key to the slave's chain was now kept in the White House, that Lincoln was the crony of chicken-hearted politicians, and that his weakness filled the hearts of liberty-loving people with funeral gloom.

An old Quaker from Pennsylvania came to the White House to see him. The man waited for three days, gradually ascending the stairway in the line of petitioners and then standing quietly in the corridor until finally ushered into Abraham's office. He wore a plain homespun jacket and a solemn look that gave him the appearance of always being at prayer, whether shoeing a horse or eating an apple pie. His gaze was patient and enduring, like his faith.

"Thee knows that slavery is evil, and that God created us all to live in freedom," he began, as if teaching a child.

Abraham scrutinized his face. Was this going to be a harangue? No, surely not. He liked the looks of the old fellow.

"Yes, my ancient faith tells me that all men are created equal," he answered. "If it were up to me alone, I would free all the slaves."

"Thee could declare them free any day."

"You seem to forget I am not a king. I cannot strip a man of property that is lawfully his. Our Constitution gives me no such power. This is no longer a government of laws when a president begins making rules of property by proclamation."

"God's law teaches us to love all our neighbors, black or white, as ourselves."

Abraham smiled. "When I took the oath of office, I promised the Southern people I would not interfere with their slaves. Do you wish me to break a promise?"

"Bad promises are often best broken."

"But as long as I keep that promise, our Southern countrymen may see that this fighting is useless and come back into the Union."

"What if they do? The evil of slavery will still be a curse on this land."

"A curse that must be removed by lawful means. If I were to declare all slaves free today, the Supreme Court would strike down my declaration as unlawful tomorrow. We've seen how the Taney Court rules."

"If Chief Justice Taney errs, that is his concern. His error should not keep thee from the right."

"That's not all. If I did as you suggest, the first thing you'd see would be a mutiny in the army. The Northern people have gone to war to save the Union, not liberate Negroes. The troops would throw down their rifles and walk off the field."

"Perhaps not so many as thee thinks."

"And then there are the border states. Would you have me lose them to the Confederacy? I would do just that if I upset slavery. Here, look at this."

He handed the old Quaker a telegram from three loyal Union men in Louisville. It read: "There is not a day to lose in disavowing emancipation or Kentucky is gone over the mill dam."

"There, do you see?" Abraham said. "To lose Kentucky is nearly the same as to lose the whole game. With Kentucky gone, we can't hold Missouri or Maryland. With those states against us, the job on our hands is too large. We may as well consent to separation at once, including the surrender of this capital."

The Quaker gazed at him with the same prayerful expression. "Does thee imagine that one good act will set off a chain of misfortunes?" he asked. "There is no need to worry about these things, so long as we keep God on our side."

"I hope God is on our side, but I must have Kentucky," Abraham smiled.

"Perhaps it is better to lose Kentucky than to keep her at such a high price."

"What I must keep is this Union, if I can. Our government has often been called an experiment. If it fails, the world will say that the idea of government of the people and by the same people is forever doomed to fail. The issue embraces more than the fate of these United States. It involves the whole family of man."

The Quaker sat quietly, willing to consider whatever his president had to say.

"This nation is the world's best hope for freedom," Abraham went on. "If we save the Union, we prove that popular government is not an absurdity. We save a government founded to elevate the condition of men—to lift artificial weights from all shoulders, to afford all an unfettered start, a fair chance in the race of life. So, you see, saving the Union must come first, or we may see an end to free government upon the earth. And what good would that do the slaves?"

The old fellow nodded his understanding.

"The hour will come for dealing with slavery," Abraham said. "We must be patient. It's like the man who watches his pear tree day after day, impatient for the ripening of the fruit. Let him attempt to force the process, and he may spoil both fruit and tree. But let him patiently wait, and the ripe pear at length falls into his lap."

"And thee believes that thy course is God's will?"

"I don't claim to know God's will. But it is my earnest desire to know it, and if I can learn what it is, I will do it."

"I will pray for thee," the old man nodded again. He rose to go, evidently satisfied. "We all are praying for thee. The Lord will sustain thee."

"Thank you, my friend." Abraham clasped his hand. "You have given a cup of cold water to a very thirsty and grateful man."

Mary felt besieged as well, though by pressures of a different sort. Washington society, the ladies in particular, was giving her a snubbing. Many refused to call on her. The women with Southern roots, who dominated the District of Columbia's social world, decided that she was coarse and ill-mannered. Never mind that she could read French and had more education than most of them. In their view, she had sprouted amid the grasses of the Western prairies and was just as fit for a log cabin as her husband. The Republican ladies gossiped that she was a secret rebel sympathizer. Her own brothers, after all, were fighting in the rebel army. It didn't help when Tad got hold of the blood-stained Confederate flag Elmer Ellsworth had torn down at the Marshall House, which Ellsworth's comrades had given to Mary as a cherished memento, and waved it gleefully from a window during one of his war games. That had certainly caused some talk.

Abraham saw her disappointment, but there was little he could do about it. "I'm sure that every president's wife takes some slings and arrows, just as every president does," he suggested.

"If that's true, it does not add much to the honor of our country," she said.

"Give it more time."

"I will, but it won't change the fact that it's painful to be treated in this manner." She touched her brow gingerly. "I'm beginning to think this place makes my head hurt."

She found relief in more shopping trips to Philadelphia and New York. Each foray unloosed a new stream of fabrics and china for the White House. The East Room, the Green Room, the Red Room, and the vestibule were all soon filled with workmen and clouds of plaster dust. At times it seemed to Abraham that Mary's closest confidantes were John Watt, the gardener, who helped her keep her accounts, and Lizzie Keckley, a former slave who had bought her freedom and gone into business as a seamstress. Lizzie had made dresses for Jefferson Davis's wife, Varina, when Davis was in the Senate. She was a kind, dignified woman. Abraham wondered if society was whispering that the first lady had had been forced to resort to a mulatto for a best friend.

He and Mary did their best to make time for each other. Once the city was over the initial fear of invasion, it flowered with operas, concerts, and plays that drew crowds needing diversions. An hour or two of Shakespeare was the best way to escape war worries. He loved sitting in the corner of a dark box, wrapped in a shawl, losing himself in *King Lear* or a minstrel show. Mary was gratified by the way audiences rose to cheer when they entered a theater, although once a man started yelling, "He hasn't any business here while men are dying! That's all he cares for his poor soldiers!" The audience booed the protester down while soldiers carried him to the door.

"Doesn't he realize I must have a change of some sort every once in a while?" Abraham grumbled. "If I don't, I'll die."

On afternoons when they had a free hour, they took a carriage ride, sometimes with the boys and sometimes without. It was a chance to get some fresh air and catch up with each other. Mary chattered about the latest carpets and bowls she had purchased. Abraham could only half-listen. No matter where they rode, signs of war marked the land: rickety barracks springing up beside the river; artillery frowning from behind jagged earthworks; a big slaughterhouse and heaps of rotting offal on the grounds of the unfinished Washington Monument, where herds of army cattle waited to be turned into beef for the troops.

Then there were the Negroes. They seemed to be everywhere, toting baskets to and from market; unloading vessels at wharves; waiting outside hotel doorways for masters. Some were free and some slaves. Some had abandoned the fields and made their way north as the Union army nudged its way into Virginia. Now they wandered the capital, unsure of what to do with themselves. Their dark inscrutable faces, too, had become emblems of war.

One afternoon, as Abraham and Mary's carriage rumbled along Maryland Avenue, they came upon an old Negro, a house servant perhaps, sitting on a stone beside the road. His black coat and tall silk hat were splattered with dried mud. Under each arm bulged a fat green cabbage. One hand clutched a rope tied around the neck of a young bellowing pig, and the other hand held an open book, which the old man leaned over, deciphering.

Abraham started to laugh at the sight, but just then the Negro looked up. For an instant recognition passed over the face that just as quickly went blank again, a face without malice or condemnation or complaint, but composed from years of servitude. He set the book in his lap, reached up, and raised his hat without spilling the cabbage tucked under the arm.

It took Abraham a second to recall where he had recently met the same expression. It was the enduring, patient gaze of the old Quaker.

He raised his own hat and nodded back as their carriage rolled by.

CHAPTER 21

AUTUMN 1861

The swarm of office seekers and petitioners continued, as thick as locusts on Pharaoh's Egypt. He tried to greet each visitor with a smile and a polite "What can I do for you?" Then he crossed his legs, clasped his hands around a knee, and listened.

An outspoken woman came to see him, insisting that her husband receive a promotion, which all the world knew to be his due. Abraham sighed and penned a note to the War Department: "Today Mrs. Major Paul of the Regular Army calls and urges the appointment of her husband as a Brig. Genl. She is a saucy woman, and I am afraid she will keep tormenting me till I may have to do it."

A farmer called wanting restitution because some Union troops had taken his hay and a horse. Abraham gave him the name of the office where he needed to file his claim.

"My good sir," he told the man gently, "if I should attempt to consider every such case, I'd have work enough for twenty presidents. This reminds me of the boy who tugged on the coattail of a steamboat captain who had his hands on the wheel as he guided his vessel through a stretch of rapids. The boy hailed him with, 'Say, Mister Captain! I wish you'd stop your boat a minute—I've dropped my apple overboard!'" The farmer went away looking chagrined.

Occasionally he lost his temper. "Look here! What do you take me for?" he barked at a man who called seeking permission to sell ale to the army. "Do you think I keep a beer shop?"

But most of the time he managed to endure the interviews with good humor. "They're my public opinion baths," he told his cabinet. "No hours of my day are better employed. They put me in direct contact with the people and give me an idea of what they think."

A massive Connecticut shipbuilder named Cornelius Bushnell appeared one day. He carried a paste-board model of the strangest vessel Abraham had ever seen. He said it was the design of John Ericsson, a Swedish-born engineer.

"It looks like a tin can on a shingle," Abraham commented. Right away it intrigued him.

"It does," Bushnell admitted, "but, by God, she'll float, and she'll fight. This is the ship to answer a Confederate ironclad."

Abraham nodded. Troubling rumors out of Norfolk indicated that the secessionists were busy fitting iron plates onto the hull of the frigate *Merrimack* to make a warship that could blow wooden ships to pieces. The Union needed an ironclad to stand up to her, and fast. Abraham studied the bizarre model, flat as a raft with its hull below the water line and a single revolving turret on its deck.

"Well, as the girl said when she put her foot into her stocking, I think there's something in it," he allowed. A naval board scrutinized the design, asked a hundred questions, and gave grudging approval. Up in New York, John Ericsson went to work building the USS *Monitor*.

A committee of soldiers and citizens came begging for a life. Private William Scott, a Vermont farm boy, had been on sentinel duty at three a.m. one morning near the Chain Bridge, on the Potomac, when the officer of the guard found him asleep. Scott had been court-martialed and condemned to be shot. The sentence was causing an uproar in the ranks.

"He's a good boy, and he's only been in the army a few weeks," a captain explained. "He volunteered the night before to stand watch for a sick friend. So it's only natural that he was tired the next night, don't you see?"

Good God, Abraham thought. We're releasing rebels on parole when we capture them. Are we going to shoot our own good men meanwhile?

"I don't think a brave lad ought to be put to death for falling asleep when he's weary," he said. "The country has better uses for him. Captain, your boy won't be shot. I'll see General McClellan about it."

Willie and Tad got wind of Private Scott's pardon and came with their own committee of neighborhood boys. They brought with them a doll dressed like a Zouave, in red trousers and a blue jacket.

"Papa-day, this is Jack," Tad announced. "We need you to fix up a pa'don fo' him."

"What's he done?"

"Desertion, spying, treason, sleeping on picket duty," Willie said. "We've already court-martialed him six times."

"And shot him with my cannon eveh'y time!"

"Jack sounds like a pretty tough character," Abraham said.

"We were going to shoot him again," Willie said, "but Mr. Watt says he won't have us digging up his rose bushes every time we bury him in the garden. Besides, it's getting his uniform awful dirty."

"That's why we need you to fix up a pa'don!"

Abraham stroked his beard. "Well, boys, his offences are rank, that's for certain. But it's a good law that no man shall be twice put in jeopardy of his life for the same offence. Since you've already shot and buried him several times, I think he's entitled to a pardon."

He took a sheet of Executive Mansion stationary and wrote it out: "The doll Jack is pardoned. By order of the President. A. Lincoln." The boys went off in a blaze of rebel yells and Indian war-whoops.

I never considered this part of the job when I ran for this office, Abraham thought as he watched them go. Never really thought about having to decide cases of who would live and who would die. It's a terrible responsibility. At least I could spare Private William Scott. And Private Jack.

But the pardon did poor Jack no good. A week later the boys court-martialed him again. This time they hung him from a tree.

❧❧❧

Senator Edward Baker came by the White House to see him on a glorious autumn afternoon. They went outside and stretched out on the lawn to talk, Abraham with his shoes kicked off and his back against the trunk of a maple tree, like he used to do in his younger days, and Ned lying on his back with hands behind his head and his handsome face turned to a faultless blue sky. Mary wandered nearby in the White House gardens, picking a bouquet of asters and mums. Willie rolled happily through crisp piles of red and gold leaves. The warm glow of an Indian summer mixed with the sheen of the river in open spaces between scarlet trees.

They talked with ease, as old friends do, of winding paths traveled together. Of their old circuit-riding days, and lawyers as slick as owl grease, and politicians with ways as dark as God's pockets.

"You were the best speaker of us all, inside a courtroom or out, back when we were younger codgers than we are now," Abraham said.

"Yes, I was the biggest gas bag of us all. Still am, some say."

"If you hadn't been born in London, you might be president instead of me."

"If that is true, Mr. President, I must thank the good Lord every day for merry old England."

Abraham smiled. He knew his friend would thank the Lord for no such thing. It was commonly said that Ned Baker had wept like a child the day he learned that his foreign birth disqualified him from ever being president.

He had emigrated to Philadelphia with his parents at age five, toiled for a while in a cotton mill, then moved west with his family to Indiana and Illinois, where he studied law. At age nineteen, he had been admitted to the state bar. When Abraham had first met him, Ned was a determined young lawyer, an inveterate gambler at cards, a writer of poetry, and a lover of champagne and oysters. His good-natured smile and generous impulses made it impossible not to like him.

It was pleasant to think back to an evening in Springfield twenty-two years earlier when Ned had delivered a fiery political address in a meeting room directly below Abraham's law office. When things got hot and the Democrats in the audience started to lay hands on the speaker, Abraham had dropped through a trap door in the ceiling to his friend's side and threatened to break some heads with a stone water pitcher. Ned, for his part, had proved a steadfast ally and helped Abraham get to Congress.

It had been Mary's idea to name their late boy Eddie after him, partly out of genuine affection, partly out of a desire to strengthen a valuable political connection with one of the brightest stars in Illinois politics. A part of Abraham, his superstitious side, had hoped that his son's name would bestow upon him the best of Ned Baker's qualities: warmth, generosity, and gallantry.

I wish Eddie could have grown up to know him, Abraham thought. They would have been good friends. It would have warmed my heart to see that.

Ambition had taken Ned to California and then Oregon, where he had been elected to the United States Senate. His fame as an orator had spread west and east as his hair had thinned and grayed. People called him the "Old Gray Eagle" in admiration of his soaring rhetoric. He had worked hard to build Republican support in the West Coast states and keep them in the Union.

"If you had not helped me get to Congress fifteen years ago, I would probably still be in Illinois and not be in the fix I'm in today," Abraham mused.

"And if you had not dropped out of the ceiling to fend off that howling mob of Springfield locofocos, I'd probably be wearing traces of tar and feathers today. I still remember the look on Mary's face when your raggedy old pants came dangling down through that trap door."

"It's a good thing she saw my better half first. It made her desire me to no end."

"Mr. Lincoln, I hear you, and you are terrible," Mary called. "Senator Baker, I cannot fathom why you put up with him."

"I put up with him so that I may visit you, Mrs. Lincoln."

Ned wore the uniform of the California Regiment, a unit he had recently formed. He had taken the rank of colonel, fully intending to lead his men into battle. "I want sudden, bold, forward, determined war," he had blustered in the Senate.

The two men talked of things old friends should not have to talk about—a torn nation, the build-up of arms, the movement of troops. The last few days had brought reports that the Confederates were up to something near Leesburg, Virginia, just forty miles from Washington. Perhaps they were digging in, or perhaps falling back. No one was sure.

"By thunder, that's one nest of vipers we should clean out!" Baker cried. "I'll do it myself if McClellan won't."

"I'm afraid that your impetuousness will endanger your life," Abraham said.

"I'd rather die in battle than anyplace else. The officer who dies with his men will never be judged harshly. I've already made out my will, you know."

"I know that's only talk, but it makes me nervous. You must be careful. I need you."

Ned rose to go. He shook hands with Abraham, then lifted Willie out of the leaves and kissed the boy goodbye. Mary gave him the bouquet she'd picked. He thanked her with a cavalier's bow.

"These flowers may wither, but my affection for you never will," he promised. He mounted his horse, and they watched him ride away.

The next day brought another azure sky and vague reports of fighting upriver near Leesburg, at a place called Ball's Bluff. Toward sunset, Abraham walked across Lafayette Square to McClellan's headquarters to see what information he could get. A couple of newspaper correspondents sat in the anteroom, hoping for news. He shook their hands and traded comments on the beauty of the afternoon until a young lieutenant ushered him into an adjoining room where a telegraph clattered away. McClellan stood leaning over a table, lines of fatigue etched in his face, reading dispatches as they came off the machine.

"Some of General Stone's boys have crossed the river above Edwards Ferry," he said. "They've run into heavy resistance."

The last two words sounded ominous.

"Are we beaten?" Abraham asked quickly.

"It's too early to know anything for sure."

The click-click-click of the telegraph filled the room. McClellan and his staff officers regarded the machine anxiously, as if it were an oracle speaking in tongues.

"I don't know why Stone sent troops across," the general said petulantly. "I didn't tell him to start a battle there. It was entirely unauthorized by me. A slight demonstration was all I wanted."

Click-click-click-click-click. A burst of fresh dispatches arrived. McClellan scanned them as they came over the wire. He looked satisfied with some, aggravated by others.

Click-click-click-click. He paused over one, seemed to read it twice. When he looked up, there was grief on his face.

"This one's brought some bad news," he said softly. "I'm afraid Colonel Baker has been shot."

Abraham's throat closed. "Is he hurt badly?" he rasped.

"Yes. I'm sorry to have to tell you. He's dead."

Abraham grabbed for the edge of the table. This could not be. A groan forced its way through his chest, ripping and slicing as it rose. The officers gaped at him. McClellan stepped close and spoke in a low tone, trying to offer words of comfort, but Abraham barely heard him.

He turned and stumbled through the anteroom, head bowed, tears starting down his cheeks. The two correspondents rose from their seats. A sentinel pacing before the door offered a salute. Abraham clutched his chest as he pushed by them onto the street. Behind him, the click-click-click of the telegraph went on, spelling out its tale of catastrophe.

He stayed up all night, pacing his room, hoping someone would bring word that the information was false. Every time he closed his eyes, he saw his son Eddie's face alongside his friend's.

They could not have the funeral in the White House. The public rooms were full of scaffolding and debris from Mary's renovations. Ned's body, torn by eight bullets, told the story of the fiasco at Ball's Bluff: the reckless blunder into Confederate forces; the troops pinned against the river; the wild plunge down hundred-foot bluffs to escape the maelstrom of lead; the blue-clad men flailing and drowning in the Potomac while rebels shot at them from atop the high banks. The bloated corpses washed downstream and lodged against Georgetown wharves.

It took weeks for the hurt to fade. Ned's death stunned him even more than poor Ellsworth's. Ellsworth's going felt tragic because he had been so young and his future so bright. Ned's death pierced deeper memories. It was not until Willie crawled into his lap to show him a poem he had written that the pain began to subside. Tears came again as he read the verse, but the simple childish lines brought succor.

> *There was no patriot like Baker,*
> *So noble and so true;*
> *He fell as a soldier on the field,*
> *His face to the sky of blue.*

CHAPTER 22

LATE 1861 AND

EARLY 1862

*T*he corpses floating down the Potomac brought with them a rising tide of dismay. Across the North, critics stormed that only incompetence or disloyalty, or both, could have allowed the tragedy at Ball's Bluff. General McClellan shot back that the officers involved, including Colonel Baker, had acted without his knowledge. Little Mac hinted strongly that he could manage things much better if Winfield Scott were out of the way.

The fat old general, feeling insulted and misused, tendered his resignation. Abraham hated to see him go, but he knew there comes a time when the venerable must give way to the vigorous. Scott boarded a predawn train in a cold, stinging downpour and chugged out of town toward retirement at West Point. Abraham named McClellan to take his place as general-in-chief of all United States armies.

"Draw on me for all the sense I have, and all the information," he told the Young Napoleon. "I fear that taking supreme command, in addition to leading the Army of the Potomac, will entail a vast labor on you."

"I can do it all," McClellan said.

The Army of the Potomac drilled and paraded through crisp autumn days while the cry, "On to Richmond!" sounded again. Editors asked why McClellan's regiments could march up and down Pennsylvania Avenue but could not seem to march onto a battlefield. Senators fumed that rebel banners still flew practically within sight of the Capitol. "For God's sake, push the traitors back before snow arrives," they demanded.

McClellan insisted that the men still were not ready, that he needed more troops. Abraham prodded him, but only gently. McClellan was the expert, and if he said the army needed more training, then it needed more training, and that was all there was to it. The last thing anyone wanted was a repeat of what had happened at Manassas.

When it came to military affairs, Abraham knew he was out of his league. The closest experience he had to battle was chasing rumors of Indians during the Black Hawk War. That bothered him keenly. If he was going to lead the nation through a war, he ought to know more about military strategy.

The old urge to dive into books kicked in. He sent to the Library of Congress, and before long, the big table in his office was piled with volumes like *Elements of Military Art and Science* by Henry W. Halleck. Late nights were given to studying maps and reports, to pondering field maneuvers and uses of artillery.

Sometimes he dropped by McClellan's headquarters to discuss what he had learned. The general listened politely, but Abraham could tell he wasn't really interested in hearing what an amateur thought. The corners of his smile said, "Well, Mr. President, aren't you a rare bird?"

One mid-November night, Abraham walked to McClellan's headquarters with Seward and Hay to get the latest news. A porter met them at the door and told them the general was at an officer's wedding but would soon return. They went in, sat in the anteroom, and passed the time by reading aloud from the humorist Petroleum Nasby, who always made Abraham slap his knee with laughter.

After about an hour, Little Mac arrived, spoke with the porter for a moment in low tones, and went upstairs, straight past the door of the room where his visitors were sitting. Abraham glanced at Seward. The secretary of state raised his eyebrows. They waited another half hour before Abraham sent the porter upstairs to remind the general they were there. The man came back down and announced coolly that the general had gone to bed.

They walked back across Lafayette Square to the White House. John Hay pulled at his bowler hat, trying to keep down his anger. "That was unparalleled insolence," he grumbled.

"I think it's better not to worry over points of etiquette and personal dignity just now," Abraham said.

"I'm not sure he understands that you're his commander," Seward said.

"Governor, I'd be willing to hold his horse if he'll bring us victory."

Shortly before Christmas, McClellan came down with typhoid fever. For three weeks he was off his feet, unable to work. The army stood still. Abraham tried taking matters into his own hands. He wired his chief commanders west of the Appalachians, urging them to advance in Kentucky and eastern Tennessee. The message came back that they, too, were not ready, and that "too much haste will ruin everything."

He had cabinet problems on top of military problems. The squabbling for patronage and influence among his department heads sometimes resembled a half-dozen hungry roosters in the presence of a single worm. His secretary of war, Simon Cameron, had become a particular worry. The War Department was a disaster. The army was paying high prices for uniforms that dissolved in the rain, tents that blew to shreds in a puff of wind, shoes with soles that wore out as soon as a man put them on and stood up. Lame horses and blind mules were being sold to the army for piles of money, and exactly where the funds were going, no one seemed to know.

More than a few critics swore that the money was finding its way into Cameron's pockets, but as far as Abraham could tell, the man wasn't really dishonest. He simply wasn't fit for the job. The War Department was woefully understaffed and incompetent, but Cameron did not seem to know how to fix it. The flood of complaints against him could turn a grist mill. He would have to go. The ministry to Russia was opening up. St. Petersburg would be a good place to send him. The question was, who should be the new secretary of war?

One name kept coming up: Edwin M. Stanton. Abraham had run into the man several years before when they had both been hired to work on a case that went to trial in Cincinnati, an important case involving the patent on the famous McCormick mechanical reaper. Stanton was a brilliant lawyer. He could also be rude, arrogant, and domineering. He had taken one look at Abraham in Cincinnati, demanded to know what such a long-armed ape was doing there, and promptly cut him out of the trial.

The irascible lawyer had gone on to serve as attorney general under President Buchanan. Recently he had been grousing to friends about the "painful imbecility" of "the Illinois Ape" in the White House, insults that had not escaped Abraham's ears. Yet by all accounts he was a brilliant administrator, unswervingly honest and brutally efficient. Just what the War Department needed.

I'll have to swallow some of my pride if I'm going to work with him, Abraham thought. But he'll have to swallow even more of his. Well, if the country was to be saved, personal matters would have to be put aside. He asked Stanton to come to the White House.

Neither of them mentioned Cincinnati when they met. As they shook hands, Abraham realized that it was for the first time. Stanton had not deigned to touch him in Cincinnati, except for one time when he had jerked Abraham's coattails to get him out of the way in the courtroom. He had the same gnomish figure as six years before, the same thick black eyebrows and sharp black eyes glaring through steel-rimmed glasses, though perhaps not quite so harshly now. His long black beard was streaked with gray.

"Everybody around here thinks you're the man to clear up a muddle," Abraham said.

"I might be, if you can stand a Democrat in your cabinet." Stanton said it with a grimace that Abraham took to be an attempt at a smile.

"I'm grateful to any man who's willing to put aside party affiliation to stand by the government in this struggle."

"I'll do it, so long as the only pledge you expect from me is to throttle treason."

They shook hands again, and his new secretary of war went off to reconnoiter his department.

❧❧

He had more problems where he least needed them—on the home front. In Washington's parlors and barrooms, the ugly whisperings about Mary continued. She was raiding the public treasury to pay for dresses and pearls. She was promising favors in return for cash and colluding with her friend, Mr. Watt, the White House gardener, to pad bills, even going so far as to sell manure from the White House stables back to the government for exorbitant sums that she kept for herself. So ran the talk, some of which reached Abraham. He did his best to ignore it. It was the kind of dung that troublemakers in the capital loved to spread.

One evening after dinner, Mary sent the children to bed early so she could talk with him about something. "There's been a mistake I must ask you to remedy," she said. "I hate to bother you with it. I know you have much on your mind."

"What is it?"

"It seems that our friends in Congress did not give us quite enough money to pay for all the renovations to this old house. We need to ask them for a little more."

"That's not possible," he said quickly. "Congress has appropriated twenty thousand dollars. That should be plenty."

"But we still have bills to pay. And, you see, the renovation fund is out of money."

He looked at her sharply. "You mean you've already spent all twenty thousand?"

"Yes."

"How much more is left to pay?"

"I'm not sure, precisely," she said evasively. "I have some bills here you may look at, if you wish—for wallpaper and moldings and such. I believe they come to about seven thousand."

"Good God!" he exploded. "How could you let this happen?"

"I managed as best I could." She assumed a wounded, indignant tone. "You don't know how much it costs to refurbish a house of this size. You've never known about these things."

He grabbed the papers from her and ran his finger down a list of expenditures. "'Elegant, grand carpet, twenty-five hundred dollars,'" he read in astonishment. "I'd like to know where one even puts a carpet worth twenty-five hundred dollars!"

"This is the president's house, Mr. Lincoln. You can't fill it with burlap and tin. Do you want the snobs in this city saying we don't know how ladies and gentlemen live?"

"This is all a monstrous extravagance!"

"The house was as run down as a barn when we moved in," she reminded him.

"It was better than any place else we've ever lived!"

She smiled, trying to calm him down. "It's common to overrun appropriations. Everyone says so. We just need Congress to pass a deficiency bill."

He gaped at her. Evidently she'd been talking to those in the know to find out how games were played in the legislature.

"Just ask Congress to pass a deficiency bill and give us a little more money." She spoke as if it were no more than wiping up a spill. "That will take care of it."

Was she serious? More money for drapes and chandeliers? In the middle of a war?

"That will never have my approval," he snapped. "I'll pay it out of my own pocket first."

"But we can't afford that!" Now it was her turn to be shocked. "It's not our house. Why should we spend our own money on it?"

"It would stink in the nostrils of the American people to have it said that the president of the United States approved a bill overrunning an appropriation of twenty thousand dollars for flub dubs for this damned old house, when the poor, freezing soldiers cannot have blankets!"

He jumped up from the table and paced the floor. How in God's name could she have done this to him? This war was costing a fortune. He had just signed the country's first income tax into law to keep the government from going bankrupt. What would people say when they heard their money was going to this?

"Why didn't you tell me about this sooner, before it was out of hand?"

"I didn't want to disturb you. I knew you were already burdened."

"Well, you got yourself into this," he shouted. "You can damn well bear the blame yourself. I swear, I won't!"

"You're talking nonsense!" Panic was setting into her voice. "Please, don't be cruel."

"It was wrong to spend a single cent! If I hadn't been overwhelmed with other business, I never would have allowed it. But what could I do? I can't attend to everything!"

"Just help get me out of this trouble," she pleaded. "I'll never get into such difficulty again."

"I tell you right now, I will not put my name to a deficiency bill."

"Please, get it settled, for my sake," she whimpered. "I won't spend a cent more without consulting you. From now on, I'll always be governed by you, I promise."

"I will *never* approve any scheme to get the people to pay for this," he said icily. "Never."

They barely spoke for three days. Mary took to her bedroom with a bad headache. In the end, however, the whole thing was swept under the rug. Congress appropriated an extra fourteen thousand dollars to pay for cost overruns. After all, it was not, as Mary had said, the first time a government project had exceeded its budget. So maybe she really did know how to handle these things, he told himself. She certainly knew how to get what she wanted. It still galled him that she had been so careless in spending public money, and that he had let it happen. But it was best to let it go, just like it was best to overlook McClellan's impertinence. There were too many other things to worry about. He had no time to stew over snubs and flub dubs.

CHAPTER 23

FEBRUARY 1862

All the French wallpaper was finally up, the paint dry and tasseled drapes hung, the new sofas and hassocks in place. Once Abraham's anger cooled, he had to admit that she had done a magnificent job remaking the place. The rooms glowed with varnished wood and gilt cornices. The frescoed ceilings and rich brocatelle had the look of a nation that had no intention of letting itself go to pieces.

Mary decided to host a grand reception for five hundred guests to show it all off. Abraham agreed to the idea, with some reservations. There would surely be grumbling in the press about partying in the midst of war. And if there were to be five hundred flattered invitees, there would no doubt be three times as many who would feel injured about being left out. But so long as he paid for the reception himself, not with public funds, he supposed it would be all right.

The invitations went out. Mary launched herself like a cannonball at the task of planning the buffet and making arrangements with caterers. She and Abraham were so busy, they hardly noticed at first when Willie went out riding his pony through a wet snow and came back with a cough. Then his cold turned into a fever, and suddenly dark memories of their son Eddie's death came rushing back. They put Willie in bed, and Mary nursed him with beef tea. He shook with chills and burned with sweats that drenched the sheets. They called in Dr. Robert Stone, who had the reputation of being the finest doctor in Washington. He ordered doses of calomel, jalap, and Peruvian bark.

"He'll be fine once the fever runs its course," he said.

Mary still worried. "I think we should postpone the reception," she said. "I don't want a commotion in the house while he's sick."

"The invitations have already been delivered," Abraham pointed out. "It would be best not to withdraw them, unless Dr. Stone advises it."

"I'd go ahead with your plans," the doctor said. "He's certainly in no immediate danger. There's every reason to expect him to recover soon."

Lizzie Keckley, Mary's mulatto seamstress, helped them take turns watching at Willie's bedside. Abraham sat with him in the evenings. He told him stories about bear hunts and Indian wars. Sometimes he sat and plowed through a stack of memoranda while the boy curled up with pencil and paper, scribbling poetry for Tad.

"I miss my pony," Willie said.

"Well, you'll be able to ride him again soon."

"Do you think he misses me?"

"Yes, but I'll go down to the stable tonight and tell him you're getting better."

After a few days, he was on the mend. The fevers dissipated, and the coughing let up. Abraham still came to his bedroom in the evenings to talk and read with him, and when the boy fell asleep, he would sit a while longer. Then his thoughts would shift back to the war. His first year in office was nearing its end, and the list of disappointments was long.

The South was really gone and wasn't coming back without a bad fight. Union armies lay idle in winter camp, led by generals who seemed inclined not to fight. Desertions were on the rise, along with public dissatisfaction. If the newspapers were to be believed, many Northerners were concluding that Abraham Lincoln might be a good man, but he wasn't up to the job.

Merchants were frustrated over disrupted markets, and farmers irritated that their field hands had gone into the army. New York bankers were threatening to lend the government no more funds, and radicals in Congress had begun to plague him about the way things were being conducted. Southerners were pressing England to side with the Confederacy. Two good friends had been shot dead.

For the first time, it looked like the secessionists might actually get their way. The bottom is out of the tub, he thought. What am I going to do?

The day of the reception, Willie took a sudden turn for the worse. His fever came raging back, along with piercing headaches that sent tears streaming down his flushed cheeks. Mary called for Dr. Stone, who came at once to look him over. He still thought there was no cause for alarm. It was too late to call off the party, at any rate. Mary sat with her boy most of the afternoon, holding his hot little hand, while downstairs caterers bustled in and out of the mansion with barrel-loads of delicacies. Men tromped from room to room, moving furniture and arranging great blue-and-white porcelain vases of flowers.

When evening came, Abraham spelled Mary while Lizzie Keckley helped her get dressed. Willie had fallen asleep, and Abraham stood with his back to the fire, hands behind him, his thoughts lost in the convoluted pattern of the carpet until he heard a rustle of satin. Mary hurried back into the room. She wore a white evening gown trimmed with flounces of black lace. A long train swept the floor behind her. The neckline was cut as low as a middle-aged lady dared, and her arms were bare. A necklace of shimmering pearls lay on her bosom, and purple-and-white crape myrtle flowers wreathed her hair. She was forty-three years old now, but she still knew how to make herself look beautiful.

"Whew! Our cat has a long tail tonight," Abraham said, looking at the gown's train.

She went to Willie's side to smooth his damp hair.

"Mother, it is my opinion that if some of that tail was nearer the head, it would be in better style," he teased softly.

"Humph!" She creased her brow, but he knew she was pleased that her dress had attracted his attention. She offered her arm, and they went downstairs together, leaving Willie in Lizzie's care.

At nine o'clock, the carriages began rolling up to the portico. The guests arrived with their cherished invitations to present at the door to Old Edward: cabinet members, senators, and representatives in black swallowtail coats; ladies in billowing fancy-colored silks; generals in shiny uniforms; princes, counts, and barons in the gilded finery of the diplomatic corps. The throng wandered from room to room, praising the new decor. Abraham stood in the East Room shaking hands. Bob was home from Harvard for the occasion and stood proudly at his side. The Marine Band, stationed in the vestibule, played selections from operas and a brand-new piece, "The Mary Lincoln Polka."

At eleven o'clock, Mary took Abraham's arm and led a promenade around the East Room before the crowd moved down the hall to the State Dining Room. The doors had been locked to keep everyone away from the food until the appointed time, and they all had to stand around for a few awkward moments while a steward ran to find the key. Someone called out, "I am in favor of a forward movement!" and someone else, "An advance to the front is only retarded by the imbecility of commanders!" Everyone laughed, even General McClellan, who had recovered nicely from his illness.

The key was located, the doors unlocked, and the guests poured through. They found heaps of turkey, duck, pheasant, oysters, venison, and ham. Fantastic replicas made of hardened sugar adorned the tables—the frigate *Union* with forty guns under full sail, Fort Pickens bristling with cannon, little cupids bearing a war helmet that waved plumes of spun sugar. A huge Japanese bowl brought from the Orient by Commodore Matthew Perry held ten gallons of champagne punch. Trays of cakes and pastries brought ladies' corsets to the bursting point. The guests gorged themselves until the wee hours of the morning, and everyone agreed that the affair was a brilliant success.

For Abraham and Mary, it was a nightmare. They took turns excusing themselves to slip upstairs and stand for a few minutes beside Willie's bed. Mrs. Keckley was there, and each time Abraham stole into the room, she looked up at him with worry on her face. The boy tossed in his sleep, sweating and whimpering. Abraham watched his labored breathing and stroked his forehead, then turned and went back downstairs. He traded glances with Mary, who was in the Blue Room conversing in French with a nobleman from Paris. Her eyes were dark with terror. He wondered if anyone else could see it. The hours crept by while the guests laughed, gossiped, and dined.

When the last senator had finally departed, they went upstairs together to sit with Willie until dawn. They both knew that, despite what the doctor had said, their son was getting worse.

CHAPTER 24

FEBRUARY 1862

The next few weeks were a descent through a landscape of deep shadows. He passed through it like a shade himself, at first with Mary at his side, but the further they traveled, the more they drew apart, until he could barely discern her.

They watched their child waste away, Mary sitting at his bedside night and day, as if she were a being that needed no sleep, Abraham treading between his office and the sickroom to look in on Willie and stroke his hair. They realized with horror that they were walking a path they had been down a dozen years before with Eddie: the violent fevers and chills, the days of false hopes when he seemed to be getting better and then grew worse, the crying out in the night, the avoiding of each other's eyes as unmentionable thoughts took hold.

Willie sensed that something was drawing near. "Is Eddie in heaven?" he whispered calmly one evening.

"Yes, he is," Abraham said.

"Will I see him there?"

"Someday you will, but not for many years."

"If I went to heaven, Eddie wouldn't be lonely."

"Don't you worry about him. Eddie's happy to wait a long time for us."

Tad came down with a fever and sore throat. It seemed to be a milder case of the same illness, but now they were doubly frightened. Dr. Stone ordered that the boys be kept apart, which made Tad whimper for his brother. Mrs. Keckley attended to him while they sat with Willie, but they could hear him fussing and crying through the wall.

During moments when both children were sleeping, Abraham did his best to comfort Mary or went to the oval library across the hall to pick up a Bible and read passages his mother used to love. Strains of her voice came in the old, worn verses. *The Lord shall give thee rest from thy sorrow, and from thy fear.*

He staggered through his duties. Nicolay and Hay tried to see that he was left alone. Whenever someone brought him something that had to be signed, he signed it. Grand news came over the telegraph wires. Troops under General Ambrose E. Burnside captured rebel forts at Roanoke Island in North Carolina. Even better, General Ulysses S. Grant forced the surrender of Fort Henry on the Tennessee River, then moved to take Fort Donelson, on the Cumberland. They were the sort of victories he had been praying for, but his prayers were needed elsewhere now.

The descent into the valley of the shadows grew steeper. They clutched Willie's hand—it was the only way they knew to help him through the last trials: the swelling abdomen and writhing convulsions; the putrid green diarrhea, streaked with blood; and the wanderings of the mind that sometimes brought sweet dreams and sometimes left their boy muttering and wildly picking at things on the bedclothes that only he could see.

Between bouts of fever and delirium, he managed a smile. "Mother, will you do something for me?"

"Of course I will, dear boy."

"Our Sunday School is collecting money for the missionaries. I've saved up five dollars. Will you give it to Dr. Gurley?"

"We'll give it to him together, the next time we go to church. As soon as you're all better."

Pneumonia set in, and he slipped into a coma. Eight days after Abraham's fifty-third birthday, the lungs filled with fluid. They sat with him while the breathing slowed to soft, infrequent rasps, then stopped. Mary crumpled to the floor, sobbing. They got her onto her feet, and Lizzie Keckley led her away.

Abraham stumbled down the hallway. He found John Nicolay lying half-asleep on a sofa in his office.

"Well, Nicolay, my boy is gone," he choked out, "he is actually gone." He went into his office and sat dazed. After a while he thought of Tad. Someone should be with him. He rose and staggered back up the hallway to tell him his brother was gone.

The screaming started a few minutes later, when the first shock wore off of Mary. He hurried to her room to quiet her. Mrs. Keckley met him at the door with a frightened look on her face. Mary stood beside her bed flailing her arms, fighting demons on the air. She was shrieking at the top of her lungs.

"Mary! Mary!" He shook her gently. "Mary! Look at me! Mary!"

She stopped flailing and gazed at him with a wild look. A guttural moan rose from her throat. He shuddered as it flowed past. She pulled herself away and ran to a corner, groaning and snatching at her hair.

"Mary! Stop! You'll hurt yourself!" He took hold and half-pushed, half-carried her to bed. "Send for Dr. Stone," he told Lizzie. "Tell him to hurry."

She thrashed at the sheets while he held her down. Her shrieks pierced the walls.

"Shsh . . . shsh. Tad will hear you!"

Dr. Stone arrived, and they forced laudanum between her lips. Within minutes, the ravings gave way to stupor. Once she was calm, the doctor ushered Abraham out the door. It would be better if she had no visitors for a few hours, he explained.

"Is there anyone you trust to help care for her, perhaps for a few weeks, until she's over her despair?"

"Her older sister, Elizabeth. But she's in Springfield."

"Get her."

He wired Elizabeth, begging her to come. Then he telegraphed Bob at Harvard. After that, he wasn't sure what to do. He went back to his office, told Nicolay he did not want to be disturbed, sat alone in the dark, and cried.

It was too soon to think about why this had happened. He had to get through the next few hours and days. *Thou, which has shewed me great and sore troubles, shalt quicken me again, and shalt bring me up again from the depths of the earth.*

He closed his eyes to picture his boy reciting his railroad time-tables, climbing onto a chair to give little fire-and-brimstone campaign speeches, riding his pony for the first time. The pain stabbed deep, cut into scars of older losses. Not even Eddie's death had hurt this much. He and Mary had been younger then, and they had known in their grief they could have more children. There would be no more now.

His son's body was still warm. He must go to him. He rose and went back to the bedroom where he had died. The women were there. Lizzie Keckley, and their friend Eliza Browning, wife of Senator Orville Browning of Illinois, and some others. That was good. The women would know what to do. They had washed his little face, combed his hair, put fresh clothes on him. Abraham went to the bed and looked down.

"My poor boy, he was too good for this earth. It is hard, hard to have him die!" He buried his head in his hands and sobbed like a child until his whole frame shook.

Numb, sleepless days followed. The doctors embalmed the body. Willie lay in the Green Room, dressed in a brown suit for visitors who came to pay their last respects. His little chest was covered with green and white blossoms of sweet-smelling mignonette. Abraham and Bob led Mary downstairs, drugged to semi-consciousness, to see him one last time in private, then led her straight upstairs again.

There was no point in even suggesting that she attend the funeral, given her state. A storm raged through the city before the service began, uprooting trees and knocking down steeples. Mary hid under her bed-covers, moaning and wailing. Downstairs, black crepe festooned the mirrors of the East Room, which earlier that month had reflected the brilliant colors of their party. Generals and high officials, drenched and shivering, filled a semicircle of chairs.

Dr. Gurley, who had befriended Willie on Sundays at the New York Avenue Presbyterian Church, stood beside the little coffin to give the oration. "What we need in the hour of trial, and what we should seek by earnest prayer, is confidence in Him who sees the end from the beginning and doeth all things well."

Afterwards, the children of Willie's Sunday school class followed the casket outside. Abraham and Bob climbed into a carriage drawn by two black horses. They followed the hearse, pulled by two white horses, through the ruins of the storm to Oak Hill Cemetery in Georgetown to lay him in a vault until they could take him home to Springfield.

Tad was getting better, but he was heartbroken over Willie and terrified by his mother's sobbing.

"Am I going to die too, Papa-day?" he wept.

"No, son, you'll be fine."

"But Willie died."

"Yes, he did."

"He died and won't speak to me anymo'!"

"He can hear you in your prayers, Taddie."

"But he can't speak to me! Why can't he speak to me?"

Abraham lay down beside him. The childhood he's known is over, he thought. It will all be different now. He stroked Tad's hair while the boy cried himself to sleep.

Elizabeth Edwards, Mary's sister, arrived from Springfield the day after the funeral. She had long been a second mother to Mary, beginning the day their mother had died, when Mary was a young girl. Elizabeth and her husband, Ninian, were living in Springfield when Abraham had moved there to take up the law. He had met Mary while she was visiting Elizabeth and had courted and married her in the parlor of the grand Edwards home. All these years later, Elizabeth stood as tall and straight as ever, still a handsome woman, still the elegant dame whose pound cakes formed the cornerstones of the Episcopal Church in Springfield.

"I'm grateful to you for coming," Abraham told her. "No one can console Mary like you."

"Take me to her."

He saw the shock on Elizabeth's face when they entered Mary's darkened bedroom. She lay in bed, hair disheveled, scratches on her arms and face. The eyes peered at them with a vacant light. For a minute he worried that Mary did not recognize her own sister. She burst into tears, shaking uncontrollably. It frightened him.

"Leave her with me," Elizabeth said firmly. "She needs time. Go get some rest. You both need it."

She's right, he thought. I've got to have rest if I'm going to go on. For the first time in days, he felt like he might close his eyes and sleep. But I should check on Tad again, he thought. I should see if he's all right. We can lie down together and rest.

He kissed Mary on the top of her head and left her with Elizabeth. He went down the empty hallway to his youngest son, his shoulder brushing against the wall, groping his way through shadows.

CHAPTER 25

MARCH 1862

He forced himself back to work. Thank God for the work. It kept him afloat. It was horrible to be grateful for the task of prosecuting a war, but part of him was.

Every Thursday, the day of Willie's death, he locked himself in the room where his boy had died and wept for an hour. Sometimes he read the Bible, and sometimes he quietly recited lines of a favorite poem he had long ago memorized.

> O why should the spirit of mortal be proud!
> Like a swift-fleeting meteor, a fast flying cloud,
> A flash of the lightning, a break of the wave—
> He passes from life to his rest in the grave.

When he was finished grieving he wiped his eyes, opened the door, and went back to work.

Criticisms of McClellan were rising. The Army of the Potomac kept drilling and parading. Dispatches from the general's headquarters read the same every evening: "All quiet on the Potomac." Republican senators noticed that the Young Napoleon wasn't spending quite so much time in the saddle anymore, but nearly every evening was giving lavish dinner parties that left empty a dozen bottles of wine, and that most of the guests had not voted for Abraham Lincoln. Rumors spread that the general had no intention of fighting, that his heart really lay with the Southern cause. The Confederates, meanwhile, kept reinforcing their lines in northern Virginia.

"If he doesn't want to use the army, I'd like to borrow it for a while," Abraham grumbled to his cabinet.

Stanton's patience was already running thin. "This army has got to fight or run away," the secretary of war barked, pounding the big table in Abraham's office. He snatched his spectacles off his nose and rubbed the lenses with a handkerchief. "The champagne and oyster suppers on the Potomac must stop!"

McClellan at last produced a plan of action, but as Abraham studied it, his doubts grew. It was a scheme of immense complication. Rather than driving south toward Richmond, the general wanted to pick up nearly the entire Army of the Potomac, transport it by water down the Chesapeake Bay, and drive on the Confederate capital from the east. It would mean more money for boats and equipment, and more delay for arrangements.

He called his general to the White House. McClellan arrived early on a Saturday morning, full of smiling self-assurance. They sat side-by-side with a map of the Virginia theater of war spread before them.

"I find that the simplest and most direct way is usually best," Abraham began. He spoke quickly, a little coolly. Best to send the message that his supply of patience was not inexhaustible. "The enemy's army sits before us, at Manassas. It seems to me we should move against him there, or on his flanks, and drive him toward Richmond."

"That's just what he wants us to try, and what we should *not* do," McClellan said matter-of-factly. "He has too many men for us to risk a direct attack."

"How many?"

"I've told you before. At least one hundred thousand."

I still can't believe that, Abraham thought. Nothing makes a fish bigger than not being caught.

"And those men are firmly entrenched behind strong fortifications," the general insisted. "An attack on the enemy's left flank, here"—he pointed to the map—"involves a long line of communication. We can't prevent him from collecting detachments from his right to meet us in battle. If we attack his right flank, here, we'll encounter heavy resistance. He's watching the fords of the Occoquan and has batteries in place to meet us."

He went on to explain how the plan Abraham envisioned would likely result in defeat. The general's own plan, on the other hand, offered much better chances. "If we move in force down the Chesapeake, we oblige the enemy to abandon his entrenched position. He must hasten to cover Richmond, but he'll find us already closing in. We'll smash him, if he doesn't disperse or surrender first."

"If you move the bulk of the army, doesn't it leave Washington unprotected?" Abraham pressed. "Once you're gone, what's to prevent him from moving quickly to take this capital?"

"I'll leave more than sufficient force behind to prevent that. Remember, I've ringed this city with fortifications. Besides, he *must* move his army south to meet us—if he doesn't, he loses all."

"What's to stop the rebels from reentrenching east of Richmond?" he asked in his best courtroom voice, the voice he once used to cross-examine witnesses.

"They'll try, but we won't give them time."

"We don't know the ground there as well as we do here."

"The country there is more favorable for offensive operations—much more level, with fewer dense woods. The roads are passable at all seasons of the year. Once we've landed the army, they'll afford us the shortest possible route to Richmond."

He's not entirely certain, Abraham thought. But he acts as though he is. That's his secret. He makes himself sound convincing.

"If you're beaten, you'll be a long way from home," he probed. "Won't retreat be more difficult?"

"On the contrary. We could fall back along this peninsula between the York and James Rivers to Fort Monroe, with our flanks perfectly secured by our fleet." The general swept his hand across the map, dismissing all objections. "I don't expect defeat with my plan," he said. "I'll stake my life and reputation on the result. More than that. I'll stake upon it the success of our cause."

They pondered each other, the commander-in-chief and general-in-chief. All right, let him try it his way, Abraham thought. At least the army will be on the march. At this point, I'll take any movement at all, so long as he leaves enough troops to defend Washington.

❧❧❧

He looked in on Mary and Tad several times each day. Tad's fever was gone, though he was still weak and often woke from nightmares crying, "Am I going to die too, Papa-day?" Mrs. Pomroy, a nurse from one of the soldiers' hospitals, came to help take care of him. She was a gentle woman who had lost two children of her own. Mary kept to her bedroom, crying much of every day, sometimes hysterically, sometimes moaning softly so that when Abraham approached her door, it sounded like someone was blowing across the mouth of an empty bottle. It gave him the chills.

Elizabeth did her best to help. "She's unable to control her feelings," she whispered. "She's always had trouble reining in her passions, ever since she was a girl, but this is the worst I've seen it."

Abraham took Mary by the arm and coaxed her to a window. He pointed in the direction of the lunatic asylum.

"Mother, do you see that large white building on the hill yonder? Try and control your grief, or it will drive you mad. You don't want to end up like the poor souls there."

She looked up at him, unable to speak, and at once he was sorry he had said it. Elizabeth led her back to her bed.

Terrifying news arrived from Fort Monroe, which sat at the mouth of the James River on the lower Chesapeake Bay in Virginia. The Confederates at Norfolk had finished refitting the frigate USS *Merrimack* with iron plates and rechristened it the CSS *Virginia*. The monster had steamed into the waters of Hampton Roads and made straight for the Union squadron there. There was no stopping her—shots rattled like peas off her sides. The *Cumberland* had been rammed and sunk, the *Congress* destroyed, and the *Minnesota* run aground. The Union's fleet of wooden vessels lay at the ironclad's mercy.

The cabinet gathered in Abraham's office, anxious for every scrap of intelligence coming over the wires. Seward manned the spyglass at the window, puffing urgently on a cigar and sweeping the river for signs of approaching disaster. Chase, the secretary of the treasury, stood nearby, his right eyelid drooping sadly. Stanton paced the room with a scowl. Gideon Welles, the secretary of the navy, sat on a sofa, alone among the group looking composed, like old Neptune in the midst of a hurricane.

"The first thing she'll do is come up the Potomac," Stanton fretted. "She'll destroy the Capitol. We'll have cannon balls from her guns in this room!"

"She can't get this far up the river," Welles said. "She draws too much water."

"How can you know that for certain?"

"Because I know the draft of the *Merrimack*."

Stanton sat down at a table, frantically polished his spectacles, jumped up, and started pacing again. I wish he'd settle down, Abraham thought. He's a lion in the courtroom and a bear when it comes to getting things done, but he's too excitable.

"Exactly how does the navy plan to stop that beast?" Stanton's voice was trembling. "She'll destroy every vessel in the entire service!"

"We're towing the *Monitor* down from New York," Welles said. "She should be in Hampton Roads shortly, if she's not already there."

"What sort of armament does the *Monitor* have?"

"Two eleven-inch guns."

Stanton glared at Welles. "Two guns? Did you say *two?*"

"They're housed in a revolving turret." Welles spoke deliberately. "She can fire them in any direction, regardless of which way she's steaming."

"We should be sinking barges in the river right now! Get the channel blocked!"

"I tell you, the *Merrimack* can't get up the Potomac. She can't get over Kettle Bottom Shoals carrying heavy armor."

Stanton turned on Abraham. "We should wire the mayors at New York and Boston. Tell them to sink timbers at the mouths of their harbors."

Abraham looked to Welles. "What do you think, Neptune? Should we do as Mars suggests?"

"There's not much danger of her getting that far north," Welles said coolly. "The rebels haven't designed their ironclad for ocean voyages. She'll stick to the Chesapeake Bay and the lower parts of its rivers."

Stanton threw up his arms. "If no one else will warn the mayors, I will!" He stomped out of the room.

The cabinet lingered at the White House most of the day, waiting for news of a battle. Abraham couldn't help looking out the window toward the river every few minutes. He rode out to the Navy Yard to see if its commander might have any insights, but there was nothing new to learn there. He came back to the White House, looked in on Tad, then walked over to the War Department to be near the telegraph machines.

Word finally came late in the afternoon. The *Monitor* and *Merrimack* had fought for hours at Hampton Roads, slamming iron balls into each other's flanks, bellowing fire until they both limped away, covered with dents and scars. Both ships were claiming victory, but the Union squadron was saved.

The cabinet let out a sigh of relief. Stanton offered Welles his hand in grudging respect. Abraham went back to his office and peered down the empty river again. His thoughts wandered back to his younger days on the Ohio and Mississippi Rivers, when he had stood on drifting rafts with decks of stout poplar timbers under his bare feet. The time of wooden fighting ships came to an end today, he mused. From now on, iron behemoths will prowl the seas.

There was no time to contemplate the passing of an era. Dispatches arrived saying the rebels had disappeared from their fortifications around Manassas and pulled back toward Richmond, beyond the Rappahannock River. General McClellan roused his army and marched out to Manassas to see. He found trenches with space for no more than fifty thousand men, half the force he had estimated. Several of the cannon poking from ramparts were Quaker guns—big logs painted black. Union officers wandered the deserted camps in disgust. They swore they could hear belly laughs floating over the Virginia hills south of the Rappahannock.

Half the North joined the laugh. The other half groaned that McClellan was an imbecile and called for his head. Abraham relieved him of his duties as general-in-chief of all Union armies but left him in command of the Army of the Potomac.

"You ought to get rid of him altogether," Stanton raged. "He's just fumbling and plunging in darkness."

"I don't know that I've got anyone better," Abraham said. "He built that army. Let's see what he can do with it."

He put his feet up on his big office table and rambled his fingers through his hair.

"When I was a boy, my father had a saying," he mused. "If you've made a bad bargain, you've got to hug it all the tighter."

ᴄ᷄ᴇᴏ— CHAPTER 26 —ᴏᴇᴄ᷄

SPRING 1862

*F*or weeks the docks of Washington and Alexandria were choked with wagons, mules, horses, tents, guns, bales of hay, barrels of powder, coils of telegraph wire, boxes of crackers. An armada of steamers, brigs, and barges came up the Potomac River to swallow the stores and regiments of men. Lines were cast off, big paddle wheels turned, sails filled, and the Army of the Potomac disappeared around a bend in the river.

McClellan had barely landed at the Virginia Peninsula, between the York and James Rivers, when he began wiring that he needed more men.

"He'd leave no one behind to defend Washington," Abraham groused. "If I gave him all the men he asks for, they couldn't find room to lie down. They'd have to sleep standing up."

While McClellan massed his forces, shocking news came out of Tennessee, where armies under Ulysses S. Grant and Don Carlos Buell had clashed with rebel forces near a little log meetinghouse called Shiloh Church. Thousands had been killed or wounded—no one was sure just how many. Abraham sat in his office reading newspaper descriptions of the carnage. The maelstrom of cannonballs had carried away heads, arms, legs, bowels. After the fighting, someone had counted the bullet holes in a single tree and found ninety. A long procession of steamboats was moving down the Tennessee River, away from the battlefield, with cargoes of writhing, shredded men.

Mary's half-brother Sam had been killed fighting in the Confederate army at Shiloh. He was twenty-two years old. It was his first time in battle. Abraham's heart broke for her when he read about it in a Richmond newspaper.

"Will you tell her?" he asked Elizabeth. "I can't bear to do it."

"Yes, I should be the one." She said it stoically, but he could see the strain in her face. She went to break the news to her sister and came back a while later looking pale.

"She says she doesn't care. She says any of our brothers fighting on the rebel side would kill you if they could, and she hopes they're all dead or prisoners."

"She doesn't mean that."

"I know. I don't think she knows what she's saying."

The newspapers brought reports of another death that shook him. William Scott, the private he'd saved from being shot after he fell asleep on sentinel duty, had been killed down in Virginia, fighting in McClellan's army as it crept toward Richmond. The papers said he fell with a half-dozen bullets in him. He left with the words, "Tell the president I tried to be a good soldier. Goodbye, boys, goodbye."

McClellan sent word that a huge Confederate army lay before him. The Southerners had dug in at Yorktown, not far from the old battle-field where Lord Cornwallis had surrendered to George Washington's patriot army to end the Revolutionary War. Instead of attacking, Little

Mac called for more artillery and prepared to lay siege.

"Can't he see that now is the time to strike a blow?" Abraham groaned. He fired off an impatient letter: *You must act!* It did no good. By the time McClellan was at last ready to bombard Yorktown, the rebels had slipped away, leaving more Quaker guns behind. It was Manassas all over again.

❧❧❧

He decided to go down there to see what could be done. Edwin Stanton and Salmon Chase went along to help shake things up. They sailed down the Potomac River on the revenue cutter *Miami* in darkness and drizzle, but the next morning was clear, and they lounged on deck mixing discussions of policy with recitations of Shakespeare.

It was good to be out of Washington for a few days. Abraham pulled an ax from a socket on a bulwark to show how he could hold it by the end of its handle and slowly lift it, swinging his arm from the shoulder, so that the heavy iron head rose in an arc until he held the ax straight out before him, his arm and the handle both horizontal with the ship's deck. It was a feat of strength he used to perform as a youth on the Indiana frontier, one few men of any age had the muscle to accomplish. It pleased him to know he could still do it, and that the sailors who tried could not.

By noon they were out on the Chesapeake Bay, tossing on choppy waters. He tried eating lunch, but the plates and glasses kept sliding around, and he felt too queasy to eat. Stanton ate his lunch but then lost it. The sight of the secretary of war throwing up over the rail made the navy men smile.

Fort Monroe grew on the horizon until its massive stone walls loomed over the *Miami*. The Gibraltar of the Chesapeake, men called it, set on a point where the Jamestown colonists, more than two hundred fifty years before, had come ashore looking for a home in the New World. Shadows of hulking Rodman guns fell over the ramparts, black monsters that could hurl giant shells over the sea. A city of vessels clustered around the peninsula's tip: steamers, men-of-war, sloops, gunboats, supply ships, and transports, all rocking at anchor under the guns' watch. Outside the fort's moats, another city of army camps and supply depots bustled with the commerce of war. At its fringes lay the contraband camps, tents of runaway slaves who had wandered and dodged through the Southern lines, following rumors of a giant Freedom Fortress where their masters could never get to them.

Abraham met with General Wool, the fort's commander, and Commodore Goldsborough, commander of the fleet at Hampton Roads. McClellan was thirty miles up the peninsula, inching his way west toward Richmond.

"What's holding up General McClellan?" Abraham asked. "He should be further along."

"He and I differ in our estimates of the enemy's strength," Wool said. He was seventy-eight years old, the oldest general in active command in the army. He carried his age like the sword Congress had bestowed on him, with dignified pride. "General McClellan says that he requires naval support," he added, glancing at Goldsborough.

"Why isn't he getting it?" Stanton demanded.

"There is still the *Merrimack* to reckon with," Goldsborough said. "I can't send boats up the James while she's in the way." The commodore, like Wool, had been in the service most of his life. His men called him Guts, perhaps for his courage, or perhaps for his paunch.

"The *Merrimack* is sheltered at Norfolk, isn't she?" Lincoln asked.

The army and navy nodded.

"If you can't destroy her, why don't you take Norfolk? Taking her base removes her from the scene."

"Seizing Norfolk requires the army," Goldsborough smiled.

Abraham traded glances with Chase and Stanton. Chase's right eyelid drooped mightily.

"Has General McClellan made plans to take the city?" the treasury secretary inquired.

"No immediate plans."

Abraham threw his hands into the air. "By thunder! This won't do, gentlemen! I want you to take Norfolk."

"When?"

"Tomorrow."

Wool flinched. "With all due respect, sir, I'm not sure you understand military necessities."

"I understand that if this army was a horse hitched to a funeral wagon, it wouldn't get the corpse to the grave in time for the final resurrection. By God, we're going to take Norfolk."

The next day, Union ships opened fire on Confederate shore batteries at Sewell's Point, outside of Norfolk. Abraham stood atop a rampart with Chase and Stanton, peering through spyglasses. The ships reminded him of toys set adrift on a pond by farm boys. White puffs flowered from their sides and dissolved into the still blue sky. Booms echoed across Hampton Roads like stones skipping over the water. After a while, a column of smoke came curling up from behind Sewell's Point.

"Here comes the *Merrimack!*" someone called.

Sure enough, the Confederate leviathan came steaming out of the Elizabeth River. She looked like a big floating barn with a smokestack on top. The Union's wooden ships drew back, but here came the *Monitor* sliding along, low and dark, like a shadow on the water. Everyone held their breath—it looked as though the two ironclads would go at it one more time. They both prowled the Roads, scowling and threatening, each keeping her distance, until the *Merrimack* fired off a sullen shot of contempt and headed back to her base.

"We certainly can't land our transports there, not with that thing in the way," Wool said. His tone hinted that he had known it all along.

"Very well. We'll go another way." Abraham studied a chart and ran his finger east of Sewell's Point. "What about here, somewhere on this stretch?"

Wool's officers leaned over the chart and shook their heads. "It's no good," one of them said. "The shoals will keep our boats a mile off shore."

"Have you tested it?"

"No."

"Well, an ounce of experience is worth a pound of theory. Let's go over and see."

Wool looked aghast. "Do you mean go yourself?"

"Why not?"

"Mr. President, that is enemy soil."

"Yes, and it's going to stay that way unless we do something about it."

They went under cover of night, slipping out of the harbor, then turning and steering where the charts said they should not go. Abraham's pulse quickened as they moved over the black surface. When they drew close to land, he climbed into a rowboat with Stanton. Chase stayed aboard the *Miami,* making sure the cutter's long-range gun stood ready. Two sailors heaved at the oars, and within minutes the rowboat touched shore.

They walked up and down the beach for a while, staying quiet and keeping a lookout for rebel patrols. The moon was up. It washed the stars from the sky but cast a thousand little sparkling lights across the water. Wavelets ran up onto the muddy sand, sighing as they came.

The troops can land somewhere in here, he thought. They'll come splashing up on this beach, and from here it's only eight miles to Norfolk. The rebels won't be expecting them to come this way. And that will be the end of the *Merrimack.*

The next day, General Wool loaded six thousand men onto boats and set out. Chase went with him to keep an eye on things. Abraham stayed behind at Fort Monroe. The embarking made him nervous. He rushed about on the wharves, hollering suggestions and warnings. There was a mix-up about where some of the troops should be—he threw his tall hat on the ground, yelled, "Send me someone who can write!" and dictated an order to straighten it out. By the time he was finished dictating, he realized he was making a spectacle of himself. He put his hat back on, excused himself, and went to his quarters to calm down and wait for news.

It grew late, but no reports came. That worried him. He had learned that in war, no news often meant bad news. The night was warm, the moon was shining brightly again, and he was too restless to sleep, so he sat at a table reading. It was after midnight when he heard footsteps and, looking out a window, saw Chase and Wool coming up a dark path. A minute later they rushed into the room.

"No time for ceremony, Mr. President," Wool beamed. "Norfolk is ours!"

Stanton burst in behind them, just out of bed, his long nightshirt sweeping the floor. "By God, I knew we could!" He threw himself at Wool in a bear hug. The little the secretary of war practically lifted the old general off the floor.

"Look out, Mars," Abraham grinned. "If you don't, the general will throw you."

Chase told how they had reached Norfolk and found the Confederates hightailing it. The mayor had met them on the road to give them a rusty old key to the city and read a proclamation while the rebels set fire to the navy yard. While Chase was describing the adventure, Abraham heard a low defiant boom come rolling across the harbor.

"There's the end of the *Merrimack*," Wool exalted. "The rebels have blown her up, to be sure."

"So ends a brilliant week's campaign," Chase said happily.

They sat up through the early morning hours swapping battle tales, giddy with triumph, and it seemed to Abraham that war could not get any better.

CHAPTER 27

SUMMER 1862

Mary was slowly recovering her ability to face life, or at least the routines of daily living, though there were mornings when headaches and crying spells kept her in bed. She could not bring herself to go into the bedroom where Willie had died, or the Green Room, where she had seen him lying in his coffin. She covered herself in layers of black cloth, and when she went to church or took an afternoon carriage ride with Abraham, she wore a black veil so immense it was hard to tell if there was a face behind it.

Elizabeth departed for Springfield, worn out from the weeks of caretaking. "My brain feels palsied," she told Abraham. "If I don't go home and get some rest, Mary will be the one nursing me."

"I'll never be able to thank you enough for coming."

"I wish neither of you had to stay here. It's a dismal place. God bless you both." And she was gone.

He sat with Mary to keep her company as evening came on.

"I should not have let him get sick," she said.

"You mustn't talk that way."

"It's true. I was so wrapped up in the world, so devoted to china and fabrics and gowns, and to our own political advancement, I thought of little else."

Her fingers ran over her scalp, searching, and plucked a single hair. She wound it around her left index finger while she talked.

"We never should have gone through with that party, Abraham. Not while our boy was sick."

"We did the best we knew how."

"I wish that were true!" she cried. "If it were, surely God would not have thrown us into this furnace of affliction!"

The terror in her voice touched his own fears. Had he spent enough time with his boys? Had he given away too many hours to politics and law?

Mary plucked another hair and twisted it slowly around her finger. "Perhaps God has seen fit to visit us with our child's death," she said quietly, "to remind us of how insignificant worldly honors are."

Poor Tad was lonely without his brother. He didn't want to play with any of the toys he and Willie had shared. "They make me sad, Papa-day," he explained. The boy had never slept in a room by himself, so Abraham began bringing him to his own bed at night. On evenings when he worked late in his office, Tad curled up on the floor beside his desk or in front of the fireplace, and when the last memorandum was read and letter signed, Abraham would hoist the sleeping child over his shoulder and carry him to bed.

More than once he dreamed he was with Willie again, pulling him in a little wagon around the square in Springfield or romping with him on the sitting room floor. Then he would wake with a shudder. In spare moments, he searched the Bible for hints of immortality. *I will dwell in the house of the Lord for ever.* Or Shakespeare. *And, father cardinal, I have heard you say that we shall see and know our friends in heaven: If that be true, I shall see my boy again.*

When summer came, they moved out of the city to a house on the grounds of the Soldiers' Home, a refuge the government had established for invalid and disabled veterans who could not support themselves. It was set amid shady hills that caught welcome breezes during Washington's hot, humid months. The house looked like a big rambling cottage in the English countryside, with a view of the Capitol dome and Smithsonian castle in the distance.

"It's charming," Mary said. "It should be much quieter here." It was the first note of pleasure he had heard in her voice in weeks.

Yes, this should work just fine, he thought as he strolled a graveled pathway. It was only three miles from the White House, an easy thirty-minute ride, so he could be in his office by eight o'clock and then, if he was lucky, back in the evening for dinner. There would be plenty of space for Tad to roam, and Bob would join them for his summer break from Harvard. Abraham liked the looks of the big porch and a copper beech tree in the yard—he could set up a desk and chair in its shade to read and relax. The main building where the soldiers lived was not far away. Off to one side of the house lay a military cemetery, full of fresh graves. There was no escaping the dead.

And no escaping the war. McClellan had inched his way up the Virginia Peninsula to within a few miles of Richmond and stopped. The Army of the Potomac could see the steeples and hear the church bells of the Confederate capital. Little Mac delayed his final assault while he built bridges over creeks, declared the roads too muddy to advance, and called for more men.

"McClellan's difficulty is that he prefers tomorrow to today," Abraham grumbled.

Suddenly all hell broke loose. There was bloody fighting on the

Peninsula and then more fighting in the Shenandoah Valley, where the black-bearded, Bible-toting, lemon-sucking Stonewall Jackson appeared out of nowhere with an army that, for a while, looked like it might be headed right for Washington, marching and attacking and dodging faster than rumors of its whereabouts could fly. Abraham camped day and night in the telegraph office at the War Department, puzzling over vague reports and staring at maps of the great valley beyond the Blue Ridge Mountains, trying to decipher what was going on.

Then Jackson was gone, or seemed to be until he reappeared on the Peninsula, where Robert E. Lee was driving at McClellan, attacking again and again, hurling gray lines at the blue Union lines in seven days of battles at more places to be hunted up on the maps: Mechanicsville, Gaines's Mill, Savage's Station, Malvern Hill. The Army of the Potomac retreated back down the Peninsula to lick its wounds. McClellan called for fifty thousand reinforcements. "The idea of sending you fifty thousand, or any other considerable force promptly, is simply absurd," Abraham wrote back. By midsummer, the Peninsula campaign had ended in failure.

He sat in the White House's upstairs oval library as evening fell, brooding over the defeat. Bugs large and small came swarming through open southward-facing windows, drawn by the gas lights. They covered the ceiling and walls, butted their heads against tables and chairs. It seemed that all of bugdom had organized an invasion to take the gas lights. Down the hall, Nicolay slapped at bugs as he tried to write at his desk—each slap accompanied by a loud "Humph!"

All chance of ending the war soon was gone now. He would have to call up three hundred thousand more volunteers to strengthen the army. If things kept going this way, a million more men wouldn't make any difference. The South would outlast them. He liked George McClellan, but he needed a general who would fight like Jackson and Lee did for the rebels.

Orville Browning came by the White House to see him. The Illinois senator looked disconcerted as they shook hands.

"How are you, Mr. President?" he asked.

Abraham shrugged. "Tolerably well."

The senator frowned, unconvinced. "You don't look it!"

"I don't?"

"No. You look like your troubles are crowded so heavily on you, your health is suffering."

Abraham lowered his head and stared at his big gnarly hands for a minute, feeling weighed down with melancholy.

"Browning, I must die sometime," he said quietly.

The slaves occupied his thoughts more and more. Abolitionists kept pressing him to free the poor creatures. Radical Republicans in Congress kept up their harangues. Generals besieged him with questions about what they were supposed to do with the thousands of Negroes seeking refuge in the army's camps.

He told visitors to the White House that slavery was like a large, ugly cyst on the body politic that all the physicians agreed must come off. But the doctors could not agree on the best way to remove it. Some said take a knife and cut it off all at once. Some said put a cord around it and draw it tighter every day to slowly choke it off. Others said a gentle rubbing with ointment would make it shrink away. Abraham was a man feeling and reasoning his way through a problem, just as he had figured his way through law books back in his prairie days, studying the plain facts of the case.

He still worried about losing the border states if he moved to abolish slavery. Still worried that thousands of Northern men would desert the army if they thought they were being asked to spill blood for Negroes. If he broke his pledge to let slavery alone in the states, how many Northern voters would desert him?

Yet public opinion about slavery was gradually turning in the North. He could sense it. Millions who had once been ambivalent about the rights of Southern states now hated the slaveholders for so much blood-shed. Let the plantation masters lose all, they muttered, including their human property. A new song was marching across the North, full of strains of vengeance and fire.

> *Mine eyes have seen the glory of the coming of the Lord,*
> *He is trampling out the vintage where the grapes of wrath are stored,*
> *He hath loosed the fateful lightning of His terrible swift sword,*
> *His truth is marching on.*

It was a hymn of trumpet calls and burnished rows of steel. *As He died to make men holy, let us die to make men free.*

He turned to prayer. What did God want of him? If he could learn the will of Providence, he would do it. But his prayers left him with more questions than answers. Why had God permitted such carnage? Why had He allowed the African to be made a slave?

The Constitution gave the president, as administrator-in-chief of the government's executive branch, no power to interfere with slavery in states. That had always been clear to Abraham. But it gave the president all kinds of power as the military's commander-in-chief to take the steps necessary to win a war. Perhaps there was a way forward. The Confederates were using slave labor to aid their war effort—digging trenches, transporting supplies, producing food for the troops. If he declared the slaves free, it might encourage them to desert their masters and cripple the South's ability to fight.

With painstaking deliberation, he was coming to the conclusion that emancipation was the only way left to go. He must change tactics or lose the game.

And then there was something else, something planted not in the mind but in the heart, something bound up in the old, cherished words that "all men are created equal, that they are endowed by their Creator with certain unalienable rights, that among these are life, liberty, and the pursuit of happiness."

He began thinking it through on paper at the War Department's telegraph office while he waited for dispatches from distant armies. He sat at a desk overlooking Pennsylvania Avenue, looking out the window a while, putting pen to paper for a line or two, then sitting quietly a few minutes more while the machines clicked away. It was slow going. He gave the paper to one of the officers to keep locked in a drawer until he came back. On the quiet, shady paths of the grounds at the Soldiers' Home, he thought it through more as he walked with head down.

Each time he returned to the telegraph office, he got the paper back and worked at it again, sometimes late into the night. Every day he puzzled it out a little more. He was a man praying, reasoning, writing his way forward.

CHAPTER 28

SUMMER 1862

He summoned his cabinet to the White House on a day when waves of July heat rolled through the windows, bringing fetid odors of the tidal flats and garbage floating in the City Canal. They sat amid scattered congressional bills and maps of war. Each man produced a big damp handkerchief to mop his brow while they talked matters of state.

"I haven't called you together to ask your advice, but to lay a proclamation before you," Abraham said firmly. "You can offer suggestions after you've heard it, but my decision is not up for debate. I have resolved to take this step."

He removed two sheets from his pocket, adjusted his spectacles, and began to read what sounded much like a lawyer's brief. There was nothing poetic about it. It was full of phrases like "in pursuance of" and "herewith published." But as he read, every man in the room knew his words held the power to unshackle generations of bondage—to change the course and character of the nation. The proclamation announced that unless the rebels laid down their arms and rejoined the Union, he would use his power as commander-in-chief of the army and navy to declare their slaves free.

When he finished, he put down the pages and took off his spectacles. For a moment no one said anything. Attorney General Bates was the first to find his voice.

"It has my decided approval," he declared, "so long as we deport the freed slaves. The white and black races cannot thrive in social proximity. We must send the blacks overseas."

Montgomery Blair, the postmaster general, scowled and shook his head. "Free blacks flooding the white labor markets—that's what Northern voters will see in this. It will cost us the fall elections. And most likely carry the border states over to the secessionists."

Stanton had been polishing his steel-rimmed glasses with determination. He put them back on and announced that he was all for issuing the proclamation right away. "It will do much to disrupt the rebels' supply of labor," he growled. "It is the just thing to do."

Welles stayed quiet, shifting uneasily and looking grave. That's all right, Abraham thought. I can count on Neptune. He'll stick by me on this.

Caleb Smith was another matter. The secretary of the interior also kept silent, but his eyes stared cold and hard, and his high bald forehead, glistening with sweat, was a wall holding back torrents of discontent. He looked like he wanted to resign and go home that day.

Salmon Chase spoke up. For someone who had long argued for emancipation, he was surprisingly cool to the proclamation. His right eye, peering from behind its drooping eyelid, seemed to focus on a distant purpose of its own.

"There is a measure of great danger in this," he said stiffly. "It could set off massacres across the South. It would be better to let the generals in the field proclaim emancipation whenever they conquer territory. That way their troops can control the situation."

"What!" Abraham exclaimed. "You, Chase, the father of abolitionism, object?"

"No, I don't object." The secretary of the treasury waved off the suggestion. "What you propose is much better than inaction. I give it my entire support." He had the look of a man who saw a prize being snatched away from him.

That left Seward, who crossed his legs and slowly rolled his cigar between thumb and index finger. Abraham had learned to gauge his secretary of state's thoughts by the way he smoked. Vigorous puffs signaled approval. A drooping cigar, on the other hand, was a bad sign. Throughout the meeting, the smoking end of the cigar had been cautiously rising.

Seward spoke in the formal tone of a diplomat. "Mr. President, I approve of the proclamation, but I question the expediency of its issue at this juncture."

"You want to delay? You're not turning into McClellan on me, are you?"

"Our repeated reverses on the battlefield have depressed the public mood. If you issue the proclamation now, it could be seen, both here and abroad, as the last measure of an exhausted government. A cry for help—a last shriek on the retreat."

Abraham winced. It was a good point. For all his thought on the subject, one he'd overlooked. If an emancipation proclamation was perceived as a gambit by a desperate administration, it might strengthen the secessionists' hand.

"It will be viewed as the government stretching forth its hands to Ethiopia, instead of Ethiopia stretching forth her hands to the government," Seward pressed.

"What do you suggest?"

"Postpone it until you can give it to the country supported by military success."

The meeting broke up. Abraham paced his office alone for a while. The wisdom of Seward's view was hard to refute. Nothing about this war came quickly, nothing except loss. It unfolded on its own terms, of its own accord. More and more, it made him feel like he was not in control of events, but rather that events controlled him.

All right, then, he told himself. Stand still and see the salvation of the Lord.

He rose, put the proclamation in a desk drawer, and pushed it shut. It would have to stay there for now, waiting for a victory.

Perhaps it would not have to wait long. Another battle was coming, maybe one that would finally end the rebellion. Now that Richmond was no longer in danger, Lee's army was moving north, in the direction of Washington. The capital braced itself while a Union army under General John Pope readied for a clash. Pope, who had won victories on the Mississippi, was boasting that "I have come from the West, where we have always seen the backs of our enemies." Trainloads of grim-faced, raw recruits were arriving daily in Washington and heading straight for the front, singing another new song as they went: "We are coming, Father Abraham, three hundred thousand more."

The dog days of August were full of planning and fretting. Abraham visited camps of new volunteers, studied reports of troop movements, tried to prod McClellan into hurrying his men off the Peninsula so they could be ready to support Pope. He spent most of a sticky, hot Saturday in his office dealing with visitors who demanded, as always, favors and jobs. By the time he left the White House late in the afternoon, his head was ready to split open. The driver of his carriage hit every rut he could find on the drive up the Seventh Street Turnpike to the Soldiers' Home. The still and quiet of the country house were a blessed relief.

He threw off his coat and shoes, dropped into a big chair in the parlor, and allowed himself to doze. He needed to gather his strength for the coming week.

Dusk was falling by the time he woke. His headache was nearly gone. Outside a window, the trill of *katy-DID-katy-DIDN'T katy-DID-katy-DIDN'T* flowed from an old elm tree. The heat of the day lingered inside the parlor. He reached for a palm-leaf fan and a book on a nearby table. It was *The Song of Hiawatha*. He dangled a leg over one of the chair's arms, fanned himself, and read languidly in the dim light.

> *And the West-Wind came at evening,*
> *Walking lightly o'er the prairie,*
> *Whispering to the leaves and blossoms,*
> *Bending low the flowers and grasses. . . .*

He read for a few minutes, until it was too dark to make out the lines, then closed his eyes again.

A sharp knock broke his rest. Three figures glided into the room—a servant followed by two others. One of them he recognized: John French, one of Chase's men at the Treasury Department. French introduced the other, Colonel Charles Scott of New Hampshire. The latter had urgent business.

"Mr. President, I apologize for disturbing you, but I have no one else to go to." There was anguish in Scott's voice. He spoke wearily, nervously. Abraham, groggy from dozing, had trouble following his story at first.

Colonel Scott had been with McClellan's army, down on the Peninsula, had caught fever and lain close to death in a hospital at Newport News. His wife had come down from New Hampshire, stayed by his bedside, nursed him until he was able to walk again. Now she was dead, killed in a terrible accident as they had been coming up the Potomac River from Newport News to Washington. It had been in the newspapers. The *West Point,* carrying wounded soldiers, had collided with the *George Peabody.* Seventy-three people killed.

"Some people down there have recovered her body," Scott explained. "I want to get her and take her home. She would want to be buried at home. But the War Department says no."

It was hard to make out the man's face in the twilight. It looked haggard, no doubt from his illness. Abraham felt his headache coming back.

"I went to Secretary Stanton," the colonel said. "He told me he'll issue no passes down the river while the troop movement is underway. So, you see, I've come to you."

Abraham got up from the chair, put the book and fan on the table. He thought of lighting a lamp, but he did not want the glare.

"Am I to have no rest? Is there no spot where I can escape these constant demands?"

His voice, stiff and raspy, cut through the shrill of the katydids. He stared down at the gray shapes of the men, who shifted uneasily.

"Why do you follow me out here with this? Why don't you go to the War Department? They have charge of all papers for transportation."

Scott cringed at the unexpected rebuke. "As I said, Mr. President, I've been to Mr. Stanton. He refused me."

"Then you probably ought not to go down the river," Abraham snapped. "Mr. Stanton knows what rules are necessary. It would be wrong of me to override his decision—it might work disaster to important movements."

"But Mr. President—"

"I have other duties to attend to. I can't give thought to questions of this kind. Why do you come here to appeal to my humanity?"

The colonel looked to French, unsure of what to say.

"Don't you know we are in the midst of war? That suffering and death press on all of us?"

"I didn't mean—"

"You mustn't vex me with your family troubles. Every family in the land is crushed with sorrow. You can't all come to me for help.

I have all the burden I can carry."

Scott stood mute and devastated.

"Go to the War Department. Your business belongs there. If they can't help you, then bear your burden, as we all must, until this war is over."

The two men left quickly. Abraham stood at a window, seething, and watched them ride down the driveway. What were they thinking, barging in here like that? Damn the doorkeeper for letting them in. Did any of them understand the pressure he was under?

He tossed in bed all night, plagued with visions: A bow slicing into a hull—shattered timbers—staterooms sheared away—bodies floating ashore. When he woke, his head was clear. The Sabbath dawn, restful with a cool hint of fall, bathed the room. He sighed, lit a lamp, and sat at a desk to scribble a few words.

He was downtown before breakfast, striding along a hotel corridor. Colonel Scott, black circles under his eyes, still in his nightshirt, took a step back when he answered the rap at his door.

"Colonel, I was a brute last night. Forgive me. I was tired. Hurry and get ready, and I'll take you to the Navy Yard. I've arranged everything. You can take the next boat down the river."

The colonel dressed quickly and gathered his things. They climbed into the waiting carriage and headed for the Navy Yard. "I honor your devotion to the memory of your wife," Abraham told him as they rode. They talked of losing loved ones, the defeat on the Peninsula, the awful duties of war.

He got the poor fellow on board the steamer and sent him on his way.

CHAPTER 29

LATE SUMMER 1862

The great battle they had all been expecting broke out along the stream called Bull Run near Manassas, Virginia, where the first big fight of the war had taken place. Abraham haunted the telegraph office at the War Department day and night, firing off queries to field commanders: "Do you hear anything from Pope?" "Is the railroad bridge over Bull Run destroyed?" "What news from the direction of Manassas Junction?" The thump of distant cannon rolled over the Virginia hills toward Washington. It reminded him of the sound of women beating blankets hung on a line. A southwest wind carried the hot, sharp smell of gunpowder.

At first the generals seemed confident, but then the all-too-familiar story clicked over the wires: reports from Pope's army that it had the

Southern troops on the run, followed by reports of sudden rebel reinforcements, then a Southern counterattack, and finally Union troops falling back. McClellan kept finding reasons not to send reinforcements that might make a difference. Instead he sent an appalling telegram that suggested the best course would be "to leave Pope to get out of this scrape and at once use all our means to make the capital perfectly safe."

Abraham walked back to the White House to absorb the blow. He felt disoriented. He put his head into John Hay's office.

"Well, John, we're whipped again, I'm afraid. The rebels reinforced on Pope and drove back his left wing."

Hay's smooth cheeks turned pale as a tombstone.

"He's retired to Centreville and says he'll be able to hold his men there," Abraham said. "I don't like that expression. I don't like to hear him admit that his men need 'holding.'"

"So much for seeing the backs of our enemies!"

"Pope must fight them." He did his best to sound defiant. "If they're too strong for him, he can gradually retire to our fortifications. But he's got to fight."

Signs of disaster were all around them. The exhausted troops straggling up Pennsylvania Avenue. Panicked families loading wagons with valuables amid rumors of Lee's army pouring over the Chain Bridge. Ambulances clattering over cobblestones to fill rows of hospital cots at the Capitol and Georgetown College. The Second Battle of Bull Run had turned out worse than the first, thirteen months before.

"I've heard of people being knocked into the middle of next week, but this is the first I ever knew of their being knocked into the middle of last year," Abraham said grimly.

"We'd be knocking the rebels right now if McClellan had brought his men up!" Hay cried.

"He acted badly. It's hard to believe, but I think he wanted Pope to fail."

"It's not hard for me to believe. McClellan is full of envy and spite."

Abraham stood at a window and watched a band of hatless,

weaponless soldiers amble past. A cluster of black refugees from Virginia trailed at a distance.

"I'll have to give him Pope's men and ask him to defend the city," he said.

Hay gaped at him. "You mean McClellan?"

"I must have him to bring the army out of chaos."

"The man doesn't know the meaning of the word fight!"

"Perhaps, but the men love him. There's no one who can lick the troops into shape half as well as he can."

"But you just said he wanted Pope to fail!"

"Yes, and that's unpardonable, but he's too useful to sacrifice just now. If he can't fight himself, he excels in making others ready to fight."

No one liked the decision. Stanton, Chase, and most of the cabinet fumed. Republicans in Congress howled that McClellan was a traitorous Democrat and the president as unstable as water. Mary joined the criticism.

"McClellan is a humbug!" she cried during an afternoon carriage ride.

"What makes you think so?" Abraham asked patiently.

"Because he talks so much and does so little. If I had the power, I'd take off his head and put an energetic man in his place."

"He's made mistakes, but he's faced more difficulties than we can guess."

"McClellan can make plenty of excuses for himself. He needs no advocate in you for that. I tell you he's a humbug, like most of the men around you."

"Who else is a humbug?" Let her rail, he thought. Better she say it to me than someone else.

"Stanton, for one. He's a dirty abolitionist sneak."

"He's made the War Department run like clockwork."

"And Chase. That man has an evil eye. I don't trust him one bit."

"Chase is a patriot. He's worked miracles finding ways to finance this war."

"He'd betray you tomorrow if he thought it would make him

president. He's almost as bad as Seward. At least Chase has himself for his principle. Seward has no principles at all."

"If I listened to you, Mother, I'd be without a cabinet."

"Better to be without it than confide in some of those men. You'll find out I'm right someday, Mr. Lincoln. I only hope your eyes are opened before it's too late."

News of another death arrived—Mary's youngest brother, Aleck, the favorite of the Todd sisters. He had been shot while fighting for the rebels a few miles from Baton Rouge and hastily buried near a plum orchard far from his Kentucky home. Mary uttered barely a word when he told her. She plucked a hair and wound it around a finger. An hour later, he passed by her bedroom and heard her talking with Mrs. Keckley. The seamstress had brought a new dress.

"Lizzie, I've just heard that one of my brothers has been killed in the war."

"I heard the same, Mrs. Lincoln. I hesitated to speak of it, for fear the subject would be painful to you."

"You need not hesitate." There was a stiffness in her voice. "Of course, it's but natural that I should feel for one so nearly related to me, but not to the extent that you suppose. He made his choice long ago. He decided against my husband, and through him against me."

"I'm sorry, Mrs. Lincoln."

"He has been fighting against us. Since he chose to be our enemy, I see no special reason why I should mourn his death."

Abraham passed by her room again a while later. When he stopped and put his ear to the closed door, he could hear her crying in bed.

Pain and death were closing in all around him. He tried to understand it, tried to see what he was supposed to do. At times he stayed up late at night, too exhausted to sleep, stirring ashes. A river of sulfur and fire was crossing the land, and he was caught in the middle, trying desperately to gain a footing as he was swept along.

He searched the faces of the people who came to see him: the widows and mothers with tears on their cheeks, the ministers and abolitionists with fury in their eyes. The clenched jaws of the wounded in the makeshift hospitals stayed with him. So did the inscrutable dark expressions in the contraband camps.

The first tinges of red showed on the dogwood trees, and the sycamores let go a few yellow-brown leaves to float down the Potomac toward the Chesapeake Bay. Something was changing—something ending, some new birth coming. He sensed it in the air and on the surface of the river, and tried to tell what it was.

He sounded out friends and strangers to see if they might have spotted clues he had missed, listening as if sitting beside an old stove in the back of some country store. Occasionally he let them know he was struggling to puzzle it through. He told them he knew he was a humble instrument in the hands of the Almighty. He must believe that God permitted this fiery trial for some wise purpose of his own, mysterious and unknown. Perhaps none of them would be able to comprehend it, with their limited understandings, but surely He who made the world still governed it.

Again he turned to pen and ink to harness his thoughts. During a night of lonely seeking, when trumpets were blasting and armies were on the move again, he sat at his desk writing.

The will of God prevails. In great contests each party claims to act in accordance with the will of God. Both may be, and one must be wrong. God can not be for, and against the same thing at the same time. In the present civil war it is quite possible that God's purpose is something different from the purpose of either party—and yet the human instrumentalities, working just as they do, are of the best adaptation to effect His purpose. I am almost ready to say this is probably true—that God wills this contest, and wills that it shall not end yet. By His mere quiet power, on the minds of the now contestants, He could have either saved or destroyed the Union without a human contest. Yet the contest began. And having begun He could give the final victory to either side any day. Yet the contest proceeds.

⚶ CHAPTER 30 ⚶

SEPTEMBER TO
NOVEMBER 1862

obert E. Lee's army was across the Potomac, in Maryland, moving north through hills of green cornstalks and yellow Black-eyed Susans. Vague reports of sightings reached Washington: a thousand Stars and Bars winding their way through mountain passes; long gray columns of Stonewall Jackson's foot cavalry leaving clouds of dust over apple orchards; Jeb Stuart's jaunty plumed hat waving at farm girls as it galloped by. Panicked Maryland and Pennsylvania officials sent pleas for federal troops. No one seemed to know the rebels' exact whereabouts or where they were headed, only that Lee was on Northern soil.

McClellan led the Army of the Potomac out of Washington to give chase. They were hard-bitten men now, tough as mule drivers, scarred and tempered by battle. Abraham watched them march away in worn shirts and patched trousers. Their eyes were dark with resolve.

This could be our best opportunity, he thought. Lee's troops will be strung out, in unfamiliar territory, far from reinforcements. McClellan might be able to trap them and hurt them—if Little Mac will fight.

He took his emancipation proclamation to the Soldiers' Home and worked on a second draft while waiting. There was no need for flowery words and phrases. But he had to get it right. Courts would scrutinize it, legislators pick at it, and editors criticize it. He labored over it as in his law practice days, grinding every sentence through his mind like corn between the stones of a grist mill.

If we defeat Lee, I'll issue it, he thought. And if McClellan is beaten, I'll let it go because then it won't matter. One more rebel victory, especially one this far north, and people will give in. The Union will be divided forever. He went to his bedroom, folded his long legs until his knees touched the floor, and prayed.

McClellan sent grand news—a sort of miracle, or at least a gift of fortune. He had come into possession of a copy of Lee's plans, found by a Union soldier in a field, wrapped around three cigars. "I have the plans of the rebels and will catch them in their own trap if my men are equal to the emergency," he wired.

Sounds of distant cannon floated over the treetops at the Soldiers' Home. Abraham climbed the tower of the main building, where the disabled soldiers lived, to see if he could glimpse the fighting, but it was too far away. More telegrams came from McClellan. He had won a glorious victory. . . . The enemy was in perfect retreat. . . . Lee himself was reportedly wounded.

Could it really be true? Abraham quietly read the dispatches, pushing the surge of joy back down into his chest, not daring to believe it. He wired McClellan back: "God bless you, and all with you. Destroy the rebel army, if possible."

He was right to contain his enthusiasm. Fresh reports arrived. Lee wasn't wounded, after all, and wasn't retreating. He was positioning his army near Sharpsburg, in western Maryland, along the ridges west of Antietam Creek. There was more fighting to come.

That night, Abraham had the same dream that had come before the bombardment at Fort Sumter. He was on the water again, standing on the deck of the same phantom ship, moving quickly toward a dark shore cloaked in mist. Where was the boat headed? The hills of Maryland? Or a Southern coast—Port Royal Sound or Mobile Bay? He could not tell. The water lay still and gray as a shadow. Fog rose from the surface, and as the boat glided toward land, the indefinite line of the shore slipped away.

Another dispatch arrived from McClellan. There had been a terrible battle along Antietam Creek. In country lanes and fields around Sharpsburg, men on both sides had been cut down by the thousands. They lay in rows where they fell, covering the hills as though a great, meticulous reaper had gone by. At day's end, the Union army held the field. McClellan was proclaiming a triumph, a masterpiece of art in fire and lead. "Our victory was complete," he wired.

Perhaps, Abraham thought. They would have to wait for the bodies to be counted to know how complete it really was. Lee had withdrawn, and his gray columns were wading back across the Potomac. It sounded like he might get away. But at least the invasion had been turned back.

He called his cabinet together at the White House and laid his proclamation before them.

"I think the time has come," he said. "I wish it was a better time. I wish we were in a better condition. The action of the army against the rebels hasn't been quite what I hoped. But Maryland and Pennsylvania are no longer in danger."

They listened with expectation on their faces, like a crew of strong men on a vessel at sea waiting to hear their captain explain why he had decided to change course and sail directly into a storm.

"When the rebel army was at Frederick, I determined to issue this proclamation as soon as it was driven out of Maryland. I said nothing to anyone, but I made the promise to myself and"—he paused for a second—"to my Maker. The rebels are now driven out, and I'm going to fulfill that promise."

They looked at him with surprise. "Could you repeat yourself, sir?" Salmon Chase asked.

"I made a vow, a covenant, if you will, that if God gave us victory in Maryland, I would take it as a sign to move forward with emancipation. That may seem strange to some. But God has decided this question in favor of the slaves."

He put on his spectacles and read the proclamation aloud. The South would have until January 1, 1863—a little over three months—to lay down arms. If not, the federal government would declare their slaves free. When he finished reading, they discussed tweaking a phrase or two. They spoke in tones of men weighing consequences they could barely imagine.

Abraham handed the proclamation to Seward to be published as a State Department circular. He felt half-uncertain, half-proud.

"Now this war is about union *and* freedom," Seward murmured.

The question is, will the Union survive this cause of freedom? Abraham thought.

"I can only trust in God I've made no mistake," he said. "It is now for the country and the world to pass judgment on it."

❧❧❧

McClellan had the slows again. Lee was back in Virginia, no doubt restoring his army to fighting shape, while the Army of the Potomac stayed put at Sharpsburg. In the parlors and lobbies of Washington, the ugly rumors swirled. Little Mac did not really want to bag Lee. He wanted to negotiate for peace, put the country back together, and save slavery. Perhaps he would run for president. Or march his army to Washington to make himself dictator.

"I'm going up there to find out what's going on," Abraham told Hill Lamon. "It'll make Mary feel better if you come with me. Bring your banjo. We may need it."

They went up into the hills of Maryland by train as far as Harper's Ferry, then by carriage to Sharpsburg. The remnants of fighting were everywhere. Homes with shattered windows and holes in their walls. Roadsides littered with broken wagons. Farms empty of cows, pigs, and chickens but rich in trampled fields and looted barns. Long rows of black mounds, each about the length of a man, smelling of fertile soil under the warm October sun. They saw one sign over a big mound that read: "Here lies the bodies of sixty rebels. The wages of sin is death!" Flies swarmed in fields where the carcasses of horses lay.

The troops lined up to greet him with three hearty cheers. Cannon fired and bayonets flashed at the command "Present arms!" as he rode up and down the ranks on a dark chestnut horse. McClellan rode with him, and Abraham noticed he no longer gave his cap a jaunty twirl on his finger as he passed the men.

The general explained how the battle had unfolded and showed him the places of the worst slaughter. A cornfield where men's rifles had been shot to pieces in their hands, where General Joseph Hooker said every stalk was cut by bullets as closely as could have been done with a knife. A worn, sunken road the rebels had used as a trench until their bodies made a bloody lane that stretched as far as the eye could see. A stone bridge with three arches over Antietam Creek, where Abraham's old friend, Bob Toombs, and five hundred Georgians had held off General Ambrose Burnside until the stream ran red.

Houses, barns, churches, and schoolhouses had been turned into makeshift hospitals. In a little white Dunker church, whose congregants believed that war was a sin, the wounded lay stretched on the pews. At a farmhouse on the Shepherdstown Road, he walked down a hallway where wounded Confederates lay on beds of straw. They were pain-racked, broken men. Something awful was in their eyes. Fear of dying in a place far from home? Loathing of the tall, homely man who stood before them twisting his hat in his hands?

They're my countrymen, he thought, and yet more than one of them would probably put a bullet in my chest if he had a pistol.

"We are enemies through uncontrollable circumstances," he said quietly. "I bear you no malice and would like to take you by the hand."

A minute passed. One of them rose, stepped forward, silently offered his hand. Several more followed. Abraham stooped and shook hands with those too wounded to rise.

"Try to keep good cheer," he told them. "You'll receive every possible care."

Outside, the autumn sunshine rested on glowing leaves. An ambulance wagon carried the president's party down a rutted country lane. "Hill, sing us something sad," Abraham said. "Sing 'Twenty Years Ago.'" Lamon took out his banjo and strummed as they bumped along.

> I've wandered to the village, Tom, I've sat beneath the tree
> Upon the schoolhouse playground that sheltered you and me.
> But none were left to greet me, Tom, and few were left to know
> Who played with us upon the green, some twenty years ago.

He played melancholy tunes to fit their mood, then cheerful little songs to break the spell. The notes went drifting over fields where twenty-three thousand men had fallen.

Abraham conferred with McClellan in a headquarters tent with the flaps pulled open so light could stream in. They eyed each other across a simple table that served as a field desk. Little Mac sat in a camp chair, his back straight and shoulders squared, ready for any surprise attack. Abraham leaned back in an old armchair he reckoned someone must have borrowed from a farmhouse. He looked down at his general.

"When do you plan to advance?" he asked.

"With luck, in a matter of days. You've seen what the men have just been through. There is no point in moving before they're ready to fight."

"Lee has been on the move for two weeks. His men are in worse shape than yours."

"Sometimes a wounded foe is the most dangerous," McClellan

parried, smiling. "Any premature movement could prove fatal to this army." He had on his pleasant, smug look that said civilians never knew what an army requires.

Not even the lever of Archimedes could move this man, Abraham thought. "What do you need before you can be ready?"

"Our supplies are exhausted. The men are badly off for food and blankets. Hundreds are going barefoot."

"We've sent fresh supplies."

"They may have been sent, but they haven't arrived. They do this army little good if they're sitting in crates somewhere between here and Philadelphia."

"What else?" Abraham sighed.

"The horses need rest. They're broken down with fatigue."

"Lee's horses seem able to travel well enough. Are you not overcautious when you assume you can't do what the enemy is constantly doing?"

McClellan ignored the question. "Without horses, we can't cover our flanks or track the enemy's movements."

"We'll send as many fresh horses as we can." Abraham turned to a map spread out on the table and ran his finger down into Virginia. "If you cross the Potomac quickly, you can get between Lee and Richmond. Then you can force him into one last fight."

"Perhaps, but he could easily move around us, and head up into Pennsylvania."

"Then you have nothing to do but follow and ruin him there! We must beat him somewhere. Better where he is now, or even in Pennsylvania, than letting him get to the entrenchments of Richmond."

He stopped himself. There was no point in arguing with a man who was supposed to take his orders. Simple forthrightness would best serve them both. He sat back and offered a fatherly smile.

"George, I wish to call your attention to a fault in your character. I mean only kindness in bringing it up. But it's the sum of my observations about you, so you ought to hear it."

A shadow of uncertainty crossed Little Mac's brow. For an instant he looked like a boy dressed up to play soldier.

"You are superb at getting yourself ready to do a good thing," Abraham said. "No man can do that better. You make all the necessary sacrifices of blood and time and treasure to secure a victory. But whether from timidity, self-distrust, or some other motive inexplicable to me, you always stop short of results."

"I feel some little pride in the result of utterly defeating Lee," McClellan shot back.

"Yes, of course. For that, the nation will always be grateful."

"And with an army, I should add, that a short time ago was beaten and demoralized."

"But now you must finish him off, George. You must finish it."

"That is exactly what I intend to do."

"Very good." Abraham turned back to the map. "I want you to advance within two weeks. Your army must move now, while the roads are good."

"That should be possible," the general said cautiously, "if I receive the supplies I require."

"I must speak frankly, George." He leaned in a bit, still looking down at his general. "If you don't move forward, move rapidly and effectively, there will be a clamor for your removal. I won't be able to resist it."

McClellan's eyes smoldered.

"I will destroy Lee," he said firmly.

We'll see, Abraham thought.

That night brought a chilly air that carried intimations of coming frosts and armies settling into winter camp. After so many months of sleeping in a mansion, it felt strange to bed down in a tent under shimmering stars. He woke just before dawn and roused Ozias Hatch, an Illinois friend who had traveled to Antietam with him.

"Hatch, come take a walk with me."

The smell of coffee and sizzling bacon mixed with the smoke of campfires. They climbed a hill and looked down over the great tent city.

All was quiet except for the rattling of pans over the fires and crowing from nearby farms. Tents dotted fields as far as the eye could see. As the soldiers woke, each tent glowed like a veiled candle.

"Hatch, what is all this?" Abraham whispered.

Hatch looked at him, uncertain. "I suppose it's the Army of the Potomac."

Abraham thought for a moment. "No, Hatch, no," he said slowly. "This is McClellan's bodyguard."

He was hardly back in Washington before the telegraph began clicking away with excuses for not moving the army. McClellan wired to complain that supplies had still not arrived. His depleted ranks needed filling. He would need time to drill the new men, and the horses were still fatigued.

"Will you pardon me for asking what the horses of your army have done since the battle of Antietam that fatigue anything?" Abraham wired back.

While McClellan dallied, Jeb Stuart, the Knight of the Golden Spurs, led his Confederate cavalry on a rollicking, shouting ride around the entire Army of the Potomac, galloping clean up into Pennsylvania while he was at it, liberating the countryside of shoes and clothes, paying for them with Confederate money, then heading back down into Virginia with twelve hundred Yankee horses and a good chunk of the North's pride. Abraham sat in the White House and fumed. Little Mac, showing no signs of embarrassment, finally roused his army and moved south. It took him nine days to get it across the Potomac and begin a sluggish pursuit of Lee, who easily maneuvered out of his way.

The fall mid-term elections brought a whipping for the Republicans. They went down to defeat in state after state, and Democrats made big striding gains in the US House of Representatives. Newspapers said the people had decided Abraham Lincoln was a failure as a president, that he had stuck too long with a general who wouldn't fight. What good was Honest Abe's honesty if he couldn't win a war?

It was the last straw. Abraham signed an order relieving McClellan of command of the Army of the Potomac and putting Ambrose Burnside in his place.

"I've tried long enough to bore with an auger too dull to take hold," he muttered.

CHAPTER 31

DECEMBER 1862

Burnside did not want the job. He shook the great bushy whiskers encasing his head from ears to upper lip and explained that he did not feel competent to lead so large an army. Abraham insisted, and Burnside charged straight into disaster.

At Fredericksburg, Virginia, surge after blue surge rolled up the slopes of Marye's Heights, where Lee's Old War Horse, General James Longstreet, waited with his corps behind a low stone wall, ready to kill them all. The dead and maimed grew so thick, each new Union assault had to stumble forward over quivering pieces of bodies. Wounded soldiers grasped at legs as they went by, begging comrades to turn back before it was too late. When darkness came, the air filled with the cries of men lying in freezing pools of blood, calling for help as the life ran out of them. Burnside lost nearly thirteen thousand troops, Lee fewer than half as many.

The reports of the butchery stunned Abraham. He sat alone in his office, a woolen shawl draped over his shoulders, staring out a window toward the Potomac. In his mind's eye, he was looking across the Rappahannock to the high ground beyond Fredericksburg, fifty miles away, where the fallen lay. He could hear their moans.

If there is a worse place than hell, I am in it, he thought.

Stanton appeared with the latest casualty report. He put it on Abraham's desk and sank into a chair. Lines of strain showed on his face. The iron-gray streak in his beard was spreading. His eyes were as fierce and the scowl as determined as ever. But for a moment, in repose, he looked like an old man.

Abraham took up the report, looked at the figures. Scratches on a page. Little curved marks sprawled on paper like contorted bodies on the field.

"If I had the power, I would change places with any of those boys," he said softly.

Stanton grunted. He was working twelve or more hours a day at his stand-up desk in the War Department, barking out orders and firing off memos. There were times when bouts of asthma drove him to the floor in violent gasping fits. Doctors warned him to get more rest. He told them to keep him alive until the rebellion was ended and the troops came home, and then he would get some rest.

"Stanton, why has God put me in this terrible place?"

"I don't know. Perhaps it's because you truly would change places with any of those boys if you could. Perhaps the Almighty needs a man like that."

"Well, I need you, Mars. I want you to take care of yourself. You look a little on the worn side—like old Lear come in from the storm."

"I was about to say much the same of you."

Abraham fished a small mirror from a drawer and examined his own face. His hair and beard were a little grizzled, the cheeks sallow. The eyes had turned more cavernous than ever. It was still the face of a powerful man, but it had weathered.

"I reckon we both look like we've been through a storm of troubles," he said. "Sometimes I feel like the old lady who lived by the sea. One time a big storm came up and the waves rose 'til the water began to come in under her cabin door. She got a broom and went to sweeping it out. The water rose higher and higher, to her knees, to her waist, at last to her chin. But she kept on sweeping and telling herself, 'I'll keep on sweeping as long as the broom lasts, and we'll see whether the storm or the broom will last the longest!' And that's the way with me."

An army of wounded poured into the city after the Battle of Fredericksburg. Steamers brought them by the hundreds to the Sixth Street Wharf. Some staggered off the boats, some hobbled on crutches. Many came off on stretchers. Their faces were blackened with smoke, their bandages soaked with gore.

The city transformed into one vast hospital to receive them. Blocks of long, low wooden structures, not built to last, sprang up on vacant lots. Carpenters covered church pews with temporary floors that could in turn be covered with beds. Barns were filled with hospital supplies, and cattle sheds were turned into hospital bakeries. The streets were crowded with people searching for wounded loved ones. They wandered among the clatter of hammers that spilled out of coffin-makers' doors.

"I want to visit one of the hospitals and pay my respects to those poor suffering men," Mary said.

"Are you sure you're up to it?" he asked.

"Yes. It would be wrong for me not to do it."

He hesitated. She was more skittish than ever lately, more prone to headaches. Drop a book or close a window too hard, and she nearly jumped out of her skin. How was she going to hold up to the grim sights of a hospital ward? Yet she seemed determined.

"All right. But I want to go with you. I'll make the arrangements."

The next Sunday afternoon, they rode the few blocks to the Patent Office, climbed its granite stairs, and passed between its huge Greek columns. Fifteen years earlier, during Abraham's term in Congress, he had spent Sunday afternoons here, leading Bob through the maze of glass cases where models of inventions were on display: little reapers, locomotives, printing presses. After he was elected president, word spread that he had filed a patent for his own invention: a device for buoying stranded vessels off shoals. Someone had searched the bowels of the Patent Office's storage room, located the odd-looking model of a boat with bladders attached to its sides, and placed it on exhibit.

No one came to see it now. The building had been converted into a giant infirmary. The rows of sick and injured lay between the display cases. Volunteer nurses moved among the cots wiping brows. Evergreen wreathes had been hung on pillars, and festoons stretched overhead to cheer the men for the Christmas season.

"Isn't that thoughtful," Mary said as they entered. Her voice was trembling. Abraham took her hand. She was still dressed in mourning for Willie, and he could feel her shrinking within the layers of black.

The stench of the place was terrible. A nurse gave them each a piece of cloth sprinkled with lavender water to hold to their noses. Most of the patients lay immobile on their cots. A few sat in chairs or on the floor, backs propped against a wall. Mary stared numbly at all the white bandaged stumps where arms and legs ought to be.

The doctor on duty, a short harried-looking man with dried blood on his sleeves, led them along the rows of beds. "This fellow here was shot with a Minie ball through both ankles," he explained in a clinical tone. "We'll most likely have to take both his feet. This one had a shot pass through his left lung and out his back. I don't know how he's managing it, but it looks as though he may recover. This one here had his spine severed."

The last man gave a soft moan. Occasionally someone let out a shriek of pain or cried, "Oh, God help me!" The throats of unconscious men rattled for air. A man delirious from morphine, or perhaps gone insane, mumbled as he counted his fingers over and over.

"We have a good many cases of dysentery," the doctor said. "Some of these boys have severe frostbite. They lay on the battlefield at Fredericksburg for two days and nights before anyone could get to them. And some got badly burned in grass set afire by cannon."

One poor lad lay perfectly still with bandages wrapped around most of his head. His eyes were both shot out. A nurse bathed his arms with cool water, and when she was done, he politely said, "Thank you." On a bed next to him lay a figure covered from head to foot with a blanket, waiting for the stretcher bearers to come take it away.

Abraham began moving from bed to bed, shaking hands with men who could, asking questions about where they were from or how long they had been in the army, and offering words of encouragement.

"You must live, my boy," he told a youngster who was coughing blood into a handkerchief. "You must live."

"I intend to, sir," he said.

A man with no apparent injuries lay on his back, staring morosely at the ceiling. "These doctors kill more men than they cure," he sighed. "They may as well leave us alone to die."

Nearby lay a man guffawing over a piece of paper. "A nice lady came by and gave me this tract on the 'Sin of Dancing,'" he grinned. "And lookee here—both my legs are shot off."

Mary had been staying close, saying nothing. There was a boy, wasted and pale, lying curled up in his bed, looking at them with large brown eyes. He could not have been more than eighteen or nineteen—about the same age as their own Bob. The flesh on his face had drawn tight against his skull.

Mary moved to his bedside. "What happened to you, dear boy?" she asked gently.

"I got hit in the gut, ma'am," he said weakly.

"Does it hurt much?"

"Yes, ma'am, it does, mostly when I try to eat. I can't hold anything down."

She nodded, started to move away, hesitated. "Is there anything I can do for you?" she asked.

"You might help me write a letter to my mother."

"Of course."

Abraham brought a chair, and she sat by the boy's side writing as he dictated.

"Dear Mother, I have been shot bad, but I am bearing up. I tried to do my duty. The doctor says I cannot recover. God bless you and Father. Kiss Rachel and Benjamin for me. We will see each other again in a better place. Your loving son, Jacob."

Getting out the few words exhausted him. Mary folded the paper and promised that it would be mailed.

"Is there anything else I might do for you?"

"I guess you might hold my hand and see me through until I can fall asleep."

She took his hand while he closed his eyes. Abraham touched her lightly on the shoulder. She looked up at him, smiling sadly.

"I'll stay," she whispered. "You go on. When you get home, send the carriage back for me."

He left her there, sitting quietly among the wounded and the dying.

CHAPTER 32

NEW YEAR'S EVE
1862 AND NEW
YEAR'S DAY 1863

A rowdy throng jammed Pennsylvania Avenue on New Year's Eve. The night was full of men shouting and firing pistols into the air. They smashed empty bottles against cobblestones and hurled crates onto roaring bonfires. Songs about days gone by and friends departed rose with the sparks. There was something desperate in the voices—the tone of a celebration in a castle while the turrets are falling.

Abraham stayed up all night pacing the second floor of the White House, listening to the old year struggle to its end. There was little good to remember about 1862. Some victories in the Western theater, like the capture of New Orleans, and in coastal regions, like the fall of Fort

Pulaski in Georgia. But more than enough loss in the East. And no sign of the carnage ending soon. Some of the newspapers were calling it "Mr. Lincoln's War." Was it? How much blood was on his hands for refusing to give up Fort Sumter, for sticking too long with McClellan? How many men had he ordered to their deaths instead of merely accepting what the country had accepted for decades?

Turmoil was spreading across the North. Critics bellowed that the administration was illegally suppressing dissent about the war, that it had blighted the country with trampled freedoms of speech, arbitrary arrests, and political prisoners rotting in jail. Up in Minnesota, the Sioux had gone on the warpath, massacring hundreds of white settlers. The Indians were desperate for food and irate over broken promises. The army had crushed the uprising and condemned three hundred three captured Sioux to die. Abraham pared the list down as far as he could, and thirty-eight Indians were hung.

His own cabinet had come to near-revolt. The ambitious Chase had been whispering into the ears of hostile senators that the president listened to none of his advisors except Seward, who played him like a fiddle. Abraham had called the cabinet and senators together and forced Chase to back down. Chase and Seward both tendered their resignations. Abraham had accepted neither and put everyone back into line. But rumors were sweeping the capital that the government was in chaos, that Congress was plotting a coup, that Uncle Abe himself would soon resign.

Confusion now hath made his masterpiece, Abraham thought.

The year had brought a few accomplishments he could regard with satisfaction. He had signed a homestead law that gave any citizen a farm in the Western Territories nearly for free, so long as he was willing to break the land, till the fields, and reap what he sowed for five years. He had signed an act granting public lands to states for establishing colleges of agriculture and mechanical arts. And he had put his signature to the Pacific Railway Act, so men with vision and nerve and muscles of iron could start building a railroad that would span the whole continent.

Tomorrow, he would officially issue his proclamation emancipating the slaves. In North and South, people were bracing themselves for what might happen. Many predicted that blood would flow and shrieks pierce the darkness, that the Negroes would suddenly feel free to slaughter their masters and mistresses in their beds, as Nat Turner had done three decades earlier. Abraham did not believe it.

At any rate, I've given my word, he thought. I can't back down now.

His pacing led him into the room where Willie had died. He sat on the edge of the bed, eyes closed. Outside, someone was pounding deep, slow booms on a drum, a funeral dirge for the old year. Good riddance to it. Maybe a new year would bring better times.

He realized with a shudder that 1863 was beginning on a Thursday, the day of Willie's death.

By morning, the crowd was lining up at the gates for the annual New Year's Day reception. At eleven o'clock, Abraham took up his station at the center of the Blue Room. Hill Lamon stood to his left as official marshal of the levee, ready to make introductions. Mary stood to his right, dressed in black silk with ruffles of black satin. It was her first public reception in nearly a year.

"Are you ready for this?" he asked her.

"As ready as I'll ever be."

"You don't have to put yourself through it, if you'd rather not. People will understand."

"No, I want to do my duty." She wore a gracious, urbane smile.

The high-and-mighty of officialdom paid their respects first: the foreign diplomats, as proud and shiny as flags on parade; the justices of the Supreme Court, led by creaky old Roger Taney, looking as solemn as a tombstone; members of the Senate and House; braided generals and admirals. At noon, the gates were thrown open and the ordinary folk rushed the door, nearly bowling over Old Edward: red-necked carpenters, dapper government clerks, grocers smelling of onions and potatoes, fishmongers reeking of oysters, brewers perfumed with hops.

The line stretched out the front door, down the driveway, and into Lafayette Square. The people jostled their way into the Blue Room, manhandling in good humor the policemen who tried to keep order, stomping to shreds the floor covers meant to save carpets from mud and grime. Abraham shook their hands vigorously, like a man at a pump trying hard to fill a leaky bucket, then swung them along past Mary to an army officer who did his best to steer them back outside through a big window that reached to the floor.

A stout, red-headed fellow with a Scottish brogue greeted him. "A wondrous thing, your proclamation, it is," he exclaimed.

"I'm glad to hear it," Abraham said.

"There are some who say you won't dare go through with it. You must remain firm, my man. Stay firm."

"I will."

"Don't be like old Peter, who gave his pledge and then broke it before the cock could crow."

"I'll stand firm as a surge-repelling rock," Abraham promised.

A broad-shouldered, sun-burnished giant of a man from Indiana passed by.

"I think you have a little advantage of me in height," Abraham said. He stopped the procession long enough to measure back-to-back. "My friend, you can go home and tell your neighbors that you stand higher today than your president," he told the Hoosier.

An office-seeker tried to thrust a bundle of recommendations into his hands. "No, you don't," Abraham said, pitching them back. "I'm not going to open shop here. Happy New Year to you, anyway."

They came by the hundreds, eager to be a part of what they expected to be an historic day. After an hour, Mary developed a headache and excused herself. Abraham's hand throbbed from all the handshaking. But there was something addictive about it, something renovating about pressing flesh with Americans who hailed from New England to California. He kept pumping, pumping, pumping away at the well of the sovereign people.

Two leathery folks from Sangamon County, Illinois, a farmer and his wife, stepped forward.

"Why, John, I'm glad to see you! I haven't seen you since we split rails for Old Man Henderson!" They grasped hands, and Abraham stooped to kiss the missus's cheek.

"We had three boys in the army, all in the same company," the farmer said. "Johnny was killed in the Seven Days' fight, Sam was taken prisoner, and Henry is in the hospital here. We had a little money, and I said, 'Mother, we'll go to Washington and see Henry.' And since we're here, I said, 'We'll go up and see the president.'"

Abraham clasped his hand again. "John, I pray to God that this miserable war will soon be over. Come to my office tomorrow, and we'll talk some more."

As they were walking away, he heard the farmer say, "Mother, he's the same old Abe!"

A man with a dour face stepped up. "I voted for you," he said, "but for the life of me, I can't tell what your policy is."

"I have none," Abraham said, as cheerfully as he could. "I pass my life in preventing the storm from blowing down the tent, and I drive in the pegs as fast as they are pulled up. But I mean to keep pegging away, sir, pegging away."

The line finally dwindled shortly after two o'clock. He shook the last hand, climbed the stairs to his office, and sank at his desk, exhausted. A few minutes later, Seward came in with his son, Fred, an earnest young man with studious and warmhearted eyes who worked for his father as assistant secretary of state.

"Well, Mr. President, today we add a new element to this war," the elder Seward said. He puffed eagerly on his cigar. They spread before Abraham an engrossed copy of the Emancipation Proclamation. He read through the final version one last time, scouring for mistakes.

I, Abraham Lincoln, President of the United States, by virtue of the power in me vested as Commander-in-Chief . . . do order and declare that all persons held as slaves within said designated States, and parts of States, are, and henceforward shall be free. . . . And upon this act, sincerely believed to be an act of justice, warranted by the Constitution, upon military necessity, I invoke the considerate judgment of mankind, and the gracious favor of Almighty God.

He picked up a pen and dipped it into his inkwell. He paused. His hand and arm were shaking. That wouldn't do. He laid down the pen, stretched his hand a few times, and tried again. The arm was shaking even harder.

An omen of some sort? A warning that if he signed it, the country would plunge even deeper into catastrophe? No, surely not.

"I've never in my life felt more certain that I was doing right," he said, half to himself. "But I've been shaking hands all day. See there? My fingers are swollen. I can barely hold this pen."

He put the pen down again and rested his arm on his knee for a minute. Both Sewards watched him, a little uneasily.

"If my name ever goes into history it will be for this act," Abraham mused.

"I expect that's true," the elder Seward agreed. His cigar bobbed up and down from the corner of his mouth, hanging in the balance.

"This signature will be closely examined. If it's shaky, people will say I had compunctions."

"Yes, that could be."

He examined his hand. It seemed a little steadier.

"What do you think, Governor? Can you tell a man's character by the way he signs his name? Or even by his hands?"

"They say you can, though I've never made a study of it myself."

His hands were rough and large-knuckled, with dark age spots beginning to show, but still plenty strong. After all these years, they were still the hands of a rail splitter, more suited to wielding an ax than a pen. They could be the hands of a roustabout or blacksmith, he thought, or a surveyor of wide tracts of land. With such hands, a man ought to be able to offer a hearty shake to fellows well met. Or grasp the tiller of the ship of state for a while. Or even make a stab at setting four million people free.

He seized the pen. "Well, at any rate, it's going to be done!"

He wrote his name slowly, then leaned back and eyed the signature. It wasn't the most elegant job he had ever made of it. But it looked clear and firm enough.

Abraham Lincoln

"That will do," he said softly.

PART THREE

THE DISTANT SHORE

January 1863 to April 1865

❦ CHAPTER 33 ❦

WINTER AND SPRING

1863

*T*he fighting raged on, heedless of any paper he signed. Word came that the Union Army of the Cumberland and the Confederate Army of Tennessee had collided near Murfreesboro, Tennessee, in rocky fields and thick cedar forests along Stones River. The Union boys had managed to repulse the Confederate attacks, thank goodness. After the disaster at Fredericksburg, it was desperately needed good news. But the fighting had turned into a bloodbath, with thousands lost on both sides.

The South railed against the Emancipation Proclamation, calling it the most egregious political crime in American history. Northern Democrats ranted that "Old Ape" had turned a war to save the Union into a crusade against slavery. "A damned abolition nigger war," some of the army officers were muttering.

Congress passed a law instituting a national draft. There was no choice—the army had to have more men. Protests roiled the North. Word spread that the Lincoln administration was recruiting Negroes to fight in the Union armies. Northern critics wailed that blacks would never make good soldiers, that white troops wouldn't fight alongside them, and that using black men to kill white men was a despicable policy.

A bleak winter turned into a discouraging spring. Ulysses S. Grant plunged an army into the wilds of Louisiana and Mississippi. The Union men trudged through swamps, dug through mud, and hacked their way through tangles of vines and Spanish moss. They battled typhoid, dysentery, smallpox. Grant abandoned his supply lines, marched one hundred and eighty miles, won five battles along the way, and hurled his army at Vicksburg, perched like a fortress on two-hundred-foot bluffs along the Mississippi River. The city withstood his assaults, so he settled down to a siege in hopes of starving the rebels out.

Disaster struck in Virginia. The Army of the Potomac had a new commanding general, Fighting Joe Hooker. He ran into Robert E. Lee at Chancellorsville, where the old Gray Fox divided his army and sent it slipping through brambles, this way and that, attacking and counterattacking, until Hooker lost his wits and seventeen thousand men. The Confederates lost thirteen thousand, including Stonewall Jackson, shot by mistake by his own men. When it was all over, the rebels had won the fight.

The blood drained from Abraham's face when he got the dispatch reporting that Hooker had fallen back across the Rappahannock. "My God, my God! What will the country say!" he groaned.

The first anniversary of Willie's death arrived, bringing a sad, sweet remembrance. Abraham observed the date quietly, spending time alone in the late afternoon, when his son had died. Mary mourned the entire week.

He worried more and more about her lately. She was fading into a world of fleeting moods and shadows. She seemed quicker to lose her temper with White House servants over the way lamps were trimmed or how much vanilla should go into a pecan pie. Quicker to perceive that senators' wives were looking down their noses at her. Comfort came in shopping trips to New York and evenings at the theater. In Reverend Phineas Gurley's sermons at the New York Avenue Presbyterian Church and visits to hospitals to sit beside wounded soldiers.

Lately, she had been attending séances to communicate with the spirit world. "There really are more things in heaven and earth than are dreamt of in our philosophies!" she enthused one evening.

"What makes you say so?" he asked gently.

"I've had four sittings with Nellie Colman. She's a true medium."

"In what way?"

"A very slight veil separates us from those we have lost," Mary said knowingly. "Though unseen by us, they are very near."

"Is that what Miss Nellie says?"

"She receives messages from the departed and wisdom from the beyond. Even on matters of state."

"What do the spirits say about matters of state?" he inquired dubiously.

"For one thing, Mr. Lincoln, they agree with me about your cabinet." There was a note of triumph in her voice. "They say you must dismiss your enemies in the cabinet before you can ever succeed."

"Maybe I should attend one of these séances with you."

"I'll arrange it! When you see her, you'll understand what I mean."

They gathered a few nights later in the Red Room of the White House. Abraham asked Gideon Welles and Edwin Stanton to join them, over Mary's objections. John Hay was there, too, because he had heard that Nellie Coleman was pretty. She was. The medium glided into the room just as a servant put out the gas lights. She was a petite woman with ivory skin and dark green eyes that looked as though they hid deep secrets.

"Well, Miss Nellie, do you think you'll have anything to say to me this evening?" Abraham smiled.

"If *I* do not, there may be *others* who do," she smiled back.

"Mrs. Lincoln says you possess a peculiar sensitivity."

"I sometimes receive communications."

"She receives messages not perceived by ordinary people," Mary insisted.

"I am sometimes led by unseen guides," Miss Nellie allowed.

"That is a unique a gift," Abraham said.

"I use it to kindle the light of hope where darkness and despair reign."

She seated them around a cloth-draped table and told them to place their hands on top, palms down. In the middle of the table sat an oil lamp, which provided the room's only dim light. Near Miss Nellie lay some paper, a pencil, and a large green handkerchief.

"Do not lift your hands from the table unless instructed, or you will break the circle," she said. "If the spirits are nearby, they will answer your questions." She leaned her head back, closed her eyes, and appeared to slip into a trance.

They did not have to wait long. A loud rap burst from under the table. They all jumped in their seats, except Miss Nellie. Three more sharp raps followed. It sounded like someone hitting the floor with a broom handle. The keys on the grand piano, across the room, jingled. Suddenly the air was full of drums thumping and banjos twanging. Abraham could feel goose bumps on his arms and neck. How is she doing that? he wondered.

He made out Stanton's face, to his left. The secretary of war glared about, trying to spot accomplices in the dark. Mary sat on Abraham's right, gently swaying.

On the mantel, two unlit candles flared to life, then extinguished themselves just as quickly. Mary gasped and motioned with her head. The vague outline of the piano was rising slowly off the floor. It moved up and down several times, levitating with the rhythm of the weird music.

She can't be doing it with wires, Abraham thought. I would have seen them when I came in. There must be a lifting machine underneath. If so, it was ingeniously concealed. The inevitable fleeting thought came:

Could there really be something to all this?

The piano settled back down to the floor. The ghost music stopped. Nellie reached for the pencil, eyes still closed. She covered her writing hand, pencil, and paper with the large green handkerchief.

"An old general wishes to communicate," she announced. Several deep knocks sounded again while her hand moved beneath the handkerchief. After a moment, she uncovered the paper and laid it before John Hay, sitting beside her.

"Haste makes waste, but delays cause vexations," Hay read by the faint glow of the lamp. "Use every means to subdue. Make a bold front and fight the enemy. Less preparation, more action. Henry Knox."

"This Henry Knox is a wise soul," Abraham remarked. "Who is he?"

"The first secretary of war," the medium said solemnly.

"Oh, yes, General Knox." Abraham turned to Stanton. "That message must be for you, Mars. It's from your predecessor."

Stanton grimaced and said nothing.

"I'd like to ask General Knox if he can tell us when this rebellion will be put down," Abraham said.

The medium covered her hand again, wrote for a moment, and produced a new message for Hay to read.

"Washington, Lafayette, and I have held consultations upon this point. Washington believes the fighting will go on until a new general is found to hasten the end. Lafayette believes the rebellion will soon die of exhaustion. I foresee hope for a speedy conclusion only if a black army is raised."

"Well, opinions differ among the saints as well as among the sinners," Abraham drawled. "They sound like my cabinet. Don't you think so, Mr. Welles?"

The secretary of the navy stroked his beard until a sharp look from Miss Nellie reminded him that he was to leave his hands on the table. "I don't know," he mumbled. "I'll have to think the matter over."

"Can General Knox tell us what Napoleon thinks?" Hay asked, grinning.

The cloaked pencil moved, the message came through: "Napoleon says that the moment of greatest peril is the moment of victory."

"We must take that under advisement," Abraham said. "Miss Nellie, I'd like, if possible, to hear what Stephen Douglas has to say about this war."

"I'll try to reach his spirit."

Again the hand went under the handkerchief, the mysterious pencil took its dictation, and the Little Giant sent his reply.

"If victory is followed up by energetic action, all will be well," Hay read.

"I believe that," Abraham said, "whether it comes from spirit or human."

A stream of drum thumping and banjo twanging poured out of the darkness, then silence. Nellie Coleman opened her eyes and rose.

"The spirits have departed," she informed them. "I hope they have done you some good. You must excuse me now. I am very fatigued." She glided out of the room.

Abraham and Mary went upstairs and sat in the oval library.

"What do you think?" Mary asked in excitement.

"I'm not sure what to think." He had to be careful. "She certainly has a gift of some kind."

"You don't know the half of it! She's brought Willie back to me, Abraham!"

His heart sank a little. He had wondered if Miss Nellie's sittings had gone that far.

"Willie sends messages through her. And I can send messages back!"

"Are you sure?"

"Yes. And sometimes he comes to me, even without Miss Nellie's help."

"What do you mean?"

"He comes at night and stands at the foot of my bed with the same sweet, adorable smile he always had! And he doesn't always come alone. Sometimes little Eddie is with him, and twice he's come with my brother

Aleck. He tells me he loves his Uncle Aleck and is with him most of the time."

"How long has this been happening?"

"A few weeks. I didn't want to say anything until you could see for yourself that spirits really do exist, and that they long to commune with us."

Her eyes were wide and shining with an unnatural light.

"You can't dream of the comfort it gives me," she said. "When I thought of our little son all alone, without his mother to hold his little hand in loving guidance, it nearly broke my heart."

Her far-away look scared him. She's been through too much loss, he thought. There's been too much death and suffering. For any of us. If it keeps up, she'll go mad.

"You believe me, don't you?" she pleaded. "If the soul is immortal, there's no reason it can't return after death. Isn't that right?"

"Anything is possible."

"If Willie didn't come to cheer me, I'd still be drowned in tears."

As long as it helps her, what's the harm? he thought. If it brings her some measure of peace.

He sat up with her late into the night, assuring her that everything would be all right.

CHAPTER 34

SPRING 1863

He found his own sources of comfort and distraction. In stealing away for an hour at Grover's or Ford's Theater. In reading snatches of the humorist Artemus Ward to anyone who would listen, throwing back his head and stomping a foot as he laughed to drive away the blues. Or, in quiet moments alone, delving into Proverbs or Ecclesiastes to read verses he already knew by heart.

Issuing pardons brought deliverance. He put aside time each week to sit down with Hay or Nicolay and comb through lists of soldiers who had been court-martialed for one breach of duty or another. "Have you ever heard how the Patagonians eat oysters?" he liked to say. "They open them and throw the shells out the window until the pile gets higher than the house, and then they move. I feel like commencing a new pile of pardons today."

He grasped at any small reason to lighten a soldier's punishment, especially a death sentence. "It makes me feel rested after a hard day's work if I can find some good excuse for saving a man's life," he said.

Petitioners seeking mercy for loved ones found their way to the White House. A pretty young woman came to beg for the life of her brother, who had been sentenced to be shot for running away from a battle.

"He knew it was wrong, sir, but he was scared, and he couldn't help it," she cried.

"I'm sure he couldn't," Abraham said kindly. "In any contest between the head and the heels, the heels usually get the best of it."

"He's my only brother!"

"Well, I don't believe shooting him will do him any good. We'll send him back to his regiment if he promises to do his duty. I'll write it out now."

A father came seeking a pardon for a son who had deserted his post to fraternize with the enemy. "He was on picket duty, and he saw his cousin Lem across the creek," the man explained. "Lem's in Bragg's army. It was only natural that he'd want do go over to swap family news and a chaw of tobacco."

"But he must stick to his post," Abraham explained.

"He wanted to show Lem where he got hit in the arm at Stones River."

"You say he'd been wounded? That casts a different light on it. As the Scriptures say, in the shedding of blood is the remission of sins, so I guess we'll have to let him off this time."

Tad brought in a woman who had been waiting two days to see him. "Papa-day, this is Missus Bu'thfield," he announced. "Huh boy is in t'ouble."

The woman's son was in prison for desertion. "Oh, sir, he didn't desert," she pleaded. "He only wanted to come home for a little while to see his poor wife and his children."

"Don't you think the other boys want a little trip home, too?" Abraham asked gently. "And where would the army be if they all went?"

"But his wife is expecting their fifth child, and his little daughter is ill with the pox!"

"Well, you can't shoot a boy like that. We'll have to let him go. The country needs all her good men, wherever they are."

The woman sobbed for joy as Tad led her away. "I knew it was a lie!" she cried. "They told me he was an ugly man. He's the handsomest man I ever saw!"

Little Tad—there lay his greatest comfort now. A mischievous glint of light in a place of darkness. Doing his best to grow up like any other boy, except in the White House, at the vortex of war.

Here was Tad hitching his pet goats, Nanko and Nanny, to a sled made from an old chair and driving it through the East Room while hoop-skirted ladies from Boston stampeded out of the way.

Here he was in a uniform with a lieutenant's commission, which Stanton had given him for fun, mustering the White House servants and drilling them on the lawn.

Abraham longed for more time with his son. Between news of battles and meetings with senators, he loved getting down on the floor with Tad to spin tops or play with kittens. Loved helping him take apart a music box or clock to see how it worked, and then putting it back together to see if it would still run.

He had a hard time convincing the boy that he could not burst into his office on a whim. "Sometimes I'm meeting with the cabinet or seeing a general about the war," he explained, "and it's hard for us to decide what to do if we're interrupted. Do you understand?"

"What if I need to tell you something 'eally impo'tant?"

"Here's what we'll do. We'll have a secret knock. If you need to tell me something really important, you give the knock, and I promise I'll come to the door so you can tell me."

"What will it be?"

"How about three fast knocks, then two slow ones. Like this. *Knock-knock-knock. Knock-knock.*"

"All 'ight. I p'omise!"

Two or three times a day, it came—*Knock-knock-knock. Knock-knock*—and Tad came flying into the room, without waiting, to beg for a nickel or pelt the cabinet with peas from his toy cannon.

The boy was lonely without Willie. Sometimes he put his head in Abraham's lap and wept. On most days, he made up for the loss of his best friend with the energy of two boys.

Here he was with his little carpenter's toolbox, hammering nails through carpets and sawing the legs off chairs.

Here he was galloping across the White House lawn on his pony, legs sticking straight out as he bounced in the saddle, challenging the soldiers to race him.

He had his mother's temper and could fly into a tantrum when rebuked for fishing all the goldfish out of the White House pond or feeding his dog Jip the beef intended for a state dinner. Sometimes he broke into tears of frustration when his cleft palate kept strangers from understanding him.

Yet he had a big, tender heart, and Abraham laughed with joy the day Nicolay told him with a disapproving "Humph!" that Tad had stationed himself at the foot of the stairs and was collecting tolls from anyone wishing to come up to see the president, the proceeds to be donated to the Sanitary Commission. The cook turned grumpy whenever Tad appeared in the White House kitchen with a cluster of rag-tag street urchins and demanded that they be fed, but it made Abraham proud.

The boy was a slow learner. There was no doubt about that. He was ten now but could still barely read and write. "I hate these plaguey old tuto's and books!" he announced daily. It made Abraham a little sad to remember how he himself, as a boy, had hungered for books, and would walk miles through the woods to get hold of one. Tad, surrounded by as many books as he might like, had little use for them.

Well, let him run, Abraham thought, there's time enough yet for him to learn his letters and get pokey.

Here he was now, fresh from a session with his tutor, storming into the office with a book in his hand and a frown on his face.

"I can't 'ead this, Papa-day!" he cried.

"Why not?"

"It's too ha'd! I t'y, but I can't!"

"I tell you what. I'll read a paragraph to you. You follow along as I read, and then you read it back to me."

"All 'ight," Tad sniffed.

Abraham put the book on his knee and adjusted his spectacles. "The lion is often called the 'king of the beasts.' His height varies from three to four feet, and he is from six to nine feet long. His coat is of a yellowish brown or tawny color, and about his neck is a great shaggy mane."

Tad leaned against him, listening and watching Abraham's finger move under the words. As they read, a series of booms came rolling across the Potomac flats to rattle the windowpanes. The army was test firing some new artillery.

"The home of the lion is the forests of Asia and Africa, where he is a terror to man and beast."

Tad leaned closer, put his cheek on his father's shoulder. Abraham cradled the book in his hands as he had done long ago as a youth by a cabin fire. The windowpanes rattled, and the air shook outside while the big guns fired away.

CHAPTER 35

SUMMER 1863

Lee was north of the Potomac again, in Pennsylvania this time, somewhere behind the Blue Ridge Mountains. Panic swept before him like an advance guard. The rebels were feeding off the land as they marched, stripping barns of cows and town banks of money, politely leaving behind Confederate IOUs. Some troops were rounding up Negroes and sending them south into slavery. The Army of the Potomac set out on a hurried march north to stop the invasion. Yet another general, George Gordon Meade, rode at its head.

Abraham sprawled across a horsehair sofa in Edwin Stanton's office at the War Department, waiting for news. The secretary of war stood at his high desk, pen in hand, firing off memos and requisitions. A staccato chatter of telegraph instruments broke through an open door. The room was hot as a furnace. Flying bugs invaded at will through raised windows. They crawled up and down a big map of Pennsylvania tacked to a wall, where pins marked reports of rebel sightings—a brigade of cavalry here, a column of foot soldiers there.

"Where is he headed?" Abraham wondered aloud. "Harrisburg? Philadelphia?"

"It's our army he wants, not our cities," Stanton growled.

That's right, Abraham thought. Lee understands that better than our generals. He wants to draw us into the open. Destroy the Army of the Potomac in one crushing blow.

"He'll try to swing behind Meade, cut him off from us," Stanton predicted.

"General Lee has a habit of not doing what we expect."

"True."

"If Meade pushes his men, he might be the one to catch Lee in the open," Abraham said hopefully.

"Lee knows how to choose his ground."

"But he's in unfamiliar country."

Stanton grunted. He took off his spectacles, furiously polished the lenses, turned back to writing a memo.

Abraham rose and went to the map. "If the head of the rebel army is up here, near Harrisburg, and the tail of it on the road between Chambersburg and Hagerstown, the animal must be very slim somewhere. Meade needs to break him."

Another grunt from Stanton. For all they knew, the animal had already pounced and gripped Meade in its jaws.

"This may be our best opportunity of the war," Abraham said. "The enemy is on a long march, through days of heat and dust. They have to be exhausted."

He thought of General Lee, of what he had been told of him. Honest, courtly, a gentleman's gentleman. Never drank, always in control. Beloved by his army. The newspapers said the Army of Northern

Virginia would march through the gates of hell for him, if he so asked.

"If the rebels manage a victory, Jeff Davis will waste no time demanding peace," Stanton muttered.

Yes, it will be on my desk the next morning, Abraham thought. Peace between two sovereign nations.

"He won't get it." A stubborn growl in his own voice now. "I'd rather take a rope and hang myself on the White House lawn."

He shooed a knot of flies off the horsehair sofa and sprawled back down. Well, it was all on Meade's shoulders. No choice but to have confidence in him. A good commanding officer. Forty-seven years old, tall, bearded, balding, with the face of a respectable country doctor. Had seen more than his share of battles. Took two bullets at the Battle of Glendale in Virginia, one to the hip and one to the arm, but had stayed in the saddle directing his troops while the blood drained out of him. His men called him the Old Snapping Turtle for the way he could lose his temper. If they didn't love him, they at least respected his judgment and skill.

"Meade is a Pennsylvanian," Stanton said, reading his thoughts. "Fighting on his own soil. That ought to stiffen him up."

A clerk darted into the room with something that needed approving. Stanton signed a paper and dismissed him with a bleary-eyed scowl. He snatched his lenses off his nose and polished away again. No doubt he had been up most of the night, working. Abraham felt a sudden upwelling of affection for his little secretary of war.

"See here, Mars. You're not doing as I told you," he said.

"Me? What do you mean?" Stanton demanded.

"I've been telling you to take care of yourself. If you don't get some rest, I'll be planting you in the cemetery up at the Soldiers' Home. That won't do because I can't get along without you. More to the point, I know the army can't."

"Let's get this damned war over, and then everyone can get along with or without each other as they damned well please," Stanton barked.

Abraham grinned. He knew now what he had not known in

Cincinnati, the first time they met: Stanton barked and glared at everyone.

They measured the afternoon by the intermittent clatter of the telegraph machines. Late in the day came the message they were waiting for—a report of heavy fighting around the town of Gettysburg. They found it on the map, a spot just east of the mountains where nine or ten roads came together, like a spider's web.

Abraham's chest tightened. So that is where it happens, he thought. He tried to picture the countryside: the long ridges covered with woods and rocks; the green fields studded with fat German barns; gray, dusty roads filled with July heat; and two armies pouring toward each other.

"'All things are ready, if our minds be so,'" he said softly.

In the evening, he rode to the cottage at the Soldiers' Home, where Mary had moved the family for another summer.

"How far away is Gettysburg?" she asked when he told her the latest report.

"Sixty miles, as the crow flies."

She was quiet for a moment, steeling herself. They were used to fighting nearby to the south, but not to the north.

"What happens if General Meade can't stop them?"

"There's every reason to think Meade will prevail," he assured her.

The sun went down, and the heat dissipated. He went outside to stretch out on the cottage's lawn for a few minutes. Overhead, the Summer Triangle swam into the darkening sky. The Dipper was lowering in the west. He breathed deeply, gathering his strength for what lay ahead. No doubt this would be a momentous fight. Maybe the last big one of the war. If Meade was victorious, perhaps the South would decide that its cause was lost. If Lee won, there would be little to stop him from moving on to Philadelphia, Baltimore, and Washington. The beginning of the end, either way.

Well, there was no point in thinking about that just now. The troops knew what they needed to do. They were fighting on their own home ground. Surely they would beat the rebels—if Meade was the right man.

He went inside to his bedroom and lay on top of the sheets. A chorus of tree frogs and other night creatures lulled him to sleep, and as he drifted off, he could feel his bed moving across the floor, out a window, and over the dark lawn of the Soldiers' Home. The bed turned into the deck of a boat, and he had the dream that had come to him before the bombardment of Fort Sumter and the fighting at Antietam Creek—the same dream that had started to come, it seemed, before every important engagement of the war.

He was onboard the mysterious vessel again, gliding toward a vague distant shore. Fog hung about the ship, and everything was quiet. He tried to make out some details in the sliver of land ahead. For an instant he thought that perhaps he saw mountain peaks. There was no sign of any inlet or bay, just a long, unbroken gray line. After a minute, the shore slipped away and the image dissolved.

He lay half-asleep, half-awake, wondering what it could mean. It puzzled him that the land was always moving away, even though the boat seemed to be gliding toward it. Perhaps the vessel was the ship of state, the mists were the fog of war, and the distant shore was the peace that seemed beyond his grasp. He could not be sure. His thoughts dissolved, like the dream, and he fell back asleep.

The next morning, he rose early, gulped down two biscuits and a cup of coffee, and rode back into the city. He went straight to the War Department. Someone had hung a map of Gettysburg on a wall in the telegraph office. The names on the map sounded peaceful: Seminary Ridge, Little Round Top, Cemetery Hill. He paced the room, stopping to look over the shoulders of the cipher-operators whenever a message clicked through.

The telegraphs were ominously quiet for most of the morning. A handful of dispatches told of the fighting the day before, how the rebels had at first thrown back troops commanded by General John Reynolds, then how the Union boys had held firm while the bulk of their army streamed toward the field, though Reynolds was shot dead yelling, "Forward men! For God's sake, forward!"

Officers and cabinet members drifted into the room. Through

a window, they could hear the murmur of a crowd on Pennsylvania Avenue, near Willard's Hotel, waiting for news.

"I don't like it," Stanton fretted. "Meade has never handled a big army in a fight like this."

"Well, there's nothing we can do about that now," Abraham said. They were all nervous.

"He hasn't even had time to organize his command."

"That army's been organized ten times over. Meade just needs to give hotter shot than he gets."

By noon, the telegraph office was boiling. They mopped their necks and brows with wet handkerchiefs. Someone brought a pitcher of cool water, and Abraham gratefully swallowed a glass. Up in Gettysburg, men were dying in a rain of bullets under a blazing sun.

John Hay appeared wearing the expression of a man who had something he hated to tell.

"Mrs. Lincoln has been in a carriage accident," he whispered.

It was as though someone had thrown the pitcher of water into Abraham's face.

"Is she all right?"

"I think so. She's in her room at the Executive Mansion."

He hurried to the White House and bounded up the stairs. Mary was propped up on pillows in her bed, a bandage on her head, scrapes on her arms. She insisted that she was fine.

"What happened?"

"I'm not sure," she said groggily. "We had just turned off Rock Creek Church Road. The driver fell out. The horses started to run. I didn't know what to do, so I jumped."

She had rolled across the ground and hit her head on a stone. Doctors from Mount Pleasant Hospital had bandaged her up.

"I'm fine," she insisted. "I don't want you worrying over me."

"Are you certain?"

"Absolutely." Her voice was thin but resolute. "Go back to the War Department. You have more important things to attend to."

He felt guilty about leaving her. She was still in shock, no doubt. But he was grateful to her for putting up a brave front. Amazing that a little woman who shivered at the faintest thunder could be a tough old gamecock when it came to war.

The next thirty-six hours were an eternity. The telegraph service from Gettysburg was poor. He scrutinized each dispatch that bled through the wire, but it was difficult to fathom what was unfolding up there. Reports indicated a monumental battle. Men clinging desperately to ridges and knolls, faces black from powder, gasping in the humid air. Charging into steady fire, heads down, leaning forward like farmers pushing head-on into a stiff prairie wind. Cannon pouring out thunder and iron that plowed through living masses. Flags toppling to the ground, rising up, falling again.

Three or four times, he went back to the White House to make sure Mary was resting comfortably. He tried to grab a few minutes of sleep in his own bed. But when he shut his eyes, he could not get the clicking of the telegraphs out of his head. He rose and hurried back to the War Department for more pacing.

It came late in the night after the third day of fighting—the electric flash that announced victory. Stanton was suddenly trembling with joy, waving the dispatch in the air, and they were dancing a jig in each other's arms like schoolboys, shouting and whooping and laughing until they dropped exhausted onto the horsehair sofa. They read the telegram a dozen times, hardly able to believe it, telling each other they had believed all along. The War Department was alive with officers pumping each other's hands. They stayed up all night, too weary and excited for sleep, discussing what the victory would mean.

Outside, people were running through dark streets, shouting the news of victory at Gettysburg. Men and boys fired guns into the air. The racket kept up until dawn. Then silence fell over the city for an hour, while people assured each other in full morning light that it wasn't a mistake or a dream, and that the celebrating could begin in earnest.

It was the Fourth of July.

ↂↂↂ

More triumphant news arrived. Ulysses S. Grant had done it—Vicksburg had fallen. It had taken him months of slogging, digging, hacking, and bombarding. The Gibraltar of the South had finally capitulated, its people worn down from subsisting on rat and mule meat. Thirty thousand weary Confederates marched out of Vicksburg's fortifications and stacked arms. Days later, Port Hudson, Louisiana, capitulated, and the entire Mississippi River lay in Union hands. The Father of Waters again went unvexed to the sea.

While Northern bells pealed and torchlight parades filled streets, Lee's army was limping away from Gettysburg in a downpour. Meade was showing no signs of stopping it. Abraham fired off telegrams urging his general to take up the pursuit and finish the rebels off. A rain-swollen Potomac halted Lee's flight, left him with his back against the river. Still the Union army hesitated.

"They've plowed the field with blood and treasure, and now just when the harvest is ripe, they'll let it go to waste," Abraham groaned.

"Meade says he intends to attack as soon as his men are in position and ready," Stanton reported.

"Yes, he'll be ready to fight a magnificent battle when there's no enemy there to fight!"

In the midst of the struggle to get Meade going, Mary took a turn for the worse. He found her sitting on the edge of her bed, clothes soaked with perspiration.

"Where is Willie?" she asked calmly. "Will you send him in?"

He turned rigid with fear. She had the same vacant look in her eyes as just after their son's death.

"Mrs. Keckley has sewed him a coat. He won't be cold now. I want him to try it on." She pulled a strand of hair from her head. "We should cancel the party. I don't want a lot of noise in the house while Willie is sick."

He took her hands and pressed them gently. "Mary, look at me."

"I don't like that man over there in the corner," she whispered. "I think he wants to kill me while you're away trying cases on the circuit."

Doctor Stone came immediately and examined her. The wound on the back of her head had begun to ooze puss.

"I'll lance and drain it," he said. "The fever should subside."

"Will she recover?"

"There's every reason to think she will."

"Thank you," he said, fighting back tears.

"Though any blow to the head can be dangerous," the doctor cautioned. "We should have a nurse sit with her around the clock."

"I'll arrange for Mrs. Pomroy to come."

Stanton sent men to examine the carriage involved in the accident. Their investigation brought a fresh shock. An act of sabotage, they said. Someone had loosened the bolts on the driver's seat, no doubt hoping to injure the president.

"I don't believe it," Abraham protested. "The bolts most likely worked themselves loose. That carriage has never been properly cared for." He could not stomach the thought that malice aimed at him had hurt Mary instead.

There was little time to worry about it. A few days later, Lee's battered forces slipped back across the Potomac to Virginia soil. The news sent Abraham to the bottom of a dark well.

"It's as if Meade was trying to get them across the river without another battle!" he cried. "If I had gone up there, I could have whipped them myself!"

He stomped into his office, slammed the door, and scratched out a bitter letter to the general.

You stood and let the flood run down, bridges be built, and the enemy move away at his leisure, without attacking him. . . . I do not believe you appreciate the magnitude of the misfortune involved in Lee's escape. He was within your easy grasp. . . .

One more battle, and the war could have been over. Now it would be prolonged indefinitely.

If you could not safely attack Lee last Monday, how can you possibly do so south of the river, when you can take with you very few more than two-thirds of the force you then had in hand?

My God, how many times are we going to let this happen? he thought. It's just like Antietam. Will we never learn?

Your golden opportunity is gone, and I am distressed immeasurably because of it.

He took off his spectacles and rubbed his temples, brooding. With Lee's army still alive, the South was far from defeated. It could go on waging a defensive war for months, maybe years. Northerners would start looking for any excuse to end the bloodshed. He would have to convince them it was worth the sacrifice to go on. How was he to do that if his generals kept holding back?

He leaned back and ran his hands through his hair. Out on the lawn, a band struck up a martial tune: "The Battle Cry of Freedom," a new song wildly popular with the troops. "Yes we'll rally round the flag, boys, we'll rally once again. . . ."

Ulysses S. Grant. There was a soldier always ready to fight. A man determined to slash and thrust and claw his way to victory. Admirers were saying that the initials in U. S. Grant stood for Unconditional Surrender, because that was the only kind he would accept from the enemy.

A rap at the door. Nicolay stuck his head into the room, recognized his mood, and withdrew.

There had been rumors of Grant drinking too much. Probably jealous slanders. Well, if he drinks, find out where he gets his whiskey and send a barrel of the stuff to every other general in the army.

He put his spectacles back on and read over his letter to Meade. Perhaps it was too harsh. His blood was cooling a little. Send a letter like this, and he might lose the services of a good man. After all, Meade had fought a magnificent battle only days after assuming command. Maybe the army was too damned cut up and exhausted to pursue Lee just now. Hard to tell from so many miles away.

I don't know for certain if I would give any different orders if I were there myself, he thought. Don't even really know how I'd behave when Minie balls are whistling and those great oblong shells shrieking in my ear.

Grant. No question about how he behaved when the fighting got rough. He settled for nothing but the annihilation of the enemy. Or unconditional surrender. But he needed Grant west of the mountains just now. There was more fighting to be done there. Let him finish the job in the West. Perhaps then. . . .

He eyed the letter for moment, then carefully folded it. Writing it had made him feel better. It had done him good and answered its purpose. He put it in an envelope, wrote "To Gen. Meade, never sent, or signed" across the front, and filed it away in a pigeonhole.

CHAPTER 36

AUGUST TO OCTOBER

1863

Frederick Douglass came to see him. Old Edward the doorkeeper appeared in Abraham's office wearing a concerned expression and whispered that he was downstairs.

"Bring him up," Abraham directed. "Now."

A black man in the White House. Not as a servant, but for a face-to-face talk with the chief executive of the land. The thought brought a vague uneasiness, both disconcerting and exhilarating.

The normal clamor of applicants waiting on the stairs fell silent. Eyebrows raised on white faces as Douglass elbowed his way up. Someone sneered, loud enough to be heard all the way down the hall, "Yes, damn it, I knew they'd let the nigger through."

Let them sneer, Abraham thought. We need this man.

He was a little over six feet tall with a solid build and strong face. The skin was light, suggesting some amount of white blood in his veins. The black mane of hair was mixed, too, with spots of gray and a broad white streak above the right eye. His black overcoat and white shirt with a high, stiff collar were the work of a good tailor.

He stepped into the room looking a little uncertain, as if expecting someone to tell him, "Go home and mind your own business." But a flash in his eyes hinted, "You're going to hear what I have to say."

Abraham stood and extended his hand.

"Mr. President, I am Frederick Douglass." A rich, powerful voice. The voice of an orator. "I don't know if you've heard of me, but I—"

"I know who you are, Mr. Douglass. I've read about you, and Mr. Seward has told me all about you. Sit down. I'm glad to see you." He moved a stack of books off a chair and motioned for his visitor to sit.

Douglass had been born a slave on Maryland's eastern shore and had whip marks on his back to remind him of his youth. He had secretly taught himself to read and write, fled north to freedom, and made a name for himself as one of the great abolitionists of the age. "If there is no struggle, there is no progress!" he had cried throughout the land. "Those who profess to favor freedom, and yet deprecate agitation, are men who want crops without plowing up the ground. They want rain without thunder and lightning."

He sat with back straight, the uncertainty on his expression fading now. "I want to thank you for signing your Order of Retaliation," he began.

Abraham nodded cordially. He had signed the order less than two weeks earlier, in response to a Confederate policy of executing and enslaving captured black troops. His Order of Retaliation stated that for every captured Union soldier executed or enslaved by the Confederacy, a captured rebel soldier would be executed or sentenced to hard labor. A horrible order to have to sign.

"Of course, I wish it had come sooner," Douglass gently chided.

"You were somewhat slow about it. Lives could have been saved."

Abraham suddenly felt on the defensive. "Popular opinion was not ready for it until now," he said quickly. "Remember, Mr. Douglass, that the battles at Milliken's Bend and Fort Wagner are recent events. The country wanted proof that black men would fight and die bravely. If I had acted sooner, people would have said, 'Ah! We thought it would come to this. White men are being killed for Negroes.'"

He felt a twinge of resentment at being forced to explain. But he reminded himself: This man has known depths I'll never know.

"I signed that order with the greatest reluctance," he went on. "Retaliation is a terrible remedy. Once begun, there's no telling where it will end. If I could get hold of the rebel soldiers guilty of murdering colored prisoners of war, I could easily retaliate, but the thought of hanging men for a crime perpetrated by others is revolting to my feelings."

"I don't agree that such concerns should stand in the way of protecting black soldiers," Douglass said, "but I respect the humane spirit behind your reluctance."

They would have to let it go at that. Douglass moved on.

"You may know, sir, that I've been hard at work recruiting colored troops."

"Your efforts have been invaluable. The colored population is a resource which can help end this war."

"I must tell you it is increasingly difficult to ask colored men to enlist."

"Why?"

"They feel the government has not dealt fairly with them." Douglass was choosing his words carefully.

"What are their specific complaints?"

"They believe they ought to get the same pay as white soldiers. They get ten dollars a month, and three dollars of that is deducted for uniforms. White privates get thirteen dollars a month, plus an allowance for clothing."

"The Negro troops gain much more than pay in fighting, don't you think?"

"Yes. But there is still the injustice of it to the men and to their families."

He's right, of course, Abraham sighed to himself. How do you tell a man who's right that he must wait a while longer for justice?

"You know there has been a great prejudice against making colored men soldiers," he said.

"I know that all too well," Douglass said.

"When Congress agreed to enlist them, the fact that they wouldn't get the same pay as white soldiers seemed a necessary concession to smooth the way."

"And now black men have shown themselves equal to whites in their ability to fight—and to stop bullets with their flesh."

"They have," Abraham said. "And in the end, I assure you, they will receive equal pay."

Douglass nodded. "There is something else. When colored soldiers perform great service on the battlefield, they should be promoted. It's not right to deny them commissions as officers."

"I agree. I'll sign any commission for colored soldiers that Secretary Stanton recommends."

"Thank you." He smiled for the first time—a reserved but genuine smile.

"I hope you'll continue your recruiting, Mr. Douglass. The bare sight of fifty thousand armed and drilled black soldiers on the banks of the Mississippi would end the rebellion at once."

"I agree wholeheartedly. And, yes, I will keep pleading for new recruits." He stood to go.

"One more thing," Abraham said. "I read in one of your recent speeches that you are dissatisfied with my 'tardy, hesitating, and vacillating' policies. Or words to that effect."

"You cannot blame me for being somewhat impatient."

"Sometimes I may seem slow, and perhaps I am. But once I take a position, I don't retreat from it."

"You give me great assurance, sir," Douglass bowed.

"Then you leave here satisfied?"

"I'll never be fully satisfied until my four million brothers and sisters have been allowed a place of common equality." He clasped Abraham's offered hand. "But I'm satisfied that slavery will not survive this war, and that the country will survive both slavery and the war."

~~~

For several days, he had a feeling that something bad was going to happen. "I believe I feel trouble in the air before it comes," he told John Hay.

It came. News of a crushing defeat at Chickamauga Creek in northern Georgia—Union lines melting away before rebel onslaughts, bodies carpeting the ground, artillery shattered, and General William Rosecrans warning his men, "If you care to live any longer, get away from here." His army stumbled across the Tennessee line into Chattanooga. The rebels planted batteries on the heights of Lookout Mountain and Missionary Ridge, cut roads leading into the city, and prepared to starve Rosecrans into surrender.

It was Stanton who came to the rescue. Stanton who convened an emergency midnight conference at the War Department, insisted that something be done and proposed rushing part of the Army of the Potomac by train down to Chattanooga. He scoffed when Abraham and others said it would take forty days, argued with them, pounded his fist, roared that, by God, if merchants could ship twenty thousand bales of cotton to Chattanooga in twenty days, the army ought to be able to get twenty thousand troops there in less time.

For two straight days and nights, the little secretary of war fired off telegrams to railroad officials, gathered locomotives, pored over timetables, and determined routes, wheezing with asthma all the while. On a Friday evening, the first of the trains rolled out of Washington to begin the twelve-hundred-mile journey. Eleven days later, twenty-three thousand men plus horses, guns, batteries, tents, wagons and supplies had arrived at the railhead near Chattanooga. Never in history had so many troops moved so far so fast.

"Stanton, you remind me of an old Methodist preacher I used to know back in Illinois," Abraham said. "He got so energetic in the pulpit, his parishioners decided to put bricks in his pockets to hold him down. We may be obliged to serve you the same way, though I guess we'll just let you jump a while longer."

Stanton scowled and went back to work.

Chattanooga remained in Union hands. Whoever possessed it controlled the vital routes northward into Virginia and southward into Georgia. "If we can hold Chattanooga and East Tennessee, I think the rebellion must dwindle and die," Abraham wired General Rosecrans.

But Chickamauga had knocked the fight out of Old Rosy. Discouraging reports from officers in the field made their way to Washington—Rosecrans's orders were inconsistent, his mind was scattered, the Army of the Cumberland was unsafe in his hands.

He's as stunned and confused as a duck hit on the head, Abraham thought. I'll have to get someone else to take charge down there.

He needed a man ready to fight every hour of every day. It took little time to decide. Less than a month after the disaster at Chickamauga, he put Ulysses S. Grant in command of all Union forces between the Appalachian Mountains and the Mississippi River.

CHAPTER 37

NOVEMBER 18
AND 19, 1863

There were empty coffins stacked beside the tracks when the train pulled into the station at Gettysburg. A crowd let out a roar as he stepped onto the platform. A band struck up "The Battle Hymn of the Republic." Ward Hill Lamon was there to greet him, acting as chief marshal of ceremonies, a couple of pistols and daggers squirreled away in his coat pockets, no doubt. To his left stood white-haired Edward Everett, the renowned orator, looking in his sixty-ninth year like noble Cicero of ancient times. To Lamon's right stood David Wills, local attorney and leading citizen, a man with energy and determination in his eyes.

They walked through the dusk two blocks up Carlisle Street. Gettysburg's town square was packed. People everywhere, cheering and thrusting out hands. Lamon and some soldiers cleared a path. Wills shouted over the noise as they walked, telling the usual facts a host gives a visitor about his town. Eight churches, six taverns, three weekly newspapers, two banks. A college and a seminary. Twenty-four hundred citizens, although many more—perhaps fifteen thousand—had come for the dedication.

"When the fighting started, a good many of us climbed onto our rooftops to glimpse the action," Wills recounted. "When it got close, we went down into our cellars. That's where we were as the rebels pushed through town and raised their flag over the square." He pointed to buildings scarred by artillery fire. "When it was all over, we came out to scrape the mud and blood off the pavement."

The Wills home, a handsome three-story brick house, stood on the edge of the square.

"It's three-quarters of a mile to the cemetery from here," Wills said as they went inside. "We were hoping to have all the graves filled by now, but we're only about a third of the way through. Moving that many bodies is a difficult process, as you can imagine."

Mrs. Wills presided over a dinner party and reception. She was pregnant, and fatigue showed through her smile. After the battle, her house had been used as a hospital, and the provost marshal had made it his headquarters. Her husband had convened dozens of meetings in their parlor to organize the national cemetery that would hold the remains of so many fallen soldiers. This night, she would find places for thirty-eight guests to sleep under her roof.

Outside the 5th New York Artillery Band serenaded the town from the square. Word spread that the president had arrived, and the crowd swelled. Throats lubricated with whiskey called from the street. "Come out, Old Abe!" "We're waiting, Father Abraham!" "Speak to us!"

He stepped to the door and bowed to loud huzzahs. "I have no speech to make just now," he called out. "In my position, it is somewhat important that I should not say any foolish things."

"If you can help it!" someone yelled amid laughter.

"It very often happens that the only way to help it is to say nothing at all," he called back. More laughter. "Goodnight, my friends."

He went upstairs to the bedroom that Mrs. Wills had set aside for him and sat at a small writing table to work on the brief address he was to make the next day. It was mostly written, but he hadn't had time to finish it before leaving Washington. He knew what he wanted to say. The thoughts had been rambling around in his head for years, some of them long before the war had begun.

His pen etched the phrases onto the page. He wanted to use the occasion to remind the Northern people of the true meaning of the war. To give them strength to shoulder the burden. He had to tell them why it was necessary for this horrible fighting to go on. Why it was necessary for so many to suffer and die. This war could destroy the country—or redeem it.

Every now and then he put his head in his hands and closed his eyes to rest the brain. The train ride had been tiring. Mary had not wanted him to come. Tad was sick with a sore throat and fever. Had not wanted any breakfast. Mary had panicked and wept that the boy would die if his father left him. She had grabbed Abraham's arm and begged him to stay. But Dr. Stone said there was little danger. The occasion was too important to change plans over a woman's hysteria. So he had come.

He got up and stepped to a window. The square was a mass of bodies whooping and singing by torchlight. "Hurrah for Old Abe!" "God save the Union!" A good many of them had sons, brothers, or husbands who had died here four and a half months before. Now they had come to mourn and find purpose. Many were drunk, staggering from tavern to tavern. It was hard to blame them for letting off steam. They had taken more than most people could take. There was something inside them fierce and resilient and fundamentally just. The town had nowhere near enough beds for them all. They would lie down in wagons, in barns, on church pews. Or walk the streets all night.

He went back to the table and took up the pen. He wanted to tell them that they must fight on, not merely to save the Union or liberate the slaves. They had to salvage the ideals on which the country was founded.

And even more. It was up to them to prove that people really could govern themselves. To show that liberty and equality were more than glimmering fables. To preserve the fact of democracy for the whole world.

A knock at the door—a sergeant was there with some telegrams. One from Mary saying that Tad was better. That was a relief. No need to worry about that now. And word from Stanton that all was quiet on the battle fronts. Good. Very good.

He finished his remarks and climbed into bed. The yelling and serenading on the square kept up, but it did not bother him. A rough chorus set him drifting.

John Brown's body lies a-moldering in the grave, John Brown's body lies a-moldering in the grave. . . .

The sun brought a gleaming dawn, then slipped behind gray clouds. A bugle call and cannon salute woke the town. Abraham was up by then for a brief carriage tour of the battlefield with Seward, who had also come from Washington for the ceremony. They rode west toward the high-domed cupola of the Lutheran Theological Seminary, set on a long ridge where the Confederate army had positioned itself during the battle last July. A soft haze floated over rocky hilltops and vacant fields. The wreckage of war covered the ground: ragged jackets, rusting pistols, boots, canteens, the skeletons of horses. Thousands of boards marked shallow graves, hastily dug wherever men had fallen. Many of the Union bodies had already been dug up and reinterred in the new cemetery, or taken home.

Perhaps fifty thousand were dead, wounded, or missing on both sides. How could it have come to this? He looked across a long, undulating rise toward a clump of trees and low stone wall nearly a mile away—the objective of George Pickett's daring, catastrophic charge. Years ago, Pickett had studied law in Springfield. Abraham remembered his flowing hair and boyish eyes. Well, they most likely weren't so boyish these days.

He went back to the Wills house, ate a quick breakfast, and wrote out a clean copy of his speech. The sun had reappeared by the time he took his place for the procession to the cemetery. The crowd lining Baltimore Street was in a much different mood now, solemn and respectful. Many wore black mourning bands, including Abraham, who had one on his tall silk hat in memory of Willie. The bay horse he was given to ride was small, and his feet hung near the ground.

Lamon gave the signal that all was ready, and the parade started forward while the Marine Band played a dirge. Black banners hung from windows. People cheered despite the somber mood as the long line of dignitaries and soldiers made its way to Cemetery Hill. Thousands had gathered in an open area around a wooden platform erected for the speakers and distinguished guests. Nearby, on the slope of the hill, more than thirty-five hundred plots lay in perfect semicircular rows.

The Chaplain of the United States Senate gave a prayer, the Marine Band played the hymn "Old Hundred," and Edward Everett began his address.

"Standing beneath this serene sky, overlooking these broad fields now reposing from the labors of the waning year, the mighty Alleghenies dimly towering before us, the graves of our brethren beneath our feet, it is with hesitation that I raise my poor voice to break the eloquent silence of God and Nature. . . ."

Everett spoke for two hours. It was a moving speech, full of history and pathos and descriptions of the great battle. When it was over, Abraham stepped to the front of the platform, adjusted his spectacles, and read his address slowly, throwing his tenor voice as far as he could over the heads of the crowd.

Four score and seven years ago our fathers brought forth on this continent, a new nation, conceived in liberty, and dedicated to the proposition that all men are created equal.

Now we are engaged in a great civil war, testing whether that nation, or any nation so conceived and so dedicated, can long endure. We are met on a great battlefield of that war. We have come to dedicate a portion of that field, as a final resting place for those who here gave their lives that that nation might live. It is altogether fitting and proper that we should do this.

But, in a larger sense, we can not dedicate—we can not consecrate— we can not hallow—this ground. The brave men, living and dead, who struggled here, have consecrated it, far above our poor power to add or detract. The world will little note, nor long remember what we say here, but it can never forget what they did here. It is for us the living, rather, to be dedicated here to the unfinished work which they who fought here have thus far so nobly advanced. It is rather for us to be here dedicated to the great task remaining before us—that from these honored dead we take increased devotion to that cause for which they gave the last full measure of devotion—that we here highly resolve that these dead shall not have died in vain—that this nation, under God, shall have a new birth of freedom—and that government of the people, by the people, for the people, shall not perish from the earth.

Silence when he finished. A hesitant, awkward silence. Was the audience moved? Or disappointed? Had they been expecting more?

"Lamon, that speech won't scour!" he whispered as he sat back down.

Then the applause started, deep and sustained, building as it swept through the crowd, rolling across the vast battlefield, across the opened and unopened graves. When it was done, three long cheers went up to the crystalline autumn sky, and he knew his words had struck home.

A dirge from a choir. A benediction from the president of Gettysburg College. An artillery salute and somber recessional. The column of dignitaries slowly made its way back into town. Men uncovered their heads as the president passed, women clasped hands to their breasts, and it seemed to Abraham that the faces wore thoughtful looks.

That evening, he boarded a train for Washington and left the people of Gettysburg to finish the task of burying the dead.

CHAPTER 38

NOVEMBER AND
DECEMBER 1863

*H*e issued a proclamation fixing the last Thursday in November 1863 as a national day of Thanksgiving. Even in civil war, there were blessings to be grateful for. The fighting had not stopped the work of the ax or the plow. Harvests were bountiful. On the far end of Pennsylvania Avenue, engineers were hoisting a twenty-foot statue of Armed Freedom, a woman holding a sheathed sword, to the top of the new Capitol dome. Whenever he saw the colossal dome taking shape amid the tower of scaffolding, it gave him hope that the Union would go on.

From Chattanooga came news to be thankful for. Grant's armies won a fierce battle above the clouds on the heights of Lookout Mountain, then stormed up Missionary Ridge to drive the rebels toward Atlanta. Tennessee lay firmly in Union hands. The gateway to the lower South had swung open.

Someone sent a turkey to the White House to be fattened for a holiday feast. Tad quickly made friends with the bird, which he named Jack. It was hard not to laugh whenever he came tromping across the lawn with Jack following like a pet.

One morning, the boy came bolting into a cabinet meeting with tears on his cheeks.

"They'a going to kill Jack!" he wailed. "You have to stop them, Papa-day!"

Abraham halted the meeting to put down the riot. "Jack was sent here to be eaten," he explained.

"I can't help that! He's a good tu'key, and we mustn't kill him!"

"Don't you think he wants to make us a nice dinner?"

"It would be wicked to kill him!"

The cabinet peered at the chief executive. Seward leaned back and puffed merrily on his cigar. Chase's right eye brightened under its sagging lid. Even Stanton, who did not suffer interruptions lightly, hid a smile behind a handkerchief while he polished his spectacles.

"Son, you've eaten turkeys before."

"Not Jack! You have to stop them, Papa-day! You'a the p'esident. You can save him!"

There was no choice. He wrote a reprieve on a card: "The turkey Jack is pardoned, and his life is to be spared." The boy scampered away with the order to save his friend.

There was something to be thankful for, too: a son with compassion for street urchins and mothers of soldiers and turkeys doomed to the chopping block.

Sad news dampened the first family's holiday spirits. General Benjamin Hardin Helm, husband of Mary's sister Emilie, had been killed fighting for the Confederates at Chickamauga. Word came that Emilie was desperate to leave Atlanta, where she had gone for Ben's funeral, and get back to her home in Kentucky. Abraham telegraphed a pass so she could get through the Union lines. She made it as far as Fort Monroe, in Virginia. Officials there detained her when she refused to take an oath of loyalty to the United States, insisting that it would be treason to her dead husband. Someone had enough wits to telegraph the White House to ask what they should do. Abraham wired back at once: "Send her to me."

She arrived two days later with her young daughter, Katherine. Two waifs, broken and stunned. Emilie hid behind deep layers of black. Mary rushed to her, and the sisters held onto each other while they wept.

"Thank you for helping us," Emilie cried. "I know our being here causes difficulties for you."

"That's not true!" Mary said. "You are always welcome in our home, wherever we are."

They made a tour of the mansion to help her feel welcome. In the Red Room, they showed her the portrait of George Washington that Dolly Madison had saved from the oncoming British in the War of 1812.

"Dolly's first husband was a Todd," both sisters said at once.

"So I've been told a few times," Abraham said, and they all managed smiles.

They talked of anything but war: old family stories about how the Todds had helped settle Kentucky; friends in Kentucky and Illinois; a visit Emilie had made to Springfield nine years before, when she was nineteen and the belle of every ball.

"Do you remember that velvet bonnet with white plumes I gave you?" Mary asked.

"Yes."

"You were a picture of loveliness when you put it on. Whatever happened to it?"

"I don't know," Emilie murmured. "So many things have been lost now."

Abraham built a fire in the Prince of Wales room, and they put her to bed with Katherine.

"It breaks my heart to see her face so creased and worn," Mary whispered. "She used to be so pretty and full of life. All the boys clustered around her."

"Yes," he said. It made him sad to realize that anyone seeing Mary for the first time in several years would think the same.

She did all she could in the following days to distract her little sister. They took a few carriage rides but mostly stayed inside, away from the public gaze. Whenever Abraham found them talking, Mary had on a cheerful face. But he knew that, behind closed doors, they were weeping over their dead together. Knew from an awkward strain in the house that they could not open up to each other as freely as they would like, that each steered clear of so much that could be said. The rebellion had come between them.

The first chance he had, he pulled Emilie aside. "I worry about Mary," he said. "Her nerves have gone to pieces."

"She's suffered as much as anyone," Emilie said cautiously. "She makes her best effort to lift all our spirits."

"She can't hide the strain from me. It's been too much for her."

"She does seem very nervous." She groped for words. "There is fright in her eyes."

She's right, he thought. There is fright in her eyes, even when she smiles.

"She worries a great deal about you, too," Emilie said. "She says you always look tired."

"We're all tired."

"She's afraid that new sorrows will be added to those we already bear. If anything should happen to you or Bob or Tad, it would kill her."

I wish I could take her away from here, he thought. It's become nothing but a house of sorrow for her. But he said: "It's good for her to have you with her. Stay with her as long as you can."

The divided loyalties were hard to ignore. One evening, Tad and little Katherine settled down beside the fire in the library to look at some photographs. Tad showed off one of himself in his army uniform, looking as sharp as McClellan ever could. Then one of his father seated at a table, looking pensive.

"This is the p'esident," he commented, proudly.

Katherine looked at the picture and shook her head. "No, that is not the president," she said with certainty. "Mr. Davis is the president."

Tad gazed at her for a minute, trying to remember if he had ever seen such a dimwitted girl. "Ev'one knows Mistuh Lincoln is p'esident," he explained.

"No, he's not. He's not my president."

"Who told you that?"

"My mother, that's who."

Tad got to his feet. "Mistuh Lincoln is p'esident!" he shouted.

"Mr. Davis is!"

"Hu'ah for Abe Lincoln!"

"Hurrah for Jeff Davis!"

The boy ran to his father. "Papa-day, Kathe'ine says you a' not p'esident!"

Abraham glanced at Mary and Emilie. The sisters put on half-amused, half-embarrassed smiles. He pulled the boy onto a knee.

"Well, Tad, you know who is your president." He pulled Katherine onto the other knee. "And I am your little cousin's Uncle Abraham." He gathered the belligerents closer and tickled them both until they laughed and forgot their quarrel.

The next evening brought a visit from two friends. One was General Daniel Sickles, who had lost a leg at Gettysburg but was more famous for shooting his wife's lover, Philip Barton Key, son of the author of "The Star-Spangled Banner," in Lafayette Square, across the street from the White House. The other was Senator Ira Harris of New York, a plodding fellow with a broad, likeable face, a good ally on Capitol Hill. They asked to meet Emilie, who reluctantly agreed.

"I told Senator Harris that you were here from the South," Sickles said pleasantly. "We hope you can give him news of his old friend, General Breckinridge."

"I have not seen General Breckinridge for some time," Emilie said stiffly. "I can give you no news of his health."

"Well, what news can you give us?" Harris asked. "Are we close to the end?"

"I'm not sure what you mean. The end of what?"

"The rebellion. Are your rebel friends close to surrender?"

"I can assure you, sir, I've heard no talk of surrender." Her voice was trembling.

Harris's face darkened a shade. "Well, we've whipped them at Chattanooga. And I hear, madam, that the scoundrels ran like scared rabbits."

"It was the example, Senator Harris, that you set them at Manassas."

The room froze. Harris looked at Sickles, then at Abraham. "Do you have any sons, Mrs. Helm?" he asked, coldly now.

"Why do you ask?"

"I was wondering if you are raising more rebels to fight against their country."

Mary intervened. "Senator Harris, Mrs. Helm has suffered a grievous loss—"

"I have one son, and he is fighting for his country," Harris interrupted. "I believe that that every young man should fight for his country, don't you, Mrs. Lincoln?"

Mary's face turned white with rage. "If you are alluding to our son Robert, sir—"

"I allude to no one in particular." He turned back to Emilie. "But I can tell you, madam, that if I had twenty sons, they should all be fighting the rebels."

"And if I had twenty sons, Senator Harris, they would all be opposing yours," Emilie shot back.

She turned and stumbled out of the room. Mary hurried after her, glaring over a shoulder. The general and senator turned toward the president.

"The child has a tongue like the rest of the Todds," Abraham offered.

Sickles stumped across the room and slapped a table. "You should not have that rebel in your house," he barked.

It was too much. Abraham pulled himself up to his full height.

"Excuse me, General, my wife and I are in the habit of choosing our own guests," he said. "We don't need advice or assistance from our friends in the matter. Besides," he added, "she came because I ordered her to come. It was not of her own volition."

The men left quickly, no doubt with a story to tell. Emilie came to Abraham early the next morning.

"My being here has become a trouble for you," she said. Her voice was still trembling.

"It's nothing we can't handle," he told her. "We want you to stay."

"I want to go. I'm longing for Kentucky."

"Yes, of course." His heart sank. Mary would be crushed. "Perhaps you could come back this summer and stay with us at the Soldiers' Home," he said. "It's quieter there. We get few visitors."

"That's very kind of you," she said. They both knew it was an impossible request.

"I'll give you a pass," he conceded. He wrote it out quickly and handed it to her. There was no point in bringing up the oath of loyalty. She would never sign one, especially after what Harris had said.

"Little Sister, I never knew you to do a mean thing in your life," he said gently. "I know you won't embarrass me in any way when you arrive in the South." It pained him to have to say it.

"I'll never do anything to betray your kindness," she said quietly.

"You know, I tried to keep Ben with me. I offered him a commission. I hope you don't blame me for all this sorrow."

"Of course not," she said. "Ben was always grateful to you. He felt bound to side with his own people."

She left the next day. Abraham tried to distract Mary with a performance of *Henry IV* at Ford's Theater. They made themselves laugh at the carousing of fat old Falstaff, but it was hollow laughter.

> *So shaken as we are, so wan with care,*
> *Find we a time for frighted peace to pant*
> *And breathe short-winded accents of new broils*
> *To be commenced in strands afar remote. . . .*

CHAPTER 39

FEBRUARY 10, 1864

wo nights before his fifty-fifth birthday, at about eight-thirty, as he finished reading a stack of reports from the battle fronts, he looked out a window in the direction of the Treasury Department and saw a glow that should not have been there. Yellow against black sky, quivering between stark tree limbs. He grabbed his coat and hurried downstairs, buttoning as he went.

A bell clanged, then another, tolling danger. He stepped outside. An acrid smell was moving across the front lawn. A guard stood on the portico, looking east.

"Where's the fire? What's burning?" Abraham asked.

"I don't know. I think maybe the stable."

He ran down the porch steps and along a dark path. The guard followed. The path turned at a low boxwood hedge, but he kept going straight and went over the hedge in an easy leap, without breaking stride.

Smoke filled the White House stable yard. The two-story brick structure was ablaze: flames on the roof, black smoke pouring from the top row of arched windows and the cupola. A crowd had already gathered. Shadowy forms clustered at the edge of the yard, keeping a safe distance, staring almost dreamily. A fire crew had arrived with a pump, but the machine stood idle. No one was moving.

The big double-door was closed. No animals in sight.

"Are the horses out?" Abraham shouted at a group of soldiers.

They looked back at him, uncertain. "I don't think so," one of them said.

"Why not?"

Again, dumbfounded looks. "Ain't no way to get them out," one of them suggested.

My God, he thought. The boys' ponies.

He pushed through the crowd, into a wave of heat. Thick smoke billowed across the building's front. It enveloped him, stung eyes and lungs. He stumbled forward, groping. Where was the door? It would be hot. He jerked off his coat, wrapped it around his hands, seized a handle. It would not give. He tried the other one, but it too held back. It scorched his hands through the coat. He kicked savagely at the timbers, seized a handle again, and pulled with all he had. The door crashed open.

The world was suddenly on fire. A blast of heat rolled over him, then a long roar as if something were rushing up out of the earth. The whole barn was trembling, full of bursts of wood ripping apart.

He backed up, gasping, trying to see through the smoke and fire. Inside, an inferno, all red, like the midst of a stove. A pile of hay burned furiously, a thousand pieces of lighted grass whirling into the air. Stalls on fire, skeletons of carriages on fire. The loft was burning. Flames dropped from the ceiling.

Where were the ponies? The horses? He heard screams, almost human. Frantic cries, high and tremulous, coming from somewhere behind the sheets of red. The horses were kicking at the stalls. Mixed with their shrieks, a mournful bleating. Tad's goats.

The soldiers were around him now, hands on his arms, pulling him back.

"Let go!" He coughed the words out.

The crowd was yelling for him to get back.

"You can't reach them!" a captain shouted at him. A man used to gauging the odds of battle. "No man can survive going in there."

They pulled him back further.

"This could be a trick," the captain argued. An urgent tone in his voice. "Someone may have set this fire to draw you into the open. We've got to get you back in the house."

He was too numb to resist. He needed to get away from those pitiful cries. The guards led him through the crowd and back up the dark path to the White House.

Mary stood in the East Room, looking out a window. She turned when she heard him come in. There were tears on her face.

"Are they all gone?" she asked.

He nodded, unable to speak. She put her head on his chest and cried silently for a while, shaking. He looked out the window at the glow of the fire. It was brighter now. Tears started down his own cheeks.

She stopped shaking, jerked her head up and peered at him. There was sudden venom in her eyes.

"This was on purpose!" she cried.

"We don't know that."

"I do know it! I know who did it! It was McGee."

"Who?"

"McGee. My coachman. I fired him this morning."

Abraham gaped at her. "Why?"

"The man was insolent and lazy! I'd ride a mule before I'd let him drive me again. He was never once ready on time!"

"That doesn't mean he burned down the stable."

"Oh, he did, I promise you he did. To get back at me. He's a low-down cur!"

"I can't believe he'd do such a thing."

"Have him arrested!" she cried. "Interrogate him! Make him confess! You'll see."

Maybe it was true. There was no telling what she could have said to the man to make him take revenge.

"I'll have the police look into it," he sighed.

"This town is filled with our enemies!"

"Shsh, don't say that, Mary. It does no good to speak of enemies."

Tad was suddenly there, pulling at Abraham's sleeve. The commotion outside had roused him, and he had come down from his bedroom.

"What is it? A' the 'ebels coming, Papa-day?" He peered out the window.

Abraham and Mary looked at each other. There was no way to hide it from him. Better he hear it from them, before he saw the charred ruins. Abraham stooped and took his son into his arms.

"No, the rebels aren't coming," he said gently. "There's been a fire. The stable is burned."

Tad blinked at him, trying to comprehend. "Is my pony safe?" he asked.

"No, my boy. Your pony is gone." He struggled to keep his voice steady.

The little face quivered. "Was he bu'ned up?"

"He died in the fire."

The child let go a cry of anguish worse than the shrieks of the doomed beasts. He crumpled in his father's arms. Mary sobbed quietly.

"What about my goats?" he pleaded. "What about Nanko and Nanny?"

"They're gone. All the animals are gone."

"Why couldn't they get out?"

"The fire was too quick. We tried, but we couldn't save them."

Wails of grief filled the room. Tad buried his head and shook all over. Abraham rocked him and stroked his hair.

"Wha-what about Willie's pony? Is Willie's pony d-dead too?"

"Yes, my boy, he is. I'm sorry."

"Willie's p-pony is dead! P-Po,' po' pony!"

"We'll get a new pony," Abraham said. "And we'll get some baby goats."

"Willie is d-dead, and now his pony's dead too!"

"He's gone to where the good ponies go."

"He's gone, just like Willie!"

The boy threw himself on the floor in convulsions, and no matter what Abraham said, he would not be consoled.

∽✦∽ CHAPTER 40 ∽✦∽

MAY AND JUNE 1864

I t was time to bring Ulysses S. Grant east and see if he could do what no other general had been able to do—crush Robert E. Lee's army. Congress passed legislation reviving the rank of lieutenant general, the same rank George Washington himself had held, and Abraham summoned Grant to the capital to assume command of all Union armies.

He arrived during a White House reception. Abraham heard a buzz of excited voices and noticed a stir on the far side of the Blue Room. The crowd parted, like the waters of the ancient sea. A stoop-shouldered, brown-whiskered man in a rumpled uniform approached.

Abraham smiled and stepped forward, hand out. "Why, here is General Grant! Well, this is a great pleasure, I assure you!"

"An honor to finally meet you, sir." A voice modest in tone, almost shy. He returned Abraham's gaze directly with penetrating blue eyes.

The crowd pressed in, men jockeying for handshakes. Seward took charge, introduced the general all around, shepherded him into the East Room, where more people waited. Cheering started, a cry of "Grant! Grant! Grant!" Ladies climbed onto chairs to catch a glimpse of the hero of Vicksburg and Chattanooga. Seward convinced his charge to mount a sofa so everyone could see him, and there the general stood, perspiring and bowing precariously in the thick of commotion. Not even McClellan had caused that kind of stir when he first came to Washington.

Maybe this is a bad sign, Abraham thought. No, it's all right. McClellan glories in adoration. Grant looks like he'd rather be fired out of a mortar than stand there on a White House couch.

It was an hour before the crush ended and they could talk in private. They sat and sized each other up, two Illinois men, the commander-in-chief and his new general-in-chief. Grant lit a cigar, slouched in his chair a bit, and puffed in relief to have escaped the hullaballoo. His clothes smelled of cigars and campfires, horses and sweat-soaked columns of infantry.

"I realize I'm not a military man," Abraham began. "I don't pretend to know anything about handling troops or waging campaigns."

"Yes, sir."

"I've never wanted to interfere with our generals, but there have been times when procrastination has forced me to issue military orders."

"I understand."

"All I've ever wanted was someone who would take responsibility and act."

Abraham leaned forward. He wanted to be clear on this next point.

"I do have enough common sense to know that swift action is an absolute necessity," he said. "While whole armies sit around, waiting for opportunities to turn up, this government is spending millions of dollars every day. There are limits to the sinews of war, and we may reach a time when the spirits and resources of our people will be exhausted."

"We are in complete agreement." Grant puffed resolutely on his cigar.

"Good, good."

Abraham leaned back, studied the face before him, liked what he saw. Something thoughtful, sensitive in the lines around the eyes. Men who knew Grant said he had never been able to make much of himself in life outside of the army, but it wasn't for lack of perseverance. Said he was the son of an Ohio tanner. A mediocre student at West Point, but had served bravely in the fighting in Mexico. Had later resigned his commission amid rumors of too much drinking. Married to the daughter of a Missouri slave holder, and had once owned a slave himself, but had freed him. Had built a house with his own hands, which he named "Hardscrabble." Right before the war, he had ended up in Galena, Illinois, working for his father in a leather shop. After Fort Sumter, he had found his way back into the army.

"Let us talk strategy," Abraham said. "What do you have in mind?"

It was Grant's turn to lean forward. Now there was doggedness in the blue eyes. "My general plan is to concentrate all possible force against the rebel armies in the field," he said. "A simultaneous movement all along the line."

"Excellent."

"We must employ all the force of all our armies, continually, without relenting so the rebels can have no rest from attack and cannot shift forces from one place to another to shore up their defenses. That's the way to wear them down."

Finally, Abraham thought. Someone who understands how to use our superiority in numbers.

"Even if an army is not fighting," Grant said, "it must advance while others are fighting, and force the enemy to commit detachments at that point."

"That's right. As we say out West, if a man can't skin, he must hold a leg while someone else does."

Grant turned to a map spread out on the table beside them. "I propose a combined offensive which I believe will meet your objectives," he said. "General Meade and I will assault Lee head-on, pushing him south through Virginia toward Richmond. General Sigel will drive up the Shenandoah Valley, to Lee's west, while General Butler will advance from the east, up the James River." He swept his arm over the map as he talked. "General Sherman will move toward Atlanta and slice through Georgia, while General Banks advances on Mobile."

"Very good," Abraham nodded. "When do you plan to commence?"

"Within two months, I'd say. I'll leave for the field right away to begin preparations."

"Good, good." He struggled to contain his elation. It was exactly the sort of offensive he wanted. Now, if Grant could only accomplish in the field what he proposed on the map.

"You can't leave quite yet, you know," he said, taking a lighter tone. "Mrs. Lincoln is planning a dinner in your honor."

Grant shifted uneasily. "I'm sorry. It's impossible for me to remain."

"But we can't excuse you, General. It would be the play of *Hamlet* with Hamlet left out."

Grant knocked the ashes off his cigar. The shyness was returning. "I appreciate the honor Mrs. Lincoln would do me. But time is very precious just now. And really, Mr. President, I believe I've had enough of the show business. Standing on that sofa was the warmest campaign I've been through."

He's a true field commander, Abraham thought. Not like some of these armchair generals.

"You're right, of course," he said. "More pressing matters await you."

They rose and shook hands.

"We all pray for your success," Abraham said.

"Thank you, I'll need your prayers." The general smiled for the first time. "Mrs. Grant says I'll succeed because I'm too obstinate to lose."

"Give Mrs. Grant my regards, and tell her I've been trying to scare up an obstinate man. If there is anything wanting that's in my power to give, don't fail to let me know."

"I'll do the best I can with the means at hand," he promised, and he was quickly gone.

Winter snows melted, roads thawed, and the great spring offensive began. Grant and the Army of the Potomac crossed the Rapidan River and disappeared into the Wilderness, a stretch of Virginia tangled with scrub oaks, jack pines, and cedars, where Lee's army lay waiting. Abraham paced corridors day and night, hands clasped behind him, head down, black rings under his eyes. For three days, no word came on what was happening. It was as if Grant had crawled down into a hole, lowered the ladder, and pulled in the hole after him.

Reports of terrible fighting trickled out of Virginia. It was a new kind of warfare, ghastly and unrelenting. Two armies thrashed blindly in the smoke-filled Wilderness, blundered through a maze of swamps and ravines, fired into thickets without knowing who they were shooting at. The underbrush caught fire, and the woods filled with the terrified shrieks of wounded men who lay watching as flames crept toward them. Grant lost over seventeen thousand troops but could not break through Lee's lines, so he marched around the enemy's right flank and pushed south toward Richmond.

He ran into Lee again at Spotsylvania Court House. Men scrambled over breastworks slippery with blood, stabbed each other through gaps between logs, hurled bayoneted rifles like spears into trenches where the dead piled up three and four deep. Grant lost another eighteen thousand troops but kept pushing south. He sent word back to Washington: "I propose to fight it out on this line if it takes all summer."

At Cold Harbor, Virginia, Union troops pinned names and addresses to their uniforms in dread of what was to come. They threw themselves at the Confederate trenches, and seven thousand fell in one day. In Washington, the dirge of the steamboat whistles played as the dead and maimed arrived at the Sixth Street wharves. Ambulances clogged the streets. Across the Potomac, on the heights of Arlington, where Robert E. Lee's columned mansion stood, green hillsides turned brown with the earth of fresh graves. The North shuddered at the carnage.

"Grant is a butcher!" Mary cried during one of their afternoon carriage rides. "He's not fit to be at the head of an army."

"At least he's moving forward," Abraham observed.

"Yes, and in the process, he loses two men to the enemy's one."

No, not two to one, he thought. But close enough to make us all wonder if it's really worth the cost.

"The rebels are determined," he reminded her. "There's no way to beat them without losses. Grant knows that."

"The man has no regard for life," she scoffed. "If he keeps this up, he'll depopulate the North."

He rubbed his temples. Mothers and wives across the country were no doubt saying the same thing about Grant—and about Abraham Lincoln.

"Grant's our best hope," he said. "He has the grit of a bulldog. Once let him get his teeth in, and nothing can shake him off."

"I could lead an army just as well myself. According to his tactics, there's nothing under the heavens to do but march a line of men up to a rebel breastwork to be shot down as fast as they get there, and keep marching until the enemy grows tired of the slaughter."

He smiled wearily. "Well, Mother, supposing we give you command of the army. No doubt you'd do much better."

She ignored the comment. "I know what he thinks! He thinks he'll be president someday. I can tell you this, if that man is ever elected president of the United States, I'll leave the country!"

Grant kept moving south, through the swamps of the Chickahominy River, where McClellan had failed two years before, then across the James River to swing around Richmond and take aim at the rail lines supplying it from the south. For four days, he hammered the earthworks protecting the town of Petersburg. He lost several thousand more men before settling in for a siege.

Summer came on. In Washington, the heat rolled in waves across the hills along the Potomac. The odor of tidal flats and refuse in the canal hung about the city, a rotting smell of swamp water and gunpowder and death. The days grew longer, and when the sun finally went down, it was hard to fall asleep. At night, when everyone else was in bed, Abraham paced the corridors, picturing in his mind the dying and wounded, and agonizing over the awful arithmetic of the war. Sometimes he slipped outside and wandered the dark streets of Washington alone, or walked the banks of the Potomac River the way he had once tromped alongside the Ohio River in Indiana and the Sangamon in Illinois, gazing into currents and thinking hard.

If the North could stand it, the war could be won through horrible slaughter. He knew that. Grant knew it, too. That was a ruthless, hard fact. The North could afford to keep losing men this way; the South could not. The South was bleeding to death. Grant could go on attacking, inflicting damage on Lee, even though the Army of the Potomac sustained even greater losses. The North could go on losing men and replacing men, day after day, until Lee's army would be wiped out to the last man, and the Army of the Potomac would still be a mighty host, and the war would be over. At a cost of rivers of human blood.

And then there is this, he thought. Grant is in the field, ordering all those men to their deaths. But I am the one who sent him there, who has demanded victory. In the end, their suffering is on my hands.

He paced the White House corridors, searching for answers and causes. Sometimes he fell to his knees for a while, searching more, then rose, overcome by sadness, and resumed his pacing.

CHAPTER 41

SUMMER 1864

From time to time, old friends from Illinois made the long trip to Washington to say hello. Whenever one showed up, Abraham made room in his schedule for reminiscing and storytelling. Mary was always welcoming, too. Their life in Springfield was so far away now, even though they had been gone not even four years. Old friends brought memories of the town square and cornfields under prairie skies.

Billy Herndon, his law partner, came to see him and stayed several days. So did Mary's cousin John Todd Stuart, who had urged Abraham to study law and given him his start as a young attorney in Springfield. And portly Judge David Davis, who had ridden the Eighth Circuit with him, laughed at his jokes from the bench, and managed his campaign for the presidency.

Most of the time, visitors wanted something besides a chance to see the White House, like appointments for friends or contracts to do business with the government. Abraham suspected he would do the same if in their shoes and obliged as best he could. He made David Davis an associate justice of the Supreme Court, partly from a sense of obligation, and partly because he figured that a man who could cut through arguments over stolen hogs and bad horse trades could handle the United States Constitution.

One day, Old Edward the doorkeeper brought word that a man who claimed to be a relation from Illinois was demanding to see him, and the next thing Abraham knew, his cousin Dennis Hanks was standing in his office, grinning.

"I woke up with an itch on top of my head and told myself I'd have good luck today," Dennis grinned. "And here you are."

"Mighty poor good luck, Denny," Abraham grinned back.

They clasped hands and gave each other bear hugs. His cousin was dressed in a stiff jean suit, made just for the occasion. His hair had mostly grayed, and the skin of his neck was beginning to look wizened, but his eyes flashed with wit and fun. They talked of old times in Indiana, of going to mill and shucking corn and writing with buzzard quills, and of their cousin John Hanks. Mostly they talked of Abraham's stepmother, Sally Lincoln.

"She's getting mighty feeble, Abe," Dennis said. "Her mind wanders sometimes, back to days when you was just a boy reading books on tree stumps."

"I wish I could get back to see her," Abraham said wistfully. "I will as soon as this damned war is over." A surge of guilt and sadness came over him. He spent so much time worrying over troop movements and casualty lists, so little thinking of the woman who had raised him.

"She fears she'll never see you again. She must have asked me a hundred times to remember her to you when I got here."

"I'll write her more often," he promised. "I'll write her a good, long letter to send back with you. Do you make good use of the money I send for her?"

"She cries like a child every time we show her a check. We take good care of her, Abe, as best we can."

His cousin had come on somewhat official business. Bad feelings over the war had led to a riot in Charleston, Illinois, with several dead or hurt by the time it was over. Fifteen of the instigators had been imprisoned at Fort Delaware. The people of Coles County had sent Dennis to Washington to see if the president might release their friends.

"They're good old boys, Abe," Dennis explained. "Most are gentle as a babe in a cradle, when not drinking. They're needed at home, and there's no sense in keeping them locked up."

Abraham sent for Stanton to see what could be done. The secretary of war appeared, glared at Dennis, snorted that every damned one of the prisoners ought to be hung, and stomped away.

"He's a frisky little Yankee, ain't he?" Dennis said. "Why don't you spank him and kick him out?"

"If I did, it would be hard to find another man to fill his place. Don't worry, Denny. I'll work on him."

Dennis stayed a few days to lounge about the office and chuckle at the workings of government. When it was time for him to go, they traded words they must have traded a hundred times in younger days.

"Well, Abe, I see you got yourself some books here."

"The things I want to know are in books, Denny. My best friend is a man who can get me a book."

"I swear there's something peculiarsome about you, Abe. Mighty peculiarsome."

His old friend Josh Speed came to visit, too. He arrived from Kentucky as hot weather came on in earnest, just after Mary had moved the household from the White House to the cottage at the Soldiers' Home for the third time in as many summers. Abraham sat with him in the parlor at dusk, sifting memories in faded light: their first meeting nearly three decades before on the day Abraham had arrived in Springfield with seven dollars and a couple of law books in his saddlebags, and Josh had immediately befriended him; the nights they had stayed up late talking about Abraham's courtship of Mary Todd; the time Abraham paid a visit to Farmington, the Speed plantation in Kentucky, and had been astounded to discover that he got a bedroom all to himself.

"You look tired, Speed," Abraham said after a while, with the casual honesty good friends can use. "Though I don't wonder why. No one's worked harder to rally Kentuckians' support for the Union."

"You don't look too fresh yourself. If I didn't know how strong you are, I'd be worried."

"Oh, I never feel good these days. Sometimes I worry a little about it. My hands and feet are always cold. Just feel my hand."

"It's overwork. You're exhausted."

"I suppose. But there's nothing to do about it."

They sat quiet for a moment, thinking of the strain of the last few years. Josh motioned to a Bible on a nearby table.

"You stay profitably engaged when not fighting rebels," he observed.

"Yes, it is profitable," Abraham smiled.

"Do you remember that my mother once gave you a Bible when you visited us at Farmington?"

"Yes, it was an Oxford Bible. She said it would help me with my troubles. It's taken me many years to discover how right she was."

"I'm sorry to say I haven't made the same discovery. I have too many doubts."

"You're wrong, Speed," Abraham said gently. "Take all of this book on what reason you can, and the balance on faith, and you will live and die a happier and better man."

"You may be right. I want to think so."

The night sounds began outside—a chorus of tree toads and crickets filling the darkness. Abraham rose and lit a lamp.

"I don't pretend to understand why all this is happening to us, to this country," he said. "But I've come to see that some Divine purpose is at work. Three years of struggle, and the nation's condition is not what either party or any man devised. God alone can claim it. Surely He intends some great good to follow this mighty convulsion."

"I hope so. I have a hard time seeing that much good can come from it."

"No good at all?" Abraham smiled again. "Surely you see some."

"You mean the finish of slavery. Yes, in the end, that will be a relief. A relief for us all, no matter how hard the aftermath." It was a difficult admission for any slaveholder to make. "But emancipation by military proclamation is a bitter pill for Southerners to swallow. I have my doubts about it, as well."

"Give it some time, my friend. You'll see the harvest of good we'll glean from it."

Abraham sat back down and stretched his long legs until his feet went almost beyond the lamp's glow. His mind drifted back again to his younger days in Springfield, to a time in his life when he had been feeling very low.

"Josh, do you remember that once, when I was in a very bad state of mind, you were worried I was ready to give up living? I told you I felt like I'd never done anything to make anyone remember me."

"Yes, I remember."

"And I told you I planned to be around until I knew the world was a little better off for my having been in it."

"Yes."

"Well, Speed, I firmly believe that in the Emancipation Proclamation, my fondest hopes will be realized."

They both made an effort to steer the conversation away from the war. They talked late into the night, just as they used to do in the back of Josh's store in Springfield—about favorite lines of poetry, and how they used to worry over girls, and old political brawls with the likes of Steve Douglas. It was almost like old times, and for a brief while, Abraham felt happy.

CHAPTER 42

JULY 1864

A rebel force moved down the Shenandoah Valley toward Washington, and at first, no one panicked. The city had grown used to the idea of armies clashing nearby. It was probably a raiding party looking for shoes, socks, and whatever else the Confederates needed. The stout ring of forts around the capital would keep out any danger.

Then the telegraph wire from Harper's Ferry went dead. Bargemen floating down the C&O Canal to Georgetown brought word of gray columns in the mountain passes. It was General Jubal Early with fifteen thousand, maybe twenty, maybe even thirty thousand men. The rebels swept down on Hagerstown, Maryland, and demanded twenty thousand dollars to spare the town from burning. Frederick was next—they got two hundred thousand dollars from the terrified citizens there. The invaders met a Union force at the Monocacy River, sent it reeling toward Baltimore, then headed for Washington, forty miles away.

The defeat on the Monocacy threw the capital into turmoil. More telegraph wires went down. Trains from the north stopped running. Refugees from the countryside rumbled into town in wagons heaped with belongings, their cows and hogs lumbering behind. They told of seeing Confederate pickets just outside the District.

Abraham followed the vague reports coming out of Maryland and grew increasingly anxious.

"The forts will hold, won't they?" Seward asked him.

"It's not the forts I'm worried about, it's the men inside them. Grant has practically the whole Army of the Potomac below Richmond. The garrison here is mostly green. I'm not even sure they know how to work the heavy guns properly."

"I hate to say it, but right now I miss McClellan."

"I feel like a man trying to plug eleven leaks in his roof with ten fingers," Abraham confessed. "Every time I move a finger, water starts running in through the hole I left behind."

"What do we do?"

"I'll wire Grant and ask him to send what force he can."

The War Department called the city's male population to arms. Rifles were issued to government clerks. Wounded veterans picked themselves up from hospital beds and trudged to the ramparts. Stanton advised that it was too dangerous for the first family to sleep at the Soldiers' Home. They packed up in the middle of the night and returned to the White House. Abraham was appalled to learn that the navy had ordered a gunboat to stand by in the Potomac so they could flee, if it came to that.

He lay in bed wondering if it would be his last night in the mansion. If Early's troops managed to breach the defenses and enter the city, the Confederates surely would not be able to hold it for long. But they could do much damage in a day or two. If the rebels sacked the capital, it would terrorize the North. Grant would likely have to pull the army back from Petersburg. The South would gain the confidence it needed to fight on. Europe might finally decide to recognize the Confederacy.

Muffled booms of artillery woke him the next morning. The scattered firing lasted through breakfast—Early's skirmishers probing the strength of the garrison, no doubt. Abraham listened while he peeled and ate an egg. Each dull boom knocked away a little piece of the anxiety inside him and filled the space with indignation until he had had enough.

"I'm riding out to the lines," he announced to Mary.

"You'll do no such thing! That's absurd!"

"Don't worry, I'm not planning to enlist. I'm just going to show the colors—and find out for myself what's going on."

"You'll find out what a bullet tastes like, that's all," she scoffed. "The country doesn't expect you to hazard yourself like that."

"There are old men and invalids manning those trenches. I won't stay here cowering in the rear."

She perceived he was determined. "Well, then, I'm going with you," she said.

"Now you're the one being absurd."

"If you're going to be shot, Mr. Lincoln, I want to be shot as well. Don't argue with me. That's the end of it."

Good Lord, he thought, how does a woman plagued by headaches and spooked by thunder think she can stand the roar of a Parrott gun? Well, the old girl still had pluck in her when she got her back up. He was glad to see it. It was the old courage he had loved in her from the start.

"All right," he conceded. "But I want you to stay in a safe place."

They rode up the Seventh Street Turnpike, toward the sound of the firing, without a military escort. Abraham had sent the presidential bodyguard to help man the fortifications. It was a hot day. Dust hovered above the road and mixed with a sticky haze. Curtains were drawn across windows on the houses they passed. No sign of life in yards. They overtook some government workers walking north, headed for the front with rifles over their shoulders. An ambulance rattled the opposite way into town, followed by a wagon of forlorn refugees. Several militiamen, overcome by the heat, rested under a big walnut tree.

The artillery blasts grew louder as the carriage reached Fort Stevens, about a mile from the Maryland line. The coachman pulled up at the door of the fort's infirmary, and the first couple went inside. The surgeon in charge, a slender man with a long, clean-shaven chin, looked startled by their appearance. He rubbed the chin for an instant, then sent an orderly to fetch General Wright of the Sixth Corps. Mary began moving from bedside to bedside, offering words of encouragement.

A minute later, the general hurried into the room. It was a relief to see him. His men were veteran troops, dispatched by Grant. They had just landed at Washington's docks.

"The main body is coming up the turnpike now," Wright said. "It should be here any time. We need only hold off the rebels until it arrives."

"That's the best possible news you could bring us," Abraham beamed.

"Would you care to observe the action?"

"By all means."

He left Mary in the infirmary and followed Wright up an embankment to a parapet. From there he could see the layout of Fort Stevens—a stronghold of packed earth and timber with eleven big guns mounted on its walls. Trenches surrounded the ramparts and extended from the fort's sides to Fort DeRussy, west, and Fort Slocum, east. To the north, trees had been felled in a vast two-mile arc to clear the range for the gunners.

A crackle of picket fire drifted up from the field below. In the distance, a thin gray line was forming at the edge of the clearing. The general raised his field glass. An unexpected thrill surged up Abraham's back. Something was about to happen. General Wright gave a signal, and the fort's big guns erupted in fury.

The blasts shook the air like the roar of Niagara, only louder. A wave of hot black smoke rolled over the parapet, stung the eyes, burned the lungs. Abraham had been around cannon fire before, at reviews and demonstrations, but never like this, not this close. It pounded into his head, through his jaw, and down his back.

He looked at the soldiers around him to make sure it was all right. The gunners scurried about the heavy pieces, loading and firing, sweat pouring down powder-stained cheeks. Some wore big handkerchiefs over their noses and mouths. They worked rapidly, frantically, until General Wright gave another signal. All the guns stopped at once, leaving behind a sharp ringing in the ears. When the smoke cleared, the gunners began a round of slower, intermittent firing.

Across the field, little gray figures began to pick themselves up and move forward. Some lay writhing in places where the earth was scarred. Some lay still and would never move again. Rifle fire started in earnest, and little puffs of smoke flowered over the broken field.

Abraham stood watching, transfixed. It was almost like watching a play. The rebels ran with heads down, sometimes throwing themselves on the ground while a shell passed over their heads, then pushing forward some more. Union rifles snarled from the trenches outside the fort, and Confederate rifles snarled back.

"The Southerners fight bravely, don't they?" someone said. Abraham turned and discovered the surgeon from the infirmary standing beside him. Between the gunfire and ringing in the ears, the man's voice sounded far away. "They fight as though they are in the right, and we are in the wrong."

"No doubt they see it that way," Abraham answered. He spoke loudly to be heard over the firing, but his own voice, too, sounded distant.

"They've learned to fight like men defending their homes," the doctor observed. "Although today we're the ones defending our homeland."

A shell from one of the fort's big guns landed near a mass of rebels without exploding and went skidding across the ground, ripping away a man's arm as it hurtled by. The man whirled around, crumpled in a heap, then rose and staggered back and forth, as if looking for his lost arm. After a moment he ran toward the rear, flapping his remaining limb, until he lost his balance and fell face-forward.

So this is what war is, Abraham thought. And this isn't even a big battle. It's a terrible thing to see.

"I still have a hard time thinking of them as enemies," the doctor said, motioning toward the Confederate line. "They're our countrymen after all."

Yes, whether they know it or not, Abraham thought. Our countrymen.

"A good many of them are Virginians, I expect," the doctor mused. "My wife is a Virginian. I lived there for a while, in Winchester. I might even know some of those boys out there."

Over on the right, a rebel flag met a fresh volley and went down like a falling tree. Cheers broke out from the fort.

"Well, I suppose there's nothing awfully strange in it," the doctor went on. "Men have been fighting and killing men they know since the day Cain struck down Abel."

Abraham saw a rebel grab his chest and fall backwards. He landed on top of another body, and the two dead men lay back-to-back, one with his face in the dirt, the other with face upturned to the sky.

"Still, it's a hard thing to watch," the doctor said. "And hard to have to clean up the aftermath. I don't like looking into the eyes of young fellows in hospital beds. Some look back at you in a puzzled way, like you should be able to explain it to them."

A Parrott gun let out a shattering roar, and for a minute the doctor's mouth moved while no words came out, until the thunder and ringing faded, and Abraham could hear him saying, "But after a while you get used to it. That's the troubling thing, I suppose."

A bullet whizzed overhead, giving a little high-pitched song as it went by. They both flinched.

"There's something else you get used to—the sound of a Minie ball," the doctor laughed grimly. "Though they say you never hear yours coming."

More bullets snipped by. Some thudded into the ramparts and made little fountains of splinters and dirt. Confederate sharpshooters, firing from barns and farmhouses outside the fort, were trying to pick off the Union gunners. Abraham could see a little gray figure on a roof, crouched behind a chimney, taking aim. It still seemed like watching a play, a ghastly, blood-soaked tragedy.

"A soldier told me there's a Minie ball for every man in this war," the doctor said, "but that fortune is a strange quartermaster, and one man might be fighting in Tennessee when his Minie ball gets fired from a gun in Georgia, while another man might be fighting on the same field as the gun that fires his ball, and then it will find him."

The Union cannon took aim at the buildings where the sharpshooters were. A shell went flashing in a streak of red into a house, caving it in.

"Death will have his day, that's for certain," the doctor sighed.

The house disappeared in a tower of black smoke.

"*Richard the Second*," Abraham said.

"What?"

"It's from *Richard the Second*. 'Cry woe, destruction, ruin, and decay: the worst is death, and death will have his day.'"

"Really? I didn't know that. That's good to know." The doctor rubbed his long chin and watched the house burn. "Well, it's all in God's hands, is it not? We can only pray He'll make an end of all this soon."

"Amen to that."

A bullet came flying along, ricocheted with a zing off a cannon, and hit the surgeon in the left thigh. He cried out, swayed precariously, and sat down hard with an astonished expression. A private rushed over, saw the blood on his leg, and called for a stretcher. The doctor looked up, managed an embarrassed smile, and said, "Well, goodbye," as they carried him away.

Bullets filled the air now, whistling past Abraham's ears.

"Get down, you damn fool!" A captain glared at him, motioned for him to take cover. The young fellow looked like he wanted to come knock Abraham's tall black hat off his head. General Wright strode to Abraham's side.

"Mr. President, it isn't safe for you here. You must come down now."

Of course it's not safe, Abraham thought. It's not safe for anyone here. Why should I be safe when others are not?

"Mr. President, I am in command here," Wright said firmly, "and I order you to come down."

The soldiers nearby were gawking at them. He saw with sudden, painful clarity that he was making a nuisance of himself. And a target, no doubt.

"Of course, you're right, General. I'll take cover."

He stepped down and sat behind the parapet, out of harm's way. Wright gave him an incredulous look and went off to issue an order.

The fort's big guns blazed away, trying to keep Early's troops at a distance. The clatter of rifle fire floated over the top of the wall, mingling with distant yells. At times the battle raged, and sometimes there were lulls, as in a storm.

Every once in a while, when he thought General Wright was probably not looking, Abraham stood and took a quick look over the parapet. Fragmented lines of gray and blue lay on the torn field. Rifle barrels flashed in the sun, letting go ribbons of smoke. Near the fort, a body missing half its head sprawled at the edge of a trench. Another lay with arms spread wide. Its side looked like it had been clawed open by a bear.

On the far edge of the field, a horse made a sudden twisting leap, kicked its front legs in the air, and came down sideways on top of its rider. Little figures of men, covered with dust and grime, fired savagely at each other. Each shot seemed not a fight over a capital, or any constitution, or liberty, but a terrible little struggle for life and death.

A bugle called, and the main body of the Sixth Corps came marching up the turnpike. Ranks of seasoned veterans poured into the fort while cheers broke out from the garrison of clerks and mechanics. Abraham raised his hat and cheered with the rest. The Confederates, seeing fresh troops on the ramparts and in the trenches, began to fall back. There was no doubt now that the defenses would hold. Washington was again safe.

It was time to go, to get out of the way. Abraham offered thanks to Wright and a word of encouragement to the troops, then climbed into the carriage with Mary for the drive back to the White House. She looked relieved to get away, but if she was shaken by all the sound and fury, she said nothing about it.

Jagged, fleeting sights of battle settled into his mind as they rattled through the heat. Before today, he had seen men march off to war more times than he wanted, seen them return bloodied and torn, had sat beside them in hospitals while trying to keep his eyes off their ghastly wounds. Now he had seen men die on the battlefield, seen them go down with limbs blown away, their stomachs hanging out, gaping holes in their chests.

An unexpected image flashed into his mind, one from childhood, when he was eight years old in Indiana. One day a flock of wild turkeys had appeared outside the cabin. His father wasn't home, so he had asked his mother if could use Tom Lincoln's rifle. He took a ball out of the shot pouch, poured powder from the horn into the gun's long barrel, and rammed the ball and charge down with the hickory ramrod. Placing the barrel through a crack in the cabin wall, he pulled back the hammer, took careful aim, and squeezed the trigger. Then he ran outside and knelt to see what he had killed.

The great bird's fine, iridescent feathers lay shattered about the carcass. Blood much darker than the bright red wattles seeped from a gash in the breast. It stained the white in the wing feathers and matted the breast tuft. The grand chestnut-tipped tail looked crooked, like a crippled man's leg. It made him sad to see.

He had never since pulled a trigger on any larger game.

CHAPTER 43

AUGUST 1864

Yet weapons interested him. He found himself drawn to machines of war that could fire bullets faster, hurl shells further, move men with greater efficiency. In a way it was a perverse interest, he realized—to be fascinated with instruments of destruction when the thought of harming any creature gave him pain. But if a piece of ordnance could bring a speedier end to the fighting, lives might be saved.

Throughout the war, inventors sent him ideas for contraptions that they predicted would change the course of the war. Some were fantastical: boots shaped like little canoes to let troops march across the water; steel vests to protect soldiers from bullets and bayonet thrusts; ironclad balloons for floating artillery to battlefields. One invention showed promise—a gun that looked like a coffee mill stuck on wheels, with a crank on its side and a hopper on top. When a man turned the crank, rounds dropped out of the hopper and fired at a rate of more than a hundred a minute. Abraham ordered ten of the guns for the army, at thirteen hundred dollars apiece.

He enjoyed pouring over diagrams of new weapons. The same curiosity that, in years past, had made him ponder the innards of grist mills and invent his own device for floating steamboats off sandbars now led him to scrutinize the mechanics of detonators, gun carriages, and signal rockets. Whenever he got a chance, he rode to the Navy Yard or the Arsenal to observe a test firing of artillery. Sometimes he took Tad with him to watch the huge black shells go hurtling into the river, throwing up thirty-foot columns of spray while booms echoed over the tidal flats.

On summer evenings when work was done but there was still plenty of light, he liked to walk down to a ragged, weedy stretch of ground near the White House to shoot one of the new breech-loading rifles. It was strangely diverting, in the midst of war, to try his hand at hitting a target propped against a big woodpile a hundred yards away. The rifles were things of beauty, elegant in design, polished in craftsmanship. It was astounding how quickly they loaded, how accurately they shot compared to the old flintlocks of his childhood. His hands itched to take one apart, like one of Tad's toys, to see just how it worked.

One evening, he shot with John Hay until dusk, then walked to the White House stables to get a ride to the Soldiers' Home. The livery was deserted, so he saddled a horse, the one the guards had nicknamed Old Abe, mounted up, and started off alone. It was dark by the time he turned off the Seventh Street Turnpike onto Rock Creek Church Road. There was no moon, and the road was pitch black. It was hard to make out even the trees and low fences slipping past. But Old Abe knew the way, and Abraham's thoughts jogged along to the cadence of the horse's slow gait.

The behemoth iron guns and sleek rifles were portents, he knew, of a North where factories were only beginning a new system of mass production for spewing out trainloads of firearms, cloth, plows, clocks, pots, churns, scissors, and countless other products desired around the world. In reapers, sewing machines, and blasting apparatuses, America was on the rise as a great industrial and military power. That is, if he could hold the country together. If not, America would be known around the world for manufacturing a splintered people.

The summer of 1864 seemed to be one discouraging setback after another. Jubal Early's force had gotten away after retreating from Fort Stevens. His men had ridden into Chambersburg, Pennsylvania, demanded a ransom of a half million dollars in currency or a hundred thousand in gold, and burned the town when the citizens could not pay. Down in Georgia, William T. Sherman was leading a Union army toward Atlanta, but the Southerners were putting up a stiff fight, and progress had stalled.

In Virginia, Grant was bogged down before the Confederate trenches at Petersburg. His men had tried digging a five-hundred-foot tunnel and exploding four tons of gunpowder beneath the rebel line. A column of fire had shot into the air, carrying arms, legs, and torsos with it, and leaving a hole in the earth thirty feet deep. The Union troops that pushed into the crater found themselves trapped with Confederate fire raining down on them. Before it was over, four thousand Union boys had been killed or wounded, and the Confederate line had held.

If the military situation did not improve quickly, Abraham knew his presidency would in all likelihood soon be over. It was hard to believe, but the four years of his term were drawing to an end, and his reelection campaign loomed darkly. The Democrats planned to run George McClellan against him. It was Little Mac's revenge. If McClellan won, he would probably negotiate a peace that would recognize the South as a separate country.

The thought was too depressing to bear. He pushed it out of his mind. No, he must somehow win reelection and have a chance to win this war. It might take months of more bloodshed, but the North could win. There was no doubt of that. Then he must find a way to bring a bitter South back and reconcile it with a vindictive North. That would be even harder than winning the war.

A blast exploded out of the darkness, shattering his thoughts. The wind of a bullet skimmed past his ear.

The horse screamed and went into the air. Abraham felt himself going with it, leaving the saddle and being thrown very far and fast, tumbling backwards through space. When he came down, he was somehow back on the horse.

He threw his arms over the neck, flailing for the reins. The horse plunged up the road, galloping in a blind panic. Branches slashed by. He felt himself going out of the saddle again but yanked himself forward and grabbed hold of the reins. Feet groped to catch the tossing stirrups. He wrenched himself upright.

His mind raced. Just hang on, he thought. Let him run. No point in trying to stop him. He'll tire in a minute. Beginning to wheeze. Not used to moving this fast.

He squeezed the reins a little, relaxed, squeezed again, matching the rhythm of the horse's surges. They hurtled forward, instinct spurring the horse on. By the time they got up the hill to the Soldiers' Home, it was exhausted enough to bring under control.

They came through the gate at a fast trot. Abraham jumped off, breathing hard, and handed the reins to the sentinel.

"He came pretty near getting away with me, didn't he?" His voice was shaky. "He got the bit in his teeth before I could draw the rein."

The private looked at horse and rider uncertainly. "I heard a rifle shot," he said.

"Yes, some fool fired off a gun. It scared the horse."

The sentinel peered through the dark toward the bottom of the hill, then back at Abraham. Now he looked alarmed.

"You've lost your hat, sir," he said.

Abraham felt on top. Sure enough, his tall silk hat was gone. Of course it is, he thought, after all that.

"Must have jerked off when the horse reared," he said. "I'll likely spot it on the way into town tomorrow. Goodnight, son."

He went straight to bed and lay on top of the sheets, perspiring and shaking. The shock gradually wore off, and he tried to think it through. It was one thing to be under fire at Fort Stevens, where bullets were supposed to be. Something else for a shot to come alone, out of a dark place. There was something malevolent about it. Something solitary and watching in the night.

Early the next morning, the same private was waiting outside. He had a corporal with him. They both looked uneasy.

"We walked down the road and found your hat," the private said, fingering the wide brim. "You had a close call."

Abraham went rigid. There were two holes in the crown, where the ball had passed through.

"The shot was fired upward," the corporal said. He pushed a stick through the holes, to show the bullet's path. "Whoever fired it was close, probably hiding by the roadside."

He offered the hat back. Abraham took it, numbly.

"I'm sure it wasn't intended for me," he said, trying to sound unconcerned. "Most likely it was just someone with a careless finger on the trigger."

The guards shifted their feet, not convinced.

"I want to keep this quiet, boys," he said firmly. "There's no sense in anyone making a fuss over it. I especially don't want Mrs. Lincoln to worry. Do you understand?"

The soldiers glanced at each other before nodding.

"Can I trust you to say nothing about it?"

They nodded again. "Yes, sir."

When he got to the White House, he called Ward Hill Lamon to his office and quietly told him what had happened. The big Virginian's good-natured face turned dark.

"Damn it, Lincoln, I won't stand on ceremony!" he cried. "It's a damned fool thing to go without a military escort."

"I can't believe anyone would deliberately shoot at me," Abraham insisted.

"That's ridiculous. You know your life is in danger. You have enemies within our lines."

"It was probably an accident. Most likely just someone coming back from a day's hunt, firing off his gun for safety before reaching home."

"Are you serious?" Lamon snorted. "You can't really think that."

"I don't know what to think. Except that I'm minus an eight-dollar plug hat."

"Damn it, Lincoln, you've made me marshal of this district. I'm telling you—officially, as marshal—you can't go out unprotected."

"All right," he conceded, mainly to pacify his friend. "But, Hill, I made up my mind a long time ago that if anyone wants to kill me, he'll do it. If I wore a shirt of mail and locked myself in an iron cage, it would all be the same. There are a thousand ways to get to a man."

"You're not making any sense. First you say you can't believe anyone would shoot at you, then that there are a thousand ways to get to a man. Which is it?"

"I refuse to live in fear," Abraham said resolutely. "It is the unalienable right of every man to choose to be happy or miserable, and I for one choose the former."

"That's a devil of a poor protection against a gun in time of war. That fellow on the roadside was a philosopher like you. He exercised his right to make himself happy by trying to kill you. If you're not more careful, within a week you'll have no unalienable rights, and we'll have no Lincoln."

Lamon stalked off, muttering under his breath. Abraham rose and went to the old upright mahogany writing desk where he kept stacks of correspondence in pigeonholes. He picked up the bunch marked "Assassination Letters." Every one of them a threat against his life. He weighed the bundle in his hand.

Hill's right, of course, he thought. I really should be more careful. A few inches another way, and I wouldn't be here now.

He thought of the doctor hit at Fort Stevens. What was it he had said? There's a Minie ball for every man in this war, and if fate puts a man near the gun that fires it, the ball will find him.

He put the stack of letters back in the pigeonhole.

Well, whether it was aimed or not, he thought, that bullet last night wasn't mine.

CHAPTER 44

AUGUST TO
NOVEMBER 1864

*T*he Democrats were calling him Abraham Africanus the First and saying that his First Commandment was "Thou shalt have no other God but the Negro." They said he was a miserable failure, a cruel tyrant, a man without brains. Democratic editors wrote that "his face is that of a demon, cunning, obscene, treacherous, lying, and devilish." A second Lincoln term would bring four more years drenched in blood.

He did not care about their insults. But the closer the presidential election drew, the more he thought about a second term. He desperately wanted one, desperately wanted to finish the job he had started. If he lost reelection, and the South were allowed to break away, the nation might end up disintegrating into a half-dozen little dictatorships, republics in name only. The grand American experiment with democracy would be over. And his presidency would forever be viewed as a failure. The thought of it tortured him.

The Democrats nominated McClellan in the same Wigwam in Chicago where Abraham had won the Republican prize four years earlier. The North seemed in a mood to make the Young Napoleon the next president. He was still popular, especially with the soldiers. And the North was war-weary. Weary of slaughter and of losing. Millions were ready for peace at any price and convinced that McClellan would bring it. Besides, they told themselves, eight years of any man was too much. There had been no two-term president since the days of Andy Jackson.

Even Republicans were saying publicly that they doubted Lincoln could be reelected. More than a few urged him to get out of the way and let someone else run. Salmon Chase, his own treasury secretary, had gotten it into his head that he should be the next president. His strong will and machinations to promote himself had become so disruptive, Abraham finally had to accept his resignation from the cabinet. He hated to do it. Chase had done a brilliant job of finding ways to finance the war.

Defeat was coming. He could feel it, the way Billy Herndon could feel truth in his bones. He tried not to act discouraged about it and reminded those who asked about his chances that it was never a good idea to swap horses when crossing a stream.

Then came a telegram from General Sherman: "Atlanta is ours, and fairly won." The news electrified the North. Cannons fired hundred-gun salutes. Supporters came out of the woodwork, praising the steadfastness of Father Abraham and shouting, "No Peace without Victory!" A sullen *Richmond Examiner* reported that Atlanta's fall had come just in time to "save the party of Lincoln from irretrievable ruin."

By mid-October 1864, he was feeling more hopeful but still unsure. He scribbled two columns of electoral vote figures, making his best guess as to how each state would go, and added them up. It would likely be close, one way or another.

Election day came, dark and wet. The White House seemed strangely empty, as if people were avoiding the place. The streets of Washington were mostly deserted. Government employees had boarded trains and gone to their hometowns to vote. Abraham sat for a while with Mary in the family library, listening to the wind and rain. They both felt anxious.

"They say the Democrats in New York plan to keep Republicans away from the polls with guns," Mary fretted.

"Those kinds of reports usually turn out to be unfounded."

"I'm afraid we will lose, Abraham."

"Well, that's up to the people," he sighed. "If they turn their backs to the fire and get scorched in the rear, they'll have to sit on the blister."

"If you're defeated, I don't know what will become of us." She pulled on a strand of hair, grimacing as it left her scalp, and wound it around her finger. "I don't know how I will bear up. I've gone down on my knees to ask for votes again and again."

"You'll make yourself ill worrying too much, Mary. If I'm reelected, it will be all right. If not, we must bear the disappointment."

They distracted themselves with talk of past elections, both victories and defeats, for the Illinois statehouse, the Congress, the Senate, the presidency. No matter how it turned out, this one would be their last. Once the votes were counted, a part of the life they had shared for more than two decades would pass away.

They looked out the window at the rain, and their dim reflections in the pane made Abraham think of something that had happened four years earlier, though it seemed ages ago now.

"Have I ever told you how one night, not long before we left Springfield, I saw something very strange?"

He told how he had flopped down exhausted on the lounge in his room and found himself looking at an unearthly double-reflection of his face in the mirror on his bureau—one image vivid, the other dim and gray, like a ghost.

"I wonder if it was an omen," he said.

"I think I know what it means," she said after a minute. Her voice was hollow. "It's a sign you are to be elected to a second term, but the paleness of the second face is a sign that you won't live to see its end."

He winced. The same thought had crossed his mind. He should not have mentioned the incident.

"I'm not going to the trouble of getting reelected just so I can die in this old house," he smiled.

"Perhaps it's better if you're not reelected, after all."

The rain slackened a bit in the afternoon, and he went to his office to catch up on some correspondence. Tad bounded into the room, pulled him to the window, and pointed at the tents of the Pennsylvania soldiers quartered at the bottom of the lawn.

"Look, Papa-day, the soldia's a' voting fo' you!"

They were lined up in their blue cloaks and overcoats, waiting patiently in the cold drizzle to record their votes with commissioners sent from their home state.

"How do you know they're voting for me, son?" Abraham asked. "They might be voting for General McClellan, you know."

"No, they a' not," the boy said happily. "They a' voting fo' you. They told me so."

Tad's pet turkey, Jack, was with the soldiers. They had adopted him as a mascot. The bird strutted up and down the line as if reviewing the troops.

"Look at Jack," Abraham chuckled. "What business does he have stalking about the polls that way?"

"He's gua'ding the ballots, and making sua' the Democ'ats don't cheat."

"Does he vote?"

"No, he's not of age," Tad said solemnly.

The rain picked up again in the evening. At seven, Abraham and John Hay slogged through puddles and mud to the telegraph office at the War Department to get the election returns straight off the wire. Stanton and Welles were there, and a few military officials, along with several orderlies, clerks, and cipher operators, all waiting nervously as if for news from a battle.

The rainstorms had played havoc with the telegraph system, and the news was slow coming in. There were no reports of disturbances at the polls. That was good. Dispatches arrived from Baltimore and Philadelphia. They told of encouraging results there.

"You'll win," Hay said. His voice was full of swagger. "I'm certain of it."

"I'm far from being certain," Abraham said. "I wish I was certain."

He sent a messenger to the White House to deliver the first returns to Mary. "She's more anxious than I am," he said.

They traded predictions while they waited, listening with one ear for the chatter of the telegraph instruments.

"If they put you out, they're fools," Stanton growled. "That's all I can say." He polished his spectacles with his handkerchief and glared around the room as if looking for fools.

"Every client has to judge for himself whether his attorney is up to his expectations," Abraham said, trying to be stoic. "I've managed the case for the people to the best of my ability. If they decide my management is not satisfactory and want to put me out, I don't see that I can do anything but respect their judgment."

"I don't trust the people to make a sound judgment in these circumstances," Stanton retorted.

"I didn't say their judgment would be correct," Abraham said with a melancholy smile. "Only that I must respect it."

If I'm beat, it will sting more than a little, he thought. But at least the burdens of the last four years will be lifted off my back.

Rain beat against the windows. The wind picked up. Stanton called for a pot of coffee and passed out cups. It was too hot to gulp down, so the men blew on it and sipped.

"It has long been a grave question whether any government that is not too strong for the liberties of its people can be strong enough to maintain its own existence in great emergencies," Abraham mused between sips. "Tonight we'll give the world an answer to that question. We'll find out if a people's government can sustain a national election in the midst of civil war."

There was a lull in the dispatches until after ten o'clock, then the telegraphs sprang to life. The news was good—better, in fact, than he had allowed himself to hope for. His chest filled with elation as the returns clattered in.

Pennsylvania would go for him. So would Maryland, Indiana, Ohio, and New York. All of New England, and nearly the entire West—every loyal state, in fact, except Kentucky, Delaware, and New Jersey went for him. It was a solid victory, with no room for dispute.

The men grasped his hand and lit cigars. "Now I'm tolerably certain," he grinned to John Hay. He sent another messenger to the White House to give Mary the grand news.

He felt relieved, vindicated, and humbled all at the same time. Editors and politicians might not have faith in him, but the people did, as well as the soldiers. He could not have won so decisively without the soldiers' votes. On a day of gales and downpours, in a time of bloodshed, when anger and hate and betrayal had reached full tide, the people had gone to the polls, stood in line together, and deliberately cast their votes. The majority had decided to let him carry on, despite the failures, despite the criticisms and doubts. The people had spoken; the wheels and gears of democracy still ran. Government of the people would not perish from the earth—at least not yet.

Towards midnight, Major Eckert, chief of the telegraph office staff, brought in a platter of fried oysters. Abraham shoveled heaps onto plates to pass around, and the room was full of munching and slurping while they waited for more returns. The rain let up again. Around two, a crowd of Pennsylvanians gathered outside with a brass band, singing and calling for a speech. Abraham stepped to a window to give them a few words.

"I give thanks to the Almighty for this evidence of the people's resolution to stand by free government and the rights of humanity," he intoned over their cheers.

He put on his coat and pushed through the crowd back to the White House, shaking hands along the way. Mary had already retired to her chamber. She was no doubt sleeping well for the first time in several nights. He went to his room, undressed, and fell into bed, exhausted. I'm getting too old for this, he thought. It's a good thing it's my last one.

Tired as he was, he was too worked up to fall right asleep. He lay still awhile, listening to shouts of revelers outside. There would be more celebrating tomorrow and the next day. He would have to work up a proper victory speech for the newspapers. It must not sound triumphant. Better to assuage hurt political feelings. He must remind his supporters not to plant thorns in the bosoms of the McClellan men.

He heard a rustling in the hallway, floorboards creaking. Something bumped against his door.

Suddenly he was wide awake. Was someone lurking there? He listened a minute more, thought he heard a stifled cough. He rose quietly, threw on a robe, pressed his ear to the door. More rustling. And breathing. Someone was definitely there. He turned the knob, yanked the door open.

It was Hill Lamon, rolled up in his cloak and some blankets, fast asleep on the floor. A small arsenal of pistols and bowie knives lay around him, at the ready. And a glass nearly empty of whiskey. The big marshal grunted, turned over, and went on snoring.

Abraham closed the door gently and went back to bed, grateful for his old friend's devotion.

CHAPTER 45

NOVEMBER 1864 TO FEBRUARY 1865

His reelection brought back the hordes of office seekers. Once again, the stairway was jammed with a brazen, pushing crowd of men who wanted clerkships, judgeships, postmasterships, or any other appointment.

"I don't know if I can stand this squabbling over the distribution of loaves and fishes," he grumbled. "It would take a greater miracle than the feeding of the five thousand to satisfy that hungry lot." He did his best to put on a smile, ask "What can I do for you?" and listen patiently.

The last four years had worn out some of his aides and advisors. Replacing them demanded care. His private secretaries, Nicolay and Hay, were ready to go. Nicolay's faithful "Humph!" was growing weary, and Hay wanted to move on, as young men often do. Abraham would miss them, but he understood. He rewarded them by naming Nicolay to be the American consul in Paris and Hay the secretary of legation there. Noah Brooks, a journalist and friend from Illinois days, would make a good replacement for Nicolay.

The attorney general, Edward Bates, seventy-one years old, turned in his resignation. Abraham asked Josh Speed's brother, James, a loyal Kentucky lawyer, to fill the post. The chief justice of the Supreme Court, Roger Taney, died and flew the bench like a shrunken old crow headed for nether realms. Abraham thought long and hard, and finally appointed Salmon Chase to take his place. He could depend on Chase, as much as any man, to uphold his administration's policies when tested in court.

The telegraph wires crackled with news of a string of victories in the field. Union forces devastated the Confederate Army of Tennessee at battles in Franklin and Nashville. In Georgia, William T. Sherman left Atlanta blazing behind him and slashed his way through the heart of the state to the sea. On Christmas Day 1864, Abraham received a telegram from him: "I beg to present you as a Christmas gift the city of Savannah." Three weeks later, in North Carolina, a massive amphibious assault captured Fort Fisher, sealing off the rebel blockade runners' last major entry point on the Atlantic coast.

Surely now it was only a matter of time before the Confederacy would fall. The question was, how much time—and how much more bloodshed?

Bob was pressing hard to go into the army. He had graduated from Harvard, had seen his classmates march off to battle, and wanted more than anything to join the ranks. Mary resisted the idea just as hard.

"I've lost two sons, and that's as much as I can bear," she told Abraham one evening on the way to Grover's Theater to see *Hamlet*. "You can't expect me to sacrifice another."

"Many a poor mother has given up all her sons," he said gently. "Ours is not more dear to us than other boys are to their mothers."

"That may be, but I couldn't bear it if something happened to Robert."

She's only being truthful, he thought. If he were killed, it would break her.

"The newspapers accuse him of shirking his duty," he pointed out. "They wound him more than bullets could."

"That's political claptrap, and you know it. His services aren't needed in the field. The sacrifice would be needless."

"The sacrifices of every man who loves his country are required in this war."

"Yes, yes, I know," she said, tearing up. "I know his plea to go into the army is manly and noble. But I'm so frightened he'll never come back to us!"

"Of course he will. The war is almost over. Let him put on a uniform for a short while, and then he'll take up his plans to study law."

"Put him in that uniform, and he may never get to study law," she said gloomily.

He wrote an awkward letter to Grant, asking if he could put Bob onto his staff with some nominal rank. The general took him on as a captain and gave him headquarters duty to keep him out of harm's way. Mary surrendered grudgingly.

The new year brought a struggle over the passage of a Constitutional amendment to abolish slavery once and for all. The Senate had already passed the measure, and now Abraham took up the fight to get it through the House. He knew that once the war was over, his Emancipation Proclamation might well be challenged in court. A Thirteenth Amendment was needed to drive a stake through the heart of slavery.

He went to work logrolling harder than he had since his days in the Illinois legislature, cajoling and promising like an old prairie horse trader to get the needed support. On the day of the vote, a roar of artillery from Capitol Hill told him the amendment had passed and could go to the states for ratification.

"It's a king's cure for all the evils," he said happily. "It winds the whole thing up."

A weary longing for peace filled people's hearts. He could see it in the soldiers' faces when he reviewed their ranks, and in the eyes of mothers and wives who called on him. The hankering to fight, so vigorous four years ago, was all but dead.

Word came that Jefferson Davis had appointed three men to approach the United States government about the possibility of ending the war: Alexander Stephens, vice president of the Confederacy and Abraham's old friend from his days in Congress; John Campbell, Confederate assistant secretary of war and former justice of the United States Supreme Court; and Robert Hunter, Confederate senator from Virginia and former Speaker of the US House. Abraham had doubts about talking with them. They would surely angle for a pact that would leave the Union severed, but a refusal to hear what they had to say might give the appearance of being disinterested in peace. He agreed to rendezvous with them at Hampton Roads, Virginia.

They met onboard the steamer *River Queen*, at anchor under the guns of Fort Monroe. The morning was cold. Patches of thin ice lay on the sidewheeler's decks, and streamers festooning its lines hung stiff with frozen spray. Abraham could not help grinning as he watched little Aleck Stephens come aboard and shed a heavy gray woolen overcoat, a long, thick muffler, and two or three shawls.

"I've never seen so small a nubbin come out of so much husk," he chuckled.

The two men shook hands, and the clasp stirred memories of their time in Congress together, of long walks in the shadow of the Capitol dome to discuss politics and philosophy, of rays pouring through the House chamber's skylight onto rows of mahogany desks. Stephens looked more pale and shrunken than ever. The war was sapping the life out of him.

They all exchanged greetings, asked each other about friends not seen in four years, and sat down at a table in the ship's saloon. William Seward sat with them, and except for a black steward who came in to bring water and cigars, the five were left alone.

"Well, Mr. President," Stephens began, "is there no way of putting an end to the present trouble?"

"I know of only one way," Abraham said, wanting to sound firm from the outset, "and that's for those who are resisting the laws of the Union to cease that resistance."

The Southerners absorbed the words with blank faces. Stephens lifted a small, thin hand as if to catch a fleeting chance. "But perhaps there is a means to ease both parties toward reconciliation," he probed. "Is there no continental question that might divert attentions for a time, until passions cool?"

"You mean Mexico."

"Yes."

If this is all they have to offer, it will be a short conference, Abraham thought. It was an old idea—bring North and South together by starting a war to drive the French out of Mexico.

"I won't consider any proposition without first having a pledge to restore the Union," he said flatly.

"But if there is a chance to restore the Union, is it not advisable to take it, even without that pledge?" Stephens pressed. "France's attempt to build an empire in Mexico is a gross violation of the Monroe Doctrine. Let North and South enter a treaty to join forces and defend the continent from European dominion. Once we are on the same side again, it may well lead to a solution to our own difficulties."

Abraham shook his head. "You speak of a treaty between North and South, as separate powers. Any peace settlement must be based on the reestablishment of the national authority throughout the land."

Hunter cleared his throat. "Does not Mr. Davis, in fact, represent a government?" he asked. "The recognition of his power to make a treaty is the first and indispensable step to peace."

"The very fact of his government is the reason that armies are in the field," Seward said. He knocked the ashes off the end of his cigar.

"There is nothing to prevent you from entering into an agreement with a people in arms against you," Hunter insisted. "Charles the First, for example, negotiated with those fighting against him."

"I don't profess to be posted in history," Abraham said drily. "On all such matters I will turn you over to Seward. All I distinctly recollect about the case of Charles the First is that, in the end, he lost his head."

There was a minute of silence.

"If the Confederate states agree to rejoin the Union, what terms might they expect?" Campbell asked. He sat tall and straight in his chair, gray-haired with a balding crown, looking as dignified as he had once appeared on the bench of the Supreme Court in Washington.

"The states will be immediately restored to their practical relations to the Union," Abraham said.

"And what of the Confederate leaders?" Hunter asked. "We understand that you regard us as traitors."

"That's about the size of it." It was painful to say, especially to Aleck, but there was no way around it. "You can count on my offering all the power of mercy and pardon that my office wields," he added.

The commissioners glanced at each other.

"Well, Mr. Lincoln," Hunter smiled, "we've about concluded that we shall not be hanged as long as you are president—if we behave ourselves."

"I believe you'll better your chances by returning to the Union at once, rather than risk continuing the war. The time might come when the people of the North no longer regard their Southern brethren as an erring people to be invited back as citizens, but as enemies to be ruined."

Another painful minute of silence.

"And what of the South's slaves?" Campbell asked. "There are many who fear we will not survive emancipation."

There it is, Abraham thought. The same old problem that has vexed us from the beginning. We will pay for it a very long time. Men like these most of all.

"Whatever may have been the views of your people before the war," he said matter-of-factly, "they must be convinced now that slavery is doomed."

"So you offer nothing but an unconditional submission on the part of the Confederate States," Hunter protested, "and subjugation for their people."

"No one has used words like 'unconditional submission,'" Seward interjected. "Yielding to the laws under the Constitution, with all its guarantees of rights, as the Northern states do, can hardly be considered subjugation."

So it went, all morning. They were groping for something that was not there to be found. The Southern commissioners, half-prideful, half-desperate, spoke as men who knew they had nothing with which to bargain. The men of the North spoke of reunion in determined, patient tones. The *River Queen* rocked softly on the sheltered waters of Hampton Roads while they talked for four hours, until the talk ran out, and the Southerners rose to go.

"Well, Stephens," Abraham smiled sadly, "there has been nothing we could do for our country today. Is there anything I can do for you personally?"

"Nothing." Little Aleck looked grim, then brightened. "Unless you can send me my nephew. He's been a prisoner of war for twenty months at Johnson's Island, Ohio."

"I'll be glad to do it. Let me have his name." He wrote it down in a notebook.

They shook hands all around again, and a colonel came to escort the commissioners back to their steamer. Abraham stood at the rail for moment watching Aleck, bundled up in his gray coat, climb down into a rowboat. The little Georgian sat hunched in the bow, looking forlorn.

Melancholy gripped Abraham. They all wanted peace, but something stubborn and violent had to play itself out. The killing would have to go on a while longer.

❧ CHAPTER 46 ❧

MARCH 4, 1865

The morning of his second inauguration dawned with rain that lashed Washington's columns and spires before tapering to a drizzle. The weather failed to discourage the crowds. They straggled through Pennsylvania Avenue's black mud: ladies in ruined velvet and laces, gentlemen in soggy hats, soldiers in great dripping overcoats. Stanton had posted guards at every corner to keep watch. Confederate deserters wandered the streets, eyes down. Fresh rumors of assassination plots were abroad.

Abraham felt tired and cold to the bone, but he put on his shawl and drove through the rain to the Capitol to sign some bills passed in the waning hours of the Thirty-eighth Congress. As he worked, he could hear bands playing and a cannon blazing—the inaugural parade churning its way up the Avenue without him. There would be more than enough time to be seen by the people later in the day.

Shortly before noon, he stepped into a packed Senate chamber to watch his new vice president, Andrew Johnson of Tennessee, take the oath of office. A Democrat, Johnson had worked hard for the Union in his home state. Putting him on the presidential ticket had been a way to attract Democratic voters and promote national unity.

Johnson had managed to get himself drunk. He launched into a jumbled speech, babbling on about being a mere plebian thrust into an exalted position until Hannibal Hamlin, the outgoing vice president, tugged at his coattails to make him stop.

Abraham closed his eyes and tried to block it out. Andy Johnson was a better man than this. He'd shown a stiff backbone to the rebels in Tennessee. Well, it wasn't the first time whiskey had confounded a fellow's tongue.

"Don't let Johnson speak outside," he whispered to Senator Henderson of Missouri, one of the inauguration marshals.

A line of dignitaries formed and escorted Abraham out of the Senate chamber and onto a big platform erected on the east front of the Capitol. A band struck up "Hail to the Chief," and a sea of humanity filling the plaza let out a roar. The drizzle had finally stopped. Flags had sprung up in place of umbrellas. Half the faces in the crowd were black—an astounding sight. There was Frederick Douglass standing near the front, easy to pick out with his thick mane and stern gaze.

The sergeant-at-arms of the Senate doffed his black hat and bowed to the multitude, a signal for quiet. Abraham approached a small iron table with a glass of water set on it. A wave of applause rolled over the crowd. As if on cue, the sun broke through the clouds and flooded the grounds with light.

Well, there's a happy omen if I've ever seen one, he thought.

He adjusted his spectacles, focused on the large sheet of paper containing his address, and began in a clear, ringing voice.

"Fellow Countrymen: At this second appearing to take the oath of the presidential office, there is less occasion for an extended address than there was at the first. . . ."

Four years earlier, he had come to office in the midst of national crisis, and it had seemed fitting to outline a course to be pursued. Now, after so much loss and suffering, he wanted to share his thoughts, born of sleepless nights, as to the reasons for such a long, terrible conflict. And he wanted to tell his countrymen that, as the war drew to its close, the victors must treat the conquered not with enmity, but with mercy and compassion.

Nobody had wanted such a war, yet it had come. Nobody had expected it to last so long, and yet it had continued. Both sides had prayed to God for aid, but the prayers of both could not be answered, and the prayers of neither had been fully answered. Surely the war was God's will. No one could tell the mind of God. The Almighty has His own purposes. But perhaps this war was God's way of purging the land of the offense of slavery. Perhaps He had given to both North and South this terrible war as the woe due to those by whom the offense of slavery had come.

Fondly do we hope—fervently do we pray—that this mighty scourge of war may speedily pass away. Yet, if God wills that it continue, until all the wealth piled by the bond-man's two hundred and fifty years of unrequited toil shall be sunk, and until every drop of blood drawn with the lash, shall be paid by another drawn with the sword, as was said three thousand years ago, so still it must be said "the judgments of the Lord, are true and righteous altogether."

With malice toward none; with charity for all; with firmness in the right, as God gives us to see the right, let us strive on to finish the work we are in; to bind up the nation's wounds; to care for him who shall have borne the battle, and for his widow, and his orphan—to do all which may achieve and cherish a just, and a lasting peace, among ourselves, and with all nations.

A brief silence, then an explosion of applause. Chief Justice Chase stepped forward. Abraham laid his hand on a Bible, swore the oath of office, and kissed the open book. Cannon began to fire. The cheers mounted. He turned, bowed to the people, and left the platform to begin his second term.

❦❦❦

From eight until eleven that night, he stood in the East Room wearing a black dress coat and white kid gloves, shaking hands. Thousands of them. Country folk in homespun cloth. Dandies in fresh store-bought suits. There had never been so many people in the White House. They were packed so tight, the reception line could barely move. Every once in a while, a lady fainted and had to be passed over heads out a door or open window.

Mary stood nearby in a white satin gown, a wreath of pink roses in her hair. Four years ago, her eyes had shined with triumph. Now they looked tired. He wondered if she could last through another four years of this.

A farmer thrust out his hand. "How does it feel to be reelected?"

"A little like the man tarred and feathered and ridden out of town on a rail," Abraham said in his best prairie philosopher voice. "When the crowd asked him how he liked it, he said, 'If it wasn't for the honor of the thing, I'd just as soon walk.'"

After a few dozen shakes, he began to feel the strength that came from contact with the people. A lieutenant who had lost a leg at Petersburg hobbled by. "God bless you, my boy," Abraham told him. "I'm always pleased to shake hands with a soldier. It's the soldier who has made us what we are today."

A man who had come all the way from California proudly gave him a cane with a grizzly bear carved on its head.

"I used many a walking stick when I was a boy," Abraham mused aloud, running his hand over the wood. "My favorite was a knotted beech stick, and I carved the head myself. There's a mighty amount of character in sticks. Dogwood clubs were favorites with the boys. I suppose they use them yet. Hickory is too heavy, unless you get it from a sapling. Have you ever noticed how a stick in one's hand will change his appearance? Old women and witches wouldn't look so without sticks."

A venerable, white-haired gentleman stepped forward and introduced himself as John Brackenridge of Indiana. Abraham beamed with pleasure.

"I know who you are, Mr. Brackenridge. When I was a boy, I used to walk a dozen miles or more to watch you in court. I once saw you try a murder case in Boonville—you made the best speech I had ever heard. I told myself that if I could ever make a speech that fine, my soul would be satisfied."

He shook and shook hands, until the palms of his white kid gloves turned brown from greeting the crowds that had struggled through the mud to greet the head of their government.

A congressman from New York broke into the line and pulled him aside. "Frederick Douglass is being detained by officers at the door," he said in a low tone.

Of course he would come, Abraham thought. They'd have to weigh him down with stones and throw him into the Potomac to stop him now—which some of them would gladly do.

"Should they let him in?" the congressman asked.

"By all means. Bring him here."

The handshaking stopped. All heads turned.

"Here comes my friend Douglass," Abraham said loudly.

The mass of white faces looked on with a measure of revulsion as a former slave entered the East Room to be received by the president. The crowd parted before the light-black skin like wheat before the scythe.

Abraham clasped his hand. "I'm glad to see you," he said, still loudly. "I saw you in the crowd today, listening to my address. How did you like it?"

The orator demurred. "Mr. Lincoln, I must not detain you with my poor opinion when there are thousands waiting to shake hands with you." He said it with great dignity.

"No, no, you must stop a little, Douglass," Abraham insisted. "There is no man in the country whose opinion I value more than yours. I want to know what you think of it."

Douglass looked him square in the face. He spoke in his rich, sonorous voice.

"Mr. Lincoln, that was a sacred effort."

CHAPTER 47

MARCH 1865

Grant sent an invitation to visit his headquarters at City Point, Virginia, just east of Petersburg and Richmond. Abraham wired back his acceptance at once. It would be a good chance to confer with his general-in-chief and get a first-hand look at how things stood at the front. He might even be able to help nudge the war toward its end.

Mary got wind of the trip and decided to go along. "We both need a change of air," she said. "It will get us away from the ravenous wolves of this city for a while."

"I don't think you would be very comfortable," he said.

"Comfortable enough. Some of the officers' wives are there. If they can stand it, so can I. Besides, we'll get to see Robert. We'll take Tad with us and make it a family reunion."

That settled it. They boarded the sidewheeler *River Queen* for the journey down the Potomac, along the Chesapeake Bay, and up the James River. Tad scampered happily over the ship, inspecting every screw of the engine, and listened wide-eyed as the grizzled captain spun yarns of pirates and blockade runners. The weather turned frigid and the bay choppy, but after thirty-two hours, the vessel arrived at City Point, where the James and Appomattox Rivers came together to form a broad, sheltered waterway.

It was night when they tied up to the wharf. The lights of boats at anchor shimmered across the harbor; hundreds of campfires flickered along the shore and atop high bluffs. Somewhere off to the west, not far away, where the rivers narrowed among dark hills, two armies faced each other, one well-armed and well-fed, increasingly confident in its eventual triumph, the other much smaller, hungry, and increasingly desperate.

Grant came aboard as soon as the *River Queen* had tied up. His wife, Julia, a plain-looking, cross-eyed woman, came with him to welcome Mary. The general wore a dusty blue coat and old black felt hat which he removed as he stepped off the gangplank. He looked exhausted. His eyes, always shy and awkward at first meeting, carried dark circles.

"Petersburg is still the key," he reported. "Cut the rail lines and roads flowing through Petersburg, and Richmond will fall in no time."

"Is Lee's hold on Petersburg beginning to loosen?" Abraham asked.

"I don't see how he can last much longer," Grant said. "We've choked off his supply lines, and his desertions mount daily."

"Then he'll surrender," Abraham suggested.

"Not yet. He'll try to break through our lines and join up with Joe Johnston in North Carolina. We expect an attempt any hour now." There was a trace of worry in the blue eyes. But the doggedness was there, too.

"If he gets away, the war could go on for another year," Abraham said. More months of killing and bleeding and dying. It was almost unthinkable.

"We're ready for him," Grant said. "The last thing I want is to wake up and discover that old fox gone and nothing left but a picket line."

"And if he fails to get away?"

The tiredness went out of the eyes. "Then he'll have played his last card. The next few days should prove decisive."

The following day started off misty and damp. By midmorning the sun had burned the fog away, and the spreading base of operations that the army had constructed at City Point came into view. Steamers, barges, sailing ships, and gunboats coming and going by the score. Giant wharves stacked high with bales of hay, crates of rifles, and barrels of cured ham. On the hills above the two rivers perched a city of tents, cabins, and barracks. Warehouses bursting with everything from socks to gunpowder. Smithies clanging with anvil and hammer. Bakeries with ovens glowing around the clock. The streets of the army town thronged with soldiers, some hurrying, most sauntering, and Negroes driving mule trains. At the railroad yard, trains set out with supplies for the men at the Petersburg siege lines, eight miles away.

Bob came aboard the *River Queen* during breakfast, looking grown up and handsome in his captain's uniform. It filled Abraham with pleasure. Even Mary smiled, despite her misgivings over their son's enlistment. He brought good news.

"The rebels mounted an assault before dawn, but our lines pushed them back." His voice was deep with pride. "General Grant wanted you to know."

"That's excellent, Bob!" Abraham pumped the young man's hand as if he had whipped the whole rebel army himself. "Let's go see the battlefield."

"I don't know if Grant would allow it just yet. The generals don't like the public getting in the way."

"Perhaps he'll make an exception for this public. Let's go ask him."

They climbed the bluff to Grant's headquarters, which was in a cabin much like the ones that dotted the Illinois prairies. The general was reluctant at first, but the latest dispatches from the front were reassuring.

"I'll order up a train and go with you," he said. "Meade's headquarters are south of Petersburg. We can confer with him there."

Mary, Tad, and Julia Grant decided to go along. They chugged slowly out of City Point, Grant explaining the progress of the siege as they rode. Tad poked his head out the car's windows, eager to see a little bit of the war. The morning turned pleasantly warm. The troops waved as they passed, and for a while it felt almost like being on a holiday, riding out to inspect the lines on the verge of final victory.

Before long, they entered a region where the earth was gouged by massive siege lines. The trenches ran for miles, zigzagging behind walls of earth and logs. Rows of sharpened stakes bristled from ditches, and stubby black mortars with nicknames like "the Dictator" and "the Widow-maker" lurked behind embankments. Wooden towers dotted hilltops, with little figures on top frantically waving little flags to signal distant forts. The trenches were filled with infantrymen, some digging, some passing time, a few sticking their heads up like prairie dogs to take a look around.

They came to a place where, just a few hours earlier, the fighting had spilled over the railroad embankment. The train lurched to a stop. Corpses lay on the ground, both Union and Confederate. The bodies were twisted, with limbs folded underneath or splayed at unnatural angles. Faint booms of artillery sounded in the west. Tad sat still in his mother's lap while Mary stroked his hair.

I should not have brought them, Abraham thought.

The train started up again and reached a little station. From there the men rode on horseback a short way to Meade's headquarters, Abraham atop a smallish black pony named Jeff Davis. The women followed in an ambulance wagon. General Meade looked weary, like the rest of the officers, but he brandished a handful of dispatches confirming that the rebel assault had been turned back. A few hundred Confederate prisoners squatted in the dirt nearby, waiting to be herded away. They were a rough-looking lot, with tangled beards and slouched hats. They looked glad to finally have a rest.

The women stayed behind while Abraham, Grant, and Meade rode forward, Tad riding at his father's side. Soldiers jumped to attention as they passed. Drummer boys beat salutes, and flag bearers dipped their regiments' colors. A regiment of black soldiers that had captured some enemy cannon cheered louder than anyone else.

They passed through an area where the worst fighting had raged and more dead lay scattered. Rifles and cartridge boxes littered the field. Some of the wounded cried "Mama! Mama!" as members of the Ambulance Corps loaded them onto stretchers to be carried to a dressing station.

They stopped at Fort Wadsworth, an earthen fortification with four large bastions that offered a clear view of the surrounding terrain. In the distance, infantrymen of the Sixth Corps were pushing slowly, stubbornly across a field toward a rebel picket line in some woods. The sharp *crack-crack-crack* of rifle fire echoed over the hills. Little puffs of white smoke rose from the field and the tree line. Shells exploded over far-off treetops. Every once in a while, one of the infantrymen would flop down, his march to the grave over.

Abraham held Tad's hand and tried to answer his questions.

"What a' ou' soldia's doing, Papa-day?"

"They're trying to drive those men out of those woods."

"Why do they want them out of the woods?"

"If they stay in the woods, they can fire on our lines. So, you see, we want to get them out."

"Whe' will they go?"

"I hope that before long they'll go back home."

Tad waved his cap over the parapet, shouting "Hu'ah fo' the Union! Hu'ah fo' the Union!" The soldiers in the fort grinned.

Abraham pulled Meade aside. "Is my boy safe here?" he asked.

"Perfectly safe."

"There's no chance of a stray Minie ball coming this way?"

"No, sir, they're too far away."

"Any chance of a shell reaching this far?"

"No, the rebels have had no chance to bring up their guns. If General Grant and I weren't certain, we wouldn't allow you here."

They stayed for two hours, until the rebels had been driven back. The firing slackened, and quiet came. Flags of truce appeared. Ambulances lumbered onto the field, then the burial parties, moving among the fallen, checking to see who was still alive and who was dead. Men with picks and shovels dug shallow graves. They put the bodies in, covered them with dirt, and put up rough boards with names scrawled in pencil. Maybe someone would come and reinter them later. The burial squads worked quickly, mechanically, like men well used to their jobs. Abraham watched them perform their duty while lines of poetry ran through his head.

> 'Tis the wink of an eye, 'tis the draught of a breath,
> From the blossom of health to the paleness of death,
> From the gilded saloon to the bier and the shroud
> Oh, why should the spirit of mortal be proud?

They rode back to the train, where Mary and Mrs. Grant were waiting. Mary looked agitated.

"We could hear the guns firing," she whispered. "It made me nervous for you and Tad."

Several cars filled with wounded had been attached to the rear of the train for transport to the hospitals at City Point. The soldiers' groans mixed with the hiss of the locomotive.

We've had enough of the horrors of war, Abraham thought. Oh, God, let this be the beginning of the end.

He helped Mary aboard, and they rode back to City Point in silence.

CHAPTER 48

MARCH 26, 1865

T he next morning he was up early. He had breakfast aboard the *River Queen,* then walked up the hill and found Grant in conference with General Meade, General Edward Ord, and Admiral David Porter. General Philip Sheridan was there as well—"Little Phil," to his men—a short, bandy-legged cavalryman who looked like he might have to scale a ladder to get on his horse. He had just arrived from sweeping the Shenandoah Valley clean of rebels.

"General Sheridan, when this war began I thought a cavalryman should be at least six feet four inches tall," Abraham drawled. "But I've changed my mind. Five feet four will do in a pinch."

Meade offered a proposal. "The rebels are likely to stay quiet for a while, after the pounding we gave them yesterday," he said. "I suggest you go up the river to General Ord's encampment at Malvern Hill and review his troops. It's well behind the lines. Mrs. Lincoln might enjoy it." Grant, Sheridan, Porter, and several of the other officers would go with them. They would take Grant's headquarters steamship, the *Mary Martin*.

Abraham walked back to the *River Queen* and told Mary the plans.

"Stay close to me," she said, frowning a little.

"I will."

"I didn't like it when you left me for so long yesterday."

"General Meade says all will be quiet," he assured her. "Mrs. Grant will come along again. She'll keep you company."

They steamed up the broad and winding James, following the water path that Captain John Smith and his gentleman adventurers had explored more than two and a half centuries earlier in their quest for gold and the fabled Northwest Passage. Abraham's mind drifted back to his childhood schoolbooks, to the old stories of those settlers and the troubles they had endured, the starving time and the clashes with Indians. The settlers had found their gold in planting tobacco; now their descendants were planting corpses the length of the James, and it seemed as though the river's banks had known little but misery and blood flowing past.

After an hour they came to a sharp bend at a place called Deep Bottom, where General Sheridan's cavalry was crossing the river on a pontoon bridge. A long column of horses, thousands of them, clomped over the floating timbers. The banks teemed with soldiers laughing and calling to each other, watering their horses, washing the grime of a hundred-mile ride from their faces. When they realized the president's party was coming by, they hoorayed at the top of their lungs. The shouts lifted Abraham's spirits.

The bridge opened, and the *Mary Martin* steamed through. All along the river, buds were unfolding on trees, and a yellow-green mist hung at the tips of branches. Two miles past the bridge, Admiral Porter's flotilla waited in a double line, dressed with flags snapping on the breeze.

The crews lined the decks, cheering as the *Mary Martin* steamed by. Abraham waved his tall silk hat at each vessel, and the men cried louder.

The officers and ladies had a sumptuous luncheon of oysters and pheasant aboard the *Malvern,* Admiral Porter's flagship, then went ashore for the ride to the parade ground. Abraham and the generals went ahead on horseback, with Mary and Julia Grant again following in an ambulance fitted up as a coach. Rough terrain made for slow going. The road was barely more than a path through the woods, full of stumps to jar wagon wheels and roots to catch horses' hooves. In swampy places, battered corduroy roads oozed with muck.

The men reached General Ord's encampment, a wide field where the troops were drawn up at parade rest, standing with feet shoulder-width apart, chests out, shoulders back. They had been waiting for some time.

"We'll begin the review as soon as Mrs. Lincoln and Mrs. Grant arrive," Grant said.

"Where are they?" Abraham asked, looking back.

"Their carriage has fallen behind. They'll be along shortly."

"Have these men had lunch?"

"No, sir," General Ord said.

"Then let's get the review underway," Abraham said. "I'm sure the ladies wouldn't want to keep them from eating any longer than necessary."

They wheeled their horses and started, Generals Grant and Ord leading the way. Abraham followed along with General Sheridan. General Ord's wife joined them. She was a handsome young woman who cut a good figure on a bay horse. On her head perched a green chapeau, the kind made popular by the French Empress Eugénie, trimmed with a long ostrich plume that jounced as the horse pranced along. It never hurt the troops' morale to see a good-looking girl every once in a while.

They rode down the long blue line, bands playing and colors dipping as they passed. Colonels and majors snapped off crisp salutes. The troops stood at present arms, as rigid as painted tin soldiers, holding rifles in front of chests. It was a sight that stirred pride, these ranks of the Army of the James swelling across the field. Abraham sat stiff and erect in the saddle, reins hanging slack from his hands. He tried to look into as many of the men's eyes as he could to let them know that he saw them, to establish even the briefest connection. Their jackets were patched and mud-stained. Their flags showed battle scars. But their faces had confidence written on them. They had the look of men who could sense that the end was near.

The ambulance carrying Mary and Julia Grant finally arrived.

She'll be disappointed we started without her, Abraham thought as it lumbered onto the edge of the parade ground. But she'll understand.

Mrs. Ord promptly reined her horse out of the procession and galloped across the field to greet the ladies. The eyes of a thousand men standing at attention followed the ostrich plume as it jounced along.

Abraham watched her dismount. Mary and Julia Grant climbed out of the ambulance. Right away, even at a distance, he could see trouble. Mary gesticulated forcefully at Mrs. Ord, who took a step back. The small band of officers escorting the ambulance beat a rapid retreat.

"Excuse me for a moment, General," he said quickly to Grant. He turned his horse and trotted across the field to the ambulance, doing his best to look casual about it.

There was scarlet rage all over Mary's face and pallid shock on Mrs. Ord's. He could hear his wife berating her as he rode up.

"What do you mean by riding with the president?" she snapped at the young woman. Her voice was shaking. "Who gave you permission to ride at his side?"

"But, I wasn't—"

"Do you not know your place, madam?"

"I—I believe I do, Mrs. Lincoln."

"You seem to confuse it with mine."

"Hello, Mother." Abraham dismounted and stepped into the fray. "I trust you had a nice ride."

"I did not!" she fairly shrieked. "We were jolted out of our seats the entire way. What do you mean by allowing this woman to ride at your side?"

"She wasn't at my side," he said soothingly.

"She most certainly was. I saw her."

"Well, if she was, I didn't notice her—no offense to you, Mrs. Ord," he added. "I was paying my respects to the troops."

He tried to take Mary's hand. She pushed it away.

"You distinguish her with too much attention!" she cried.

Tears had started down Mrs. Ord's pretty cheeks. "I didn't mean to give offense," she pleaded. "If you'll just tell me—"

"Other ladies should not be in my husband's presence without me," Mary said regally. "You surely know that."

Julia Grant came to the young woman's aid. "She was there only because of her husband, Mrs. Lincoln," she said pleasantly. "General Ord was at the head of the party."

Mary swung toward her, eyes spitting fire. "Does she think the president wants *her* by his side?" she demanded.

"I'm sure she doesn't." Mrs. Grant smiled weakly.

"That's a very equivocal smile, madam." Mary lowered her voice. "I suppose you think you'll get to the White House yourself, don't you?"

The words shocked them all into silence. Abraham could not believe he had heard correctly.

An iciness went over Mrs. Grant's face. "I'm quite satisfied with my present position," she said after a moment. "It's far greater than I ever expected to attain."

"Oh, you had better take it, if you can get it," Mary hissed. "It's very nice at the White House."

"Mary, Mary—" Abraham whispered.

Mrs. Ord broke down in tears and fled.

"Now, now, Mother, I was only reviewing the troops," he assured her, "as you must do with me, now that you're here. Come along."

"I will not! Now the soldiers believe that *she* is the president's wife."

He gaped at her. Surely she couldn't mean that.

"No, Mother, no one has made that mistake," he said gently. "They all know who is the lady president. Let's go finish the review."

"General Ord should be removed from his command!" she insisted. "He's entirely unfit for such a high station, to say nothing of his wife."

"You're just upset. Let's get you back into the coach."

She pushed him away again. "I won't have you around a strumpet like that!" she shouted. She had lost all control. "Oh, I know what she is. I know!"

"Quiet, Mary, quiet," he entreated. Mrs. Grant's face had flushed with horror. "They'll all hear you. Let's get you back into the coach."

"I know what she is!" she screeched. "I know a slut when I see one!"

"Get back into the coach, Mary," he ordered, firmly now. "I'll tell the driver to ride alongside me. I'll stay close to you."

She turned from him, trembling, and climbed into the ambulance on her own. Abraham felt numb. What sort of insanity was this?

"You'll have to excuse her," he mumbled to Mrs. Grant. "She isn't feeling well. The strain on her is great." Mrs. Grant hesitated, then climbed into the ambulance, looking like she'd rather ride with a bear.

They concluded the review as quickly as possible and returned to the *Mary Martin.* Mary sulked alone on deck all the way back down the river. When they reached City Point, she fled to her cabin on the *River Queen.*

As soon as he could get away from the generals, he knocked on her door.

"Mary, are you all right? May I come in?"

He pushed the door open. She was sitting on the edge of her bed, head down. The cabin was dark. There was just enough light to see her swollen eyes and puffy cheeks.

"How are you feeling?"

"Humiliated," she sniveled.

That makes three or four of us, he thought.

"I should not have raised my voice," she cried. "I didn't mean to do that."

"You were upset, that's all."

"Yes, I was. You should not have begun the review without me."

"I'm sorry. The men were hungry. I thought we should get it over so they could eat."

There was no point in trying to make her see that she was in the wrong. She was too crushed. Besides, it might set off another explosion.

"And you should not have let that woman take my place!" Her voice began to rise.

"Now, now, Mother, no one can take your place." He patted her shoulder.

"That woman had no right to pretend to be me!"

She's too fragile to be this close to the front, he thought.

"She never would have had the chance if that driver had not made us so late," she said, wringing her hands. "I never want to set foot in one of those contraptions again."

"I'm sorry," he said again. A shiver passed over him. The gathering darkness seemed to thicken the despair in the cabin. He stooped and lit a lamp.

"That driver must have been drunk, banging us around like that," Mary went on. "He tossed my head against the ceiling. My head still hurts."

She pressed her fingers gently to her temples.

"My head always hurts," she whimpered.

He sat on the bed and reached to hold her. This time, she did not push him away.

"Shall I ask General Grant to send a doctor?" he offered.

"No! I don't want to be beholden to him, or his wife."

"Now, Mother, we must all be friends."

"They mock me behind my back!"

"No, they don't."

"If General Grant were any kind of friend, he would relieve Ord of his command."

"He can't do that. He says Ord is a good officer."

She sat quietly for a minute, frowning as she plucked a strand of hair.

"Perhaps I shouldn't be here," she said, new tears coming. She looked at him, searching. "Perhaps I should go back to Washington."

A painful silence. Thank God she had been the first to say it.

"If you think that's best," he said finally. "You could get some rest there." Her eyes filled with hurt. "I'll be here only a few days longer," he added quickly. "As soon as possible, I'll go back to be with you."

It was as though he were sending her away. They both felt it. And perhaps that's what it came down to. But there was no help for it.

"I'll go back, then," she said resolutely.

She drew a little away from him and dabbed her eyes.

"What about Tad?" she asked. "He won't be happy about leaving."

"He can stay here with Bob and me. You'll get more rest if you don't have him underfoot for a few days."

She remained in her cabin for the rest of her time at City Point, until suitable transportation could be arranged. A few days later, he put her aboard the USS *Monohansett* and stood on the wharf, holding Tad's hand, watching her disappear downstream. He had never felt so great a distance between them.

CHAPTER 49

LATE MARCH AND EARLY APRIL 1865

With Mary gone, he spent a good bit of time in the cabin Grant's staff had turned into a telegraph office, scrutinizing reports from the front and trading messages with Stanton back at the War Department. Sometimes he read to Tad or got down on the floor with him to play with three stray kittens that had taken up residence in the hut. Bob came by when he could and told them of camp life, of living on essence of coffee, make-do stew, and biscuits so hard they could split a board or fell a steer at forty feet. He told them how the picket lines traded jibes, the Union boys calling out to the Southerners, "How come you rebs never have decent clothes?" and the rebs shouting back, "We don't put on our best to kill hogs in."

The huge Depot Field Hospital, which could treat as many as ten thousand patients, lay at the mouth of the Appomattox River, not far from Grant's headquarters. Abraham went to visit the sick and wounded. Those who could make it up from their beds stood in line outside to shake his hand. Then he went inside the big tents and moved from cot to cot, shaking hands with those who were able, asking, "How are you, son?" and "Are you getting well, sir?" He had seen so much torn and mangled flesh by now, the wounds no longer shocked him, but the pain in the soldiers' eyes still hit him hard.

He was heading toward a group of tents set aside from the rest when a young surgeon tried to stop him.

"Mr. President, you don't want to go in there."

"Why not, my boy?"

"Those are sick rebel prisoners."

"That is just where I want to go."

He went inside and moved down the rows of cots, bowing and saying good morning to the surprised Confederates. A colonel who lay with his knees drawn up and arms folded across his chest gave him a frown.

"Mr. President, do you know who you're offering your hand to?" the man asked.

"I do not."

"You offer your hand to a Confederate colonel who has fought you as hard as he could for four years."

Abraham nodded and looked more closely. The fellow had been shot in both hips.

"Well, I hope a Confederate colonel will not refuse me his hand."

The suspicion drained out of the man's face, and there was only weariness left. "No sir, I will not," he said.

They clasped hands.

"I hope you will soon be restored to health and your family," Abraham told him.

He shook hundreds of patients' hands. When he was done for the day, the young doctor said he knew his arm must ache.

"No, not a whit," Abraham said, and to prove it he grabbed an ax from a woodpile and took a few swings at a log. When he had hacked through it, he gripped the end of the ax's handle in his right hand, swung its head up shoulder-high, and held it out horizontally before him with arm straight while the troops cheered.

"Still some fiber left in these gnarly old limbs, eh boys?" he smiled. But in truth his arm ached badly.

I should really stop doing that trick, he told himself.

General Grant, Admiral Porter, and General William T. Sherman came aboard the *River Queen* to talk strategy. Sherman's army was in North Carolina now, driving through what little resistance Joseph E. Johnston's Confederate forces could offer. Sherman had left it there and come up by boat to consult with Grant. Abraham sized him up as they all sat down in the *River Queen*'s after-cabin: tall, lean, scrawny, with finger-combed red hair atop a high forehead and whiskers that looked to have been close-chopped with a broadax. There was a restless look about him. His men called him Uncle Billy. Some of them called him Crazy Sherman and said he mumbled to himself too much. Abraham was certain of one thing. The man could whip rebels.

Grant crossed his legs and puffed on a cigar. "Sheridan's cavalry is moving around Lee's flank to sever his last supply lines," he said. "As I've told you, my only fear is that Lee's army will manage to slip out of Petersburg and unite with Johnston's force."

"But you say you are ready for him," Abraham said.

"We'll give him hot pursuit."

Sherman nodded, leaned forward. "My army at Goldsboro is strong enough to handle Lee's army and Johnston's combined, provided that General Grant comes up within a day or so," he said. "Then we'll have them in a vise."

"Perhaps we won't have to face that," Abraham suggested. "Lee must know it's only a matter of time. He may surrender now."

"Perhaps," Grant said. "But General Sherman and I are both of the opinion that one of us will have to fight one more battle."

Abraham closed his eyes. "My God, must more blood be shed? We've had so much of it."

"That's up to the enemy," Sherman said. "If he won't quit, we have to fight him. But it will be his last fight."

"In that case, General, I'd feel better if you were back in Goldsboro with your army."

"General Schofield is capable of handling things in my absence. But I'm starting back this afternoon."

"Good. What if Johnston slips away in the meantime? He could go south and keep the war going indefinitely."

"I have him where he can't move without breaking up his army," Sherman said. The man was all confidence. "I've destroyed the Southern railroads. The rebs won't be using them for a long time."

"What's to prevent their laying the rails again?" Admiral Porter asked.

"My bummers don't do things by halves," Sherman grinned. "They've put every rail over a hot fire and twisted it crooked as a ram's horn. No, those rails won't be used again."

Abraham chuckled. The name Sherman wouldn't be worth much in the South for a generation or two, that was for sure.

"What do you want us to do with the rebel armies once we defeat them?" Grant asked.

"Let them go home," Abraham said. "They won't take up arms again. Let them go, officers and all."

Sherman glanced at Grant and Porter. He looked uncertain, but said nothing.

"We want them back in their homes," Abraham said, "at work on their farms and in their shops. Let them have their horses to plow with and their guns to shoot crows with. Treat them liberally. We want these people to return to their allegiance and submit to the laws. They'll do that if we give them favorable terms."

"What about their political leaders?" Grant asked. "What should we do with Jeff Davis?"

"I hope Mr. Davis mounts a fleet horse, reaches the shores of the Gulf of Mexico, and drives so far into its waters that we never see him again."

"Do you mean we should let him escape?" Sherman asked, astounded.

"I didn't exactly say that," Abraham smiled. "But it brings to mind what the temperance man said when a friend pouring a glass of lemonade for him asked if he'd like a little brandy in it. 'I'm bound to oppose it,' the temperance man said, 'but if you could manage to put in a drop unbeknownst to me, I guess I wouldn't object.'

"Now, gentlemen, I'm bound to oppose the escape of Jeff Davis. But if you could manage to let him slip out unbeknownst to me, I guess I wouldn't object."

They talked a while longer, until he was satisfied they understood that once it was all over, he wanted the Southerners treated with generosity. When they were done, he scraped back his chair.

"Sherman, do you know why I took a shine to Grant and you?" he asked.

"I don't know, Mr. Lincoln. You've been kinder than I deserve."

"Well, I'll tell you. Unlike just about every other general, you never found fault with me. Or at least none that I heard of."

Sherman left that afternoon to rejoin his army in North Carolina. The next morning, Grant moved his headquarters from City Point to the front at Petersburg. Abraham walked him to the train and gave him a warm handshake. He shook the hands of all the headquarters staff, Bob among them.

"Goodbye, son. God bless you. Remember to always do your duty."

The whistle sounded. Grant and his staff raised their hats, and Abraham returned the salute.

"Goodbye, gentlemen. God bless you all! Remember, your success is my success."

Clouds moved in that evening, followed by rain. Abraham sat for a long time on the deck of the *River Queen* watching it fall on the wide, black river. The night was as dark as a moonless, rainy night could be. At ten-fifteen, a furious cannonade began off to the west, soon joined by heavy musket fire. The booms rolled across the water, and the flashes of the guns lit the clouds. The firing kept up past midnight. An end of some sort, once distant, was approaching.

CHAPTER 50

APRIL 4, 1865

Richmond had fallen. The long-awaited dispatch flashed over a wire to City Point. Jefferson Davis and the Confederate government, informed that Lee could no longer hold Petersburg, had abandoned their capital. Federal troops under General Godfrey Weitzel were moving into the city to take control while Grant went after Lee's army.

Abraham held the telegram like a man who has been handed a key to his cell, almost afraid to believe it was true. "Thank God I've lived to see this," he said quietly. "I feel like I've been living a horrid dream for four years, and now the nightmare is gone. I want to see Richmond."

The *River Queen* started the thirty-mile trip up the James River, accompanied by Admiral Porter's flagship, the *Malvern,* and two other vessels. Tad scampered from wheelhouse to boiler deck and back as the *Queen* pounded along. He was turning twelve years old that very day.

"A' the 'ebels giving me 'ichmond fo' my bu'thday?" he asked in high excitement.

"You might say that," Abraham smiled.

"I hope I get some 'ebel flags," the boy said happily.

By early afternoon they reached the part of the river that, only hours before, had been under Southern control. The ships picked their way past sunken boats and crates of rocks put down to obstruct the channel. Union gunboats were sweeping the river for mines that could shred a hull in one blast. Some lurked on the surface, some infested the waters just beneath. The *River Queen*'s crew turned jittery and muttered that the river was as full of mines as catfish. Abandoned fortifications slipped by, their cannon looking down from high bluffs, savage and mute. Omens of destruction came floating downstream: dead horses, charred timbers, a broken paddlewheel, wrecked boats.

The obstructions halted the progress of the *River Queen* and the other large steamboats. Abraham and Tad clambered into a small barge with Admiral Porter, a few other officers, and twelve sailors. A tugboat took the barge in tow and churned upstream, past the shattered hulks of Confederate ironclads the rebels had blown up.

They swung around a bend in the river, and Richmond came into view. Black smoke hung over its steeples, an immense, grotesque smudge against the sky. Grayish-white flecks of ashes drifted on a breeze coming down the river, bringing with them the sharp smell of burned wood. Ahead loomed the skeleton of a bridge, its spans collapsed into the water. The clamor of rapids filled the air.

The tug ran aground. Admiral Porter ordered the sailors to cut the barge loose and take up oars. They rowed to the nearest landing, and the party stepped ashore amid the smoldering wreckage of the city.

A dozen black men digging with spades behind a shabby little house paused to watch them land. One of them, an old man, bolted upright.

"Bless the Lord! There is the great Messiah!"

The man dropped his spade and rushed down the bank. Before the sailors could stop him, he fell at Abraham's feet.

"Bless the Lord! I knew him as soon as I saw him! He's come at last to free his children!"

Abraham, surprised and embarrassed, looked down at the upturned face. How in the world did the old fellow know who he was? Photographs? In an instant, the others had dropped their spades and were falling to their knees around him. The old man bent low to kiss his feet.

"Don't!" Abraham told him. "Don't kneel to me. That isn't right. You must kneel only to God."

They got up, reluctantly.

"Excuse us, Master Lincoln, we mean no disrespect," the old man beamed. "But after being so many years in the desert without water, it's mighty pleasant to be looking at last on our spring of life."

There were more coming, by the score it seemed, pouring out of streets that a second ago had seemed deserted. Black faces shining in wonder, black hands reaching to touch his sleeve. Negroes shouting and clapping, belting out hymns, yelling "Glory Hallelujah!" and "I've seen Father Abraham!" They grew frantic with joy. Abraham felt someone grab his hand, looked down, and saw Tad's face peering up at him, a little frightened. The officers shouted at the crowd to get back, but they pressed closer, reaching and jostling. It was getting hard to move. Someone was going to get hurt. Admiral Porter ordered the sailors to fix bayonets and form a circle.

Perhaps if I speak to them, Abraham thought. He raised his hand, and at once the shouting stopped. They stood still, gaping at him.

"My poor friends, you are free—free as air. You can cast off the name of slave and trample on it. It will come to you no more. Liberty is your birthright. God gave it to you as he gave it to others."

The crowd shrieked in ecstasy.

"There, now, let me pass on. I have little time to spare. I want to see the capital, and then must return at once to Washington to secure that liberty which you prize so highly."

They inched their way up a hill, six sailors in front and six behind, the crowd following, clapping and dancing. Tad held tight to his father's hand. They came to a farmer's market and turned onto Main Street. The crowd kept growing. There were some white faces now, most peering with sullen curiosity. People were climbing trees and telegraph poles, hanging from windows to catch a glimpse.

The smoking ruins of the business district lay before them. An avenging angel had passed that way. Blackened walls and fallen chimneys lined the road—burned office buildings, warehouses, saloons. Scores of them, as far as the eye could see. The street was littered with smashed furniture, broken windows, shattered liquor bottles. Red cinders went up from scattered fires. The afternoon was growing hot; the smoke and the dust made it hard to breathe. Abraham fanned himself with his hat.

A few whites offered greetings. A young white lady stood at the edge of the crowd, an American flag draped over her shoulders. Another girl struggled forward to present a bouquet of flowers. A white man bolted toward Abraham from the sidewalk, and Admiral Porter drew his sword, but the man cried, "Abraham Lincoln, God bless you! You are the poor man's friend!" The last they saw of him, he was throwing his hat into the air.

Where were General Weitzel's troops? Porter and the other officers looked tense. Ahead, to the left, a gray figure moved at a second-story window. The guards jumped to close ranks.

"What is it?" Abraham asked.

"That man had a rifle."

He looked but saw nothing. The figure was gone.

"If I had my pistol, I could shoot him!" Tad said happily.

"We don't want to start our own war, Taddie," Abraham said, moving forward.

A squad of Union cavalry finally arrived and pushed the masses back. The horsemen led the way up the hill to Jefferson Davis's house, which

General Weitzel had turned into his headquarters, though the general was not there just then.

It was a gray stucco, three-story mansion with a small front portico flanked by columns. They went up a short flight of marble steps and through an entrance hall, past two gas lamps held by statues of Comedy and Tragedy, into a small study. A leather-covered armchair beckoned, and Abraham sank into it, grateful for a few minutes of rest. He felt suddenly parched.

"I wonder if I could get a drink of water," he said.

He surveyed the room while he drank. An inviting place. A small desk on one side. A divan and a few chairs pulled around a tea table near the fireplace. Prints of Confederate ironclads on the walls. A shelf full of books. The Davises had probably come to this room often to find some quiet. Or to serve coffee and tea to visitors—Robert E. Lee, Stonewall Jackson, and a good many others the North had been fighting for so long now.

It all seemed unreal. He could not quite bring himself to believe he was sitting in what, until the day before, had been the White House of the Confederacy.

"This must have been President Davis's chair," he mused, running his hands over the arms.

An old black manservant gave them a tour of the house, explaining that Mrs. Davis, as she departed, had ordered him to make sure the mansion was in orderly shape for the Yankees when they arrived. Downstairs, he showed them a large dining room with a portrait of George Washington hanging over a sideboard. The parlor mantel was covered with jewelry and carvings fashioned by Confederate prisoners of war.

Upstairs, in Davis's office, a gas lamp sat on a handsome desk, connected by a tube to a gasolier hanging overhead. The old manservant told them that Mr. Davis had eye troubles, was blind in his left eye, in fact, and that he needed the extra light. Next door, in the nursery, some toys lay on the floor, waiting to be played with.

"Look, Papa-day, Jeff Davis's boys had a little cannon like me!" Tad cried in delight.

"It looks like they did."

"And one of them had a 'ebel Zouave unifo'm!"

"That's so."

These poor people have known as much misery in this house as we have in ours, he thought. And now they've lost everything.

A solemn look came over Tad's face. "I'm glad we a' beating the 'ebels," he said. "But I'm sad they had to leave tha' toys behind."

General Weitzel arrived. His cheeks, framed by a thick black beard, were flushed with embarrassment.

"I'm sorry we weren't there to meet you when you landed," he said. "We thought you were coming later."

"There's no need to apologize," Abraham said. "Congratulations on taking the city."

"That's kind of you, sir."

"How did the fire start? I trust it was not by our hands."

"No, sir. As best I can tell, the rebels fired some tobacco warehouses, and the flames spread from there. We've got most of it out now."

"Good. That's good."

With the general's arrival, the house was suddenly full of officers. Weitzel ordered up lunch for his staff and the president's traveling party. The old manservant located a bottle of whiskey, and everyone but Abraham and Tad took a swig. Tad went outside to stand on the back of an open carriage and make a jubilant little speech to the soldiers and freedmen crowded around the mansion.

John Campbell, assistant secretary of war for the Confederacy, appeared and asked for a conference. Two months earlier, when he had come with Aleck Stephens to talk peace aboard the *River Queen* at Hampton Roads, he had looked tall and distinguished. Now he looked pale and broken. He bowed very low before taking a seat.

"The war will be over any day now." He sounded relieved to get the words out. "General Lee can't possibly hold his army together."

"We surmised as much," Abraham said.

"The public men of Virginia stand ready to help restore their state to the Union. You can rely on that."

"That is very welcome news."

"I am an Alabaman, Mr. Lincoln. It would be better if a Virginian were here to deliver this message." For an instant his voice was tinged with bitterness. "But I am the only person of any prominence in the Confederate government who has remained in the capital. So I must speak for Virginia."

"I understand."

Campbell glanced around the room like a man struggling to comprehend where he was. He had no doubt been in the house many times.

"I hope it is not presumptuous for the vanquished to offer counsel," he said. "But if I may, I believe that the quickest way to restore the Union now is leniency and moderation on your part. It is true that 'when lenity and cruelty play for a kingdom, the gentler gamester is the soonest winner.'"

"That is true," Abraham nodded. "For those who are prepared to rejoin the Union, they can expect all the leniency I have in my power to give."

"Thank you," Campbell said humbly.

"But I cannot negotiate with men who are fighting against us. My conditions for peace remain the same as they were at Hampton Roads. The rebels must lay down their arms. They must recognize the national authority. And they must realize that on the question of slavery, there will be no receding on my part. All other questions can be settled on terms of sincere liberality."

Campbell lowered his head. "I wish to God the South had found a way to make peace before it came to this," he murmured. "Now each man will have to make his own peace."

When he had gone, Abraham climbed into a carriage with Tad, Porter, and Weitzel for a tour of the city, escorted by cavalry. The streets thronged with people, mostly black, calling "Glory! Glory!" and "Thank

God, Jesus Christ has come at last!" A black woman stood on a street corner holding up her sick baby, crying, "Look there, honey, look at the Savior, and you'll get well!" In the finer neighborhoods, the blinds on the windows were drawn, and the houses stood silent.

The lawn of the Capitol was covered with people, black and white, whose homes had burned. They huddled beside piles of belongings— blankets, clothing, chairs, precious heirlooms. Over their heads rose a great bronze statue of George Washington on a horse. Someone had placed the Stars and Stripes in one of its hands. Inside the Capitol, where the Confederate Congress had met, looters had done their work. The members' desks and chairs were overturned, some of them hacked to pieces. Official papers littered the corridors. Bundles of Confederate money lay scattered across the floors.

The carriage passed through the burned district of the city. Block after block of scorched ruins, collapsed roofs, toppled walls. Smoke rose from piles of bricks. Near the waterfront stood Libby Prison and Castle Thunder, where Union prisoners of war had suffered harsh treatment and near starvation. The prisons were full of Confederates now.

The navy had managed to clear the James of enough obstructions to get the *Malvern* upstream. General Weitzel escorted Abraham and his party to a wharf, where a rowboat waited to ferry them to the flagship.

"I don't think the rebels believed they would ever be conquered," the general said as they shook hands.

"Perhaps not," Abraham said. "At least not like this."

"Do you have any instructions as to how you want me to handle them?"

"No, nothing specific."

He looked back up the hill toward the Capitol. Two ashen figures, a woman and child, sat paralyzed on the carcass of a broken wagon, as if waiting for someone to haul them far away.

"If I were in your place I'd let 'em up easy," Abraham said. "Let 'em up easy."

Four days later, the *River Queen* set out for Washington, departing City Point under cover of night. Abraham stood alone for a while on the ship's deck, watching the busy port and the high bluffs covered with tents and barracks slip away. Beyond the dark hills to the west, Grant's army was racing to catch Lee. With luck, soon it would all be over. But not before hundreds of thousands had died. Ned Baker was dead. Elmer Ellsworth was dead. Ben Hardin Helm. And two of Mary's brothers. Countless brothers, husbands, fathers, sons. All dead.

He tried to distract himself by browsing a volume of Shakespeare. In *Macbeth,* he read the passage in which the tortured Macbeth, who has murdered Duncan, the king of Scotland, comes to envy the sleep of his victim.

> *Duncan is in his grave;*
> *After life's fitful fever he sleeps well.*
> *Treason has done his worst: nor steel nor poison,*
> *Malice domestic, foreign levy, nothing*
> *Can touch him further.*

Yes, treason has done his worst, he thought. And the worst was worse than any of us imagined it could be. But at least those who have been sent to peace, so the living could gain their peace, sleep well now. Nothing can touch them further.

He read the lines again as the *River Queen* crawled north.

CHAPTER 51

APRIL 9 TO
APRIL 13, 1865

*W*hen the *River Queen* docked at sundown the following day, the streets of Washington were alive with people singing, "The Union forever! Hurrah, boys, hurrah!" and shouting, "Let Richmond burn!" Abraham took a carriage straight to William Henry Seward's house on Lafayette Square. A few days earlier, the secretary of state had broken his jaw and dislocated his right shoulder in a carriage accident.

The house was still when he arrived. Seward's wife, Frances, and his son, Fred, moved softly and spoke in whispers. They showed Abraham to a dimly lit bedroom where the invalid lay with a steel frame around his jaw to keep it immobile. It was shocking to see how swollen and cut the face was. The bandaged right arm projected from the side of the bed to keep it free of all contact; even the pressure of blankets caused pain.

Abraham put on a smile to greet his friend. "Well, Seward, you look hale and hearty. Your cheeks are as red as apples. I'm surprised the birds don't come peck at them."

"My head is too hard to peck at," Seward rasped faintly.

"That's true. I'm told that when you fell out of that carriage, your head hit a rock, and the rock broke."

Seward's eyes glimmered.

"Are they are taking good care of you?"

"Yes. Stanton was here." The swollen tongue labored to get the words out. "He was like a woman in a sick room. He stayed for hours, fretting over me."

"If Mars ain't careful, he'll lose his reputation for being meaner than a hog."

He could tell that it was hurting Seward to turn his head and look in his direction. He gently eased himself onto the bed and stretched out beside his friend, propped up on his elbow so the wounded man could see him better.

"So you are back from Richmond?" Seward whispered.

"Yes, and I think we're near the end at last. I believe we should proclaim a Day of Thanksgiving."

"Perhaps . . . perhaps . . ." The lips barely moved inside the bulky metal contraption holding the jaw in place. He won't be smoking any of his beloved cigars any time soon, Abraham thought.

"Take your time."

"Perhaps you should wait for a final surrender before proclaiming a Day of Thanksgiving. A proclamation might drive the remaining Confederate armies to greater desperation."

"There, you see how much I need you?" Abraham smiled. "Even flat on your back, you give excellent counsel."

"Tell me about Richmond."

He told about going into the city, the blocks of destruction he saw, the freedmen crowding the streets, and the shocked resignation on so many faces. After a few minutes, Seward's eyelids began to flutter, and he drifted off to sleep. Abraham rose carefully and slipped out the door.

He was exhausted by the time he got back to the White House, but he went straight to his office to survey the backlog of work. His heart sank when he saw the leaning piles of documents on the big table. It would take a week to plow through it all. Tired as he was, he sat down to see what was there and lost himself in some reports from Congress.

About ten o'clock, Stanton came thumping up the stairs and burst into the room waving a telegram. There were tears in his eyes.

"It's done! It's over!"

He shoved the telegram into Abraham's hands. It was from Grant: *General Lee surrendered the Army of Northern Virginia this morning on terms proposed by myself. The accompanying correspondence will show the conditions fully.*

Suddenly all the fatigue was gone, and in its place surging, profound relief.

"Is it certain?"

"Yes, absolutely."

"There's no doubt?"

"None at all."

"By jing, Mars!"

He jumped out of his chair, pumped Stanton's hand, thought better of it, and wrapped the little secretary of war in a giant bear hug. When he let go, Stanton dropped onto a sofa, out of breath. Abraham read the dispatch again.

"Appomattox Court House. That's where the surrender took place?"

"Yes," Stanton wheezed.

"Where is that?"

"About seventy-five miles west of Richmond."

Abraham went to a map of Virginia tacked on a wall and put his finger on the village where the end had finally come.

"Grant gave them generous terms," Stanton said. "Lee's officers and men will be paroled and allowed to go home."

"Good. Good."

"The officers may keep their side arms, and the men their horses for plowing."

"Very good," Abraham said happily. "I knew I could count on Grant to treat them well."

Stanton had recovered his breath. He put on a grimace.

"I'm irritated with you for walking into Richmond the way you did," he fussed. "And with Porter and Weitzel for letting you get away with it."

"I've lived to tell the tale."

"Anybody could have taken a shot at you, at any time," Stanton insisted.

"That would not have done the people of the South any good. I reckon they realized that."

"It was a damned foolish thing to do."

Abraham grinned. "Well, Mars, you're probably right," he said. "You most always are. You've been the rock that's stood firm against the dash and roar of our national storm. I'm grateful to you, even for fretting over me."

When Stanton was gone, he eased himself back into his chair and gazed out a window toward the dark Potomac. News of Lee's surrender would be spreading across the South tonight. To Montgomery, the Confederacy's first capital, where Jeff Davis had delivered his inaugural address while the American flag was given a funeral. To Vicksburg, where the citizens and rebel garrison had tasted shoe leather before giving in to Grant's siege. Through the ashes of Columbia and Atlanta. Through the woods and fields of Shiloh, Stones River, Chickamauga.

Men who had once sworn they would see Pennsylvania Avenue paved ten fathoms deep with mangled bodies before they would submit to the North were shivering in despair tonight. But surely they, too, must feel some relief that the bloodletting was finally done. Thank God. Thank God.

Mary would want to know the news. It would lighten her heart. After a while, he got up and went down the hall to tell her.

Dawn came with five hundred cannon blasts, Stanton's way of announcing the news of Lee's surrender. When the cannon were finished, the air broke loose with church bells, cow bells, tin horns, drums, steam whistles, squirrel guns, and pistols all firing, ringing, shrieking, pounding, and blaring at once. A crowd marched up Pennsylvania Avenue, swelling to thousands as it came, flags waving, bands playing, hats flying, children laughing, women and men weeping for joy. People covered the White House lawn, filled the portico and carriageways. They roared when Tad appeared at a window and waved the Confederate flag that had cost Elmer Ellsworth his life. When Abraham came to the window, they jumped and danced in each other's arms.

"I'm glad to have an occasion so pleasurable that the people cannot restrain themselves," he called, and they cavorted some more.

"I have a request for the band," he announced.

Cheers from the crowd. "Let's have it! Play it!"

"I've always thought that 'Dixie' was one of the best tunes I've ever heard."

Boos and catcalls from the crowd. "No! Down with 'Dixie!'"

"Our adversaries across the way attempted to appropriate it, but I say we've fairly captured it."

"That's right! Yes! We won it!"

"I presented the question to the attorney general, and he gave it as his legal opinion that it is our lawful prize."

"That's right! Hooray!"

"Now I ask the band to favor us with its performance."

"Let's hear it! Damn right!" The crowd hollered and danced while the band played "Dixie," followed by "Yankee Doodle."

They came back the next night to hear him give a victory speech from the same window. A sea of candles and lanterns spread around the White House, setting the misty air aglow.

"We meet this evening, not in sorrow," he began, "but in gladness of heart."

He read by candlelight, dropping the pages one by one as he went along. Tad scrambled about the floor picking them up, happily whispering "Anothe,' anothe'!" as they fluttered down.

He told the people he could take no part of the honor for winning the war. "To General Grant, his skillful officers, and brave men all belongs."

The crowd roared its approval. But he was not going to give them a triumphant speech recounting the glories of the soldiers. He wanted to turn their thoughts, instead, to making the nation whole. It would be a task fraught with great difficulty. There were people in the North bent on revenge. The only way to restore the country was to act with forgiveness.

"We all agree that the seceded states, so called, are out of their proper practical relation with the Union," he told them. The best way to remedy that now was to act with generosity of spirit. "Let us all join in doing the acts necessary to restoring the proper practical relations between these states and the Union."

The crowd cheered again, but it began to look a little bored when he offered some thoughts on reconstruction. Some in the audience shook their heads when he mentioned the idea of allowing black men to vote and said that he himself preferred to confer the franchise "on the very intelligent, and on those who serve our cause as soldiers." It was not exactly the kind of address the throng was hoping for. Here and there, people grew restless and wandered away before he was done. Those who stayed to the end offered polite applause.

"I guess I don't blame them," he told John Hay afterwards. "They came hunting bear and think they got a turkey instead. But it was a turkey with a good bit of meat on it."

He did not let it bother him. There was too much to do and think about, too many questions to be answered now. How should the nation go about the job of getting the South back on its feet? What was the best way to reestablish authority in the Confederate states? What would happen to the four million blacks now free from slavery?

He decided to send Ward Hill Lamon down to Richmond to get a sense of how to begin reconstruction in the state. The burly Virginian dropped by the White House to get his instructions.

"I want you to promise me something," Lamon said solemnly.

"What?"

"Don't go out after dark while I'm gone."

Abraham waved him off. "Oh, Hill, is that all you can think about, someone trying to kill me?" he asked, half-petulantly.

"You should think about it more, if you want to stay alive," Lamon snorted.

"You've become a monomaniac on the subject of my safety."

"I promised our Illinois friends that I would protect you, and I mean to do it."

Abraham sighed. If Stanton and Lamon had their way, he'd have guards with drawn sabers at his door, like an emperor in his palace.

"The war is over, Hill. I can't believe any human being would do me harm now."

"You're in more danger now than ever," Lamon insisted. "Passions are running high. The Southerners have tasted the bitterness of defeat. We have to assume that someone will try something rash."

"If they kill me, the next man will be just as bad for them," Abraham shrugged.

"That may not be the way they see it."

"Besides, I've told you before, if anyone wants to kill me, he can do it any day or night he's ready to give his life for mine. There's nothing I can do about it."

Lamon stood there, not budging, hat in hand. "Promise me anyway," he pleaded. "Promise to stay out of the public eye as much as possible for the next several nights."

"Well, I promise to do the best I can toward it," Abraham grumbled. He clasped his friend's hand. "Goodbye. God bless you, Hill."

Every day brought good news now. The city of Mobile, Alabama, surrendered after a long campaign. In North Carolina, federal troops took Raleigh. Washington celebrated the war's end with a grand illu-mination. Thousands of candles lit windows. Huge lighted transparen-cies hung from public buildings, proclaiming slogans like "VICTORY BRINGS PEACE" and "GLORY TO GOD, WHO HATH TO U.S. GRANT-D THE VICTORY." Fireworks arced over the half-built shaft of the Washington Monument.

After the illumination, when the last candle had been extinguished, Abraham crawled into bed tired but content, and again he had the dream that had come to him several times during the war. He was standing on the deck of the phantom vessel, moving silently across the gray, still water. For an instant the mists seemed to part, but just as quickly closed around him, though not before he caught a glimpse of the distant, receding shore.

CHAPTER 52

APRIL 14, 1865

ood Friday came, balmy and serene, with purple lilacs blooming in the White House gardens. He rose and dressed quickly—it was going to be a busy day. The chatter of several early-bird petitioners waiting in the first-floor vestibule drifted up the stairs. He slipped down the hallway, past Mary's room, went into his office, and closed the door.

A new stack of mail occupied a corner of his desk: congratulatory letters, requests for autographs, and advice from friends and strangers. He glanced through the pile and scribbled a few quick notes.

"Please assemble the cabinet at 11 a.m. today. General Grant will meet with us."

"I thank you for the assurance you give me that I shall be supported by conservative men like yourself."

The clatter of iron wheels on cobblestones slipped through a half-open window. A locomotive starting for Baltimore let out a brisk whistle. Pleasant, comforting sounds. The sounds of a nation at peace—or, at least, on the verge of peace—going about its early morning business.

At eight o'clock, he went downstairs for breakfast with Mary and Tad. Bob appeared as they sat down, just returned from Appomattox, looking weary but exuberant in his dusty uniform. They all jumped up to kiss him.

"I brought you a picture of General Lee," he said with a mischievous grin, and he laid it on the table. Tad leaned forward, eyes wide. Abraham put on his spectacles to study the photograph.

"It's a good face," he said after a minute. "It's the face of a noble, brave man." He took off the spectacles and looked at Bob with satisfaction. "Tell us about the surrender."

Bob told how the generals had met for more than an hour in the parlor of a three-story brick house set back from the Richmond-Lynchburg Stage Road; how when General Lee finally emerged onto the porch of the house, looking somber and dignified, several blue-coated officers jumped to attention; how Lee stood on the porch for an instant, pulling on his gauntlets and striking his right fist into his left palm three times as he gazed in the direction of his waiting army; and how when Grant came out of the house, he raised his hat in salute, and Lee, now mounted on Traveller, his big gray charger, lifted his own hat in return before passing through the gate and up the road, out of sight, to tell his men that it was done.

"General Lee wore a spotless uniform with a red sash and a glittering sword," Bob said. "Grant wore a rumpled old tunic with muddy trousers and no sword or spurs. Oh, it was great."

"I'm sad it's ove'," Tad scowled. "I neve' got a chance to shoot a 'ebel."

Mary ignored the comment. "We've invited General and Mrs. Grant to attend the theater with us tonight," she told Bob. "*My American*

Cousin, with Laura Keene, is playing at Ford's. Will you join us?"

"Perhaps. I'm not sure."

"It should be worth a few rib-crackers," Abraham put in. "We'd love to have you with us."

"I'm awfully tired," Bob said.

"Well, you can make up your mind later," Abraham said. "We're just glad you're home from the front, safe and sound."

He took a piece of bacon to eat with his usual egg and coffee, in celebration of his family being together again.

"Now that the war is closed, you can lay aside your uniform and return to your studies," he said happily.

"Yes, sir."

"If you still aim to be an attorney, you must read law for about three years. At the end of that time I hope we'll be able to tell whether you'll make a lawyer or not."

"That sounds better than living on army beans and hardtack," Bob said.

After breakfast, it was back to the office to face the usual hordes. Well-wishers came to offer congratulations and ask a favor or two. There were appointments to be made and questions to be settled about pardons and discharges. He took a few minutes to slip away to the War Department, in hopes of getting news from Sherman about Johnston's army in North Carolina, but there was nothing.

At eleven o'clock, the cabinet gathered. Grant joined them, again looking uncomfortable at having to sit in an armchair instead of a saddle. They were all eager to hear his version of Lee's surrender, so he told it briefly.

"What terms did you make for the common soldiers?" Abraham asked.

"I told them to go back to their homes and families, and they would not be molested if they did nothing more."

"Good, very good," Abraham nodded. "Do you have any news from Sherman to give us?"

"No," Grant said, "but I expect word from him any hour."

"So do I, and I believe it will be good news," Abraham said. He hesitated an instant, then went on. "Last night I had a dream I've had more than once during the war. It's always come right before something important occurs, usually something favorable."

"What kind of dream?" Gideon Welles asked.

"It relates to your element, Neptune, the water." He told them about being on the indescribable vessel, gliding toward the indefinite shore. "I had the dream right before Sumter, Antietam, Gettysburg, Stones River, Vicksburg—just about every significant victory, I suppose."

"Stones River was certainly no victory," Grant pointed out. "A few more like it would have ruined us."

"However that might be, the dream preceded that fight."

Maybe it was a mistake to tell them, he thought. Oh well, some men believed in portents, some did not. He did.

"Since I had it again last night, we're likely to have news soon," he said. "It must relate to Sherman. My thoughts are in that direction, as are most of yours, and there's no other important event that's likely to occur just now."

They turned to the business at hand, a speedy restoration of the Union. Military governors would have to be appointed in the South until civilian governments could be reestablished. Trade must be restored, post offices reopened, revenues collected, and courts reestablished. It was a daunting task.

"There is a limit to what Washington can do," Abraham said. "We can't undertake to run governments in all these Southern states. Their people must do that, though I reckon that at first some of them may do it badly."

"There are men who would like nothing better than to crush the South under the North's boot," James Speed, the attorney general, said, "and keep that boot there for a long time."

"Yes, and some of them are in Congress," Abraham said. "Men who possess feelings of hate. We must extinguish our resentments if we expect harmony and union."

"We can't allow the rebel leaders to come back into power," Stanton insisted.

"That's right, we can't," Abraham said. "Perhaps we should let the worst of them know it would be in their best interests to leave. Frighten them out of the country, open the gates, let down the bars, scare them off." He waved his hands, as if shooing sheep. "But I want no bloody work, gentlemen. Enough lives have been sacrificed."

They met for three hours, talking through the expected troubles of reconstruction. He was elated to find that his cabinet was in agreement about the general approach to take, and that every man showed kindly feelings toward the vanquished.

"It's been a tough time," he said as the meeting broke up, "but we've lived it out. Or some of us have."

They all fell quiet.

"But it's over," he went on, firmly. "We're going to have good times now, and a united country."

Grant lingered as the others made their way out the door, looking as if he had something to say. The general fidgeted with his collar.

"I'm afraid we won't be able to join you at the theater tonight," he said.

"I'm sorry to hear that. Are you sure?"

"Yes. We've promised our children in New Jersey that we'd come see them." He sounded a little uncertain.

"Can't it wait one day?" Abraham pressed gently. "The people would take great pleasure in seeing the man who won the war."

"Mrs. Grant is anxious to see our sons and our daughter," the general explained, shuffling his feet. "We told them we'd catch the afternoon train."

So that's it, Abraham thought. Well, I can't blame her, not after the way Mary treated her.

"I understand," he said. "Of course, you must see your family."

They shook hands, and the general went on his way, looking embarrassed and relieved.

There was no time for lunch, so he munched an apple before turning back to the rounds of petitions and interviews. Vice President Johnson came to see him, and Governor Swann and Senator Creswell of Maryland, and some congressmen and businessmen, all wanting something. He happily signed a note for two Southerners who wanted to travel to Richmond: "No pass is necessary now to authorize any one to go and return from Petersburg and Richmond. People go and return just as they did before the war. A. Lincoln." He signed a pardon for a deserter sentenced to be shot.

"Well, I think the boy can do us more good above ground than underground," he told himself.

By late afternoon, the thermometer had pushed into the upper sixties. A mild southwest wind came off the river, and white clouds billowed overhead like sails on the ocean. Abraham and Mary crossed the White House portico and climbed into a waiting barouche for a drive.

"Would you like anyone to go along with us?" she asked.

"No, I prefer to ride by ourselves today."

He nodded to the coachman, and they set out with two cavalrymen following at a short distance. The open carriage rattled east on G Street, then south along New Jersey Avenue. Flags waved from windows and roofs in celebration. Men lifted their hats when they saw the carriage, and Abraham lifted his in return. A column of soldiers marched toward the B&O train station, stepping lively because they were going home. The great Capitol dome stood welded against the sky, permanent and immovable. Abraham took Mary's hand.

"I haven't seen you look this happy in a long time," she said.

"I should be happy," he smiled. "I feel that the war has come to a close today."

He patted her hand, and she nestled closer as the matched blacks trotted toward the Navy Yard.

"We must both be more cheerful in the future," he said gently. "Between the war and the loss of Willie, we've both been very miserable."

"Yes, we have," she said softly.

"But now we can look forward to four years of peace. Four years of happiness. And when those are over. . . ."

They talked of their lives together after the presidency. He told her he would like to do a little traveling in Europe, and perhaps visit the Holy Land. It would be wonderful to see Jerusalem. And someday he wanted to go over the Rocky Mountains to California and see the gold mines. His old wanderlust, dormant since youthful days when he dreamed of setting out on wide rivers, twinged inside him.

"After we travel a bit, we'll settle down in Springfield, and I'll practice law again." The sign with the names *Lincoln & Herndon* on it, swinging on rusty hinges outside his old office, flashed into his mind. And old friends riding the Eighth Circuit together, trying cases by day and swapping stories by night. "Or we could move to Chicago, and I could practice there." Jostling, blustery, surging Chicago. The metropolis of the West. It must have grown like corn in July since they last saw it. Chicago would be a fine place to live. Maybe he and Bob could practice law together there.

The carriage rolled to a stop at the Navy Yard, where some monitors had come in for repairs. Turrets and smokestacks rose from the Eastern Branch like a floating city of iron. Abraham helped Mary down, and they stretched their legs on the deck of the *Montauk,* a two-hundred-foot ironclad that wore scars from fighting at Charleston. It was strange to think that four years before, ships like this one did not even exist. What would become of them now that the war was over? He would have to talk it over with Gideon Welles.

By the time they started the carriage ride back, the sun was declining, and a chill touched the air. Abraham tucked a blanket over their legs. He suddenly remembered that the Grants could not go to the theater.

"Yes, I know, Mrs. Grant sent word," Mary said with determined cheer. "It's all right. I've invited Major Rathbone and Miss Harris to join us. They'll make better company, anyway."

Back at the White House, they found two friends from Illinois, Governor Richard Oglesby and General Isham Haynie, waiting to see Abraham. The men were the sort of visitors he welcomed, and he spent a while jesting and laughing until Mary pulled him away for a quick supper.

"I feel a headache coming on," she confessed, picking at a slice of pork.

"Does it hurt much?"

"No, not much, but I'm afraid it will get worse. Perhaps we shouldn't go to the theater after all."

"Unless it hurts badly, I think we should try. The newspapers have announced that we'll be there." In truth, he didn't feel much like going out, either. But their plans were made, and they might as well stick to them. They would probably end up having a good time.

"I'm going to the theate,' too!" Tad cried.

"Is that right?" Abraham asked.

"Yes, he's going to Grover's Theater to see *Aladdin,*" Mary said. Alphonso Donn, a White House doorman, had agreed to take him.

"Well, you be extra good, Taddie."

"I will, Papa-day."

He made another quick trip to the War Department after supper. Stanton was at his post, driving away with a pen.

"Any message from Sherman?" Abraham asked.

"None."

"I hope he hasn't run into a bad row of stumps."

"If so, we would have heard from him."

"I expect you're right. I'm going to the theater. Will you send word if you hear anything?"

"Of course." Stanton scowled at the thought of Abraham making a public foray, but he held his fire. "You're still convinced that Johnston will surrender his army today?"

"Not convinced so much as hopeful."

"Whether tonight, tomorrow, or next week, it's still over."

"Yes, that's right." It was hard to believe, but it really *was* over. There would be no more killing. He dropped a long arm onto Stanton's shoulders. "Mars, for the first time since this cruel war began, I can see my way clearly," he smiled.

He walked back to the White House, where two more visitors appeared, Schuyler Colfax, Speaker of the House, and George Ashmun, a former congressman from Massachusetts. It took several minutes to speak with them. A doorkeeper brought word from Mary that it was getting late, and they must leave for Ford's. Abraham excused himself and stepped to a mirror to run his fingers through his scraggly hair.

The face that peered back at him looked gaunt and pale. His hair was thinning, had more gray in it. Well, no wonder, after what they had all been through. He must make an effort to put on a little weight, get more fresh air.

He put on his overcoat, stuffed some white kid gloves into a pocket, and picked up his high silk hat. On the way down the hall, he stuck his head into Bob's room.

"Sure you won't go to the theater with us?"

The young man was sprawled on his bed, half-dressed, smoking. He looked tired. They all looked tired.

"This is the first time in two months that my back has felt a mattress," he said. "I think I'll just finish my cigar and go to bed."

"All right, my boy. Do just what you feel like. Good night."

"Good night, Father."

Mary emerged from her room wearing a light gray dress and black velvet cloak. She took his arm, and they went downstairs together. It was dark outside now. As they were stepping into the carriage, a voice called. Here came Isaac Arnold, a fellow Illinois lawyer and political ally, hustling across the lawn, evidently anxious to talk about something. Mary's brow creased. Would they ever get away?

"Excuse me now, I'm going to the theater," Abraham called to Arnold in a friendly tone. "Come and see me in the morning."

He ducked his head, climbed in, and settled down beside Mary. The wheels crunched over gravel as the coach rolled down the driveway and through the White House gates.

CHAPTER 53

APRIL 14, 1865

hey stopped two blocks northeast of the White House at the home of New York Senator Ira Harris to pick up the senator's daughter, Clara, and her fiancé, Major Henry Rathbone. The young couple was popular among Washington's social set: Clara pretty, kindhearted, and full of wit; Rathbone tall, rich, and unassuming despite his mutton-chop whiskers and a walrus mustache. Both were excited to be going out with the first couple.

"I can't wait to see Laura Keene on the stage again!" Clara said. "I saw her in New York in *The Seven Sisters*. She's the best all-around actress of our time, don't you think?"

The ladies chatted as they bumped along over cobblestones, first south on Fourteenth Street, then east on F Street. A chilly fog had come over the city. Streetlamps made yellow smudges on the air, and men walking in the streets were ghosts.

The carriage swung around a corner onto Tenth Street and stopped in front of Ford's Theater. Several people, including a few soldiers, milled about the entrance. A bodyguard waited to escort them inside, through the gas-lit lobby and up some winding stairs to the first balcony. The play had already started. As they crossed the rear of the balcony toward the state box, someone in the audience began to clap. Heads turned, and the applause spread from row to row. On stage, Laura Keene broke off her performance to join the ovation. The band struck up "Hail to the Chief," and the whole theater rose to cheer.

The usher led the way through a narrow vestibule into the box, which looked directly over the stage. The applause did not let up. Abraham stepped to the box rail, hat in hand, and bowed. The cheering grew louder. He scanned the rows of faces, and each one seemed to look up with an affectionate smile. Several officers in attendance were hooraying the loudest. Some of the women were wiping their eyes.

For an instant all the bitterness of war, of lives lost and families torn apart, all the grief and anguish and desperation of four terrible years was gone, and in its place long-awaited joy. It stunned him a little to discover that for the first time since becoming president, he felt like the Father Abraham that newspapers depicted, watching over the people.

He stepped back, took off his overcoat, sank into a rocking chair. Mary perched in a seat beside him. Clara Harris and Henry Rathbone settled down on the other side of the box, and the play picked up where it had left off.

Our American Cousin was a clunky farce about a rough-edged, warm-hearted Yankee backwoodsman, Asa Trenchard, who sailed to England to claim an inheritance and ran into all kinds of shenanigans. The lines were less than brilliantly written, the plot not quite memorable, the jokes a trifle worn. But the acting was good, and Laura Keene, who had starred as the comedy's heroine more than a thousand times, lit the stage with grace and charm. The audience, eager for something to chuckle at, was determined to have a good time.

"I'm Asa Trenchard, born in Vermont, suckled on the banks of Muddy Creek, about the tallest gunner, the slickest dancer, and generally the loudest critter in the state."

For a while, the play held his attention, and he laughed along with the others as the uncouth American cousin tangled with English nobility. But soon his thoughts wandered off in the direction of all he had to do in the coming months.

It was lucky the war had ended while Congress was adjourned. It would not be back in session until December. If he moved quickly, he could get his reconstruction policies in place without too much interference from those in the House and Senate who wanted a harsh peace for the Southerners.

"I struck a pump in the kitchen, slicked my hair down a little, gave my boots a lick of grease, and now I feel quite handsome; but I'm everlastingly dry . . . dry as a sap-tree in August."

Virginia was the key. If he could help it get back on its feet, it might set the tone for the rest of the South. Stanton wanted to combine Virginia and North Carolina into a single military district, but that did not seem practical. They needed to restore the Southern states, not redraw their boundaries. They must give careful thought to Virginia.

The theater was drafty, the box on the chilly side. He rose, put on his overcoat, sank back into the rocker. When the gaslights went up between acts, he scanned the audience for familiar faces and traded conversation with Major Rathbone.

The lights dimmed again, and he fell back into his reverie. He must bring the country together, or his administration would be called a failure. His critics would say that Grant had won the war, but Lincoln could not restore the peace. That might open the way for the Democrats to retake the White House in 1868.

"Oh, Mr. Trenchard, why did you not bring me one of those lovely Indian's dresses of your boundless prairie?"

The door to the box clicked open behind him. He glanced over his shoulder—it was a White House footman with a telegraph message. A dispatch from Sherman? He fumbled for his spectacles and bent over the page in the dim light. No, it was just a report from Richmond. Nothing that could not wait until morning. He thanked the footman and slipped the paper into a pocket.

"I'm a rough sort of a customer, and don't know much about the ways of great folks. But I've got a cool head, a stout arm, and a willing heart."

Mary nestled lightly against him, and he took her little hand in his big one. It felt good to be close to her. They had moved apart from each other in the last four years. They both realized it. There had been too many demands, too little time for each other. Now that the war was over, they must remedy that.

"What will Miss Harris think of my hanging on to you so?" Mary asked in a teasing whisper.

"She won't think anything about it," he whispered back, giving her hand a gentle squeeze.

"I am aware, Mr. Trenchard, you are not used to the manners of good society, and that, alone, will excuse the impertinence of which you have been guilty."

She had grown so fragile. He must somehow carve out more time for her, bring her back to her old self. She wasn't the only one who needed care. Tad needed him, too. The poor rascal still missed his brother. And Bob would need guidance reading the law. They must all make more time for each other—more time for laughing, for afternoon drives, for evenings at the theater.

"Don't know the manners of good society, eh? Well, I guess I know enough to turn you inside out, old gal—you sockdologizing old man-trap—"

❧❧❧

The play was suddenly done, and he was falling asleep. It must have been sleep, because he was dreaming again, standing on the deck of the mysterious vessel, gliding rapidly over dark water. Only this time it seemed different. This time a warm breeze stirred the mists, and a gentle rocking set his mind at ease. The sliver of shore ahead seemed to be pulling closer.

Woods and fields covered the deck of the vessel, and there was a long-limbed boy in a cornfield, pulling fodder with one hand, holding a book in the other. Then the boy had an ax in his hands and was splitting rails, stacks and stacks of rails for miles of zigzagging fences. The vessel's deck became a prairie stretching to the sky; the youth had another book in his hands and was sitting on a woodpile, reading aloud to himself, soaking up words.

Then the youth was standing barefoot on an overturned box, giving a speech to a knot of interested men. He wrestled one of them—a good-natured contest full of laughing and whooping—while the deck widened even more, and then he was crossing big tracts of land with a compass and chain, but it was all too vast to survey. A girl with corn-silk hair came by, waved to him, and slipped out of sight before he could say hello.

The vessel glided across an expanse wider than the shining Ohio, or even the grand Mississippi. Fields stretched into a continent. Farms, towns, and great cities dotted the countryside. Ships sailed from ports. Railroads crisscrossed the land. The scourge of war had passed away, and the land was full of people. Some of them were binding up wounds, caring for those who had borne the battle. But most were hard at work building, shaping, writing, and planning while church bells rang out the news that something precious and indivisible had endured.

He was surprised to see his father among them, toiling behind his plow. His sister Sarah was there, too, stirring a big iron kettle, while little Eddie and Willie played nearby. And here was his own mother, Nancy Hanks Lincoln, sitting beside a log fire, her blue eyes full of lights and shadows, smiling.

The vessel slowed, and overhead the sun broke through the mist. He could feel its rays touching the hillsides, warming the soil. One last time he picked up an ax, raised it high, and brought it swinging down, just to show himself that he could still do it, just to remind himself that he possessed the strength and the spirit of a free people. The blow split the raft to pieces, the dream came to an end, and he stepped onto the far shore.

EPILOGUE

*N*ews of the assassination stunned the country in a way that not even the horrific casualty lists from Shiloh, Antietam, and Gettysburg had. Shaken telegraph operators tapped the report over the wires. Newspaper boys stood mute on street corners with black-bordered special editions in their hands, tears running down their cheeks. The color drained from men's faces when they read the headlines. People heard church bells tolling, asked "What's happened?" and stumbled away murmuring, "Oh God, no!" Shopkeepers closed their stores for the day. Children ran home crying, "Mama, they've killed Old Abe!"

Gloom thickened across the South. A few rebels, bitter over defeat, muttered that it served the tyrant right. But most shuddered with the expectation of harsh retribution from the North. Confederate General Joseph E. Johnston got word of the murder straight from General William T. Sherman while negotiating the surrender of his army in North Carolina. "This is the greatest possible calamity to the South," Johnston said.

At the White House, Edwin Stanton oversaw the dressing of his friend's body. They clothed him in his best suit, the one he had worn to give his second inaugural address six weeks earlier, and laid him in an ornate coffin barely long enough to hold his six-foot-four-inch frame.

Twenty-five thousand people filed past the casket as it lay in the East Room, which was draped in black. It was the same room where Willie Lincoln's funeral had been held, and Elmer Ellsworth's. Then the public was shut out, and six hundred dignitaries gathered for a service. Mary was not among them. She stayed in her room, too distraught to attend any of the memorial ceremonies. General Grant sat alone at the head of the coffin, eyes filled with tears. At the same hour, millions gathered in churches across the United States to pray and listen to eulogies.

When the White House service was concluded, the mourners escorted the casket outside, placed it on a black hearse pulled by six white horses, and moved in solemn order up Pennsylvania Avenue to Capitol Hill. Fifty thousand veterans, officials, and citizens joined the procession, which was led by the 22nd US Colored Troops. Another fifty thousand lined the avenue wearing black armbands, badges, and ribbons. Onlookers covered every roof and tree limb. Red, white, and blue decorations celebrating Lee's surrender had been hurriedly torn down and black crepe hung in their place at windows and doorways.

His body lay in state for a day in the Capitol Rotunda, the coffin resting on a catafalque, draped in black, under the newly finished dome. People streamed through the hall by the thousands to pay their last respects, still barely able to believe what had happened, even after they saw him lying there. Then the doors to the Capitol were closed, and it was time to go home to Springfield.

A special nine-car train, draped in black, set out from Washington for the journey, which would largely retrace the route of his inaugural trip in 1861. Friends like Ward Hill Lamon, David Davis, John Nicolay, and John Hay rode along, quietly sharing memories as the locomotive chugged west. Little Willie's casket was aboard as well. Lincoln had planned to have his son's body, which had been temporarily entombed at Oak Hill Cemetery in Georgetown, taken to Springfield for interment at the end of his second term. Now father and son would make the trip together, sooner than expected.

At major cities—Baltimore, Harrisburg, Philadelphia, New York, Albany, Buffalo, Cleveland, Columbus, Indianapolis, and Chicago—the presidential coffin was unloaded for public viewing. Huge crowds turned out to stand silently, sometimes in pouring rain, and watch a grand procession. They filled sidewalks, balconies, and windows. Banners with inscriptions like "Millions Bless Thy Name" and "With Malice Toward None, With Charity For All" hung on buildings. Muffled drumbeats accompanied the clatter of the hearse's wheels. When it reached the statehouse or some other large public hall, the casket was placed on a catafalque and opened to reveal the fallen leader. The mourners stood in line for hours, sometimes through the night, to gaze for an instant on his face, restful in death. When the allotted time was up, the hearse took the casket back to the train to continue the journey.

In the dozens of smaller towns and vast stretches of countryside where the train did not stop, people offered tributes that would have pleased him the most. For hundreds of miles they lined the tracks, many waiting all day or night to catch a glimpse of the funeral car: rough-edged farmers, leather-skinned tanners and blacksmiths, mothers whose sons were buried on distant battlefields. Families sat quietly in wagons or huddled around bonfires, patiently waiting, often in the rain. They made arches of evergreens over the rails for the train to pass under, or covered the tracks with flowers. When the locomotive finally appeared, its black ribbons and crepe fluttering as it came, the men doffed their hats, and the women waved handkerchiefs. Many parents held up infants so that in years to come they could tell them, "You were there when he passed by."

Well before the train left Washington, the intensive search for the assassin was underway. While the remains of the president were lying in Albany, New York, a quarter of the way through the journey, federal troops cornered John Wilkes Booth in a tobacco barn near Port Royal, Virginia, and shot him through the neck. "Tell my mother I die for my country," Booth whispered to his captors at the end. That same day, near Durham Station, North Carolina, Joe Johnston finally surrendered his army to Sherman. It was the largest surrender of troops in the war.

The train rolled on, heading west across New York and Ohio, past town depots where little bands played dirges as the cars rattled by. Past Utica, Batavia, Dunkirk. Through Ashtabula, Wickliffe, Urbana, Piqua. Between towns, more country folk lined the tracks—men bearing torches throughout the night, women singing hymns, and girls holding bouquets of flowers. Voices calling out, "Goodbye, Father Abraham."

The train reached Indiana, where he had grown up in the wilderness just a stone's throw from the Ohio River, where he had learned to use the ax and the plow, and had tramped miles through the woods to get hold of books like "The Life of Washington" and "Lessons in Elocution." Then at last came the prairies of Illinois, the state that had been his home for three decades. Here he had studied law, had made a name for himself in politics, and had courted his wife and raised a family.

In Chicago, where he had won the Republican Party nomination for president, an inscription over the south door of the Cook County Courthouse read: "Illinois Clasps To Her Bosom Her Slain But Glorified Son." Thirty-six young women in white dresses and black sashes, representing all the states in the now-reunited country, each placed a flower on the coffin. The *Chicago Tribune* estimated that more than 120,000 people—whites, blacks, Germans, Irish, Swedes, Norwegians, mechanics, tailors, masons, carpenters—joined or watched the city's funeral procession.

By the time the train reached Springfield, it had traveled more than sixteen hundred miles in thirteen days, using sixteen different rail lines. Some five to seven million people—no one is sure exactly how many—had gathered in city streets or at rural crossroads to pay their respects to the fallen president as he passed by. Never before in all of history had there been a journey like it.

Banners reading "Come Home" and "Home Is The Martyr" stretched over the tracks as the locomotive approached Illinois's capital. Every house and building in town was draped in black, including the Lincolns' home at Eighth and Jackson streets. Over the front door of the law office he had shared with Billy Herndon hung a banner that proclaimed: "He Lives In The Hearts Of His People."

For twenty-four hours, the body lay in state at the capitol building, where he had delivered his "House Divided" speech. Friends, neighbors, and clients came to pay their respects. These were the people who had seen him pulling his boys around the square in a little wagon and had heard him tell countless jokes and stories around cast-iron stoves. They climbed the grand staircase to Representatives Hall, filed quietly past the casket, went back down the stairs and, once outside, cried in each other's arms.

Thousands lined up for a final grand procession to Oak Ridge Cemetery, two miles from the town center. Even his horse, Old Bob, took part. His stepmother, Sally Lincoln, was too old and weak to make the trip from Coles County. When Dennis Hanks told her of her boy's death, she said, "Yes, I know, Denny. I knowed they'd kill him. I been awaiting for it."

Six black horses adorned with black plumes drew the hearse down a country lane. The fields around Springfield lay freshly plowed; out on the prairies, the grasses were beginning to push toward the sky. The mourners passed under an evergreen arch at the cemetery's entrance, then along a path between two ridges until they reached a stone vault that looked like a small Greek temple built into a hill. Willie's casket was already waiting inside. It had been nearly four years and three months since Abraham had told his friends farewell and set out for Washington. Twenty days since the assassination. It was time for the last goodbye. They gently lifted him and carried him into the tomb, into history and legend.

ACKNOWLEDGMENTS

Anyone who has ever written a book knows it is not a solitary endeavor. Many people help along the way.

In researching this novel, I drew on the work of Lincoln scholars, living and dead. Their works fill several shelves in my office. Some are professional historians, some devoted amateurs. I am deeply indebted to them.

For a bibliography of works I consulted, please see my website, www.johncribbauthor.com.

Over the past several years, I have visited many Lincoln and Civil War sites, places like the Lincoln Home National Historic Site in Springfield, Illinois; President Lincoln's Cottage in Washington, DC; Gettysburg National Military Park in Pennsylvania; and City Point at Petersburg National Battlefield in Virginia. The staff members and volunteers were unfailingly helpful, knowledgeable, and enthusiastic. They helped bring Lincoln alive for me.

Marly Rusoff is not only an extraordinary literary agent, she is an extraordinary person. This is the first time I've had the honor to work with her, and I've quickly come to understand why she is so revered and loved in the book world. I'm grateful she took this book under her wing and grateful to call her my friend.

There is no way for me to adequately thank Eric Kampmann, Al Regnery, and the team at Republic Book Publishers. They took a risk on this project when others would not. I'm grateful for their dedication to Lincoln's legacy and to our country.

This book may never have seen the light of day without Kathie Bennett, publicist extraordinaire and founder of Magic Time Literary Publicity. Her friendship, encouragement, and guidance made all the difference. Thank you, Kathie.

Likewise, I doubt this book would have come into being without my dear friend and colleague, Bill Bennett. He has taught me much, including about Lincoln. Outside of my family, I have learned more from him than anyone else. Bill is a wise, generous man and wonderful friend.

Several people read and critiqued portions of this book as it moved through various drafts. In particular, I'd like to thank Bill Bennett, Marshall Evans, Mary Beth Klee, Seth Leibsohn, Andy Myers, and Chris Scalia. Their careful reading and spot-on feedback were invaluable.

Noreen Burns, who is from Lincoln territory, offered her wise counsel, as she has done so many times.

This book was born at the Spartanburg County Public Library, where I've spent many happy hours and where I found the books that first inspired this novel. The staff there is amazing. It's a wonderful place.

The Hub City Writers Project in Spartanburg, South Carolina, is also a marvelous organization full of extraordinary, talented people. It has become a national model for literary organizations—for good reason. They nurture writers, including this one.

I owe no end of thanks to my family. Kirsten read and reread drafts, and offered encouragement that only a wife can give, without which it would not have been finished. Molly and Sarah pretty much grew up with this book as I worked on it, on and off, over the years. God makes all things possible. One way he made this book possible was to bless me with my family.